Angelglass

To Muriel and Malcolm,
Or as I know them, Mum and Dad

Angelglass

David Barnett

IMMANION PRESS
Stafford, England

Angelglass
David Barnett

Cover Art: David Gentry
Cover Design: Andy Bigwood
Interior Design and Layout: Storm Constantine

Set in Garamond and akaPotsley

IP0079
An Immanion Press Edition
http://www.immanion-press.com
info@immanion-press.com

ISBN 978-1-904853-49-7

Immanion Press
8 Rowley Grove
Stafford ST17 9BJ
UK

Also by David Barnett

*Hinterland

*Available as an Immanion Press edition

Praise for David Barnett and Hinterland

"An intriguing psychological thriller."
- The Sun

"An ambitious, interesting, compelling read, written with passion and integrity."
- Eric Brown, Infinity Plus

"This walk on the weird side is a well-crafted and highly enjoyable page-turner, written with a light touch and a distinctly dark heart."
-Yorkshire Post

"A dark, engrossing tale full of shrewd observation and sly humour, the product of what must be a genuinely brilliant skewed imagination."
-Joolz Denby, Telegraph & Argus, Bradford

"Highly recommended high strangeness - 10/10"
-The Fortean Times

"A dark, funny and kaleidoscopic search for answers, written with lavish originality and page-turning passion. An undoubted cult in the making."
- The Gazette, Blackpool

"A tender, relevant anti-fantasy that doesn't trip on its own hipness and comes off like an alien abduction party."
- Interzone magazine

"Hinterland is an insidious black magic spell of a book. Long after you've read it the story stays with you and imprints itself on the world around you."
- AOL.com

"The novel's strength - to veer from the ordinary to the extraordinary so seamlessly - is gradually unsettling and the bemusement and uncertainty that it throws up is ultimately deeply poignant and not a little troubling."
- The Big Issue

"Now that I am far from her, perhaps forever, I catch myself wondering whether Prague really exists or whether she is not an imaginary land..."
- Angelo Maria Ripellino, *Magic Prague*

One
The Prague House

On balance, I know more than I do not, I think.

I know that I lie on damp grass. I know that the sky is blue and that the sun burns cold and distant, its power diminished by late autumn. That the tree which casts its spindly shadow across my body is dead, its calcified branches scraping at the sky like the fingers of something long forgotten to human knowledge. That the orange roofs which cluster at the edge of my vision hold people and life, and that the towers and halls which cling together on the hill above the labyrinthine streets form the castle.

I know that I am in Prague.

I know that I am naked.

I know that I have been born from white light and whispers.

What I do not know is my own name, or how I came to be here.

My heart hammers so that I can hear it clearly, and it makes me think that I know I must be alive. But no, it is not my heart. It is the steady beat of a horse's hoofs, coming closer.

Presently, a larger shadow falls across me, absorbing the grey fingers cast by the dead tree. I shield my eyes against the sun, squinting at the rider, who speaks in hushed tones to calm the skittish mare. When the horse settles, the rider addresses me with a concerned voice, "Hey, are you okay? It's a little chilly for sunbathing."

With my gradual awakening comes a growing sense that my nakedness is not right or proper, and I hasten to cover myself with my hands. The sun fades momentarily behind cottony clouds and the rider emerges from the blinding, fresh light as a woman of singular beauty. She dismounts expertly and squats beside my ditch, ignoring my bareness and gazing intently into my eyes with her own of a rather startling green. She brushes auburn locks back off her face then hesitantly waves her hand in front of my eyes, as though testing for blindness. Or perhaps madness.

"Erm, let's see... *Jak se mate*?" she asks, then: "How are you? Are you okay?"

She speaks in English, then Czech, then English again. It is all the same to me. I don't know how I know the difference, nor really care. She seems to favour English, so that is how I reply.

"I'm fine, I think," I say, now becoming more aware that my nakedness is not appropriate.

She notices, as though for the first time, and says, "Hang on a minute."

She goes to her horse and from a saddlebag pulls a pair of shorts and a T-shirt, immaculately folded. She hands them over, saying, "I always carry extras. They're mine, but we're not too different in size. Put those on and we'll get you some help."

I struggle into the shorts while she strokes her horse and whispers into its ear, then I pull on the T-shirt, stealing sly glances at her. She's pale and English, her lush curls almost red in this light. She wears jodhpurs and a tight shirt.

Shirt. Jodhpurs. Curls. English. I see a thing, and it is named. Words well from within me, unbidden. Horse. Shorts. Saddlebag.

I look at the girl. More words come.

Beautiful.

The only thing I have no name for, no word for, is myself.

"So, what happened?" she asks, turning back to me once I'm decent. "You have a fall? Were you mugged?"

I shrug, standing uncomfortably in her clothes. "I, uh, I'm not sure. I can't remember anything. ."

She looks straight at me again, with her unnerving green eyes. "Nothing? I think we should maybe get you to a doctor. Come on, get up behind me on Rose. I'll take you to the hospital... um, I don't suppose you've got any money have you?"

I shrug helplessly. She says, "We'll need a thousand crowns to get through the door of the Diplomatic Health Centre for Foreigners... I don't have anything like that on me."

She pauses for a minute, thinking and looking at me, before hooking her right foot in the stirrup and deftly lifting herself on to the saddle. "Come on. I'll get Jenny to look at you. She'll be able to decide whether it's worth spending the cash at the hospital."

Awkwardly, I climb up on to the horse behind the girl. "Thank you, ah...."

She twists round to shake my hand. "Karla. Don't worry about it. When we get there you can have a bath, get some food, then I'll get Jenny to look you over and decide what we're going to do with you."

"Get there? Get where?" I ask as Karla spurs Rose into a trot across the grassy plain, towards the orange roofs far below us.

"Home, where else?" she shouts as the horse begins to gather pace. "Home to the Prague House."

At the edge of the park, the grass and trees abruptly give way to concrete and noise and the humming web of electricity cables suspended criss-cross above the tight, winding streets. I draw back at the sight of the distant, thundering trams that rattle along the cobbles. There is a collection of low wooden buildings on the park side—a stables? —and Karla hands over the reins of the horse to a sullen youth, then leads me towards the tumult.

"I love to ride on Sunday mornings," says Karla as we negotiate the busy road. "Sometimes I get out to the countryside, but mostly I ride Rose here on Letna Park. It's kind of my communing with nature thing? You sort of need a bit of fresh air after a few days in the city. It's so polluted, you know?"

I confess, I'm hardly listening to her words, so captivated am I by the gracefully tarnished stone buildings, the cracked pavements, the honking traffic as we stride down the stone steps from Letna Park on to the busy roads. A slender woman wearing a pin-striped skirt and jacket hurries past, coffee cup in her hand. A shuffling, swarthy woman wrapped in layers of rags and blankets peers at me through heavy-lidded eyes. A trio of black-clad young men on skateboards weaves through the tourists.

Karla ignores it all and drags me by the elbow across the road. We cut in through a series of narrow alleys, away from the din and the shouts. "We could get the tram," she says, putting a hand on my chest to stop me walking into a man carrying a stack of crates from the back door of a bar, "but they're full of Germans this time of year. Besides, it's only a short walk to Mala Strana. What's the point of living in Prague if you can't walk through it? Apart from the pollution, of course. Like I already said."

We emerge from another alley on to the bank of the Vltava river (I see it, it is named), shimmering in the cold sun, not far from a wide bridge bedecked by statues and thronged with people. "Can't avoid passing by the Charles Bridge on this route, unfortunately," mutters Karla. "Just don't buy anything. If I take home one more cheap marionette or painting of the Tyn Church, Cody'll kill me."

As we push through the crowds and the hawkers, under a high arch and past shops and cafes, I wonder vaguely who Cody is. Suddenly a small, wiry man is pushing his face into mine. "You like? You like?

Picture postcard of Praha?"

He brandishes a sheaf of gaudy views of the city in my face. I push him away, startled, and he's digging into a rough sack he has slung from his shoulder for more tat when he stops and squints at me. He lets loose a stream of rapid Czech, his eyes widening. Then he's backing off, waving his fist at me, the forefinger and little finger extended. I look around in panic, suddenly alone in the crowd, when Karla emerges from a knot of tourists, looking first at me and then at the hawker before he disappears into the throng. "Jesus, I thought I'd lost you. What'd you do to upset that guy?"

"Upset him? I didn't say a word. He was trying to sell me something and then he... well, I don't know what he was doing."

Karla looks at me sidelong for a moment. "Come on, let's get you home. You sure you didn't say anything to him?"

I allow her to take my hand and lead me into a side-street off the busy main drag. "Not a word. What was he saying?"

"I barely know enough Czech to get me to a bar and then get me drunk in it, so I didn't catch what he was shouting. But you can't mistake that sign he was making at you. Unless I'm very wrong, you've just been cursed with the evil eye." Then she laughs and leads me off into a labyrinth of cobbled streets, towards the Prague House.

The house stands alone, awkwardly, on a corner, not quite in step with the other buildings that jumble haphazardly around it. We walk around it from the street, into a covered alleyway, the shuttered windows betraying nothing. "Where's the door?" I ask.

Karla fishes out a set of keys from her rucksack. "We don't have a front door, as such. That's the beauty of the place. You can only get in this way, and if we don't want you here, you're not getting close."

She has stopped outside a large wooden gate, set solidly into the peeling, yellowing wall, a good twenty feet high, which surrounds what must be the grounds of the house. As she inserts one of the keys into the gate's lock, she says, "John found the place, God knows how. And the rent we pay, it's like you couldn't get a shoebox for that kind of money in the New Town, or even Zizkov or Karlin."

She lets us into the garden, a beautiful, fragrant bower where suddenly the noises of the city, the traffic and the bustle and shrill voices of tourists, cease to exist. It's like the garden of the house is a vacuum, soaking up the sounds of the outside world. It's unreal.

"Come on, then," says Karla, leading the way to the elaborate doorway set in the centre of the old house. "Let's see who's home."

The door opens into a large living room, and I'm suddenly taken aback to see it full of people. I lurk in the doorway, feeling suddenly foolish in Karla's ill-fitting cast-offs. She sees me draw back, and grabs me by the wrist, hauling me into the room. A young man about Karla's age looks up at us, suspicious. He has long hair and is poring over a guitar, strumming it quietly. "More waifs and strays, Karla?" he says, without looking at me. He speaks English but with an accent. American. She shoots him a look. This, then, I take to be Cody.

Behind him, leaning on the back of the huge, battered sofa which dominates the room and helping Cody to place his fingers on the guitar neck is a curly-haired man with a twinkling smile. "How about you, Karla?" he asks, but he's looking at me. "One more for Sunday dinner, is it?"

Sitting at the back of the room, lounging on a dusty red chaise longue, is a long, thin man with the beginnings of a beard and scraggly, dark hair. He sucks tightly on a hand-rolled cigarette and waves languidly at us, but doesn't speak. Instead, he stares intently at the dead flowers which droop in a vase on a low polished table, or perhaps beyond them to the sleeping, grey box of an unplugged television set angled awkwardly in the corner. At the edge of my vision, I notice a door hanging ajar into another interior room.

Karla throws her rucksack in a corner and stands on the faded rug before the hearth. "Guys, is Jenny about? I need her to look over, uh...." She glances at me. "Look, he doesn't have a name. I found him in Letna Park, he's lost his memory. I thought we'd get Jenny to look at him before we take him to hospital."

Cody discards the guitar. "Jesus, Karla," he spits. "I think I preferred it when you were filling the place with those fucking marionettes."

I feel like I should say something. "Look, maybe I should go...."

Karla replies, but glares at Cody. "No, it's fine. It's just that some of us seem to have forgotten our manners."

The short-haired lad who was helping Cody with the guitar bounds over the couch and thrusts a hand at me. "Karla's right. I'm Padraig. How about you?"

His voice is different again. Irish. The words come without effort, now. I offer my own hand and he shakes it vigorously. "Welcome to the house. Now, let's see. Karla you've already met. This paragon of virtue and etiquette trying to learn the guitar behind me is Cody, and at the back's Petey. Jenny's in the bath, so no doubt she'll be out by Thursday or so."

Cody resignedly waves a hand at me. "Hi, guy," he sighs.

Padraig leans into me and whispers loudly: "Cody and Petey are Americans, but don't let that put you off. You're English yourself?"

"I think so," I say awkwardly. I look to Karla for help, but she's disappearing through a door at the back of the living room.

Padraig nods to himself. "Ah yes, the amnesia. Still, no doubt you can remember what this is." He hops off into a room to the left and emerges with four cans of beer. "Guinness!" he proclaims, pulling a can free from the plastic and tossing it to me.

I stare at it. "Alcohol? Stout?"

"That's the fella!" Padraig laughs, slapping me on the shoulder, and tossing cans at Cody and Petey before cracking open his own. "If there's one thing guaranteed to make you feel better…."

Padraig is cut short by a piercing scream from the back of the house, in the direction taken by Karla just a few moments earlier. Cody looks up and then bounds after her, closely followed by Padraig and myself. Petey stares, momentarily startled, then blinks at the beer can in his hand.

I follow Padraig through a twisting corridor which ends at a door. Cody is there already, and Karla is banging on the door, shouting, "Jenny! Are you all right? What is it?"

"Should I bust it down?" asks Padraig, rolling up his sleeves, but eventually there's a click as the bolt slides free and the door opens a crack, steam billowing out. Behind the steam a figure appears; perfect brown almond-shaped eyes wide in a pale, Oriental face framed with wet hair so black it almost looks blue.

"Jenny!" says Karla again. "Whatever's the matter?"

She opens the door fully, holding a towel around her wet body, and rubs her face with her free hand. "There was someone at the window, watching me. It was horrible."

Karla takes Jenny into a hug, ignoring her wetness. After a moment she turns to us. "Guys? What are you waiting for?"

Cody springs into action. "Come on, he might still be on the premises," he shouts, leading us back to the living room and the front door, where we pick up a rather confused Petey. "What's happening, man?" he wonders, scratching his head, but there's no time to explain. The four of us spill into the walled garden and Cody leads us around the corner of the house. "Come on, the girls' bathroom is on this side."

He stops outside a steamed-up ground floor window. Padraig explains to me, "The girls have their own toilet and bathroom. I can hardly blame 'em after the state the one upstairs is left in sometimes."

"There's no-one here, man," observes Petey, rubbing his whiskers. Cody punches his balled up fist into his hand. "Shit., shit, shit, shit."

We wander back to the door, but not before Cody sees the gate flapping gently in the breeze. "Aw, man!" he cries, slapping his forehead. "Karla only went and left the fucking gate wide open."

He glares at me with hostility, as though her finding me on Letna Park has driven all sensible thoughts of security out of her head, then storms back into the house, no doubt for a confrontation. Petey flops down on an ornate, rusty bench outside the window of the living room, plucking a hand-rolled cigarette from the breast pocket of his check shirt and lighting it with the dancing flame of a shiny metal cigarette lighter. Padraig fishes a set of keys from his jeans pocket and quietly goes to lock the gate, leaving me standing awkwardly among the rose bushes. Waiting for Padraig to return and take me back indoors, I spot something lodged in the gutter that runs along the garden path. Frowning, I stoop to pluck it from the ground, turning it over in my hands. A small pack of postcards showing views of Prague, shrink-wrapped in polythene. Then Padraig's in front of me, smiling. "Been souvenir hunting?"

I shove the postcards into the pocket of the shorts. "Uh, no. Should we see how Jenny is?"

"'Course. Come on. It's nothing a pint of Guinness won't solve, I'm sure." I follow Padraig into the house, past Petey, off in his own little world, but sense that behind the Irishman's jocularity there's a measure of tension I'm not yet privy to.

Back in the living room, Jenny has changed into a big bathrobe and is sitting on the couch with Cody, while Karla brings in from the kitchen a large tray with six mugs of tea on it. "Strong and sweet, just the thing for shocks," she says, passing one to Jenny. Padraig picks up his can and wiggles it at Karla. "This is just the thing for shocks," he corrects.

"Can we just find out what the hell happened?" says Cody.

Jenny takes a mouthful of the hot tea and says, "It seems a bit silly now, really. I was just sitting in the bath when I noticed a movement outside the window. I hadn't bothered to shut the blinds, in fact I never do since you boys got over the habit of peeking in the windows." Petey snickers to himself from the doorway.

Jenny goes on, "Anyway, I just thought it was a cat or something, but then there was this face at the window, staring at me. I threw the loofah at him but he wouldn't go away, and, uh, I just screamed. Sorry, guys."

"What did he look like?" presses Karla.

Jenny shrugs, taking another sip of tea. "He looked sort of old—he had a really wizened, wrinkled face. But that was it. The window was sort of steamed up and he didn't hang around after I'd screamed."

"Do you think we should call the police?" Karla says, addressing the query to the room at large. Padraig frowns, Petey shakes his head to himself. Cody avoids meeting her eyes. Eventually, Jenny says, "I'm sure it was a one off, just some guy who climbed over the wall or something."

Cody is quick to play his hand. "You left the gate unlocked, Karla," he says accusingly, glancing at Jenny as though to get her on his side. Jenny waves away Karla's apologies and Cody's not-so subtle recriminations, and instead turns her attention to me. "And who's this, then?"

Cody mutters something under his breath which I don't catch. Karla glares at him, then says, "This is our mystery man, Jenny. I need you to have a look at him, if you're up to it."

"Of course," says Jenny, leaning forward to look at me more closely. "What's the problem?"

Karla says, "I found him on Letna Park this morning. Naked, in a ditch. Not a shred of memory left. Doesn't even know his own name. I was going to take him to the hospital, but I thought you might want a look first."

Jenny gives Karla a long, curious look and raises one eyebrow. Her eyes dance as she mouths the word "naked?" at Karla then says out loud: "Give me a few minutes to get some clothes on, then bring him up to my room, Karla, if you will."

Petey returns to the couch at the far end of the room, Cody picks up the discarded guitar, and Padraig takes a swig of his Guinness. As Karla leads me out of the living room, it's as though everything has settled again, as though I was never there.

"Try not to blink," says Jenny as she shines a white light into my eye. She is wearing a shapeless white coat and peering into my pupils. She has already taken my blood pressure, tested my reflexes, and felt all over my head for bumps or injuries. There are none. She clicks off the light and shapes swim in front of my eyes, before coalescing into Jenny, standing there making notes in a little book, and Karla, gazing absently out of the elaborate leaded window that looks down onto the garden. Jenny's room is more cluttered than I expected it to be; shelves of hard-backed books, a desk piled high with papers and files, an unmade bed, clothes spilling out of a huge wardrobe.

"Well?" says Karla, turning away from the window. Jenny makes a clucking sound at the back of her throat and sighs. "Physically, he's in great shape. Early to mid-twenties. No evidence of any injuries, no knocks to the head, blood pressure fine, heart rate okay." She looks deep into my eyes again. "He just has no idea who he is."

Karla stands. "The hospital, then?"

Jenny shrugs. "I don't know how much good it would be. He'd just end up taking up a bed. There's nothing wrong with him, as such. Eventually the British embassy would have to fly him home, and he'd end up in hospital back in England. Presumably." Jenny pauses and looks at me. "You are English, aren't you?"

I hold out my hands and say nothing.

"There's also," says Jenny quietly, looking pointedly at Karla, "the problem of... well. You know. Attracting too much... attention."

"What, then?" asks Karla.

Jenny sucks gently on the pencil she's been making notes with. "I think it's time for a house meeting."

They ask me to wait in the kitchen while the five of them have a conference in the living room, but I can hear every word they say through the closed door anyway. They're pondering whether or not to let me stay. Jenny thinks it would be a good idea, because the hospitals won't be able to do much for me. Cody accuses her of just wanting to be able to carry out experiments on me, which I don't like the sound of, but everyone laughs and shouts him down. Padraig asks if I shouldn't be having some kind of brain scan, but Jenny reckons she can get me one through her connections quicker than if I was stuck in a hospital bed. Petey wonders if I can play the drums. Karla, strangely, says nothing.

Eventually, there's some kind of vote, and then Karla opens the door to the kitchen. I busy myself reading the back of a packet of spaghetti. "Um... can you come in here for a minute, please?"

I follow her into the living room. Jenny speaks. "We've had a chat and a, uh, vote, and we've decided to offer you a place to stay for a while, if you want. I'm a medical student, and I can possibly get you some treatment through the back door. We think it would be a good idea."

I ignore Cody's gentle snort. "I don't really know what to say. It's a very kind offer. Is there room for me?"

Karla says, "John is away travelling. He's not due back for a couple of weeks yet. We've decided you can stay in his room for a bit, if you like."

It hadn't really crossed my mind what I was going to do, after waking up in the ditch. "I suppose... yes, thank you. Thank you all."

Padraig claps me on the shoulder again, beaming. "That's settled then! Only problem is, what're we going to call you? Fella's got to have a name."

Jenny sits down on the couch. "That's right. Until your memory starts to come back, we'll have to call you something. Have you any ideas?"

A name... I'm sure I have a name. But there's nothing there. I shrug idiotically.

"What about Mr. X?" suggests Cody.

"Not practical," says Padraig. "Something simple. Joe, or Bob or…."

Jenny interrupts. "No, it can't be anything that might interfere with his memory coming back, nothing that gives him false recollections. It needs to be something... neutral."

"Poutnik," says Petey then, uncertainly. Everyone turns to him, me included.

"What did you say?" I ask him.

Petey seems embarrassed. "Poutnik. It's, like, Czech for... wanderer. Pilgrim. I always thought it was a pretty cool word. I was going to call the band Joe Poutnik and the Wanderers at one stage."

"Poutnik...." I say thoughtfully to myself. "Poutnik. I like it."

Cody shrugs. "Sounds pretty dumb to me, but we've got to call you something. As long as you're staying."

Jenny claps her hands on her knees. "Right, that's settled then. Does somebody want to show, ah, Poutnik to John's room?"

"I'll take him, I'm going up anyway," says Karla. "Come on, Pooty, let's go."

John's room is vast, a tumbledown labyrinth of books and magazines, papers, scrawlings and etchings. Thick drapes hide the sun. The bed is ornate and dusty.

"It's a bit of a mess, but best not to move too much around," suggests Karla. "I guess you might be a bit tired. Why not grab a bit of rest, then we'll have dinner later? Our room is just across the hall if you need anything."

"Our room?"

"Uh, mine and Cody's. See you later."

Then I'm alone again. I sink into the heavy mattress of John's bed, the dust rising and settling as I lie there silently. Poutnik. The wanderer. The pilgrim.

At rest, I close my eyes.

And sleep.

And dream.

Two
The Castle

An awakening, then; a meadow, gently sloping, trees losing their leaves and growing brittle in the fresh air. Woodsmoke drifts on the breeze, obscuring the shapes of towers and spires far beneath me. I catch the glint of a wide, sluggish river somewhere on the edge of my sightline.

The damp grass, and the grainy mud beneath, grinds against my nakedness and I seek to cover myself with my hands as the sudden whinnying of horses rises up from behind me.

A troop of men pass by, a caravan weaving unsteadily across the grass in their wake. I am not worthy of their notice, it seems, until the man at their head pauses some distance past me and reins in his brown stallion, peering back through the curling smoke which mingles with the early morning mist.

"Ho," he calls, raising his hand and halting his train. He canters to me and I look up at him, framed by the cottony sunlight. He is joined by another man on horseback, tidier in appearance, of more sumptuous dress.

"Mother of God, man!" says the second, his eyes piercing me cruelly. "They told me this Rudolf gave houseroom to all manner of freaks and sports, but this skinny little piglet must have escaped from his famed cabinet of curiosities and headed back to the mud in search of its mamma!"

I squint up at the man resting on the back of his big brown stallion, at the head of thirty or so others. A third of the men are on horseback, the infantry divided between pikemen and musket-bearers. Behind them rolls a caravan of three bulging wagons. Fighting men, evidently, their half-harness breastplates glinting in the light, their boots and cloaks grey with road-dust. They laugh easily into their beards at their commander's words. I struggle to my feet and cover my crotch as best I can.

The man who has yet to speak almost has a look of concern in his eyes. His clothes appear fine and expensive, although travel-worn and tired. He loosens the chin-straps of his burgonet helmet and pulls it from his head, shaking free a lustrous, blond mane. He continues to regard me with vague interest, as his lieutenant vaults down from an impatient, black horse and, quite unexpectedly, boots me lightly in my bare chest, so I fall back into the mud.

The men laugh again, apart from their leader, who frowns at this. The man who kicked me leans into my ditch and shouts at me, enunciating each word as though conversing with a deaf man, or an idiot.

"Pray, do not just sit there in the midden, scuttlebutt! You are now in the presence of greatness! Comport yourself with a little more dignity."

The others laugh again, and the man, possessed of dark, thin hair and cold blue eyes, continues his baiting of me: "Is this how you Bohemians disport yourselves before the gentry?"

This has gone quite far enough. Struggling to my feet, I attempt a clumsy bow, to the amusement of my audience. Directing my comments to the man on horseback, I say as clearly and as loudly as I can, "Forgive me, sir. I am a little disorientated, having awoken quite unexpectedly in this ditch. Should you care to call off your pet dog…." At this, I nod at the fellow whose boot mark I still wear on my chest. "I would gladly afford you the respect a member of the English nobility in a foreign land so deserves."

If my words surprise them, they surprise me even more. The men on the horses are Englishman; this I seem to know. I speak to them in the language they use among themselves. The big man dismounts, and pushes my tormentor to one side, then reaches down to my ditch, offering his gloved hand. I take it hesitantly, and he hauls me out, standing me before him. "Percy," he growls at the other. "Clothing."

The one called Percy frowns and fingers the ornate hilt of his rapier that hangs loosely beneath his cloak, cut short in the Spanish style and bound at the neck with a gold brooch.

I marvel at the things I know, the style of the cloak and the words I use, the very facts of the matter. Of rapiers and horses and soldiers and gloves. With each new thing I see, its name is added to the slowly awakening lexicon in my mind. If only I could remember my name, or who I am, or what I am doing here.

Now, Percy," the man warns. "I have put up with your cowardly chauvery of these people for long enough. We evidently have an Englishman before us, and an educated one at that, by the sounds of him. He has evidently suffered some misfortune, and I should think —if he is willing—that we would only be correct in taking him with us. You would not have him ride with us to court with his prick flapping, I trust? Especially as he will be on your horse?"

The other men laugh and Percy reluctantly strides to the foremost of the covered wagons. After some moments he returns with breeches, a simple shirt, and a long French cloak, thrusting them at me. I dress awkwardly and Percy says with a sneer, "I trust the gallygaskins will be comfortable enough without a doublet and paned hose?"

"Now, Percy," says my benefactor. "Boots. Perhaps the ones you are wearing."

"Sir Anthony…." protests Percy, but one warning glance and he is kicking them off. He offers them to me with a look of barely disguised contempt.

"There's no need…." I begin, but the man waves his hands. "Percy has untold pairs of fine boots in his luggage. You look about the same size, and I know he does not mind."

As I take the boots, without meeting Percy's gaze, the man he called Sir Anthony climbs back on to his horse. "So what happened? Bandits? We have had our trouble with rogue landsknechte these past few days, God knows."

"I confess, sir, that I cannot remember," I say, immediately feeling stupid.

"A woman, then!" roars the man, slapping the neck of his horse and causing it to spook slightly. He tugs the rein and whispers to it, until it calms. "I've known many a tart myself who'll get you pissed then make off with your purse when you're snoring in the stew. They normally stop short of the entire kit and caboodle, mind. Mayhap these Bohemian wenches are a particularly feisty breed, eh?"

His men laugh again, and the man beckons me to mount Percy's steed. "Get up on there. Percy will take the reins. You might as well come with us."

As I climb up awkwardly, I say, "But sir, I neither know who you are or your business…."

"Ah, this time it is I who misplace my manners," he says, pulling off his thick glove and offering me his be-ringed hand. "I am Sir Anthony Sherley, well known at the court of dear Elizabeth and late on the business of Shah Abbas of Persia. And as to where we are bound...."

He gestures behind me, and for the first time since awakening, I look down the grassy slope. And see the golden city.

"God's wounds, sir, have you never been on the back of a horse before?" Percy spits as we meander through the streets of Prague towards the castle. I am slipping and awkward, grasping his tunic tightly. Whether I have been on a horse before, I could not say. Sir Anthony rides at the head of the group, behind us his retinue and caravan. "How did you come to be in Prague anyway?"

This too I do not know, I concede miserably. I do not know anything. Not even my own name, although I do not tell them that. I do not wish to be seen as an airling among these men of honour and valour. And yet, what am I but such a creature? I awake in a ditch, bereft of identity and memory. Now I am riding through the streets of Prague, awash with sewage and bustle. The cobbled road to the castle is narrow and packed with people, hawkers, merchants, peasants. A soldier leans on his pike and gooses a servant girl; she gives a gap-toothed grin and makes a show of outrage before turning to her friends and giggling. Rich woodsmoke wreathes itself between the lurching buildings, masking only slightly the stench of the open drains. There is a shout and Percy's horse bucks slightly, as the contents of a jordan come splashing down near us.

"Dear God," mutters Percy, putting his gloved hand to his nose and mouth. "This is worse than London."

There is music and shouting, a man juggles flaming torches. "Buy my remedies!" calls a fat man from the back of a gaudily-painted cart. "Potions for what ails you! Powders to restore the whore to a maiden! Herbs to give you the second sight, a window on that which is yet to be! No reasonable offer refused!"

I am still watching the travelling apothecary as we ride by, twisting to listen to his proud boasts, when Percy hisses, "Hell's teeth, man, sit straight, or you'll have us both arse down in the shit!"

I do as I am bid, and suck in the sour air at the sight that greets me, the castle rising up in front of us as we trek up the narrow road, hailed by purveyors of mulled wine or marionettes or dancing pups wearing ruffs. Whores call to Sir Anthony and his band, lifting their skirts and pulling down their blouses to show their wares.

"Keep on the road!" roars Sir Anthony at the head of the caravan. "There shall be plenty of time for you buggers to fritter your coin in the leaping houses, but later, after we have our royal audience."

"Royal audience?" I ask Percy.

He turns his head only slightly. "You think we have traversed Persia and Europe these long months simply to do some sightseeing in Prague?" he asks wearily. "We are on a mission from Shah Abbas himself."

"A mission ?"

"We are here to see Rudolf II, the mad emperor of Prague," he says, enunciating his words slowly again, by now convinced I am some moron if he was ever in any doubt at all.

I look at him, as dumbly and wretchedly as ever.

"Rudolf," spits Percy. "He's a bloody magnet for the weird and wonderful. The place is full of frauds, charlatans, despots who inveigle their way into his house with tales of impossibilities and talk of miracles. They say he's got a menagerie of dwarfs and a regiment of giants. He who showers alchemists with gold in his thirst to understand the dark arts, while his people thieve and murder and rut in the cesspit below his golden castle."

Ahead of us, Sir Anthony holds up his arm and the caravan slows and halts. The suffocating narrowness of the street has widened somewhat into a small square.

"Rest here for a moment," says Sir Anthony, dismounting expertly. Percy slides smoothly from his mount and I follow suit gracelessly, slipping on the oozing cobbles. "Percy, come with me." Sir Anthony pauses for a moment, watching me from beneath his burgonet, then says, "And you, if you please. You may find this interesting."

Sir Anthony, Percy and myself leave the company to water the horses and exchange banter with the whores who melt out of the stews in the narrow alleys leading from the square. We climb the steep and slippery stone steps towards huge wrought iron gates.

"St Vitus's Cathedral," murmurs Percy, indicating the two towers rearing up from within the castle grounds. "A man is no closer to God anywhere on Earth, I have heard it said."

As I marvel at the gigantic statues of men frozen in close combat over the gates in front of us, Rudolf's palace guard wave us in with barely a check on our credentials, which nonplusses Sir Anthony slightly.

"The court is in uproar," confides the captain of the guard. "We have just had news."

"What news?" frowns Sir Anthony, alarmed. "Vienna? Spain?"

Percy whispers to me, "If there is to be war, Sir Anthony will not want his company here. Our fealty lies with Elizabeth in London by nature, and Shah Abbas of Persia by purse. Any other conflict is not our concern."

"Doctor Dee," whispers the captain, a broad, square-faced man in tarnished breastplate, leaning on his keen-edged pike. "Messengers have arrived from Cracow. Doctor Dee is coming to take up residence at the court of Emperor Rudolf."

As Sir Anthony leads us through the courtyard towards the stone towers of the palace, I ask Percy, "Who is this Doctor Dee?"

He laughs bitterly. "Have you spent your entire life in that ditch? Even those whores in the street know of Doctor John Dee, one-time court magician of Elizabeth. They say he converses with angels, you know, and can turn lead into gold. More nonsense, of course."

We assemble in the courtyard and the gates swing shut behind us. Percy strides in the direction of a set of huge double doors, guarded by two sentries wearing outlandish tunics of a strange blue, and tall, furry hats of an almost comical nature, but brandishing fierce-looking pikes which invite little in the way of ribaldry. A dialogue which I cannot hear ensues between Percy and the guards, and I take the opportunity to examine the castle in detail. Rising up behind the walls of the courtyard are the impressive twin spires of St Vitus's Cathedral, which seem to gaze down with almost ominous disdain. The rest of the palace seems vaguely asymmetrical; walls careering off at angles which are not quite right, as though the architects were afeared of true geometry, or else simply lunatics let loose from the asylum and armed with set squares and pencils. Beyond the walls, the smoke of Prague lingers in the air, fuzzing the views of the pan-tiled roofs of the houses which are cast higgledy-piggledy about, jostling for shoulder-space along the banks of the shining Vltava. Truly, this seems a wondrous place, the air thick with something as dense as soot. A word comes to me, but I am once again unsure if it is the right one: Magic.

Percy's voice is rising with indignation and weariness as he argues with the stony-faced sentries, and eventually Sir Anthony stalks towards them himself, his cloak flapping about him and lending more volume to his already-imposing stature. Within seconds of his arrival, a few quiet words have despatched one of the guards through a smaller, man-sized door set into the huge wooden portals, and Sir Anthony, seemingly satisfied, casts a small, yet unmissable, glance in my direction.

Within minutes the door is flung open again and the guard emerges ahead of a tall, thin, wiry man, dressed in tight-fitting breeches and tunic and seemingly borne aloft on a shifting, flowing, ebbing cloak of fine black silk. Almost mesmerising is this cloak, the effect it has on me. I watch as patterns emerge from the random swaying of the material, as the black seems sometimes blue, sometimes green, and sometimes even a bright white in the faint sunshine. An expertly cropped beard and silver thatch frame predatory eyes and a hawk nose, beneath which hangs the thin, bloodless line of a mouth. His head darts like a raptor, cocks to one side as he considers me, listening to Percy's ministrations, which are lost to me in the hustle of the courtyard. He continues to look at me as Percy introduces him to Sir Anthony, and there is a moment's pause as the English noble holds his hand out in greeting, before the hawkish features snap away from their study of me and acknowledge Sir Anthony with a brief nod and without movement of the hard mouth. Visibly disgruntled, Sir Anthony jams his hand back into his thick riding glove and frowns, towering over the tall newcomer by a span or so. He intercedes between the man and Percy, speaking in a low voice to the hawk-man, who resumes his examination of me from afar. Is this, then, the Emperor Rudolf I have heard so much about since my arrival in this city? Although, it seems unlikely that one so important would receive visitors personally in a busy courtyard. Eventually, some kind of agreement is reached, and the man disappears back through the door.

Percy strides back up to me. "Poxy little bureaucrat," he seethes through his beard, speaking largely to himself. Then he looks up at me, and demands, "Come along. We've finally been granted admission into this carnival of a court. We're to have an audience with the mad old bastard himself."

I make to follow Percy, but trip myself on the hem of my borrowed cloak, losing my footing and sliding to my backside on the cobbles of the court, to the amusement of the palace guard. Percy raises his eyes to the heavens in despair. "At least we shall soon be shot of you," he mutters to himself.

Then Sir Anthony himself is there, reaching down with his big hand and hauling me to my feet. "A word, lad, in private, if I may."

Pulling Percy's cloak about me, I stroll with Sir Anthony a short distance from Percy, who is having word sent to the company that they are to bring their wagons to the courtyard. "I don't know how much Percy has told you on the journey down from the plain," he begins, "but we are here to see Emperor Rudolf of the Habsburgs on a very delicate mission from Shah Abbas of Persia. Although Elizabeth's men we are and shall remain, we do a little, ah, freelance envoy work on the side, if the coin is right. You understand me?"

I nod and Sir Anthony goes on, "This Rudolf is a strange old bugger, but he is head of one of the most powerful houses in Europe. The Shah is after an alliance with the Habsburgs to see off the Ottoman Empire, who are threatening his borders, and that's where we come in. A few gifts from the Shah, wind-up toys, whimsies and the like, and hopefully we get the old boy on side, the Shah gets his little war, Rudolf gets to show his family he isn't completely useless and can hold his own in a ruck, we get handsomely paid, and everyone is happy." He pauses.

"Well, apart from the Turks, of course, who hopefully get a good whipping."

"Sir Anthony," I begin carefully. "As privileged as I feel to be given this insight into your mission, I, ah...."

"Fail to see what you've got to do with it all?" he finishes for me. "I thought you might. Listen, lad, I'll be straight with you. When we first picked you up in that ditch, I was simply doing you a favour, one Englishman to another. But on the ride into town, something occurred to me. You're a bit of an odd-looking cove, a bit taller and thinner than we usually breed 'em. We found you in a ditch, and you don't seem to have much idea of who you are or how you got there. Rudolf's got some of the best physicians and magicians and what have you in the world here, and I'm sure they could take a look at you. But in return, I'd like you to do something for me."

We're disturbed by a shout from Percy. The men have brought the horses and wagons to the courtyard and are noisily dismounting, handing the steeds to stable-boys and gazing in wonder at the castle sights. The hawkish man has appeared again, his piercing eyes on us immediately. "This is Philipp Lang, Rudolf's Chamberlain," explains Sir Anthony, steering me back towards the throng. "He's something of a likely character, and we shall need to watch our step with him. But it looks like he's secured us an audience with Rudolf at least."

Sir Anthony stops and hauls me around to face him. I look him straight in the eye and he says quietly through his beard, "By your leave, whatever I say in there, just go along with it, no matter how odd it seems. Remember, this Rudolf has strange ideas. Play this well and we'll all be handsomely rewarded. And Lang speaks English like a native, so watch what you say. All right?"

I nod and let Sir Anthony lead me to where the hungry gaze of Philipp Lang awaits.

The labyrinthine halls of the castle are cluttered with what might be works of art but which equally might be abandoned junk. Statues battle for elbow room with suits of glistening armour, dark paintings depicting heavenly battles and mythological passions play out their dramas along the walls, and even the carpet on the floor writhes with shapes and patterns. As we turn a corner we draw back at the sight of a dwarf clad in fool's clothes, cartwheeling down the corridor towards us. He squeaks an apology as he pinwheels past, executing a perfect turn at the bend and continuing on his way. Percy ducks as we pass an open door and three or four magpies flap out in a shower of feathers and shit. "Fie me," mutters Sir Anthony's lieutenant. "This place is a madhouse."

Philipp Lang stops abruptly before a set of dark, closed doors. He turns and summons a servant from the shadows. "Sir Anthony, his deputy, and the boy shall accompany me to see the Emperor in his inner chambers," he announces in impeccable English to no one in particular. "The rest of the company shall be taken to the scullery, where food, wine and ales shall be laid on."

This seems most agreeable to Sir Anthony's men, and the scrawny servant leads them away down another set of twisting corridors, leaving Sir Anthony, Percy and myself with Lang. "Your tithes have already been assembled in the chamber," he says. Then with a glance at me he adds, "I suggest you save your best until last. The Emperor appreciates dramatic effect."

Lang sweeps open the double doors into a dark chamber lit only by shafts of autumn sunlight lancing through gaps in the heavy drapes which hang over tall, thin windows reaching from the floor to the ceiling some thirty feet above us. Dust motes dance in the light, imprisoned in the swathes of pale yellow, some managing to escape only to be ensnared in the intricate junctions of the thousands of spider-webs which criss-cross the gloomy room. Paintings so dark they are almost entirely composed of black fill each wall, like windows into the abyss, and heavy dust-sheets are cast over the barely discernible shapes of tables, chairs and bureaux. Our feet rustle on the rushes cast on the floor, and strewn among them I can discern basil and marjoram, cowslips and sage, sweet fennel and pennyroyal.

A sigh like the death rattle of a damned soul draws our eyes to the centre of the room where a large chair, almost a throne, crouches in a pool of light from a tear in the drapes. Arranged on the chair is a large man, wrapped in more furs and robes than the mild weather demands, his head resting wearily on a right hand cluttered with rings. Never have I seen so melancholy a visage. He ignores our entrance, rather, he does not notice it, staring into the middle-distance with deep, heavily-lidded eyes, his jowls dragging his mouth down into a permanent frown beneath the full beard. Standing a few feet in front of him an artist, draped in a paint-splattered white apron which is at odds with his black frock-coat, conical hat and shabby, white ruff, works at a canvas. He turns at the interruption, casting his severe face to the heavens at our entrance.

"I faith!" he swears in Italian, throwing his brush down to the floor in temper. Then he seems to compose himself and says in careful

German: "How many times, Chamberlain, how many times have I told you that I must not be disturbed while I am working on this portrait of His Excellency? The Emperor has insisted that only in this room can I complete the work, and that gives me but an hour a day of sunlight over that chair!"

Lang clasps his hands together as if in treaty, but his piercing blue eyes offer no apologies, despite his words. "Pray pardon, I am sorry for the interruption, Master Arcimboldo, but the Emperor has promised an audience to the emissaries of Shah Abbas of Persia. It is a matter of state which simply cannot wait."

The grumbling painter sighs and throws a sheet over his half-finished work, but not before I catch a glimpse of it. If it is a portrait of the Emperor, I fear the artist shall not have long to reign in this world. He has rendered Rudolf in caricature, a pear for his nose, cherries for his lips, rosy apples for the Emperor's cheeks. I glance back at Rudolf to see if there is any likeness at all, no matter how comic. He has not moved since our entrance, and I doubt if he even knows we are here. As the painter packs up and leaves, muttering curses, Percy sidles up to Lang. "Could we perhaps have a little more light in here, Chamberlain?" he whispers.

Lang shakes his head sadly. "I am afraid not. This was the room in which his beloved Katrin died, and his melancholia has been so profound since then that he cannot bear to have it changed from how it was on the very day she passed over."

"His wife?" whispers Percy.

"His Excellency has taken no wife, nor do I expect him to," replies Lang in hushed tones. "Katrin Strada was the most beloved of his concubines. She bore him six bastards, and died in labour with the last one. I fear it may have broken his heart."

"And what tongues does His Excellency speak?" asks Percy. "English, it is to be hoped. I can do German, but not with as much conviction... and I have no idea about this Bohemian tongue."

"English it shall be," says Lang, but with a slight frown. "Although German would be better and High German better yet. But if you have failings in that area...."

Percy bridles and opens his mouth to speak again, but without warning, Rudolf stirs, and Lang snaps to attention. "Philipp?" rumbles Rudolf, coughing into his beard and peering into the gloom. "Philipp, is that you? Who do you have with you? I want to be alone, Philipp. Take them away."

"Your Excellency," calls Lang so loudly that I presume Rudolf must be a little deaf. "These are the envoys of Shah Abbas of Persia. They have travelled many weeks and bring you gifts and important news from the East. His Excellency may recall that he has already granted them an audience."

Waking properly from his reveries, Rudolf straightens himself on the wooden throne as best as his proliferation of robes will allow. "Gifts, did you say? Gifts from Persia? Let me see their gifts."

Sir Anthony steps forward, clears his throat, and begins: "Rudolf II, most holy Emperor of the mighty Habsburg realms, I, Sir Anthony Sherley, do bring you on this day October the fourteenth in the year of our infant Lord fifteen hundred and eighty four—"

"Gifts!" roars Rudolf in his heavily accented English before lapsing into a bout of coughing. "I will hear your appeals from your Shah of wherever after I have seen his gifts."

Percy claps his hands and some attendants from the caravan melt out of the shadows, dragging with them large boxes and chests. They must have been hidden away here since we arrived at the castle. Percy nods to the attendants, who begin dismantling the boxes. "Emperor Rudolf, the East has long been known to harbour some of the most arcane secrets of the occult world. It is a wild, chaotic place, populated by thieves and bandits, yet also a magical world where princesses languish in windowless towers, awaiting rescue by daring princes on winged horses, and carpets sail through the air, flying on the breath of the djinns that howl like tortured spirits as they criss-cross the earth burned by a sun so hot and merciless it would flay the skin off a pure Habsburg virgin in a matter of minutes."

I am, I have to say, impressed by Percy's delivery, which belies his earlier oafish behaviour. It is obvious, too, that Rudolf is as equally impressed. The sluggish Emperor has been animated by Percy's fanciful descriptions, and he now sits perched on the edge of his huge chair, his eyes twinkling as Percy spins rather ludicrous yarns of spirits trapped in bottles and brass horses. Lang leans into Sir Anthony and whispers almost imperceptibly: "You have done your homework. Your man is very good."

"I'm sure I don't know what you mean, Chamberlain," whispers Sir Anthony with exaggerated innocence.

Percy's tales of the wonders of the East draw to a close, and he claps again, signalling for two attendants to carry a huge, rolled carpet up to Rudolf's chair. "A flying rug?" asks the Emperor eagerly.

Percy says, "The carpets of Persia hold many mysteries, Your Excellency. Shah Abbas sends this, one of his finest. Every time it is unfurled, a new wonder emerges."

Percy then claps his hands and the two attendants roll the carpet towards Rudolf, and when it unfurls to its length a woman of ample charms lies at his feet, bedecked in violet silks that barely hide her figure. Rudolf is beside himself as the girl nimbly stands and lays a ringed finger on his jowly cheek. The Emperor becomes the most animated I have seen him during our audience and grabs the girl's behind, chortling, "Now this is the sort of wonder I like! Do it again!"

Percy glances at Sir Anthony, then says, "His Excellency will appreciate the work that goes into a wonder of this kind. As powerful as the Shah's carpet is, it can only be used once in a calendar month. Wonders must be worth waiting for, is Shah Abbas's sage advice."

Rudolf has his hands all over the girl, who I now recognise as one of the whores who hailed us from the street. Sir Anthony has concocted a quite elaborate con to win Rudolf over to his arguments, and it appears to be working. Percy claps again, and another rug is unfurled. "It's empty," says Rudolf in dismay.

"Ah, but this is a flying carpet," says Percy knowingly. "If your scientists can unravel the mysteries locked in the hieroglyphics that border the tapestry, then His Excellency shall be floating with the birds in no time at all."

"Take it down to Golden Lane immediately and get them working on it," roars Rudolf. "What's next?"

Over the next half hour the attendants unveil all manner of wonders. A clockwork monkey that gambols around the room. A tall hat from which Percy produces a brightly-plumed parrot. A staff that becomes a hissing serpent when banged on the ground (I later learn that Sir Anthony has brought with him a Persian who can mesmerise snakes into going rigid, and that they take on the appearance of staffs until the spell is broken with a sharp knock to the tail).

But Rudolf has slumped into his chair again, and the girl is becoming irritated by his groping hands. Whatever gold Sir Anthony promised her to carry out the deception is obviously not enough, she has decided. Lang leans over to whisper to Sir Anthony again. "His Excellency is becoming bored. I suggest you play your trump card if you wish the audience to continue."

Sir Anthony nods and winks at Percy, who abandons whatever whimsy he is desperately trying to talk up and instead says, "And our final wonder, Your Excellency, I am sure will titillate you."

"Is it a girl?" drawls the Emperor.

"Not quite, Emperor," says Percy. "Not a girl, but a man—a man of mystery. He knows not who he is or from whence he came. An enigma wrapped in a puzzle, a code to be cracked."

Suddenly, I feel Sir Anthony's strong hand in my back, and he propels me forward with a hard shove that sends me sprawling at Rudolf's feet.

"Discovered in a ditch, sprawling naked in the clay," announces Percy, warming to his subject with malice. "Not entirely human—is he the product of some unholy union? Woman and beast? Angel and goatherd? Demon and virgin? No-one knows, Your Excellency. He is yours for your menagerie."

Rudolf leans forward, puzzlement and growing interest creasing his brow as he stares into my eyes. "Have you brought me a foundling?" he says with wonder.

"That we have, Excellency," interjects Sir Anthony. "A foundling—and he's yours to keep."

Three
The Lady and the Lamp

The sun shining through the dust-encrusted window, fractured by the thick velvet curtains. A heavy candlewick bedspread, edges touching bare floorboards. Shelves of lustrous pine, groaning under the weight of books, of Mallory's Mort d'Arthur, of Crowley's Magick, of Waugh's Scoop, of National Geographic and Penthouse and the Silver Surfer. Compact discs scattered like the shattered tiles of a Pompeii bath-house, a dead-looking PC forgotten in the corner. A tree tapping insistently on the leaded glass of the window. Silver birch.

The cascade of auburn curls on white cotton shoulders.

These things I name, I know. Words come unbidden, the right words.

These things I do not know: Who I am, what my name is, where I come from, where I am going. I feel I belong here, yet am out of place, out of time. Poutnik, they call me. The wanderer. The pilgrim. Always travelling, yet with no destination, no embarkation point, no stamp on my papers.

I come properly awake to a dull, insistent rhythm. It's like a heartbeat, or the cadence of horses' hoofs across a grassy plain. The sun is low and red outside the drapes, and I rise from the bed, still wearing Karla's shorts and T-shirt, and open the door that leads out from the mysterious John's room. The corridor outside is dark, the rhythm louder, the creaking of a bed. From the room across the hall. "Our" room. Closer to the door I can hear indistinct words, gasps, moans. This thing too I know, I can name. I withdraw back into my room, and quietly close the door.

I wait, because I don't know what else to do. I watch the sun sink, staining the spires and towers of Prague. I wait until I hear a smart rap on the door, and a voice calls, "Poot? You awake in there?"

I open the door to Padraig, wearing a check apron and wiping his hands on a tea-towel. "We're having dinner," he beams. "I'll be dishing up in ten minutes. That okay?"

I nod wordlessly, then look down at my crumpled shorts and T-shirt. Padraig frowns and says, "Well, it's not black tie, but you'll probably be wanting a change. Tell you what, we're about the same size. I'll bob you up some jeans and a shirt in a couple of ticks."

He turns and skips across the hall, banging on Karla and Cody's door. "You two! Dinner in ten! Don't be late!"

He looks back at me and raises one eyebrow, nodding his head in the direction of their room with a *what are they like?* expression, then heads back down the dark stairs.

Waiting for Padraig to return with the clothes, I sit on the bed with the door to my... John's room, open, wondering about the man who lives here. He's travelling, they said, off around the world. What does that mean? Striding through foreign lands, struggling through carpets of shrubbery and rubber plants with his luggage, slashing at the undergrowth? Perhaps he travels by horse or by... aeroplane or... bus. Or maybe on wings of pale, cold sunshine like... like... I seem on the verge of remembering something, someone, but it disappears in a twinkling with the arrival of a polite cough at the open door. It's Padraig.

He steps in and places a bundle of clothes on the bed beside me. "Those should fit," he says. "Not exactly Armani, but it'll get you by."

I thank Padraig, and as he's about to leave, I ask, "What's John like?"

He looks at me for a long moment from the doorway, a brief flash of suspicion, maybe, or perhaps wariness, in his eyes. Then he shrugs and says, "John's John. There's not too much to say, other than that. If you're still around when he comes back, you'll find out for yourself."

He turns to go and then turns again. "He's a good guy, deep down, Pooty. You might hear a lot of stuff about him, but he's a good guy. Now, dinner in five, okay? I can't be too late because I'm working the night. See you down there."

The clothes—a pair of jeans, a T-shirt with Budvar picked out on the front in faded print, socks and shorts and a pair of battered trainers—are functional but comfortable, which surprises me because the act of dressing seems inherently...odd. But the garments give me a sense of belonging, of settling. Looking at myself for a long moment in the dusty mirror, I quietly leave the room and creep down the stairs.

The dining room is at the rear of the house, shuttered windows letting in cracks of streetlight. Everyone is seated at a huge, dark table, lit by the glow of a dozen or more candles scattered around the room. Padraig, wearing a floral apron, is dishing out soup from a huge tureen, and Cody is already viciously tearing up hunks of bread and mopping up his dishful. They all look towards me as I enter and the hubbub of gentle conversation fades slowly away.

"You're just in time," says Padraig, and the conversation bubbles up again. "Park your arse."

I take the indicated seat, beside Jenny and across the table from Karla, who sits by Cody. Petey is to my left and Padraig sits at the other end of the wide mahogany table, after ladling me a dishful of thick soup.

"Potato and leek," Padraig announces. "My mother's recipe. Tuck in, but leave some space for the main course, because tonight is speciality night."

Cody groans. "Aw, no, man, I don't think my stomach can handle another one of your lamb roasts. I'll be fit to burst."

"And snoring by eight o'clock," chips in Karla. They all laugh again.

Conversation flows easily between the five of them, and I'm content to sit and eat Padraig's delicious fare, nodding my head and laughing politely at the right bits, drinking the seemingly endless bottles of chilled white wine which people keep bringing out from the kitchen. Cody drapes his arm across Karla's shoulders, and as soon as the dessert, a heavy fruit pudding, is despatched, Petey begins to roll up a cigarette.

Suddenly putting down the coffee she's been sipping, Jenny suddenly half-shouts, "Hey, you lot, I almost forgot. It's rent day tomorrow. Cheques, cash and IOUs in the vase by first thing, please. And I'm not bailing anyone out this month because I had to buy all those new books for my course last week."

"Ah, that's me hustling me poor old arse on Wenceslas Square again tonight, then," sighs Padraig with mock melancholia. "And me mother wonders why I never sit down when I go home to visit."

Karla makes pleading, puppy dog eyes across the table at Jenny. "Aw, Jenny, pleeeease can I give it to you on Thursday? We don't get paid until then and I've got to go to this gallery opening tomorrow and pay Rose's stabling fees and…."

Jenny holds up her hands in mock surrender. "Okay, okay. But this is the last time, Karla. Why that damn horse should pay its rent before you pay yours is completely beyond me."

She looks towards Petey, delicately licking the cigarette papers. "And your excuse is…?"

"Uh-uh," he shakes his head and, still rolling the cigarette, digs into his back pocket and tosses a wad of notes across the table.

"Jesus," says Cody, mid-way through writing a cheque. "I don't fucking believe it. Petey has cash."

"And there's more where that came from," he smiles, finishing off his handiwork with a twist of paper. "We've got a regular gig at that basement club on Celetna, every Wednesday. We're hitting the big time, my friends."

There are cheers and congratulations from the table. "Petey plays guitar in a band," explains Karla. "What are you called this week, Petey?"

"Tristessa," he replies. "It means 'sadness' in Spanish."

"Petey's band changes its name more often than he changes his underpants," Jenny whispers mock-confidingly to me.

"Which ain't no big deal," puts in Cody, completing his cheque and handing it over to Jenny. Padraig stands at the head of the table, and says, "I'll get paid after my shift tonight and pop the rent in the vase when I get back, Jen, okay?"

She nods her head. "'Course." And then there's an awkward pause as people try not to look at me. My cheeks burn and I stutter, "Ah, I haven't, um...."

Karla leaps to my rescue. "Don't be stupid, Pooty. We don't expect you to pay any rent. You're a guest."

Cody holds up his hands. "Now, folks, I don't want to appear, ah, unfriendly, but, hey, why shouldn't he pay rent? He's going to be living here with the rest of us, eating the food and drinking the Guinness. Everyone should pay their way."

Karla shoots him a look of almost contempt. "Don't you fucking dare, Cody Doyle. If you didn't have that fucking trust fund shoring you up you'd be out on the street, probably sleeping naked in a ditch too."

"No I wouldn't," smiles Cody smugly. "You'd let me sleep in your bed because you love me."

"Don't push it, arsehole," Karla mutters, taking a swig of wine.

"Hey, hey," shouts Padraig, placatory. "Peace is breaking out! Enough! We're embarrassing our guest."

I feel it is time to speak. "I don't want to cause divisions in your household," I say, slowly. "Cody is right. If I am to stay, I should pay my way. I will search for work in the morning."

"Hey, man, what about at the bar?" asks Petey.

Padraig shrugs. "They were looking for someone, glass collecting, cellarwork, that sort of thing. I could have a word."

"Padraig's a barman at The Leopold Bloom, you know the Irish pub just off Karlova?" says Karla. I look at her blankly and she balls a fist and hits her forehead. "What am I saying, of course you don't know it. Anyway, that's where Padraig works. As a barman."

She seems a little drunk, and I must admit that the wine is going to my head a bit too. True to her prediction, Cody is starting to nod off at the table, despite his outburst of just a few moments before. "I'll try anything," I say. Padraig nods. "That's sorted, then. In fact, you could come down with me tonight. I'm on at nine. I'll have a word with the boss."

"That's a good idea," Jenny chips in. "I wouldn't mind a drink myself. Anyone else?"

Karla pulls a face, pushing the now-dozing Cody off her shoulder. "I'd better stay here and look after Rip Van Winkle. Besides, I've got an early start tomorrow."

Petey is sucking in the sweet-smelling smoke of his cigarette. He shrugs. "Naw, man, gotta work on that new song we've been doing. We want to play it Wednesday."

"Just the three of us, then," says Padraig, nimbly hopping around the table and plucking the cigarette from Petey's fingers. "And just time for a toot on this before I go and get ready for work." He screws his face up as he takes a long drag, coughing as he lets the smoke out. "Jesus, Petey, that sure'n'hell is some stuff."

Petey takes it from him and hands it onto Karla. "Finest skunk weed, man. Straight in from Afghanistan. Rowed up the Vltava by a man in a coal boat."

Karla keeps the smoke in after a couple of goes and hands it to Jenny, a smile creasing her face which eventually erupts into a guffaw. "A coal boat? A fucking coal boat? Petey, do you expect me to believe some guy rowed this weed up the Vltava in a coal boat?"

Petey nods sombrely and starts rolling another cigarette. "I swear, man. That joint in your hands has been lovingly hand-crafted by experts every single step of the way."

Padraig lets a beaming grin spread across his face and starts chortling along with Karla. Jenny too is laughing quietly, as Petey swiftly finishes rolling another joint and lights it up. Cody sleeps on.

Jenny passes the burning joint on to me. "You ever done puff before, man?" asks Padraig, wiping the tears from his eyes. I stare blankly at it.

Karla recovers enough to slap the table to get my attention, and manages to squeeze out, "What he... what he means, is, do you smoke, smoke dope?"

Taking a deep lungful of the new roll-up, Petey leans across the table, letting the white smoke drift out of his mouth and up his nose, and looks seriously at me, his hollow eyes fixing mine. "What they're both trying to say, man, in not so many words is, Poot, do you toot?"

Then they're all laughing, Padraig, sinking to his knees and holding his gut with his arm, fighting to catch his breath, Jenny leaning back in the chair, howling at the top of her voice, Karla spread out on the table, knocking wine glasses over with her flailing arms and trying to repeat Petey's words through her tears. "Do... you... Poot... do... you... you... toot...."

Petey stays impassive, staring me down. I look at the joint again, then suck it deeply, taking the hot smoke down and coughing slightly. A second later I'm blinking and reeling, and smiling at Petey as I hand him the joint. "I think I do, Petey," I smile. "I think I toot." And they're all roaring with laughter again; even Petey allowing himself a smile, and Cody's waking up and rubbing his eyes, and saying, "What the fuck's got into you fuckers... Aw, you went and got stoned without me, you bastards...."

The cold air of the Prague night is as sobering as any I've tasted. An hour later, and I'm walking with Jenny and Padraig towards a biting wind that blows off the Vltava, Jenny between us, linking us both and jamming her hands into the pockets of the voluminous fur coat— "fake, of course," she assures me—that she has wrapped herself in. I'm wearing a reefer jacket kindly and—it seems—uncommonly loaned by Cody, although at Karla's instigation I think. Padraig is telling a story, a joke, about some footballer or other shipped in from a war-torn country: "...so his poor old mother's on the phone saying, 'Yeah, son, and we're glad for your success and all, what with winning the FA Cup and the Premiership, and the Champions' League and fuck knows what else, but have you stopped for a minute to think about us? Your sister was molested in the street, the house was burned down and looted, your old dad got shot when he tried to stop a mob running off with our possessions'. So the lad, he breaks down and says, 'Oh God, mother, that's terrible. Here I am, thinking about my own success and glory, and my own family is being put through these terrible indignities'. There's a pause, like, and then the old dear says, 'Well, son, it was your fucking idea we all move to Manchester with you.'...."

Jenny laughs and playfully hits Padraig. I assume she's from Manchester. The joke doesn't really mean anything to me, but I laugh along with them as well, more from bonhomie and comradeship than understanding. After punching Padraig a couple of times on his arm, until he shouts, "Ow, ow! Dead arm, dead arm!" she entangles hers with mine again. We walk along in silence for a while, crossing the Charles Bridge. There are one or two tourists pausing besides the glass-eyed statues, a couple of tramps and beggars sharing vodka and sheltering from the biting wind that howls along the course of the wide, glittering river and leaps over the bridge like a streaming army of vengeful spirits.

"Watch the lamp!" squeals Jenny.

"Aw, Jenny, surely you've lived in Prague long enough to not shout that every single time we walk over the Charles Bridge," sighs Padraig. He turns to me and points at a little electric lamp affixed to the wall of a house on the bank of the Vltava on the Mala Strana side of the river. Besides the lamp is a mangle, and a small statue of the Virgin. "See that lamp there? Mean anything to you?"

I search the vast, white tundra of my memory. Nothing stirs. I shake my head. Padraig goes on, "Legend has it that if that lamp goes out while you're passing, you'll be dead within the year."

We watch it flicker for a moment. It doesn't go out. "Now," says Padraig. "It's fucking freezing and I'm going to be late for work. So are you coming or not?"

The Leopold Bloom is tucked away in a dark, cobbled alleyway, just off a wider thoroughfare that the signage tells me is "Karlova". I roll the exotic names around my tongue as Padraig hauls open the door to warmth, steam and voices, the brittle clink of glass, the raised expectations of drink. No sooner are we in the door than a voice booms out, "Padraig! It's about fucking time! Get behind this bar and get these good people some refreshment."

There's a murmur of agreement from the punters lined against the oak bar waving notes at the single barman behind it, a huge, bald, sweating man with a goatee beard. Padraig waves at him, winks at us, then disappears into a back room behind the bar, emerging a second later wearing a white apron and rubbing his hands in front of his first customer.

Jenny sheds her fur coat and hangs it on an ornate wooden hat-stand. The pub is warm and loud, and I follow suit with Cody's reefer jacket.

"Come on," she says, forging a path to the bar. "I suppose the drinks are on me tonight."

By the time we're at the bar, Padraig has dispensed with his customers and serves us up two pints of Guinness. "On the house," he winks, pretending to clock up the money into the till. "When it's a little quieter, I'll have a word with Noel there about the job, Pooty, all right?"

I nod and sip the stout. Jenny contemplates the shamrock Padraig has expertly woven into the froth on the head of her pint before taking a mouthful herself. "Do you think you might like living in the house?" she asks without looking at me.

"Yes, you're all very kind. I can't thank you enough."

She looks at me. "I wasn't fishing for gratitude. I meant it. Do you think you'll like living with us?"

I'm a little nonplussed. "I don't know," I say honestly. "I'll feel better when I'm earning a bit of money and can pay my way, and when my memory starts to come back... But all I can do is try to get on with people."

"Do you like everyone?" she digs a little further.

"You're all very... nice. Petey's very easy going, Padraig can't do enough for people, you've been very helpful, Cody... well, Cody seems okay."

She smiles at me. "Don't let Cody worry you. He's just defending his territory."

I drain my pint and Jenny signals to Padraig to fetch another pair, which she pays for this time. "What do you mean, defending his territory?"

She laughs and touches me lightly on my arm. "You know. Karla. They're an item and, well, let's just say he probably won't like having a handsome, young man like you around the house."

Handsome? For the first time since waking in that ditch this morning, I look at myself in the slightly warped mirror behind the bar. Between the M and the L of the Bushmills lettering, I regard my image; dark, longish hair, thin face, twinkling eyes. Eyes you could trust, I like to think, yet eyes which give nothing away. No windows to the soul these eyes. "Karla is very... nice," I say absently.

"You're not the first to think so," says Jenny. "Unfortunately, Cody won't let anyone else get close to her. Californian insecurity, I suppose. Either that, or...."

"Or he's an arsehole," I say, still staring at my reflection in the mirror, remembering the word Karla used about Cody at dinner. Jenny laughs, spitting her stout everywhere. "Yeah," she agrees, wiping her mouth. "Yeah, either that, or he's an arsehole. You know something, Pooty, I think I'm going to like having you around."

A pint later and Jenny is heading off to the toilets. I watch her go, and suddenly become aware of Padraig leaning on the bar opposite.

"Having a nice time?" he beams.

"Yes, thank you Padraig. It's a nice place you work in."

"I'm glad you think so, because I've just been talking to Noel. Can you start tomorrow?"

I sit up straight and look at him. "What? Start here? A job?"

"Well, it'll be collecting glasses and hauling shit up from the cellar and suchlike, but it'll pay the rent, get Cody off your back. You keen?"

I lay a hand on Padraig's shoulder across the bar. "Definitely. Thank you Padraig. Just one thing; I don't have any papers or documentation or anything. Will that be a problem?"

"Not at all. Noel's a good sort. I've explained the situation a bit, and he's fine. He won't ask too many questions. So I'll tell him you'll be here with me at about ten tomorrow, shall I?"

"Yes! And thank you again, Padraig."

He leans further over the bar, glancing towards the women's toilets. "Oh, and one more thing."

I follow his gaze and see Jenny, adjusting her skirt as she approaches us. "See Jenny? Don't try too hard with her."

I sense a warning . "What, you and her…?"

He laughs his Padraig laugh. "No, man. Not me, not Cody, not Petey. That's not her bag, man. She bats for the other side, if you get my drift." He winks and moves off to serve a gaggle of Germans just as Jenny slides back onto her barstool.

"What are you boys talking about, then?" she asks, glancing over at Padraig.

"I've got a job here," I say proudly.

"Well done!" she says, touching my arm and giving me a light kiss on my cheek. I can smell her scent: spices and nutmeg. "Come on, it's been a long day. Let's get back to the house."

We climb back into our coats, wave at Padraig, and set off back towards the Charles Bridge. The wind is even fiercer and colder on the way back, and Jenny moves in close, linking my arm again. As we cross the bridge she points out the statues, Saints Vitus, Augustine, Wenceslas and Nicholas of Tolentino. She's a little drunk, swaying on my arm, and as we approach the Mala Strana end she stops and looks skywards.

"Look at the stars!" she gasps, and it's true, away from the streetlights there are millions of them, jostling and winking in the blackness. Still linking me, she steers herself backwards so she's leaning on the bridge, with me in front of her.

"I think I'm going to like you living with us, Pooty," she whispers. I look into her eyes, but I can't read anything in their inky, almond centres. Then she kisses me, her cold lips meeting mine. Unsure what to do, I kiss her back, closing my eyes.

But not before a small, electric lamp fixed to the wall of a house behind Jenny flickers and goes out for the briefest of moments.

Four
The Mirror of Prague

"Well, that went most desirably," says Percy through a mouthful of chicken. "The old fool has more than enough to stuff his Kunstkammer."

There are shouts and sniggers from the men of Sir Anthony's company, who are assembled on trestle tables laid out in the draughty bare-stone hall where they have been quartered for the duration of their stay. Sir Anthony smirks, raising his eyebrows at Percy. "Sounds bawdy," he says, mopping up the remains of his stew with a hunk of manchet bread.

"You know full well what I refer to," sighs Percy, taking a mouthful of sack. "Ugh. This Jerez wine needs more sugar. I talk of Rudolf's famed cabinet of treasures and curiosities."

Sir Anthony sniffs at his mug of sack and empties it on to the reed flooring by his rough wooden chair. "Someone hand me the beer. How is it?"

A broad-shouldered soldier with a flattened nose grimaces and passes a stone jug across the table. "Flavoured with lupins, sir. Wherefore, God only knows."

Sir Anthony takes a swig and throws back his head, swallowing noisily. "I can see I shall have to send you out for supplies, captain," he says to the soldier who passed the beer. "This Habsburg fare is a little rich for my tastes."

Sir Anthony reaches beneath his cloak and withdraws a pouch bulging with coins, which he tosses over to the captain. "Take the men and get them some proper ale. Have a barrel sent to me and procure for Percy some claret. We have done well, I think."

The captain grins broadly and the men let out a cheer, standing and saluting Sir Anthony with their mugs.

As they busy themselves noisily around us, Sir Anthony looks at me for a long time, picking his teeth with a piece of dried straw from beneath his boot. "I expect you're feeling a little disturbed right now, young man."

"To say the least, Sir Anthony," I reply through gritted teeth. "You appear to have given me as a gift to the mad emperor, Rudolf. I do not recall being yours, or anyone else's for that matter, to give. I am no slave, Sir, I am—by your own admission—an Englishman. I am not to be bartered as... as a rooster."

Sir Anthony waves a placatory hand. "Calm yourself, boy. Look, things are never what they seem around this place. The whole city feels like a stage setting, sometimes. Truth and consequence are often blurred; strange things happen, but when you delve behind the scenes it's quite often all done with smoke and mirrors.

"True, you are an Englishman born and bred, or so you seem to me. But you have no memory of who you are or from whence you came. We did you a good turn by rescuing you from that ditch before you were chanced upon by some cutpurse or rogue landsknechte—God knows, the countryside around here is full of mercenaries. Rudolf attracts them like flies. All I'm asking now is that you play along with our little charade, for a few days at least."

Percy leans in to join the conversation, helping himself to another hank of greying chicken. "Rudolf is insane, you saw as much from our meeting with him earlier. If he thinks you're some hell-spawn of a demon and virgin, let him. It can't do us any harm. He'll be bored of you in a couple of days, anyway."

"What Percy says is the truth," adds Sir Anthony. "Rudolf is a melancholy soul; not much stirs him for very long. At the moment he sees you as his new toy, but within a week or so some other fancy will have caught his eye, and you'll be abandoned. By then our work here will hopefully be done; Rudolf will have agreed to send forces to help Shah Abbas take on the Turks and we can be away. We are voyaging to England next, and you will be most welcome to journey with us."

England... Sir Anthony fancies me to be an Englishman, yet I have no recollections of the place. Distant memories of brightness and light are all that I can summon, yet they seem to be a world—or a lifetime—away from this dirty, nightmarish place of noise and lights. Perhaps journeying to England will re-awaken my slumbering memories.

"So what do I do until then?"

Sir Anthony shrugs, contemplating another mug of the beer. "Tarry a while. Do whatever the old fool wants, I suppose. Tell him nothing of what we have spoken of, naturally. But keep your ears open. Information is worth money, these days, and you might well pick up a few tid-bits that might earn us a coin or two from the right people."

"Especially when Dee arrives," interjects Percy, wiping chicken grease from his beard.

Sir Anthony frowns. "I'll hope to be away from here by the time Doctor Dee enters Prague. He has the ear of Queen Elizabeth, and it would not do for her to know too much of what her nobles get up to in Europe. Relations with the Habsburgs are uneasy at best, and I would not have England look too closely at our dealings here in Prague. Her spymaster Walshingham would have our hides, though our interests are purely for the coin that Shah Abbas pays us. In truth, their politics bore me...."

"Doctor Dee...." the name is like a bubble rising to the surface of some dark lake. I have... not so much a memory of Dee, more of an inkling, although I cannot fish it out of the murk. Noise and bright light confound the picture. "I seem to have knowledge of Dee, although it is dim."

"A strange man," says Sir Anthony. "I met him, on occasion, at Elizabeth's court. A magician, they say, who speaks with angels through a magic scrying glass. They dictate to him lost or forbidden works, folderol. A man of little good humour, as I recall, but of a strange power I could not put a finger on. Best to be avoided, I think."

"A charlatan," insists Percy. "Talking with angels through magic mirrors? Pshaw. A fairy tale. More fool Bess for giving him the time of day, I say. Although I'm sure Rudolf will welcome him with open arms. The pair are made for each other."

"They say he raised a dead man from the grave and ordered him to point out where he had buried his treasure in life," muses Sir Anthony. "I have seen many strange things on my journeys, Percy. I for one would not cross Doctor John Dee."

Percy snorts and returns to picking at his chicken bones. Sir Anthony leans into me and says quietly, "And there is another I would not trust in this castle, boy. Remember Lang, the Chamberlain, who met us in the courtyard?"

I nod.

"Watch him. He has the look of the snake, or the hawk, about him. Tell him nothing, and trust nothing he says. You understand?"

Again, I nod, as there is a sharp rap at the door. A serving, man, his face dark with grime and his clothing ragged, enters and whispers in the ear of Sir Anthony. The soldier shrugs and says to me, "Rudolf wishes a private audience with you. First you are to be taken to Philipp Lang. Remember what I said. Keep your eyes and ears open and your mouth shut, as much as possible."

I pull my borrowed cloak about me, and follow the messenger. At the door I stop and turn, my eyes meeting Sir Anthony's for a moment.

"Trust no-one," he says curtly, before turning back to his stew and beer.

"Ah, the foundling," says Philipp Lang. He reclines in a large chair in his office, taking tobacco from a clay pipe. The wainscoted room is lined with books and a tidy desk faces a window that looks on to a collection of gardens and arbours, the view fuzzied by drifting woodsmoke. There is no straw on his floor, as with the lesser rooms of the castle, but a sumptuous rug. "Come in, come in," he says in the tongue of Sir Anthony and his men, flawless and clipped.

I pull Percy's cape about me as the servant quietly leaves, closing the door behind him. Lang regards me with a measured, sharp-eyed gaze.

"His Excellency has requested that you join him for dinner. He wishes to know...." -- Lang waves his hand dismissively in the air -- "...whatever secrets and arcane knowledge lie locked within your foundling brain. I do so hope you won't disappoint him."

"I'm afraid I have no..." I begin, then recall Sir Anthony's words, and my tongue falters. Lang's head cocks to one side, his impenetrable glare boring into me.

"Clothes," I finish haltingly. "Clothes for dinner with the Emperor. All I have are these borrowed items, which barely fit."

Lang stands, gazing out of the window. "Ah, yes. Discovered naked in a ditch, dropped from the heavens. We shall have to get you suitable attire for dinner with His Excellency. I shall summon a servant, then we shall take a walk around the castle, you and I, and perhaps talk before your appointment with the Emperor."

I am barely listening. Lang's earlier words have me rapt: dropped from the heavens. Another bubble pops on the surface of the black lake. But again, noise and light muddy the waters. Half-formed memories are crowding my head, and I hardly realise that Lang has rung for a servant and I am being steered down the dark corridor to a huge, candle-lit room hung with bright drapes festooned with clothing of all colours, styles and sizes.

"A bath, perhaps?" suggests Lang, looking disdainfully at me as an outfit in my size is selected from the rails. "Valet, our guest speaks English. Did whatever meagre education you might have had stretch to that?" He repeats the question in another, more guttural manner, which I surprise myself by understanding perfectly. German, I realise.

"Very good, Chamberlain," says a short man, his face lined with wrinkles, eyes bright in his wind-burned face.

"Have him back at my room in an hour," says Lang, turning on his heel.

For a long moment, the servant looks at me, then tentatively touches my cloaked shoulder. "So, you're the foundling, then?" he says in halting English.

"I suppose so. That's what everyone calls me."

"And do you have a name? I am Jakob, valet to the castle for forty-seven years." He extends his hand cautiously in greeting.

"I... I have no recollection of a name, Jakob," I say, taking his hand. "I suppose foundlings don't have much call for them."

As our hands touch my waking nightmares descend again, incoherent and panicked shouting coalescing from the white noise. A word bubbles under the surface.

"Poutnik," I say almost to myself.

Jakob looks inexplicably alarmed. "Poutnik? The pilgrim? The... wanderer?"

"It is as good a name as any, I suppose," I say, examining the clothes Jakob has selected for me. The valet has backed off some way and is still regarding me with something approaching awe.

"Poutnik," he breathes. "I have heard tell of the Wanderer. I never thought for a minute... I am an old man, I never could have believed...."

I am beginning to weary of the puzzles and riddles of my awakening. "Shall we just get on with this bath, Jakob?" I snap. "I am a pilgrim, that is all, and one with an appointment to keep."

"Of course," says Jakob, bowing low. "I shall prepare your bath."

Lang is at his desk, writing in a leather-bound ledger, when I am led back into his study. He turns on the chair at my entrance, appraising my new outfit of Venetian knee-breeches, long shirt, peascod doublet and paned-trunk hose. "Much better," he says. "Although I'm sure His Excellency would prefer you to be naked with your wings proudly unfurled, as befits the offspring of some unholy union."

Closing his ledger and replacing his quill in his gilt inkpot, he stands and gathers his black cloak about him. "Come now, let me show you something of the castle before you meet with the Emperor for dinner. It is a large and roaming place, and I would not wish you to get lost should you find yourself alone within these walls."

Lang strides into the corridor, and I hurry to keep up with him. "Did you have a name, foundling, by the way?" he asks as we head into the gloomy, torch-lit passageway.

I shrug. "Poutnik is what many call me."

Lang smiles wryly. "Ah. The pilgrim. Very good, Sir Anthony has done his work very thoroughly. A name to conjure with, certainly. His Excellency shall like that, no doubt."

Lang is leading me upwards, along ramps and flights of steps, until we reach a windowless corridor with a spiral stone staircase set into an alcove. "Up here," he says, and launches himself into the stairwell, taking the steep steps three at a time.

The stairwell is dark, and Lang in his black robes and cloak is invisible to me, not even a hint of breathlessness betraying his position. When his voice sounds, it echoes off the walls as if he is all around me, making it impossible to establish exactly where he is, although I know he must be but a few feet ahead of me.

"Are you a Jew, boy?"

The question nonplusses me. I remember Sir Anthony's words of warning, and compose myself before answering. "I am a foundling, Chamberlain. I know not what I am, in truth."

"Hmm. You have the look of a Jew about you, that black hair, those fine features. Not on an errand from that damned Rabbi in the Ghetto, are you?"

"I know no Rabbi, Chamberlain." I am unnerved, here in the darkness with Lang, not sure exactly where he is. I wait for his voice to echo around me again, but there is silence. I can hear his footfalls scraping lightly on the steps some distance above me. I hurry to catch up.

By degrees, the stairwell gets lighter, until Lang leads us out in to a turret room that affords astonishing views of Prague. The city moves beneath us like some living thing, perpetual smoke wreathing its roofs like shifting tresses. The Vltava glitters coldly in the sinking sun. I walk over to the glassless window and soak in the breathtaking panorama.

"It's beautiful," I whisper.

Lang spits. "It's a cesspit."

He joins me and points down at the lane up which I rode with Sir Anthony and Percy to reach the castle. "Zamecke Street. There the poxy whores ply their trade and charlatans defraud anyone stupid enough to glance twice at them."

He indicates to the east. "There the Jews live in squalor, practising their un-Godly arts."

My eyes follow his outstretched arm to where the towers of the Tyn church rear above the town square. "Here the rabble fight and drink and thieve and rut. Prague is the festering sore of Bohemia, boy.

But here in the castle is joy, purity, decency. Order. And as Chamberlain to His Excellency Rudolf II, Emperor of the Habsburg dynasty...." His hand suddenly clutches the back of my cloak and I feel myself pushed forward hard, so my gut hits the sill of the window and my breath is knocked out of me at the same time as the landscape comes rushing at me from a dizzying angle. "I shall not allow anything to threaten that order."

I am now leaning far out of the window, the courtyard below us seeming so very far away. "Ch-Chamberlain...."

Lang puts his head close to mine, and hisses in my ear, "Who are you spying for, boy?"

I can only shake my head, eyes bulging with fear.

"Is it Elizabeth? Sir Anthony's Arab paymasters? Rudolf's family in Vienna ? Rabbi Loew and his Jews in the Ghetto? Who is it?"

"Chamberlain!" I gag. "I promise, I spy for no-one! I was found…"

"In a ditch," sighs Lang, releasing his grip and letting me pull myself back from the window ledge. "Yes, I know. Now come, I would have you meet someone before your audience with the Emperor."

Leaving me clutching my throat, he strides across the stone floor of the tower, pausing at a door on the north side. "Come on then, boy."

A man with a golden nose is peering at me through a magnifying glass, his hybrid features warped to grotesque proportions behind it. Lang idly inspects a system of glass pipes that connect vessels filled with smoking and bubbling liquids. Armillary spheres and polished astrolabes are ranged along trestles, gold sextants and dull crucibles are cast haphazardly across desks. Charts hang on the walls of the circular room, and leaning by the largest spyglass I have ever seen, fixed to the bare stone wall by way of pulleys and gears and protruding through the wooden slats of the ceiling of this, the topmost room of the highest tower in Rudolf's castle, is a younger man with a long beard and sad eyes, who watches the Chamberlain nervously.

"I understood you had been commanded to keep these infernal experiments out of the castle and confine them to your laboratories on Golden Lane," says Lang airily, tapping a glass vial with his gloved finger and watching it bubble with his hawkish eyes.

The younger man tugs his beard anxiously and looks at his companion, who continues to glare unflinchingly through his glass into my eyes. Lang turns to the man by the telescope. "Master Kepler? I believe I am speaking to you."

The man, Kepler, nods and looks again for support from his colleague, though none appears to be forthcoming. "I, that is, we, myself and Master Brahe, we...."

The man with the golden nose, Brahe, straightens irritably and turns to Lang. "Chamberlain, we have permission from the Emperor, as well you know, to carry out this very important experiment within the castle walls. We believe we are close to a breakthrough and our calculations suggest only the rarefied atmosphere afforded by being so far above the stench of the city streets will help us to get the necessary results."

Lang bows, a mocking smile playing upon his lips. "Very well, Masters. I am but a lowly Chamberlain and you are His Excellency's most respected scientists. My only concern is for the safety of the Emperor should your experiments not go according to plan."

"They are perfectly safe, Chamberlain," begins Kepler, but he is silenced by a glare from Lang, who turns back to the evidently more senior Brahe, and says, "So what do you make of our little foundling here?"

Brahe, the man with the golden nose, has measured me, weighed me, taken samples of my spit and piss, and prodded me all over. He has taken cuttings of my hair and scrapings from my nose, and measured the distance between my eyes. And all the while, I have been unable to tear my gaze away from the nose made of shining metal that is strapped to his thin face.

He sighs, holding up the sheaf of papers on which he has made interminable notes during my examination. "I have all this information to process, Chamberlain. I cannot tell you anything from such a cursory examination. Could I not have him for longer?"

"Out of the question," smiles Lang without warmth. "He is to meet the Emperor now. I shall send him to you tomorrow, and then I expect your report by the morning after. Understood?"

Lang waves away Brahe's protestations as I dress, then he steers me outside, closing the door to the small observatory behind him.

"Who were they?" I ask.

"The Emperor's scientists," says Lang, contempt dripping from his viper's tongue. "If it isn't magicians, and adventurers, and...." here he casts a dismissive glance at me, "foundlings, then it's scientists. They are alchemists, they claim, striving to transform base metals into gold. They also study the heavens through that telescope, noting the positions of the stars and planets for God only knows what purpose."

"And the one with the, the nose...?"

"Tycho Brahe. A Dane. Too much schooling, if you ask me. He attended universities in Copenhagen and Leipzig. He lost his nose in a duel with another student, the fool, and had that gold one manufactured, which he straps to his head like a horse's nosebag. The other one is Johannes Kepler, more mouse than man. He harbours some mad notions about worlds revolving around each other, as though God were some juggler." Lang shakes his head as though in sympathy. "Now come, it is time for your audience with Emperor Rudolf."

My dinner with Rudolf is a carnival of riotous proportions. I wait nervously outside double oaken doors until Lang has informed His Excellency of my arrival, then I am led into a huge stone room hung with drapes and lit by a dozen candelabras. A huge table groans with a stunning feast of boar and venison, fruit and vegetables, sweetmeats and confections. Rudolf is in huge fur robes, slumped in melancholy disposition at the head of the table, while a midget in a red and green fool's suit gambols unnoticed around his chair. A party of tense musicians plays soft madrigals from a raised dais to one side, while servants wait silent and unmoving in the shadows.

"Emperor," says Lang, bowing low before Rudolf. The dwarf ceases his cart-wheeling and shakes a stick hung with charms and bells at the Chamberlain.

"Eyes of a shark, nose of a hawk, honey soaks the words he talks," cackles the fool, creasing into laughter at his own weak couplet. Lang glares at him, then rises, pulling me to join him.

"Excellency, I bring the foundling."

"Found in a ditch, was it from heaven he fell?" says the fool in a stage whisper into Rudolf's ear. "Neither sire nor bitch, a bastard from hell?"

The Emperor stirs and swats a huge, bejewelled hand at the jester, who somersaults away in a tinkling of bells. "Jeppe, I tire of you. Be gone now, I would talk with my new pet."

The midget bows low and scampers into the drapes. Lang indicates I should sit at Rudolf's left hand, where a place has been laid for me.

"You too, Chamberlain," says Rudolf lazily. "I would speak to the foundling alone."

Lang frowns, but nods his assent to the Emperor. "Very good, Excellency."

He turns with a flourish of his robes, leaving Rudolf regarding me with heavy-lidded eyes. I can sense the breathing of the servants in the shadows, but for all intents and purposes I am alone with the Emperor.

Rudolf examines with a baleful stare a single grape, turning it this way and that, catching the thin light shafting in through the dusty windows. "Did you know my father?" he asks.

I pause at my nibbling of a roasted chicken breast. Before I can answer, Rudolf says almost to himself, "A good man, whose heart I follow. Dead these many years, bequeathing to me this Holy Roman Empire. It is not a mantle I wear with comfort, foundling."

The Emperor calls for more wine, watching with keen interest the depths of the ruby liquid sparkling in his immaculately cut glass. Eventually, he asks, "What know you of the world, foundling?"

"Little, I confess, Emperor." I recall Sir Anthony and his mission. "I am aware of the Turks...."

"The Turk is always at the castle gates," sighs Rudolf. "And I am speaking figuratively, foundling. Do you understand me? It's always the Turk, or the Spaniard, or the English. If not them, my own family."

Abruptly he stands, swiping his plate off the table with a sudden clatter. "I am beset upon all sides!" he roars. "More wine!"

As a new plate is placed before him and a fresh wine glass filled, Rudolf tears into a chunk of roasted boar. "After my father died," he says more quietly, "and I became Holy Roman Emperor, I moved the seat of Government of the Habsburg dynasty to Prague. Do you know what they say about the House of Habsburg, foundling? That we are mad. Mad from birth. That insanity runs in the family as surely as red hair might, or a crooked nose. They called my great-grandmother Joanna the Mad. They say my mother Maria is mad, that her brother, Philip of Spain, is mad, that my brother Albrecht is mad."

Rudolf looks at me levelly. "And I am sure you have heard what they say about me, found in a ditch or no."

I decide the wisest course is to say nothing.

"Only my father understood me," says Rudolf. "Only he shared my lust for knowledge. My family is content to waste time on flippant balls in Vienna, to wring its hands at the latest incursion by the Turk, to seek its spiritual guidance from the damned Papacy. They call me a fool, or worse, for my patronage of mystics and alchemists. They do not understand my search for truth. That is why I fled Vienna with my court, to be away from them and their shallow lives, and to be here, in Prague.

"Can you not feel it, boy? The magic? I believe this city to be on the crossroads of many things, foundling. I believe the Vltava washes more than fish and driftwood along its banks. It is here that I shall conquer the mysteries of the universe. And then I shall be more than mere ruler of the Holy Roman Empire. I shall be master of the truth, boy!"

Rudolf slumps in his chair as though exhausted, and begins once again to examine his wine glass.

"But the mysteries elude me, foundling. My alchemists fail to turn lead to gold. Spirits refuse to attend when conjured. I demand answers, and my oracles can find only more questions. How can this be?"

Again, I remain silent. Rudolf looks at me curiously for a moment, then his eyes seem to light from within.

"Of course, foundling. You. You have been sent to me for a purpose. You are the key that will unlock the mysteries. Prague is indeed magic, yet it cannot be seen straight on. Like a willow-the-wisp, or a rainbow, it disappears when scrutinised too closely. You shall reflect the glories of Prague, and through you I will see what must be seen. You shall be a mirror, foundling, the Mirror of Prague, and in your eyes, all shall be revealed!"

Rudolf bangs his fist on the table with triumph. "The Mirror of Prague!" he says again, his gaze rising to things beyond my sight in the dark rafters of the room, his lips moving to an unheard song, his mind elsewhere.

We sit like this for an hour or maybe more, until Lang appears silently at the table, frowning at me.

"It is time for His Excellency to retire," he says, signalling for servants to help him guide Rudolf to his chambers. "I suggest you get some rest, foundling. It appears the Emperor has big plans for you."

Interlude one

On a vast and trackless plain of white stands a marvellous citadel of silver, populated by beings of great beauty, wisdom and goodness. The city is a paradox; itself infinite, though bordered at all points by inky, black nothingness. The citadel is as wide as it is high, its foundations run as deep as the distance between the gates in the north and south walls. The city has a name, for all things have been named, and its shining inhabitants have their names also.

A tower, high above the shining silver city. Two beings, seemingly formed of light, affect a walking not unlike dancing, on to the balcony that offers panoramic views of eternity. So alike as to hardly tell them apart, these two, except for the air of authority and power in the one and the dreams that flit like butterflies of quicksilver around the head of the other.

The first speaks in a voice that could shatter stars, yet lull a baby to sleep. "I have heard tell of... communication. Is this true?"

The dreamflies spin in agitation, the citizen of the shining spires looks down at the wide avenues of light. "No. Communication is forbidden. We both know that."

The first gathers his light about him as though a cloak, a badge of office. "We do indeed. I have business in The House. I'll take my leave."

The spirit of air and brightness steps out off the balcony, the thin air distorting around him like the dry breath of a desert disturbed by a hummingbird's wings. He turns his visage that reflects a thousands suns to the other. "No communication, Uriel. We both know it is forbidden."

Then he is gone, dandelion clocks on the breeze.

Uriel watches his passing in the by-wash for a moment, before turning and skating back into the tower, to where a pool of liquid sunshine lies in a gently singing font.

Uriel parts the waters with his fingers of delicate light, and listens.

Five
No Logo

"The thing that cracks me up, personally," Padraig is saying to me, "is that they come from miles and miles around, from all over the world, and when they get to Prague, the first thing they want is a pint of Guinness. Now how do you work that out?"

I'm washing pint glasses in the big sink at the rear of the bar area, and handing them to Padraig to dry with a tattered towel. It's mid-morning and The Leopold Bloom is quiet for a Sunday, so Padraig tells me; just a few knots of tourists huddled over guide-books and street maps, and a couple of locals nursing bottles of golden beer. Padraig, on the orders of Noel, has been showing me the ropes all morning: shifting stock from the cellar up to the bar, changing barrels, clearing the tables of glasses and wiping them down. I am not to be serving beer to customers yet, but that suits me fine. So long as I can pay my way in the house, I do not mind what the nature of the work is.

"It's become part of a universal language," continues Padraig. "Wherever in the world you go, you can get a pint of Guinness. It's a global thing, now. But the strange thing is, nobody throws bricks through pub windows on these anti-globalisation demos, like they do at McDonald's or Starbucks. Why do you think that is?"

I shrug, handing the last of the washed glasses to Padraig. "Because," he says, drying it off and holding it up to the thin light leaking in through the windows for inspection, "because, no matter how much you want to change the world, you're still going to want a good pint at the end of it. Sure, we can live without two all-beef patties, special sauce, lettuce, cheese, pickled onion, in a sesame seed bun, served up by some grinning red-haired clown who looks like he's just signed up for the Sexual Offender's Register, and, you know, a coffee's a coffee whether or not it's a double decaff special latte mochalato, but come the revolution, everyone's going to be needing a stiff drink. You see where I'm coming from?"

I have to confess that I don't. Padraig taps good-naturedly on my head with his knuckles. "Not to worry, Pooty, it'll all come flooding back, I'm sure. Now, let's see... we'd better get stocked up for the lunchtime rush. Tell you what, you go down to the cellar and bring me up four crates of Budvar, two of Staropramen, and about a dozen small bottles of tonic, then get them in the two big fridges nearest the till. Remember to pull the cold ones at the back out and put them back in at the front when you've filled up, okay? I'm going to put a couple of fresh barrels on and have a chat with your man Noel over there."

Noel, the bar owner, is sitting by himself in a shadowy corner, reading a newspaper and puffing on an enormous cigar. From time to time he strokes his goatee beard or runs his hand over his smooth head, glancing over at me and Padraig. When I showed up for work at nine this morning, he gave me the once-over and said gruffly, "So you're trying to save the world like Paddy and his mates, then?" I just blinked at him, until Padraig steered me away and kitted me out with an apron bearing the logo of the bar.

"Don't be minding Noel," he said casually. "He's old school. Grew up in Cork; ask him nicely some time and he might show you his scars. Spent the Seventies involved in some heavy shit up in Derry. But he's good people, right enough."

I'd awoken that morning with my head full of shining light, and the memory of Jenny's kiss still on my lips. On the Charles Bridge, beneath the cold stars, she'd broken away almost immediately, shaking her head as though to clear cobwebs or wine fuzziness, mumbling apologies. The kiss felt to me like some kind of exploration for her, some charting of unknown territories. We'd walked back to the house in silence, and she'd retired to her room almost as soon as we were through the door. Karla and Cody were in bed also, and Petey was sitting in darkness, the orange tip of his joint painting his face with the colour of dying embers.

"Poutnik," slurred Petey dreamily, more to himself than as an address to me. "The wanderer...."

After a few moments sitting in oppressive silence, I went to bed.

It's warm in the cellar, the distant sound of muffled boilers or generators creating a constant hum. There's no lift so I have to lug the crates up the narrow and winding staircase. Before bringing my last one up I take off my apron and use it to wipe down my sweating face and neck, then drag the clinking bottles up the stairs. The cold air blasting from the refrigerators as I load them up with fresh stock is a blessing. By the time I've finished the bar is filling up, and two more workers have come on to serve drinks. Noel has gone from his berth in the corner, and Padraig is nowhere to be seen. One of the bar staff, a young girl with a pierced eye-brow and startling red hair, calls over to me. "Hey, new guy. We're running short of pint glasses back here. Could you get out there and do a swoop on some of the tables?"

I'm about to head out when I realise I've left my apron in the cellar. Padraig said to wear it all the time when in the public areas, so I hurriedly skip down the stone staircase to retrieve it from where I tossed it, over a stack of dull metal barrels.

I hear their voices a fraction of a second before I see them, and they look up to me just as I jump off the last stair.

"...fuses...." is all I hear from Noel, who is facing Padraig over a large crate in the gloom of the back end of the cellar. Quickly, and without fuss, Padraig bends and pulls a sheet over the open box between them, grinning broadly at me to counter Noel's scowls.

"Pooty!" says Padraig with over-emphasised bonhomie. "How the devil are you?"

"I just came for my apron," I say, a little disconcerted without really knowing why. Noel seems to relax, and gives Padraig a mock-angry cuff around the ear. "Get back to work, the pair of yous. Don't you know it's lunchtime?"

We head up the stairs together. "Tell you what," says Padraig. "Soon as the rush is over, about two-ish, we'll nip out and get a bite. How's that sound?"

"Fine," I say as we enter the bar. "Padraig, I...."

But the girl with the pierced eyebrow is looking at me exasperatedly. "Glasses, new guy! Glasses!"

I nod and grab a tray and cloth, and begin working my way around the busy tables.

Padraig takes me to a small cafe off the Old Town Square for lunch. It's bright but cool, although not too cold, and we sit at a table outside the cafe, in the shadow of the towers of the Tyn Church, watching tourists stop to gawp at the Astronomical Clock performing its hourly ballet, the grinning clockwork mannequin of death pirouetting around the ancient landmark. Hawkers and their stalls jostle around the perimeters of the square, selling marionettes, postcards and tarnished military cap badges.

"October's a nice time to be in Prague," says Padraig, munching on a beef sandwich. "The crowds have thinned out a bit, and it's not yet so cold. It gets bitter over winter, mind. You'll have to use some of your wages to get a pair of gloves and a hat for later on."

I sip at a spoonful of broth, conscious that I'm still wearing the clothes Padraig lent to me yesterday. "Everybody's been very kind to me. I promise I'll start paying my way now."

"Ah, don't fret yourself. Nice to have someone new to talk to. Even if you are a Brit." He winks at me to show me he's joking, then after a pause, adds, "Not that it matters much, but... Proddy or Catholic?"

"Sorry?"

"You know—God? The big feller upstairs? Which of his teams do you turn out for, if any? That mean much to you?"

I shake my head. "I can't remember."

"Not to worry, although you'd probably know if you were a left-footer. See these shoulders? Round. I got terrible posture from carrying me guilt around all the time."

Padraig bursts into a gale of laughter at his own joke, then takes a swig of his beer. His talk of God has dislodged something in the murk of my mind, but not freed it enough for it to bob to the surface.

"Funny as it sounds, Prague reminds me of home," he announces suddenly. "I mean, Dublin's nothing like Prague, really, but the folks here have a lot in common with my lot. The Czechs have been shat on for centuries, just like the Irish."

Padraig finishes his sandwich and the rest of his beer. "I once asked a Brit what they taught him in history at school. It was all World War One this, World War Two that, Waterloo, Boer War. You know what they teach us at school? The history of everyone who's ever been screwed by the Brits. That's why I know all about the Czechs. Don't believe it when they tell you history's always written by the winners, Pooty."

He pauses reflectively, then calls to the waiter to bring us two more bottles of beer. "Is that why you came to Prague?" I ask.

He runs a hand through his mop of curly hair. "Nothing so romantic, I'm afraid. I got involved in a bit of... bother back home. Running around with a bad lot from up North. Not what you think—they were mainly ODCs."

"ODCs?"

Padraig smiles broadly. "Ordinary Decent Criminals. In other words, not Provos. But tasty characters all the same, Pooty. Thought it best to skip town for a while, and I fetched up here."

"How did you meet the others?"

"It was John and Cody I met first. Well, they found me, really. I'd been off the bus about a week and I was dossing at the station. I was just sitting there, watching the pair of 'em sticking posters up for some big demo they were involved in, when I sees one of the coppers coming round the corner, so I shouts to them to clear off. I did a runner with them, because the coppers don't much care for people sleeping rough. If you're really unlucky, they might think you're a gipsy and give you a good kicking."

"Demo?" I ask, my mind racing to keep up with Padraig's patter.

"Yeah, the anti-globalisation stuff, you know?" he begins, then stops himself. "Oh, we'll talk about that later on, probably when John gets back. Anyway, they took me to this squat they were living in, really got me sorted out. I mean, Cody might come across as a bit of an eejit, but he's a decent sort, really.

"And John?"

Padraig shrugs. "Like I said yesterday, John's John. You'll see. Look, he's a bit of a shady character, but he's got a heart of gold. I'd still be living rough if it wasn't for him. And then, when he found that house from nowhere... man, I've got a better quality of life here than I ever had in Dublin. And it's all down to John, really. God knows how I would have ended up if he hadn't taken me in."

Padraig squints up at the clock on the town hall. "Ah, Jesus, will you look at the time. I can't believe you've had me yakking for so long. We'd better get back."

He calls the waiter over and, despite my protestations, pays the bill. As he settles up, he says, "You sure you're not a priest under all that amnesia? I can't remember last time I spilled my guts like that to a virtual stranger."

"I don't know what I am, Padraig."

"Good people," he says, standing up. "That's what it seems like to me. Now come on. Noel's going to have our balls for castanets."

The feared punishment from Noel is not forthcoming, merely a raised eyebrow from the hulking bar owner as we saunter in fifteen minutes late. "I was going through procedures with Pooty!" protests Padraig, but he just waves us behind the bar. The rest of my first shift passes quickly, and at six Noel hands each of us a sealed envelope.

"Wages," says Padraig. "Noel likes to pay by the day. Cash in hand," he adds, tapping the side of his nose with his envelope. "You're a man of means again, my friend."

As we prepare to leave, Padraig takes Noel to one side, and I can't help but overhear their murmured conversation as I hang my apron up behind the bar.

"About the gear downstairs...." begins Padraig.

"You can pay me when your man John gets back," says Noel

gruffly. "But I want it out of my cellar by tomorrow night. Understood?"

"Perfectly," smiles Padraig, then to me says, "Come on, Pooty, let's get home."

We arrive to a row. Cody is lounging on the sofa, his arms folded defensively while Karla stands in the centre of the room, hands on hips, head cocked to one side, her curls falling angrily over one shoulder.

"I just can't fucking believe, it Cody! You knew about this weeks ago! Why do you think to tell me now that you have to go on some pissy little pub-crawl with a bunch of slackers you hardly even know?"

"Should we leave and go for a pint?" says Padraig.

Karla turns, surprised to see us. Cody ignores us and says, "One, Karla, they're not slackers, they're fucking Wombles, for God's sake, and two, I like know them really, really well and they're gonna be so useful next month...."

Padraig grabs me by the arm. "I think we should go for a drink."

"Stop right there!" says Karla. "If Cody's ducking out tonight, one of you has to come with me to this exhibition opening."

"Not me," says Padraig. "I'm beat. I'm on again at six in the morning for the beer deliveries. What time's your shift tomorrow, Pooty?"

"Ten."

"Ah, that'll be right, then," says Padraig. "There you go, Karla, Pooty'll come with you tonight. Give him a chance to get out and about, might jog his memory a bit."

"Well...." says Karla, glancing at Cody. He casts me a scowl but just shrugs and mumbles, "Whatever."

"That's sorted then," decides Karla. "We're leaving in half an hour."

Padraig gently suggests a shower and shave before I leave, and loans me some more clothes, a crisp, white shirt, a pair of grey trousers, and some black leather laced shoes. Jenny, who makes no mention of our brief kiss on the Charles Bridge last night, decides on taking me shopping on my next day off for clothes of my own, which she insists on buying on her credit card as a loan.

After lathering my face I stare for a long time at my reflection in the condensation-clouded mirror, but it's not really the image of the thin, white face with its long, straight nose, pale, almost bloodless lips, and bright, lucid eyes that fascinates me, nor the way my wet, black hair curls itself around my ears and the nape of my neck; rather it's the mirror itself that is captivating. I reach out to graze the damp glass with my fingertips, almost on the verge of some remembrance, something of importance...

A sharp knock at the bathroom door pops the bubble before it is even fully formed.

"Like, Poutnik, you in there?" It's Petey.

"Coming," I shout.

"Hey, no fear, guy, it's just that... you know. Karla's downstairs, ready, and... you know. Women."

After shaving, I hurriedly I dress in John's room and skip down the stairs, to where Jenny is lounging on the sofa, reading a book, and Padraig is snoring gently on the floor, his head propped on a pillow. Karla is standing in the middle of the room, and I stop in the doorway, entranced by her beauty. She wears a simple, blue dress with a white woollen cardigan, yet her presence dominates the room, and her scent fills it with flowers. She cocks an exquisitely painted eye at me, the deep curls jostling on her shoulders.

"Very nice," mutters Cody, emerging from the kitchen holding a sandwich.

"Your loss, buster," she says, winking at me. "Come on, Poutnik, we'd better get going. It's a clear night, so I thought we'd walk."

"Where to?" I ask as Karla gathers her handbag and a top-coat

"To the castle," she says.

We pull our jackets tight against the biting chill wind that has sprung up as we weave our way through the cobbled streets of Mala Strana, walking in silence until Karla says casually, "Jenny told me what happened last night. On the Charles Bridge. On the way home from the bar."

"Oh?"

She looks at me with her blue eyes, probing. "The kiss. There's something you should know about Jenny. She's gay."

"Ah."

"Look, don't think I'm interfering, Pooty, because I'm not…" Karla pauses and grabs my arm, letting a tram clatter past before we cross the road, her still gripping my coat, "But she has a girlfriend and stuff. She says she felt a bit... confused, last night."

I think about this. "Jenny doesn't seem the confused type to me."

Karla shrugs. "She isn't. Not usually. She's the level-headed type. But she said that last night there was... something that made her do it.

Like she wanted to know."

"Wanted to know what?"

Karla shakes her head, and gives a small, tinkling, embarrassed laugh. "I'm not really sure what she meant. She said she wanted to know if you were real."

We turn off Malastrana Square, past the bars and cafes and on to Nerudova, the narrow street that winds up to the castle, and the wind howls down, taking our breath away.

"Should have got a cab," mutters Karla, as though trying to change the subject. For me, the matter is forgotten anyway, at least temporarily. There before me, shining and bright in the clear night sky, rears up the castle, dominating Prague. For a long moment I forget to retrieve my breath from the wind. "The castle...." I whisper.

Karla looks at me piercingly. "Does it seem familiar? I mean, shit, the castle's familiar to everyone who lives in Prague, but... does it stir something in you?"

I meet her gaze, and we stand like that for long seconds, until she looks away. "I'm, ah, sure it'll come back eventually," she says a little too briskly. "Come on, we'll be late."

Inside the castle it is warm and bright, a string quartet playing softly as we wander around the Spanish Hall. It is the first night of an art exhibition, and Karla is to write a report for her newspaper. She secures us two glasses of champagne and we head towards where the paintings have been set up for the exposition. There are small groups of people speaking in low voices and consulting the programmes.

"Will the artist be here?" I ask.

Karla laughs softly. "I shouldn't think so, Pooty. He's been dead for more than four hundred years."

She glances at the programme as we walk up to the first painting. "Giuseppe…"

"Arcimboldo," I finish, gazing at the unmistakably grotesque production before me, the assembly of autumnal fruits and vegetables mimicking the form of a mane. It is familiar, but not through remembrance. It is as though I am looking at the portrait right now, but in another place, another time. My head feels filled with roaring wind.

"Arcimboldo," agrees Karla. "Hey, Pooty, it looks like things are coming back to you. Maybe you're an art student or something, eh?"

"I don't think so," I say absently, entranced by the painting. "He's dead, you say?"

"Just the four centuries," says Karla, looking at me quizzically.

"Hey, are you okay? You look a bit weird."

"I feel a bit weird." I look around for somewhere to sit down, and my glass slips from my hand, shattering loudly on the marble floor, spattering my shoes with champagne. People look in our direction, and mutter darkly. "I think I need to get out of here."

As a Czech waiter glowers at us and begins to clean up the mess, Karla leads me by the arm to a quiet corner of the Spanish Hall. "Wait here, I'll get you some water," she says uncertainly.

I sit at a bench, feeling the cool stone of the wall with my hands. I'm shaking. "No," I say. "I'm okay now. I just felt a little... strange. I'll be all right in a minute."

"Well," says Karla doubtfully. "I do need to get a few quotes for my article. Why don't you sit here for five minutes, I'll get my interviews done, then we can maybe go get a bite to eat or something?"

"Fine," I say. I'm shaking, and I can feel cold sweat beading on my forehead, but I wave her away. When she's gone, I steal a glance back at the painting at the far end of the room. It seems flat and lifeless now, just oils on canvas, not the leering, monstrous image that seemed to conjure so much squalling confusion in my mind just moments before. I can feel myself calming considerably, and I idly watch Karla as she conducts her interviews, a feeling of an emotion I can't quite recognise welling up in my breast as she glances back in my direction once or twice.

The dizziness has passed, and I feel able to stand and study the paintings once more. Most are as unfamiliar to me as most things I have encountered since waking in the ditch yesterday, apart from the series of pictures the artist has assembled with representations of fruits. I look around for Karla but I can't see her in the crowd, and then I glimpse her through a doorway, speaking in urgent whispers to a tall man wearing the uniform of a waiter. I wander closer to them, in time to see Karla hand a roll of banknotes to the man in exchange for a bulky parcel, which she secretes beneath her coat. They part without a word and Karla steps out of the small ante-room, blinking in surprise to see me.

"Pooty. Uh, I'm pretty much done here. You feeling better?"

I nod. "It's okay if you want to stay, Karla. I feel fine now."

She glances around. "Nah, not my cup of tea, really. I've got enough for the piece tomorrow. You up for a bite to eat?"

Twenty minutes later we're cocooned in a booth in a dark restaurant a few minutes' walk down the hill from the castle. We've an open bottle of red wine in front of us, and Karla is choosing from the leather-bound menu. "Don't tell Jenny I brought you here," she warns. "I still haven't paid the rent yet, and she'd go apeshit if she thought I was eating out."

"I can pay my way," I say. "I was paid at the bar today."

Karla dismisses my offer with a wave. "My treat, Pooty. Don't blow your wages all at once. Christ, I know you won't have got that much. Now, I'm going to have the goulash. It's completely to die for. You fancy that?"

"Sounds good," I say, refilling our glasses with wine.

"Pooty!" says Karla in mock-admonishment. "You're not trying to get me drunk, are you? Slow down!"

We chat easily, picking at crusty bread until the waiter announces with a curt cough that our meal has arrived.. "I suppose you're wondering how I ended up with the Scooby gang," says Karla through a mouthful of bread.

"The Scooby gang?"

"Yeah, you know—Scooby-dooby-doo, where are you?"

I look blankly at her. Karla giggles, her nose pink from the red wine and the intimate cosiness of the restaurant. "Cody's Fred, of course. He'd never admit it himself, but he'd be really secretly proud if he heard me saying that. He kind of fancies himself to be the leader of the pack. And Petey's just so Shaggy it hurts. I actually heard him say 'zoiks' once!" Karla collapses into a fit of giggles, putting her hand over her mouth demurely and looking at me from under her arched eyebrows. "Sorry. Jenny would have to be Velma, but don't you dare repeat that to her! She'd string me up!"

I haven't the faintest idea what she's talking about, but I like to see her in such high spirits. "And Padraig?" I say, joining in with the spirit of Karla's ramble.

"We-e-ll, he's a bit of a Scrappy Doo, don't you think?" This sets Karla off into peals of laughter again.

"So what about you?" I ask.

"Why, the delectable Daphne, of course," she says, vamping at me with that raised eyebrow again. "Don't you think I'd look delicious in a purple minidress?" This time Karla holds my gaze, and it's my turn to look away, slightly flustered.

"What about John?" I say.

Karla shrugs, her playful mood evaporating suddenly. "There always has to be a bogeyman in Scooby Doo," she says quietly.

I push my goulash around the dish for a long moment, before breaking the silence. "So how did you meet them, then?"

Karla pauses to order another bottle of wine, then says, "I came over to Prague about a year ago. I'd been working on newspapers back in Britain, and I had a relationship that had gone down the toilet that I needed to get away from. I came out here for a holiday, and ended up seeing a job advertised for the English language weekly, the Prague Gazette. I just turned up at the office and never went home."

She chews thoughtfully. "About six months ago there was a spate of graffiti attacks on advertising billboards around the city. Not just mindless vandalism, but words altered to create political slogans, the pictures tampered with to criticise the companies that were advertising. It was all big corporate ads that were targeted. I was intrigued. I eventually tracked the campaign down to John, Cody, Padraig, Jenny and Petey. Adbusting, they called it, using the big corporations' own media campaigns to damn them. Anyway, I did a piece on it for the Gazette, John loved it, and I started hanging around with them. A few weeks later the lease on my grotty apartment was up, and they invited me to move in. Never looked back since."

I sip my wine. "And you and Cody…?"

Karla shifts her shoulders again. "I'm not really sure how that happened, really. It just did. Look, Pooty, I know he can seem a bit of a pain, but he's quite sweet, really." She looks off into the middle distance. "I think he loves me, you know, I really do."

I decide to say nothing. Out of everyone at the house, Cody has by far been the least friendly. And I have yet to meet John. Karla appears to be reading my mind.

"John'll be fascinated by you, I reckon," she says, signalling for the bill. "He loves a good mystery."

"I'm looking forward to meeting him. I've heard a lot about him."

Karla nods. "It seems that whenever John's here we do what he says, and when he's not we talk about him all the time. He's very charismatic, I'll give him that."

"He seems a little fearsome, from what I've heard," I say.

"Oh, he'd love that as well. He likes to think of himself as this big mystical leader of men," says Karla airily, downing her wine and climbing into her coat. "I probably shouldn't say this before you've actually met the guy, but I think he's full of shit. Oh, don't get me wrong, he's interesting and motivating and his politics are sound, all this anti-globalisation stuff he's into, but I get the feeling he's started to believe his own hype. And add to that the fact that Cody follows him round like a little puppy dog."

As we leave the restaurant and step out into the cold night, I say teasingly, "Sounds like you're jealous."

Karla pushes me against the wall and for a moment I think I've genuinely offended her. "Look, buster," she says angrily, but I can see her eyes are laughing. "Karla Stone is jealous of nobody!"

Her face softens and she moves in so close that I can smell the fruit of the red wine on her breath as it plumes from her open mouth. "Besides," she whispers, leaning in even closer, "maybe it's high time I made Cody-boy jealous myself. What do you say, mystery man?"

I close my eyes involuntarily as Karla's lips brush mine, but abruptly she pulls away. She pinches the bridge of her nose and shakes her head, as though trying to wake up from a fitful doze. "Pooty, I... I mean... look, we'd better get back, hey?"

We walk the rest of the way back to Mala Strana in silence, but I can feel Karla's gaze burning into me. I'm glad when we arrive home and Karla immediately goes up to her room. Her's and Cody's room, I correct myself mentally. The house is in darkness, and I trudge up the stairs to retire myself, pausing at the open door of Petey's bedroom, where he sits in the blackness, only the orange tip of his joint betraying any sign of life. "Good night out, man?" he says softly.

I nod. "Yes, thanks, Petey."

"Want a toke? Help you sleep."

I wander into his room and he flicks on the bedside lamp. He's reclining on the bed, surrounded by garish magazines. His room is a jumble of clothes, books and CDs, his guitar strewn across the foot of the bed. Petey pulls his long hair back and deftly ties it into a ponytail with an elastic band. I perch on the edge of his bed and accept the proffered joint.

We sit in silence for a while, passing the cigarette between us. Finally, as though with great effort, Petey says, "So, man... you remembering anything yet?"

I shake my head languidly. "Not much. I keep getting snatches of dreams or half-memories, but they never amount to anything. I'm beginning to wonder if I'll ever get my memory back at all."

"Tabula rasa," says Petey, and chuckles quietly to himself. "A blank canvas. A virgin circuit board."

He kills the roach and immediately begins building another joint. I pick up one of the magazines littering the bed; it's a comic book, colourfully dressed champions in battle with heinous villains, unlikely situations and implausible dialogue.

"You read comic books, man?" asks Petey.

I flick through the magazine. "I'm not sure... I know what they are, I just don't know if I've ever read one before. Are they all like this?"

"With superheroes, you mean? Only the best ones." Petey picks up a comic and leafs through it. "They're the modern day mythology, Poutnik. Fables for the Twenty-first Century. Legends for a world obsessed with reality TV."

He holds a comic out to me. "Take this one. Superman. Granddaddy of them all. The last son of a dying planet, sent to Earth to save us. It's positively fucking Biblical, guy! And Batman... he's a spirit of vengeance, his humanity's gone, he's a scared child locked inside the body of a killing machine."

Petey pauses to light the joint, taking a deep drag. "They're the stories that define our age, Pooty. We don't sit around fires in caves any more, making up tales about the wind or the moon. We've got street-lights and sat-nav and MySpace and hand-held computers and twenty-four hour malls. But we still need our legends, man. We still need our heroes. And you know why?"

I accept the joint and shake my head.

"Because we don't want to be human any more. We've done human. We want the next stage. We want to fly and shoot laser beams from our eyes and leap tall buildings in a single bound. We pierce and tattoo and scar our bodies to make us something more than human. We want to transcend our flesh and take our rightful place with the gods, man, and that's what comics help us to do. They're a manual for the future."

He's the most animated I've seen him since I arrived here. He roots through a pile of comics and pulls one out, handing it to me. "Take a look at that. Green Lantern. A normal guy, chosen by a higher power to defend the cosmos, to become a member of a corps of protectors patrolling the heavens. You know what they are, really? Angels, man. Angels."

He slumps back against the wall, watching the tip of his joint grow long with ash, suddenly oblivious to my presence. I glance at the comic book before replacing it on his bed and stand to go to my room, leaving Petey mumbling to himself: "Angels, man. Angels...."

Six
The Lion King

"Where in damnation is the Mirror of Prague?" Rudolf bellows, the servants who are trying to dress him flinching from his rage and hot spittle. "Bring me the Mirror of Prague!"

Lang stands before him in the perpetual dusk of the throne room as Rudolf casts off the ermine robe his dressers are tentatively trying to lay across his broad shoulders. The Chamberlain looks perplexed, and says slowly, "The Mirror of Prague, Your Excellency....?" just as I rush into the room, fastening the buttons on my doublet.

"Here he is!" roars Rudolf.

Lang stares at me quizzically, and hisses, "What are you doing here, boy? The Emperor is giving an audience to Sir Anthony."

"This is the Mirror of Prague, fool!" shouts Rudolf at Lang. "The foundling is to be my scrying stone through which the mysteries of life will be reflected. I have ordered that he attend me at all official functions."

Lang purses his lips. "Very good, your Excellency. I shall summon Sir Anthony."

He turns on his heel and leans in to me. "And you and I shall talk later, friend Poutnik," he whispers, before stalking from the great hall.

Rudolf allows his servants to complete fitting his robes. "I shall sit on the throne, of course," he says. "The foundling shall sit by my right side—no, my left—on the floor, and Sir Anthony and his men shall stand before me. Does that sound fair?"

I look around, but the servants are mutely working on, making minute and invisible adjustments to Rudolf's extravagant outfit.

"Of course it does," he says to himself. Abruptly he cuffs one of the servants around the ear. "Away now. Away! I must prepare for the audience."

The servants bow low and scurry from the room. Rudolf inspects the robes they have laid upon him. "That foolish Jew has got it all wrong," he sighs. "What do you say, foundling? Should I cast him from the windows into the thistles and thorns of the Stag Moat? Or feed him to my lion?"

"Emperor?"

"Jakob, my valet. I expressly insisted on the mink robes today." He plucks at his sleeve and tugs it petulantly, holding it under my nose. "Does that look like mink to you?"

I study the fur with exaggerated keenness. "It seems a... fine robe, your Excellency," I say carefully.

Rudolf looks at it again. "I suppose so," he muses. "Perhaps I was a little harsh. Now then, foundling, tell me of your dreams."

"My dreams, Emperor?" I shift uncomfortably on to each foot as Rudolf settles his mass into the dark wooden throne.

"Your dreams, your dreams," he says impatiently, waving his hand to hurry me. "What visions did you see in the night? What portents? What omens?"

I struggle to recall the night-terrors that did indeed disturb my sleep. "I dreamed of Prague, Excellency...." I begin, cautiously.

Rudolf interrupts immediately. "Yes? Yes?"

"It was a Prague many years hence," I say uncertainly, unsure of where my words come from. "Centuries hence."

Rudolf's face lights like a child's. "And was it good? Was the name of Rudolf spoken with love and respect? Was I as a god to the people?"

Rudolf's questioning is making my head ache. "I...I cannot recall, your Excellency," I finish lamely.

Rudolf snorts, glaring at me with disdain. I cast around for more to say. "And there was another dream, your Excellency, of...of a place of light, a shining place... and then I remember falling, falling for such a long time, falling for an eternity...."

The Emperor is singularly unimpressed. "Trifles, foundling. Trifles. I must say, I was expecting more of you."

I stand awkwardly in front of him, the silence between us thick and edgy. I breathe a prayer of thanks as there is a brisk rapping at the double doors of the throne room, and a guard loudly announces the arrival of Sir Anthony Sherley, Percy Tremayne, and the Chamberlain, Philipp Lang.

"Assume your position," hisses Rudolf, and I hurry to squat beside him. "The other side," he whispers frantically. "The left!"

"Emperor, I am on the left," I protest urgently.

"Not your left, foundling, mine!" he snarls, and I scamper to the other side of his throne just as Lang leads up Sir Anthony and Percy. Percy raises an eyebrow at my antics as I settle into a comfortable position, brushing the dust of the floor from my knees.

Sir Anthony bows before Rudolf, and says, "Your Excellency. I trust the gifts we delivered on behalf of Shah Abbas have found favour with you?"

"Well, I have threatened my scientists in Golden Lane with rather painful tortures of my own devising should they fail to get your flying carpet to work," drawls Rudolf. "And the girl you conjured from that rug was not as... pliant as I am used to. But I have high hopes for this foundling..." here he turns his baleful gaze on me "Once he has settled in and is rested, of course."

Sir Anthony risks a momentary glance at me, his eyes seeming to convey the message *whatever you do keep the old dog happy, for all our sakes*, before responding. "Very good, Excellency."

Lang strokes his trimmed beard casually and says, "Now, your Excellency, I should think the envoys of Shah Abbas would perhaps wish to discuss the business that has spurred their epic journey from the Arab lands."

Rudolf shrugs and bids Sir Anthony continue with a nonchalant wave. Percy takes his cue and steps forward. "Excellency," he says, bowing as low as he can. "As you are no doubt aware, Shah Abbas is raising an army to teach the Turk a lesson. The Godless Ottoman Empire is snapping at the heels of civilised lands like a rabid dog, and while the Shah is under no illusion that the might of Bohemia would find it any great effort to vanquish the Turk alone, he is proposing a coalition of countries to present a united front to show the Ottoman Empire that such behaviour cannot be forgiven."

"As you say," interrupts Lang, "The Holy Roman Empire could swat the Turk like a horsefly if his Excellency but gave the word. Why should Bohemia rally under the banner of your Shah Abbas, himself no less of a heathen than the Ottoman?"

Sir Anthony glances at Percy, seemingly willing that his lieutenant's oratory skills not fail him now. Percy ignores Lang, turning his attention to Rudolf, who slumps on his throne, idly sucking his thumb in boredom. "Excellency, the Turk is becoming braver by the day. Your family in Vienna has already seen incursions into the Habsburg lands; it is only fair that we impart what intelligence we have gained from spies deep within the Ottoman Empire."

Rudolf raises an eyebrow, bidding Percy to continue. He does, leaning in closer towards Rudolf with a theatrical confidence, a stage whisper. "The Turk is driven by astrological omens, your Excellency. Godless they might well be, but the Ottoman Empire has discovered the value of the very sciences that you yourself seek to unlock here in

Prague. It is said…" and here Percy glances around, as though looking for spies within the very throne room of Rudolf's castle "…that the Turk has seers and mystics able to predict precisely the right conditions for success in battle."

Mention of astrology and mystics has Rudolf enraptured. "By God," he breathes. "And they called me a fool in Vienna when I moved the seat of the Empire here to Prague, and began my patronage of the occult arts. I was right. I was right."

Lang is looking perturbed, his lips set in a tight, bloodless line. "Excellency," he says doubtfully. "I would strongly urge caution with this venture. The costliness of financing any kind of extended war on the Turks would prove prohibitive at best, and I would argue that this is perhaps not the right time to rush the Habsburgs into a conflict the Empire may not yet be fully ready for...."

Rudolf sighs, holding up both hands. "Sir Anthony, you and your man put forward an attractive argument, yet I am once again indebted to my Chamberlain for his words of caution in this matter. It is something I shall need to dwell on for a while, and to take advice on from my generals. I shall call you again when I have made my decision."

Sir Anthony looks slightly crestfallen; he was evidently expecting a swifter conclusion than this. He shoots Lang a narroweyed glance, then bows. "Very good, Excellency. We shall await your summons."

As Sir Anthony and Percy turn and leave the throne room, Lang says, "Excellency, Master Arcimboldo has requested a sitting for your portrait this morning. If you are willing, I shall call him in at once. It will give me the opportunity to show more of the castle to your foundling, and to take him to Master Brahe and Master Kepler for more examinations."

Rudolf nods his acquiescence, his jowls slumping on his chest, already lost in some reverie. Lang grips me hard by the arm and steers me to the doors of the throne room, looking at me coldly. "Come, 'Mirror of Prague'," he mutters.

I hurry to keep pace with Lang's bold strides as he leads the way through the dark corridors of the castle and outdoors, where the sun is high but the air is chill. "Let us walk in the Royal Gardens," he suggests, his black cape sinuously winding about him as he heads over the Powder Bridge that spans the Stag Moat and into the fragrant arbours beyond.

"The Royal Gardens are a marvel of Prague, foundling," says Lang, leading me along the gravel paths deep into the bowers. "They were designed by our court gardener, Francesco, to provide colour and scent all year round. Figs we grow here, and grapefruits, and spring sees an ocean of tulips stretching as far as you can see."

Lang slows and stops, stooping to smell a rose bush. "It is beauty and goodness, like the Empire itself."

He straightens again and pauses a moment, as though considering all this beauty, then turns his head slightly, his eyes narrowing. "Foundling," he says carefully. "I do not trust you."

I am suddenly aware of being alone in this shaded garden with Lang, a man considered even by the formidable Sir Anthony to be dangerous. "There is no reason to distrust a man without memory," I say.

Lang muses for a moment. "Somehow, foundling, you have inveigled your way into the Emperor's confidence. Very convenient for Sir Anthony's cause, wouldn't you say?"

"I had not met Sir Anthony until yesterday, Chamberlain."

"As you say. Yet your tale hangs oddly on you, foundling. These are times of tribulation we find ourselves in, and the Emperor is not... a well man, at best. He is the figurehead of this great Empire, and as his Chamberlain it is my sworn duty to act in his—and the Empire's—best interests." He smiles, an unconvincing and half-hearted facade of friendship. "Look at it from my point of view, Poutnik. The House of Habsburg is one of the most influential in Europe. There are certain factions within it who are not... wholly enamoured with Rudolf's position as Emperor. There are those who would betray him, within these very walls. And that is before we make mention of the Turks, or the Catholic contingents who are unhappy with his embracing of Protestantism, or the Jews in the Ghetto, or capricious Elizabeth in London. I shall die before I allow this Empire to be hurt, foundling. And I shall kill those who make the attempt."

There is silence in the Royal Garden as Lang regards me with his impenetrable hawk's stare, a silence that is shattered by a dreadful roar that seems to shake the leaves from the trees and causes me to stagger slightly.

Lang is amused to note my expression of alarm. "Ah. Feeding time. Come, foundling, I imagine you shall find this instructive."

Lang walks on through the gardens to where they open up into a meadow, bordered by high walls, which features as its centrepiece a huge, sunken paddock bounded on all sides by a cage of strong iron. The ear-splitting roar issues again, and I stare aghast at the creature padding around the centre of the enclosure.

"The Emperor's lion," says Lang proudly. The beast is huge,

muscle and sinew coiling and flexing beneath its golden fur, its paws as big as dinner plates, its lustrous mane framing its maw lined with rows of bright white teeth. Seeing us, it lets out another growl, so low as to make my bones rumble.

"It is hungry," points out Lang, and I feel his claw-like hand settle upon my shoulder.

"Come closer, foundling. Take a look," insists Lang quietly, pushing me to the bars. The lion pads closer, sniffing the air, looking at me both curiously and menacingly.

"Magnificent, is it not? The king of all the rude beasts. It has been predicted that Rudolf shall die only when this lion dies," whispers Lang fiercely into my ear, his grip tightening on my shoulder. "Look at this lion, foundling. Does it appear near death to you? Do you think you could kill this lion with your bare hands? With a rapier? With a hundred rapiers?"

"No, Chamberlain," I gasp.

"No. No, you could not. It is as healthy and strong as the Empire itself, and not you nor Sir Anthony nor Doctor John blasted Dee when he arrives would last above a moment in that cage. That is as it is with Rudolf. He may look a sick man, he may be called mad, but he—and his Empire—are as vital as that lion. Be warned, foundling. Be warned."

There is a small commotion behind us and four of the castle guards in leather tunics and battered boots crunch up the gravel paths pulling a small cart carrying the fresh carcass of a large deer.

"Ah, about time," says Lang mildly. He speaks in the Bohemian tongue, perhaps fancying that I cannot understand. "The lion is hungry. I feared I would have to feed the Emperor's new pet to it."

The guards grin, eyeing me and glancing at each other. Word of my adoption by Rudolf has spread quickly. "No need today, Chamberlain," says one of the soldiers. "Freshly killed venison for the beast."

"Just as well," agrees Lang. "There is little meat on this one, I would imagine."

The guards laugh again, and one collects a huge pike from a lean-to beside the cage, and thrusts it in between the bars at the lion, which sits down and watches him with an air of detached boredom. It is evidently a procedure it is used to.

A second soldier unlocks a gate set into the huge cage, while the remaining pair heft the deer carcass on to their shoulders. With the swiftness and ease of practice, the gate is opened, the deer tossed into the paddock, and the cage locked again. The guard returns the pike to the lean-to and the four soldiers salute Lang and take their leave.

We watch as the lion tears into its meal, ripping flesh in its teeth and swallowing great chunks, until Lang has evidently decided I have seen enough. "Come, now. Brahe and Kepler await us in Golden Lane."

"Do you know why they call it Golden Lane?" asks the nervous, young man with the unkempt beard, Master Kepler. I sit almost naked on an examining table in a draughty room that comprises most of one of the tiny terrace of low-ceilinged houses adjacent to the main castle buildings. The houses are painted gaudily in colours of yellow, orange, green and blue, and look almost to have been shoved up against each other by giant hands.

"Most people outside the castle think it is because it is here we strive with our alchemical pursuits, our mission to turn lead to gold," says Kepler with a lop-sided grin of rotten teeth showing through his beard. "But really it's because the castle guard barracks are just up the hill from us, and their latrines empty straight on to this street. The only gold in Golden Lane is the river of piss running down the gutter. It's something of a joke, you see...."

The stench rising from the narrow, cobbled street is certainly no joke, and backs up Kepler's story. I wonder how Rudolf's scientists manage to work under such conditions.

"Quiet, Kepler," says Brahe, annoyed. He evidently has no problems with the stench, given the golden nose strapped to his face. "He's not here to make small-talk with, he's here to examine."

Kepler shrugs and grins shyly at me again. I shouldn't think he gets much chance for conversation with his stern master. Thankfully, Lang has business elsewhere and has left me alone with the alchemists. Over the past hour or more they have measured me again, noted my weight, cut my toenails and snipped at my hair, held candles to my eyes and scraped at my flesh. All of their notes have been carefully printed in a large ledger. "So are you any closer to finding out whatever it is you're searching for?" I ask.

Brahe raises his head from a series of complicated calculations on a scrap of paper, and sighs heavily. "I am not quite sure exactly what the Emperor expects us to find out without fully dissecting you, which he has expressly forbidden."

Kepler gives a nervous laugh. "He's joking," he assures me. Brahe blinks at him to suggest that he was anything but.

As Brahe goes to the rear of the cluttered laboratory to seek out an abacus to aid his calculations, Kepler hops from foot to foot, stealing sly glances at me.

"What exactly is it you do here, this alchemy?" I ask to break the silence.

"To explain would take a lifetime," says Kepler, "and then I would only scratch the surface. To people like Chamberlain Lang we are merely trying to transmute base metals to gold; that is the layman's view and we are happy to let them remain in their ignorance. Alchemy is so much more... spiritual."

Kepler halts abruptly as Brahe returns with his abacus, expecting to be berated for talking to me. The scientist with the grotesque golden nose considers me silently for a moment, then says, "I do not need calculations and tests to tell me that you're cut from a different cloth than most, Master Poutnik. Let me tell you something of alchemy."

Brahe sits himself heavily on a wooden stool, placing his abacus and calculations to one side, and thinks to himself for a moment, idly rubbing his metal nose.

"It is correct," he says, "that alchemy is often thought to be the pursuit of creating gold from lesser elements. The simple truth at the heart of this is that alchemy is about transformation, no more, no less. It is about utilising the power of invisible spirituality and impressing it upon the raw matter of nature, to effect a significant change.

"Everything in the cosmos is duality, Master Poutnik. Man and woman. Life and death. Light and shade. All dualities are in constant war and motion, and can only be balanced by a third element, a harmonizer. This threefold nature is at the heart of alchemy."

Brahe stands and points to a chart showing a depiction of a naked man. "Take ourselves, Master Poutnik. We are a prime example of the threefold nature, the triple secret, call it what you will. Man is composed of the swirling chaotic state in which he enters the world, his rude, primal, animal lusts. This, his basic life-power, we say is represented by the element Sulphur, and its base of power is here in the loins.

"His other aspect is the rational thought-process, his self-awareness, his mind, which is ultimately his death-power, for it conveys upon him an acute knowledge of his own mortality. We represent this with Salt.

"The two are constantly in turmoil; the life-force and the death-force pulling at each other, rational thought and animal passion vying for control. It is the third element, that of Mercury, the emotional centre of man, which binds them together, and keeps them apart, and strives for balance."

Brahe picks up an ingot of lead from the workbench. "As with mankind, so it is with all. Here I have the product of the earth, the worthless and base Sulphur."

He waves his hand in the air. "Around us is the spiritual Salt of thought and reason, the order that is the sacred dew of Heaven."

Brahe lays the ingot back down with a sigh. "Somewhere is the Mercury, the force that balances, that can be shaped into a tool to work the Salt and the Sulphur, to create something new. It is the third element that it is the curse of alchemists to spend their lives searching for."

After a short silence, Kepler speaks. "There are those who say the essential element required for alchemy is the fabled Philosopher's Stone. It unlocks the secrets of the threefold nature, and can grant ultimate knowledge and eternal youth. They say that Doctor Dee...."

Brahe shoots Kepler a warning glance. "No more talking. Dee is a charlatan and a fool. He shall be exposed as such in short measure. Now, I must get back to these calculations and prepare a report for the Emperor forthwith."

As Brahe immerses himself in his formulae, Kepler busies himself tidying the workbench. I sit idly, thinking on Brahe's words, until my eyes fall upon a series of charts hanging on the nearest wall, depicting coloured orbs in circular sequence with one another. "What is this?" I ask. "More alchemy?"

Brahe looks up briefly. "It seems we have not exhausted our guest with our explanation of alchemy, Master Kepler," he sighs. "Feel free to inform him of our other researches."

Kepler is by my side before Brahe has finished speaking. "We're very proud of this work," he grins breathlessly. "We are formulating what we call the Laws of Planetary Motion. I must say, a lot of this is my study. It interests me immensely."

I examine the chart. At its centre lies a representation of a flaming ball. "This must be the sun, then?"

Kepler appears taken aback, and even Brahe looks up again. "Well, yes," says the young alchemist, glancing at his master. "Ah, does not that strike you as odd, Master Poutnik? The sun at the centre of the universe?"

I shrug. Kepler goes on: "It isn't new thinking, by any means. Copernicus himself has posited it. But most people still dismiss the idea, and are loathe to abandon the concept of our world as the focal point of the heavens."

Brahe intercedes again, "Master Kepler has made painstaking observations of the planets and improved upon the work of Copernicus to the point where I would lay a fair wager on the prediction that this will be the model of astronomical study for generations to come."

As Kepler blushes with pride I study the diagrams with the planets in elliptical orbits around the sun a little closer. "I'd say you would be a wise man to do that."

There is a knock at the door and Kepler opens it to a messenger from the castle. "The Emperor has called for you, Master Poutnik," he says.

Brahe stands and accompanies me to the door. "I have taken all the tests and measurements I need, I think. I shall continue with my calculations, and make my report to the Emperor soon."

"What do you think your findings shall be?"

Brahe looks at me contemplatively. "You are a curious man, Master Poutnik. A curious man. You recall I told you of the threefold nature? Of the duality between Salt and Sulphur?"

I nod.

"I detect none of that in you, Master Poutnik. No conflict. Either you are the most supremely balanced human being I have ever set eyes upon, or...."

"Or?"

"Or... you are neither Salt, nor Sulphur. If I didn't know it to be impossible, Master Poutnik, I would have you as wholly Mercury. The balancer. The unifying force. Almost as if you have been inserted into the endless battle on this Earthly plane to add some kind of resolution."

Brahe shakes his head, as though angry at his own words. "I speak foolishness, but I would caution you with this—and this is something that will not be in my report to the Emperor. Alchemy is a fickle art, and one of the many problems is that the introduction of Mercury can indeed bring balance—but at a cost. Often the Mercury is polarised by the Salt or the Sulphur; in essence, it becomes one or the other in order to achieve the balance. Think upon that, and take care, Master Poutnik. Take care."

Seven
Nightwalking

Days pass, and I settle into a comfortable routine of working at The Leopold Bloom, relaxing in the house, and exploring Prague. I have discovered that I don't really need to sleep. If I lay down and close my eyes, sleep of a sort will come, but my dreams are filled with strange visions which evaporate soon after waking. But if I do not sleep, I do not feel tired, so I have taken to wandering the streets of the city at night, roaming across the Vltava by one bridge and returning by another, losing myself in the narrow cobbled streets of Mala Strana, skirting the edges of bright and brash Wenceslas Square, closing my eyes and feeling crowded by ghosts in the dead midnight air of the Old Town Square, and pulling my coat tight about me and taking the walk up the hill to Hradcany. To the castle.

"To the castle," says Karla. I think of Karla often on my meanderings through the small hours, puzzled by her, puzzled by all of them. Such different people, yet brought together by reasons beyond my understanding, bound by a glue I do not yet understand. Karla has explained in simple terms to me their hatred of the big corporations that control everything from the music we hear to the clothes we wear, at the expense of the poorest people in the world, who are tasked with manufacturing the trinkets that define modern civilisation, yet are paid but pennies for their trouble. Of the corporations' slow but sure destruction of the very planet, of the collusion between them and governments until the lines between them blur and shift.

"It's an evil empire," Karla says to me, and her words set me adrift on an ocean of forgotten memories, which play like fish just beyond my reach in the dark depths.

These, then, are the ties that bind them. Karla, Petey, Cody, Jenny, Padraig, and the mysterious John, of whom I understand so little. They seem in turn afraid of him, in awe of him, in love with him. He appears to be as charismatic as he is legendary.

Only Karla has displayed any healthy scepticism with regard to John. Padraig sees him as a natural leader, a rebel to whose standard the

Irishman is grateful to rally; Petey sees him as a mystic, a bodhisattva, a saviour. Karla distrusts him, I can tell. Yet still she stays.

As well as not thirsting for sleep, I have also come to realise that I don't really need to eat anything, either. I never feel hungry, and more often than not push my food idly around my plate while listening to the easy conversations around the house. When I am working or in the house alone, I have noticed that I often forget to eat or drink at all.

It is Tuesday again, and as Padraig prepares another roast lamb dinner for the entire household—the first time everyone has been in together at the same time since I met them—I realise that a week has passed since I was discovered on Letna by Karla on her horse. After the meal I help Karla clear the dishes.

"Weren't you hungry?" she says, noticing the food pulped and played with on my plate. "I ate late at the pub," I lie, scraping the leftovers into a plastic sack in the kitchen. I am unsure why I lie—perhaps because my lack of appetite would seem strange to them, perhaps because I do not wish to hurt their feelings after they have taken me in with such generosity. I feel I ought to eat more, but sometimes when I catch sight of them forcing forkfuls of food into their mouths I feel inexplicably sickened.

Karla fills the sink with hot water from the ancient iron taps, and steam billows about her as she feeds the crockery into the washing-up basin. "So, how's your first week with us been?" she asks.

I pile the plates up on the work surface. "I'm not remembering anything, if that's what you're getting at."

She turns to me, peering intently into my eyes. "You're an odd one, Pooty. I sometimes feel like you're here for a reason, for a purpose. Are you?"

"If I am, I don't know what it is."

There's a pause, then I add, "I'm not a spy."

Karla looks at me sharply. "What on Earth do you mean?"

I don't know what I mean. It seemed the right thing to say. I flush slightly, somewhat embarrassed. "I'm sorry. I don't know. Sometimes... sometimes I say things or think things but they're wrong, like I'm... having a different conversation with someone else."

"Or remembering a different conversation with someone else?" suggests Karla.

Cody pops his head around the kitchen door, glancing at Karla and scowling at me. "Jenny's after the rent money," he says, giving me a pointed stare.

"Fine," says Karla curtly. "Then you can finish the washing up,

Cody."

She tosses the cloth at him and leads me out of the kitchen. Cody grimaces and shoots me a look again. "Maybe we'll get the chance for a little chat later," he says to me.

Back in the dining room, Petey is assembling a joint while Padraig counts out money from a stack of bills for Jenny. "The Lord giveth, and Jenny taketh away," he says, handing over the money. "I don't know why we don't just get Noel to send our wages straight to her, what do you say, Pooty?"

Taking my cue, I dip into my trouser pocket and withdraw my wages. Noel has found me work every day since I started there, and I'm grateful for the money it has brought in. I peel off a number of notes and push them across the table to Jenny. She gives me a smile and says, "God, that's the first Tuesday I remember when everyone's paid their rent. We should celebrate."

"That's what we're doing, man," says Petey, holding up his finished joint. "New stock, fresh in today."

"Ah, not for me," says Padraig, standing. "I'm on the graveyard shift again tonight. How about you, Pooty? You working?"

I shake my head. "Not until Thursday."

"Oh, good!" says Jenny. "I've no classes tomorrow, either. We can have our shopping trip."

Karla purses her lips, accepting the joint from Petey. "Don't you usually see Lisa on your days off?"

"Lisa's sort of my girlfriend," explains Jenny to me.

Karla cuts in again. "Sort of your girlfriend? I thought she *was* your girlfriend. Full stop."

Jenny frowns at Karla, turning back to me. "Okay, she is my girlfriend. Full stop. But tomorrow, I'm going to take you shopping." She looks at Karla again, before adding, "If that's okay by everyone else here?"

Karla and Jenny glare at each other for a moment, before Karla shrugs and stands. "I don't know what you're asking me for," she says. "I'm going to go help Cody do the washing up."

Padraig has an amused look on his face. "Boy, Pooty," he says in a stage whisper. "It looks like you've got the ladies fighting over you."

"I heard that!" shouts Karla from the kitchen.

"Heard what?" comes Cody's voice, followed by Karla telling him to never mind and hurry up with the dishes before the water gets cold.

"Ignore her," says Jenny. "She's just jealous."

"I heard that, too!" calls Karla.

"Heard what?" says Cody, exasperatedly. "What the fuck's going on, man?"

Jenny winks at me. "See how much trouble you're causing?"

I stand awkwardly. "I, uh, think I'll go for a walk."

"Good idea," says Petey. "Mind if I join you?"

I shrug. I had intended to head out towards the castle again, where I always feel on the verge of remembrance. I don't expect to recall much with Petey accompanying me.

Petey ties up his long straggly hair with an elastic band and climbs into a thick army greatcoat. "Come on, man, let's go smoke a doobie by the river."

It's about eight by the time we stroll across Charles Bridge, dark and cold but busy with tourists. "I love Prague, man," says Petey, sucking on his joint. "Fucking love it. Can't you feel it? It's like magic, man."

I nod. Prague does have an atmosphere that's almost solid. "How long have you been here, Petey?"

We pause by the statue of King Wenceslas, watching the tourists swathed in scarves and coats hurry by on their way to restaurants and bars. I think Petey hasn't heard me as he watches through his slits of eyes, the smoke trailing from his mouth. Eventually, he says: "It feels like forever, man. You believe in reincarnation?"

"Reincarnation?"

"You know. Past lives. Rebirths. Shit like that."

"I don't know. Do you?"

Petey pauses again for a long time. "I must have come to Prague what, two years ago? The minute I got off the train, I felt like I'd been here before. It was like I knew exactly where to go, felt like I'd seen the statues and the buildings and the streets before a million times. You ever get that feeling?"

I think back to walking the streets in the cold hours of the early, early morning, my feet picking out an unerring path from Mala Strana to the castle to the Jewish quarter. "Yes," I say absently. "Yes, I do."

"It's Prague," says Petey quietly. "It's like we've all been here before in former lives, and somehow we know it, deep down, and we just make our way back here unconsciously."

"Do you think that's how the others got here?" I ask. "Because they felt... compelled?"

"Can't speak for the others, but that's the feeling I get. I'd bummed around a bit after college, fell in with the anti-capitalist network back in the States. Did the big demos in Seattle and London, then just drifted towards Prague. I'd been living down in Zizkov in a horrible squat when I met Cody at a party. He's really into it all, you know, the anti-globalisation stuff. He's rabid, man. It always just felt like the right thing to do, for me, but that kid's obsessed. I think he must've choked on a Burger King or something when he was little."

"So did Cody introduce you to John?"

"Yeah, they'd already got the house in Mala Strana. Padraig was there, then I moved in, then Jenny, then Karla. It's a good set-up, man, a good cell. John's the shit."

"I'm looking forward to meeting him."

Petey flicks the roach into the night over the sluggish Vltava and delves into his coat pocket for another one. "He's radical. He can be a bit fucking scary at times, I don't mind admitting, but we'd never get anything done without him."

I sense an opportunity to try to understand the group more. As Petey lights the joint I say, "What exactly is it you do, Petey?"

"Bit of culture-jamming, adbusting, few pranks. The usual. Cody always goes on at us to get more hardcore. 'We need to FUCK SHIT UP, guy'." Petey snickers at his own impersonation of Cody. "John calls the shots, though. He wants us to stay low-key, at least until November fifteenth."

"What happens then?"

"November fifteenth? It's the big one, man. The World Trade Organisation oil industry exposition in Prague. The N15 protest's going to be the biggest shit anyone's ever seen. You stick around, you're gonna be part of it as well. It's gonna be awesome, man. Awesome."

Having ghosted along the dark, wet streets of the city for several nights now, I elect to sleep, or at least surrender myself to the scattered images that play behind my eyes during the quiet small hours.

I am awake and staring at the ceiling of John's room from first light, listening as first Karla leaves for work at her newspaper office, then Padraig departs for The Leopold Bloom. I hear Cody shuffling around the bathroom before heading back to bed, and Petey strumming his guitar softly in his room. There is a small knock at the door, and Jenny puts her head around. "Pooty? Hi, wasn't sure if you were up. I brought you a cup of tea."

Jenny, clad in a fluffy dressing gown, perches on the end of the huge bed and I accept the steaming mug from her. "Pleasant dreams?"

I search for the right words to describe my swiftly fading night visions. "Castles... horses... giants and death," I say eventually.

Jenny looks at me with her dark eyes. "Sounds like you had too much of Petey's skunk before you turned in last night," she says reprovingly. "Never mind, I know just the thing to shake off the cobwebs. You up for some retail therapy, Jenny-style?"

"Is that your professional medical advice?"

She laughs lightly. "You'd better take it as well, buster. I'm the doctor here. Well, going to be. See you downstairs in half an hour, then? We can get a bit of breakfast in town, if you like."

I nod assent and Jenny withdraws, leaving me alone. Even my dreams have dissolved with the morning dew.

"The first thing we need to get you is some decent clothes," decides Jenny as we sit in the warmth of a small café in the huddle of streets behind the Old Town Square. "A couple of pairs of good jeans, some T-shirts, and a thick jumper or two. Then we're going to need some gloves, a scarf and a hat. Definitely a hat. It gets bitter over here when winter sets in. Christ, I thought winters in Manchester were cold until I came here. Nearly froze my arse off last year."

We sip our hot chocolate, watching as tourists bundled in woollen clothes strip off their layers as they enter the centrally-heated café. It's colder than it was last night even, and the clouds are thick and gravid with rain, or even snow.

"This is my last year of medical school," says Jenny conversationally. "I won a scholarship at university to be seconded to a European hospital, and I chose Prague."

"How did you meet Karla and Cody and everyone else?" I ask.

"The last Prague protest. A few of us from the hospital set up a voluntary medical facility in a squat just out of town, because we knew there were going to be some injuries. John got hit round the head by a copper, and I bandaged him up. I'd seen him and Cody around, and I got talking to them. I was sharing a room at the hospital at the time, and it was a bit cramped, so he asked me if I wanted to move in. That was about eight or nine months ago. They're a bit of a mixed bunch, but the house is fantastic. I think you'll like living with us, Pooty. I really hope you do, anyway."

I finish my hot chocolate. "It's been good so far," I agree. "When do you think John will be back?"

Jenny shrugs. "He's been over in Thailand and Laos for a few weeks, travelling around. He's due back anytime, though."

"Before November fifteenth, presumably?"

Jenny looks at me curiously. "Who's been talking? Karla, I bet."

"I didn't realise it was a secret. The protest."

Jenny shrugs again. "It's not, I suppose. I guess you're one of us now, anyway. You up for a bit of direct action, then?"

"I suppose. It seems a worthwhile cause."

"Oh, it is," says Jenny, her eyes lighting. "It's the oil industry we're going up against this time. They're raping the fucking planet, Pooty. Do you know, this world's going to be uninhabitable in less than forty years? And unless they build us a space rocket to take us to Mars before then, we're all going to be fucked. Even the oil barons. What's the use of having all that money when there'll be nowhere to go and nothing to spend it on? If only they could see things like John. If only they'd just listen to him. He's a bloody prophet, Pooty. But when twenty percent of the population has eighty percent of the global income, who's going to listen to a prophet? It's profits they're more interested in."

She smiles sourly, lighting a cigarette. "Do you want one of these? I know I'm not exactly setting a good example, being a medical student and everything, but once you're addicted...."

I take one of the cigarettes and look at it. "This isn't like one of Petey's," I say uncertainly.

"Nah, this is one of the legal ones," says Jenny, exhaling smoke. "Probably best if you don't have one, if you're not sure. I don't want to be the one who started you smoking. Another example of globalisation screwing the planet, this. Still, we all have our weaknesses." She pauses and appraises me. "And I'm beginning to suspect that you're Karla's particular Achilles heel."

Watching the smoke curl from Jenny's cigarette, I feel myself flush and try to change the subject slightly, "Do you and Karla not get on, then?"

Jenny sighs. "We do, usually. She's just been a bit weird recently. Well, since you came, I suppose. Cody's an arsehole, as we've already established, but he's good people. She's been a bit short with me, since I, well, since I mentioned to her...."

"About us kissing?"

Jenny puts her head down, peering at me through the straight fringe of black hair that hangs over her forehead. "Uh, yeah. I was meaning to speak to you about that."

Jenny gathers her thoughts, stubbing out her cigarette and lighting another one immediately. "Look, Pooty," she begins with resolution. "I'm gay. Lesbian. I've got a girlfriend, Lisa, who works at a bookshop in the New Town, and we've been together for six months. I haven't kissed a boy since I was fourteen years old. I knew on that rainy day in

Salford that it wasn't for me. I'm into girls. But when I was with you the other night... I don't know. Don't take this the wrong way, but I'm not sexually attracted to you."

She shakes her head, as though looking for the right words. "I just felt like I had to do it. I felt drawn to you. You're a mystery, Poutnik, and something about mysteries fascinates me. Kissing you was wrong. But it felt like the only way to get into your head. Shit, I'm not making a very good job of this, am I?"

I'm not sure what to say. "Look, Jenny, I understand. People keep telling me I'm easy to talk to, to be with. I don't know who I am or what I'm doing here, but I'm not here to cause trouble. Everything's okay, right? Matter closed."

She looks at me gratefully. "Thanks, Pooty. It was just a moment of madness, that's all. But it is true what you said about people opening up to you. There's something, I don't know, pure about you. And people tend to want a piece of that. Just be careful, okay? Not everyone's as good as you, you know."

By the time we come back to the house dusk has fallen, and our cheeks are red with cold. We burst into the house laden with bags, to find Petey, Padraig and Karla hanging around in the lounge, respectively smoking, reading, and watching TV.

"We're back!" announces Jenny unnecessarily.

Karla looks up from the TV, which is burbling quietly in Czech. "Good shopping trip, guys?"

Jenny dumps the bags on the sofa and starts to unwind her scarf. "Got Pooty some winter gear, and just in time, too, with the looks of it. It's getting a bit chilly out there."

Padraig is uncharacteristically quiet and doesn't even look up from his book. As Jenny starts unravelling the packages, he sighs loudly, stuffs a bookmark into the paperback and leaves the room.

"Is Padraig okay?" I ask. Jenny, Petey and Karla glance at each other.

"Padraig can be a little... down, sometimes," says Karla carefully. "I think there was some heavy shit back home he was involved in. He doesn't talk about it. It's best to give him a bit of space when he has a downer moment. He's generally back to his usual self within a couple of hours."

"I'll go and make some tea," I decide, heading into the kitchen. As I pass Petey he sucks on his joint and murmurs, "Did you get the shit, Jen?"

Jenny replies in a low voice, and I don't catch the words. But I do remember her packing me off to browse in a pottery shop while she said she had to run a "quick errand". She returned minutes later with a newspaper parcel in a paper bag, about which I thought little. But I'm suddenly put in mind of the crates I saw Padraig hunkered over in the cellar of The Leopold Bloom, and the package that Karla received from the waiter at the art exhibition and secreted within the folds of her coat. Still, they're entitled to their secrets. It's just that, as with Jenny, I appear to be fascinated with mysteries, both of myself and of those who have taken me in.

I return with a tray of tea. "Where's Cody?" asks Jenny as I hand her a cup.

"Out meeting the fucking Wombles," sighs Karla. "The guy's completely starstruck. He's planning N15 like it's some kind of military operation."

"Wombles—White Overalls Movement Building Libertarian Effective Struggles," says Jenny to me by way of explanation. "They turn up to all the anti-capitalism stuff. They wear these all-over white suits, padded to stop them getting a good kicking from the cops. I like them."

"I just wish Cody wasn't so far up their arses," complains Karla. "He's desperate for them to invite him to join so he can wear a fucking boiler suit."

"He is not," chides Jenny. "He's one of us."

"True, Cody's too much into following John to get into the Wombles," Karla corrects herself. "They're too non-hierarchical for him. He needs a leader."

Jenny pulls a mischievous face, glancing at me. "Things not too rosy in the love-nest, then?"

Karla pouts at Jenny and tosses a cushion from the sofa at her. Jenny dodges, spilling her tea down her jeans. "Shit. Now look what you've done. It's a good job I let it go cold, as usual. Better get changed anyway."

She stands, and pauses at the door. "Petey, don't you have some astral travelling to do or something?"

Petey blinks and looks around. "Sure, I guess so."

As they both leave the lounge, Karla shoots Jenny daggers.

"What was that all about?" I say.

"Nothing," says Karla. "Just Jenny up to mischief. So, what did you get, then?"

I unpack the bags and show Karla my clothes, all bought by Jenny as a loan. Karla pulls a face.

"They're okay," she sniffs. "Could have got you something a bit more stylish, though. Next time you come shopping with me."

"I'd like that," I say. "It was nice, today, with Jenny. We had a good talk."

Karla raises an eyebrow and looks at me. I recall Jenny's words. *She's just been a bit weird, recently. Well, since you came, I suppose.* "Oh? What about?" Karla says.

"Nothing much," I say. We sit in silence for a couple of minutes, then Karla stands up.

"Look, I'm going to go get a bath, Pooty. You okay on your own?"

"Of course. I might go for a walk."

"Okay, take care. See you later."

As Karla heads up the stairs, I hear her pausing at Jenny's door, and her muffled voice: "I want a word with you, girl."

This house is a confusion to me. It is as though there is some unspoken truth which I have yet to grasp, some secret signs being made with passes in the air at my back, some smooth shared telepathy which cuts through my clouded thoughts with such sharpness as to barely disturb them.

Like a poultice, Prague draws me from the bafflement. It is only while walking at night that I feel any measure of peace. I leave the darkened house by the garden, carefully latching the gate behind me. The shadows of Mala Strana, the Lesser Quarter, are deep and multi-layered around me as I wait quietly by the gate, until my eyes get used to the cold darkness.

The night is not quiet in Prague, at least not to my ears. Spirits whisper at my shoulder at every turn, their shoes falling into cadence with my footfalls on the echoing cobbles, drawing their coats about them along with me as the icy wind roars off the Vltava. They look upon Prague with their invisible eyes, and the Prague each of them sees is different to the one that unfolds in darkness before me. While night-walking like this I feel like I can almost see through their eyes, yet by morning they disappear as the pale sun burns the fog off the river, any understanding I might be approaching in the small hours evaporating with them.

Emerging from the side-streets I turn a clockwise circuit of Mala Strana Square, circling St Nicholas's Church. During my midnight excursions I have come to know Prague, its sights and streets, its landmarks and echoes. I pause by the Column of the Plague, hearing the death rattles of the tenth of the city's population struck by the fever three centuries ago. Outside the Gromling Palace, the House at the sign of the Stone Table, Kafka's ghost shuffles through snow long ago thawed, on his way to the café on the second floor to brood and dream.

From the Liechtenstein Palace that dominates the upper part of the square I hear the sounds of music. No ghosts these, but the very real song of the students practising in softly-lit rooms at the Academy of Music throughout the night, as restless and insomniac as myself. And always, always, the castle stands proudly above, surveying the city scattered below. As imposing as the castle is, Mala Strana is not impressed; it keeps its own counsel, squirrels its secrets away in the warren of alleys and snickets, the electric lamps bowing their heads away from the illumination of the hill-top fortifications, counting their secrets and mysteries through hooded eyes.

I turn off the square and slide into the shadowed alleys. The walls abruptly catch a sound and volley it between them: frantic footfalls, a shout, the slam of a gate. But it is impossible to tell where it comes from. I hurry to the house.

Where I find Cody in the shadows by the gate, sucking on a cigarette. "Poutnik? That you?" he says with suspicion. I step into the pale starlight. "Hello. Are you okay?"

"Where the fuck have you been?" Cody glowers at me. "It's four o'clock in the morning."

"Walking," I say. "Just walking."

Cody tosses the cigarette to the cobbles and grinds it under foot. "That intruder's been here again. Look at this."

He moves away from the gate to let me into the garden. Beneath the window is a smashed terracotta plant pot, earth spilling over the debris.

"I heard a noise," says Cody. "Guy must have been trying to stare in the window. Just saw him running through the gate as I got downstairs."

I search for something to say. "Could it be something to do with N15?"

Cody glares at me. "What the fuck do you know about that?" he snaps, then adds to himself: "Some people in this house can't keep their traps shut." He takes another cigarette out of his jeans pocket. "Christ, it's freezing."

He lights it and blows a column of smoke into the still morning. "Look, Poutnik, or whatever the hell you call yourself, I'm going to be straight with you. I don't know you, I don't trust you, and I can't say I particularly like you much. But it looks like you're staying. At least, until John comes back, anyway. But I'll say this," and he comes close to me, breathing smoke into my face. "This house, and the people in it, are very important to me, dude. There's something you're not telling us, and if it turns out that you in any way try to fuck things up for us, you're gonna have me to deal with. I don't know who this old guy hanging around is, or what he's got to do with you, but I'm not going to let you screw around with us. Is that clear?"

I shrug. "I'm not here to cause trouble, Cody," I say simply.

"Whatever," he says. "We've had our chat now, and let's say no more about it. I'm going back to bed."

Cody heads back into the house, and I stand for a long moment in the garden. Morning is approaching, though Prague has yet to waken. But I can't shake the feeling that someone is out there in the gloom, intently watching me.

Eight
The Innocents

The artist Arcimboldo is at work on his frightful caricature of Rudolf when I am announced and shown into the hall. The Emperor is still, almost dozing, on his great throne as Arcimboldo squints in the gloom of the heavily draped room, and shows no sign that he has acknowledged my entrance. I wait nervously by the painter, stealing glances at the portrait rendering Rudolf in fruit and vegetables. Arcimboldo's conical hat is askew and he casts exasperated glances at me.

"Must you hang on my shoulder like this?" he hisses. "Conditions are bad enough without you turning this into some kind of spectator sport."

"Has the Emperor seen his portrait yet?" I ask in a whisper.

"I never allow my subjects to view the painting until it is completed," says the artist proudly. "The unveiling shall be a state affair. You should not even be looking at it."

"It's grotesque," I say, involuntarily.

Arcimboldo's eyes blaze with fury. He draws himself up to his full height and fixes his hat on his head. "Grotesque? Grotesque? Philistine! This is the Emperor rendered as Vertumnus, the god of the Autumn. Those fools in Golden Lane strive to perfect petty alchemies in the stench of the midden, yet it is I, Giuseppe Arcimboldo, who is the true magician! Have I not conjured this magnificence from the thin air? Has not the Emperor's essence been captured and bottled within these brush-strokes? Is it not the glory of Prague itself that emanates from this canvas?"

Arcimboldo pauses as Rudolf stirs from his doze. "Is that the Mirror of Prague with you, Master Artist?" he drawls.

Arcimboldo shoots me an angry stare, before saying shakily, "Indeed, Excellency. And it is not good for my concentration to have such interruptions."

Rudolf rouses himself and claps his hands. "Then away with you, Master Arcimboldo. Today's sitting is over. I have important business."

His protestations ignored, Arcimboldo begins to pack away his easel and paints. "Philistine!" he hisses at me again as he stamps heavily from the throne room. I stand awkwardly before the Emperor.

"Come, walk with me, young Master Poutnik," yawns Rudolf, stretching his arms and hauling himself out of his chair. "I would show you something."

Rudolf takes up a candelabra and shuffles painfully across the great hall to a pair of wooden doors sealed with a huge padlock and hanging with velvet drapes. Today he is clothed in black; breeches and shirt and cloak, with only a white ruff in the Spanish style to break the gloom of his attire. He fumbles with his thick fingers about the ruff and pulls a brass key on a leather cord from his shirt.

"Have you heard tell of my cabinet of treasures, foundling?" he says.

"The Kunstkammer. Yes, Excellency."

Rudolf bends forward to allow him to place the key in the padlock. "Then you shall see it, Mirror of Prague."

Rudolf rights himself and removes the padlock. There is a dull sound, as of a million insects marching out of time, which sharpens as Rudolf throws open the doors. I am expecting a large wardrobe, at best a small antechamber, but beyond the doors is a cavernous room, almost as large as the great hall we stand in. The source of the noise becomes apparent; the room is lined with clocks of all shapes and styles, fixed to the wainscoted walls, standing free, piled on shelves. And between them the room is suffocating with marvels.

I follow Rudolf into the room, picking our way through the objets d'art which litter the floor, spill out of chests and hang from nails and gutted torch clasps. It is a treasure trove beyond the imaginings of any spinner of tales. Even silver-tongued Percy Tremayne, with his fables of Eastern excesses, would stutter at describing such a hoard. I pause by a wide tea-chest, its lid hanging from broken hinges. Inside, scattered like pebbles on a beach, are cut gems of breathtaking beauty. Sapphires, rubies, emeralds and diamonds, cast as carelessly as one would throw chicken-feed.

Rudolf turns and sees me looking wide-eyed. "Bah. Gimcracks and geegaws. Jewels are mere breadcrumbs at my table. Come."

We tiptoe deeper through the glittering cavern Rudolf has created, the clocks keeping their own individual time all around us, pendulums swinging and hands shifting inexorably around faces of ivory, jet and stone. The Emperor seizes a gnarled tusk and brandishes it at me. "The horn of a unicorn" he whispers, his eyes shining. In his other hand he seizes a large egg. "Ostrich," he muses. "Perhaps a roc."

One by one, the wonders are presented to me by an increasingly feverish Rudolf. Some are almost fantastical: A rude, rusting nail he claims is from Noah's Ark, a lump of clay from which God fashioned Adam, the tooth of a kraken. Others are more mundane, like the knife swallowed by a peasant and removed from his stomach, as though by Caesarean section, by a surgeon nine months later, or the petrified tangle of tails from a rat-king discovered in a house on Golden Lane.

Rudolf scrabbles through a chest, emptying drawers on to the floor and casting golden statuettes and glass figurines carelessly around him. "Where is it?" he mutters under his breath. "I could have sworn it was here."

I look up from a leather-bound manuscript of ancient, brittle pages scrawled with indecipherable script and meaningless diagrams. "What are you looking for, Excellency?"

The book I hold catches Rudolf's eye. "That's the Voynich Manuscript; its meaning has eluded my best scientists. Take it with you and see what you make of it." He continues to delve into boxes, becoming increasingly frustrated. "I had a scarab encased in amber, brought to me from the land of the pyramids. It must be here somewhere, I only saw it yesterday."

As he leans heavily on a chest of drawers to catch his breath, I lean forward to examine a glass case containing a miniscule sitting room peopled by grotesque, twisted homonculi.

"Mandrake roots in the shape of men," breathes Rudolf raggedly. "There is meant to be a way to animate them, but this once again eludes my so-called experts. Which reminds me, foundling. I have an errand of the utmost secrecy for you to run. Come, sit with me."

I seat myself on the floor as Rudolf settles himself into a jewel-studded chair, and he ruminates a while as I shift uncomfortably on the draughty stones. Finally he says, "Tell me, foundling, what do you know of Doctor John Dee?"

"Only what I have heard in the castle, Excellency. That he is an alchemist and a magician. That he converses with angels through a scrying mirror. That he was the court conjuror of Elizabeth. That he is on his way here."

"It is true Doctor Dee is bound for Prague. At my invitation. Many fear him, foundling, yet I am fascinated by his work and expect to gain much from having him reside here at my court for a while. However, he is a greatly learned man, and I would have some topics of discourse I can share with him on level ground. It is said that Doctor Dee has great knowledge of the Cabala, the esoteric knowledge of the Jews. I would have this knowledge also, my Mirror of Prague."

Rudolf pauses. I say, "And you would have me obtain this for you, Excellency?"

"I would have you aid me in obtaining it, foundling," laughs Rudolf. "I would not expect you to understand the Cabala yourself and relate it to me!"

"So what is to be my errand, Excellency?"

Rudolf leans close to me. "A secret mission to the Ghetto," he whispers. "A visit to Rabbi Jehuda Loew ben Bezalel. But secret, foundling! It must be secret! I would not have Chamberlain Lang or any other in the court know that I consort with the Hebrews on such matters. It would be seen as a sign of weakness, and I must be strong at this time when so much threatens my throne. Find Loew, and tell him to visit me here in the castle, tomorrow at nightfall."

I wait for more instructions, for details on how to find this Rabbi, but Rudolf has abruptly lapsed into a semi-comatose state. Leaving him snoring softly, I steal away from the massive cabinet of wonders, and out of the great hall.

The Ghetto. My only knowledge of it is the brief glimpse I saw from the tower with Lang. And now I am to visit there in secrecy and locate this Rabbi. I, who have no memory of the world outside these castle walls beyond that short ride with Sir Anthony Sherley and his company, must now skulk through the shadows of this immense city alone and unaided.

I ponder my errand in the corridor outside the great hall. I could ask the impassive guards, armed with pikes and rapiers, who stand sentry by the double doors, but Rudolf has sworn me to secrecy. I set off walking down the torch-lit corridors, my feet shuffling through the brittle straw underfoot, uneasy that by following the Emperor's orders I am about to make an enemy of his chamberlain.

Ahead of me, there is a swift movement and the tinkling of bells. I frown and peer into the shadows, but can see nothing. As I walk on, the bells sound again, rattling hollowly in the stone corridor. I walk forward more slowly, and jump as a dusty tapestry jerks a few feet ahead of me. I rush to it and pull the heraldic drape to one side, but there is only grey stone beneath.

The bells ring again, now distant and tinny, now right by my ear. There is a high-pitched laugh, deadened by the thin, black air. My eyes narrow. It is Jeppe, Rudolf's dwarfish fool. I spin at another sound and see a shape cartwheel through the pool of flickering torchlight at an intersection of corridors. Then there is silence, Jeppe's mischief evidently at an end. For the moment.

"Jakob! Jakob, are you there?" I hammer loudly on the door of the Emperor's valet once more, until it is opened by the surprised servant.

"Master Poutnik!" he says. "Is there some kind of problem? His Excellency does not wish a new outfit, does he? I was not told...."

"Nothing like that, Jakob," I say, pushing past him into the dark room hanging with clothes and silks. "I need your help."

I sit down on a stool while Jakob goes to make some tea in the small kitchen at the rear of the huge room. "Of course, Master Poutnik. What can I aid you with?"

As be brings the cup of tea to me, I say, "But I must swear you to secrecy, Jakob. You must tell no-one of this."

"Of course, of course. What is it?"

"I have been despatched on a mission by the Emperor," I say in hushed tones. "I am to arrange a meeting between him and Rabbi Loew. But I do not have the faintest idea where to find him."

Jakob strokes his wind-burned chin. "A meeting between the Rabbi and the Emperor, you say? Well, good luck, Mirror of Prague. It would be easier to bring the White Mountain to the castle than to persuade Rabbi Loew to set foot in here."

I moan softly. "Oh, Jakob, can you not help me? You are a Jew, are you not?"

Jakob smiles at me crookedly. "What, you think we all know each other, or something? It's not like being in a club, you know."

"Yes, sorry, that was stupid of me," I say, draining my hot tea and standing. "I apologise. I had better be off. Can you at least give me directions to the Ghetto?"

Jakob holds his hands in the air and bids me sit again. "Slow down, Master Poutnik. As it happens, I do know Rabbi Loew. Everyone in the Ghetto knows him. I was just fooling with you there. I can take you to him, as well, but not right now. I have to prepare the Emperor's robes for his evening dinner."

"Could you not give me directions, then?" I plead. "I must get this errand done today."

Jakob purses his lips. "I could, but it would not be advisable. I don't think the Ghetto is a place you should wander alone."

The ancient valet muses for a moment, then clicks his fingers. "I have a plan. I shall send you to the Ghetto with Hannah, and write you a letter of introduction to the Rabbi. That is the best solution."

"Hannah? I don't know, Jakob, I'd rather not involve anyone else...."

"Oh, do not worry, young Master," smiles Jakob cheerfully. "Hannah is most trustworthy. She is, you see, my daughter."

I wait impatiently in the room while Jakob converses quietly with his daughter in the kitchen area. She is young and small, with black hair scraped severely off her face and held in a string at the back, evidently a scullery maid in the castle by her simple shift dress.

"But father," I hear her say. "I cannot just leave the castle...."

"Hush, child," says Jakob soothingly. "I shall make things right with Mrs Hulbert in the kitchens. This is a matter of grave importance, and you must speak to no-one about it nor ask Master Poutnik too many questions."

More urgent whispering follows, and presently the pair emerge from the recess. "It is done," says Jakob, handing me a parchment envelope sealed with wax. "Hannah shall take you to the Ghetto. Give this letter to Rabbi Loew and, God willing, he shall help you in your task."

I take the envelope, glancing momentarily at the indentation Jakob has made in the seal, a number of interlinked circles in clusters of three, with one more at the bottom of the network. "Thank you, Jakob. And Hannah. I am grateful for your help."

"We had better be off, then," sighs Hannah. "I want to get back before I am missed, because I do not trust my father's ability to appease Mrs Hulbert for long."

"Oh, I have a way with Mrs Hulbert," says Jakob airily, winking at me. "Now go."

We slip out of Jakob's room... and my heart catches in my mouth as we come straight up against the dark figure of Philipp Lang, standing silently in the corridor, his hands clasped behind his black-clad back, one eyebrow raised at us.

"Ah, the Mirror of Prague," he says. He nods at Jakob's daughter. "And young Hannah. What have we here, then?"

Hannah bows her head, staring at the carpeted floor, saying nothing. I realise it is up to me to come up with some kind of excuse. "Chamberlain," I falter. "I was just with the Emperor earlier. I was just checking on this evening's apparel with Jakob."

Lang frowns. "That is another of your tasks, is it, now? To keep track of the Emperor's wardrobe?"

"It was just... I was passing...." I trail off. I look to Hannah for support, but she keeps her head down, a dead look in her eye.

Lang follows my gaze. "And this is what you found in the valet's quarters, is it, Master Poutnik? A scullery girl skiving off work? Well done."

Hannah's eyes flash angrily now, but she remains silent. "I... I got lost finding my way to the wardrobe rooms," I say quickly. "I saw, uh, Hannah, on the second floor, and she offered to bring me here."

Lang nods. "I see. And yet, you just told me you were to be passing this way, on whatever journey you were taking. How curious, that one should have to ask directions to a place one is planning to be passing by."

"I...."

Lang waves his gloved hand. "Please, Master Poutnik. You obviously have places to be, and I should not keep you from your errands. Good day."

"Chamberlain," I nod. Lang smiles viperishly, and casts a glance at Hannah, before striding off down the corridor.

"Fool," whispers Jakob's daughter as Lang rounds the corner. "You almost gave away the whole game there."

"You were hardly much help," I protest.

She looks at me, eyes dull in her pale, plain face. "It is not for a scullery maid to speak to the Chamberlain," she says simply. "Now, shall we move on lest this errand takes us all day?"

It is only when we are beyond the huge gates that I realise it is as though the environs of the castle were Prague for me; I had almost forgotten the huge rambling city spread out around its feet. I am suddenly spellbound by the hawkers and traders lining the narrow street that winds downwards, the clamour of their voices and the squawking of poultry, the woodsmoke that curls about the rooftops, the distant banging of a drum and playing of a flute. The streets are packed with people; beggars in rags and hard-faced women busying themselves with errands and gossip, haughty nobles lightly stepping through the filth, goats and dogs scavenging in piles of foetid rubbish. Hannah presses on through the throng, and for a moment I lose her and panic amid the foetid, roaring press of humanity, but she turns just a few feet ahead of me, materialising out of the anonymity she wears like a shawl. "Come on, Master Poutnik," she says sourly. "We don't have all day."

I apologise and hurry to match her pace as she strides down the lane. A sudden crack and a puff of black smoke startles me; a woman emerges from the smoke to a ripple of applause from a knot of onlookers and a man wearing a turban and cheap silks takes a bow.

"Where is the Ghetto?" I ask after a few minutes of silent pushing through the crowds.

She shoots me an angry look. "Not so loud. It isn't good to advertise the fact we're going there."

"Why not?"

She stops, hands on her hips, and looks at me with her head on one side. "Look, my father told me not to ask questions of you. I'd appreciate it if you could return the courtesy."

I shrug and fall into step beside Hannah again. She cuts off the lane and into a large square dominated by an ornate chapel. "St Nicholas's Church," she volunteers quietly. "This is Mala Strana Square. We're going across the Charles Bridge, over the Old Town Square, and up into the Ghetto. All right?"

"Thank you," I say.

The Charles Bridge is heaving with people and carts, trying to cross both ways. From its balustrades, blank eyed statues stare down at the morass of humanity, the water glittering coldly as it ponderously weaves beneath. On the muddied banks of the river women wash clothes, men fish, and filthy children sport. As we approach the Mala Strana bridge tower, I feel Hannah stiffen besides me as she spies a group of soldiers leaning lazily against the walls, their pikes propped up against them. "Oh, no. Landsknechte," she whispers.

"Landsknechte?"

"Mercenary soldiers. Prague is crawling with them since Rudolf became emperor. They answer to whoever pays them, and honour is lacking. Speak to them only if we are spoken to."

As we approach, one of the guards, an unshaven wretch with barely any teeth, holds out his rag-clad arm to stop us squeezing through a bottleneck at the entrance to the bridge. I feel Hannah's anxiety. I glance at her but she again has her head cast downwards, as she was when we were confronted by Lang at the castle.

"What's your business?" drawls the guard, eyeing Hannah's shape beneath the shift dress.

"Castle business," she mumbles.

The guard looks at his comrades, who grin back at him. They appear to be about to have some fun at our expense.

The mercenary who accosted us makes a mock bow in front of Hannah. "My apologies, milady," he says in ingratiating tones. "I did not realise I was in the presence of royalty."

Some of the pedestrians on the bridge have stopped to watch, a few openly laughing, others hurrying past so as to not be involved. I feel myself tense as the soldier rises and brings his face close to Hannah's. He makes an exaggerated sniffing noise over her dark hair.

"And here I thought I could smell a Jewess."

Hannah says nothing, but I take a step forward, and the guard seems to notice me for the first time. The others straighten their postures and one rests his hand on his pike.

"Ho, and who's this? Perhaps it is Rudolf himself, in disguise to walk among his people. That right, boy, or are you another stinking Jew?"

My heart is beating rapidly but I feel calm. I look the guard directly in his eyes. "Please allow us to cross the bridge," I say as reasonably as possible.

Hannah flinches beside me, and the soldier looks taken aback to have been spoken to. His hand plays about his rapier hilt and he wipes a greasy hand across his leather jerkin. Without really knowing what I'm doing, my left arm shoots out and grips him solidly around the throat. His eyes bulge and his three compatriots move as one man towards me, but I simply hold out my other hand, palm outwards, and they each freeze, hardly breathing. Hannah lifts her head and looks at me in wonder.

I keep my voice low and direct it to the guard who is slowly turning purple in my hand. "We are going to cross the bridge," I say quietly. "Look into my eyes. Do you see?"

Anger, wonder and then fear play across his face as he meets my stare. I feel his body slacken, so I loosen my grip and he falls to his knees, coughing violently. The crowd around us has grown and fallen silent. The other three landsknechte stand immobile, confused. When the soldier can speak, he manages to spit on to the cobbles and says, "Go. Cross the bridge. Just go."

Without waiting for him to change his mind, I grab Hannah's arm and steer her across the statue-fringed bridge, walking quickly and not speaking until we are over the Vltava and into the narrow streets behind the Old Town Square. All the while she is looking curiously at me, and when I finally stop, breathless, having dragged her down two or three dark and cobbled streets in what direction I do not know, she says without sourness or sarcasm, "What... exactly happened there, Master Poutnik?"

"I confess, I do not know, Hannah," I say, gasping for air.

"I have never seen landsknechte back down like that," she says softly. "They were terrified of you. The one who looked into your eyes...

he was in awe. What did he see there?"

She searches my eyes herself, but whatever it was that petrified the mercenaries is evidently no longer present. "Why did they stop us in the first place?" I say.

Hannah shrugs, her palms raised upwards. "Because I am Jewish. Because they thought you were, too." She studies my face again. "Are you?"

We resume walking, this time with Hannah leading the way. "I don't know. I'm sure you've heard the story...."

"...discovered in a ditch, no memory, a foundling dropped from the heavens," says Hannah. "I thought it was just one of the Emperor's fancies. What are you doing here, really?"

"I don't know. Really. It's all true. At least, about being found in a ditch. Before that happened, I can vouch for nothing."

The streets open up into another crowded square, lined with booths and stalls, and dominated by a black church with twin spires. "The Old Town Square," says Hannah. "That is the Tyn Church. You can buy anything here."

I step forward, drinking in the sights. I am almost brought low by the sheer mass of life going about its business all around me, shouting and laughing and brawling and courting, selling trinkets and buying food and picking pockets. It is almost as if I am connected to every single one of them, every priest, every cutpurse, every child, every maiden. Connected, yet apart, looking on while they live life yet unable to immerse myself along with them.

Hannah joins me at my side, taking hold of my forearm. She looks at me, her head cocked slightly, and says: "There are fortune tellers and seers here. The girls in the castle kitchens come all the time, to have their palms read and their destiny predicted. I am forbidden from visiting them, but you...."

I look into her green eyes. "But me what?"

"Perhaps they can help. Perhaps they can see the past as well as the future."

I scan the booths and tents crowding the perimeter of the square. "But there are so many. How do we know we are not going to waste our money on some charlatan? And come to that, I have no money."

"I have a few crowns," says Hannah. "And the girls in the kitchen speak highly of one particular fortune teller. They call him Ripellino."

Ripellino proves easy to find. A garishly painted board is propped outside a red and blue striped tent to the south of the square. Outside sits a squat man in workman's clothes, his nose bent from one barroom brawl too many. We approach slowly, and I whisper to Hannah, "Surely this is not...."

My whispers are not quite quiet enough, though. The man stands as we approach, revealing himself to have a tortuously disfigured spine, and he turns sightless eyes up at us. "The Great Ripellino? Me, sir? No, no, not at all. What a thought! He is inside, communing with the spirits. I am merely his help. Would you be after a consultation, and the like?"

I glance doubtfully at Hannah. She pushes me forward. "Yes, yes he would," she says. "How much is it?"

The blind hunchback appears to size us up with his milky, useless eyes. "Half a crown, my dear. Payable up front. Some don't like the bad news, you see, and refuses to pay. I told the Great Ripellino, I says 'you don't want to give 'em the bad news, then, do you?' but would he listen? Insists on telling it like it is."

He pauses and Hannah holds out a coin, which he snatches from her hand with uncanny dexterity for one apparently blind. "I'll just see if the Great Ripellino is back on the same plane as us, so to speak."

He vanishes into the tent, and I turn to Hannah. "I'm really not sure about this. I would be on with my errand...."

"It won't take but a few minutes," she assures me. "The Ghetto is only one or two streets away."

The hunchback emerges then, and says, "The master will see you now, sir. Don't fret about your young lady; I'll take good care of her while you are inside."

Shrugging, I push through the flaps of the tent into the candle-lit gloom within. Incense fills the air, and Ripellino is sitting behind a table covered with a blue cloth decorated with golden moons and stars. He is thin and pale, with a pointed beard and short-cropped, black hair. His eyes dance under thick eyebrows as his gaze follows me.

"Welcome," he says richly, and indicating a stool in front of his table, adds, "Please, be seated."

I do as he bids. On the table, to Ripellino's left, is a crystal globe. To his right, a parcel of purple silk tied with a length of cord. The candles flicker and settle as I make myself comfortable.

"So," he says. "What is it to be? A palm reading? The cards? The runes? What do you wish to know?"

"Who I am," I say simply.

Ripellino nods, and lays his hands on the purple parcel to his left. "The cards, then. A simple three-card layout with the Major Arcana to begin with."

The fortune-teller unwraps the cards and caresses them softly, murmuring under his breath. "I am Italian," he says conversationally, shuffling the cards. "We Italians perfected the use of the Tarot a hundred years ago. True, they say the art began in the times of the ancient Egyptians, and decks have been seen in the hands of the Chinese and Indian traders. But it was in Italy that the decks we use now were created."

Ripellino expertly spreads the cards in a neat fan across the table. "Choose three," he instructs. "Take your time. Pick the ones that feel right, that call to you."

My hand hovers over the fanned deck; after a moment I select three cards. Ripellino gathers the remainder up in a fluid movement and places them to one side. The three cards he arranges simply, face down, on the table between us.

"This first card is your past," he says. "Let us see what brought you to here."

He turns the card over. The colourful picture depicts a man sitting on a throne, an orb in one hand, a sceptre in the other. It is numbered with the Roman numeral IV. Ripellino raises an eyebrow. "The Emperor, reversed. The Emperor represents the highest authority, absolute power. It is the father-figure, it is governance by logic over emotion. You have been oppressed, perhaps? The victim of some tyrannical behaviour?"

He turns to the second card. "Your present," he explains, turning the card. Its number is V. A priest in long robes holds a staff. "The Hierophant, also reversed. This is the symbol of religious power, of the establishment, of order. Upright, it stands for freedom and truth, yet reversed, as here, it indicates lies and distortion. Information is being kept from you. You are being restricted. There are those who are dishonest who would gain favour with you for their own ends. Beware."

Ripellino turns to the final card. "The future," he says. "That which is to be, or perhaps that which only might be."

He turns the card. This one needs no explanation from the fortune-teller.

"The Devil," I breathe.

"Again, reversed," points out Ripellino, looking at me curiously. He gathers his thoughts for a moment. "The number of this card is XV, which represents the conflict of opposites. When the card is reversed, this is even more acute. Decisions will have to be made, and you will have to follow either your head or your heart. Act with honour, do the right thing, and the imbalance can be rectified."

Ripellino gathers the cards and puts them with the rest of his deck.

"Intriguing," he says mildly. "Does any of that help, at all? Does it have meaning for you?"

"I'm not sure, Master Ripellino," I say haltingly. "Your reading has interested me greatly. You see, I am without a past. I remember nothing up to a few days ago."

"We all have a past, whether we remember it or not," says the seer. "Why don't you remember yours, sir? What are you blocking out? Or is someone blocking the past for you? Remember the card, The Emperor, reversed. It can also mean a loss of perspective on a situation, a dilution of power or position. Who has cast you out, sir? This is what you need to find out."

"But it is all so vague...."

Ripellino gathers the deck again. "Another reading, then, sir. No extra charge. A simple question-and-answer layout. You ask the question; I shall turn over a card and give you an answer."

Ripellino shuffles the cards, again murmuring gently, either to himself or to the deck. He looks up. "Question."

"Why am I here?"

He turns the card. "Justice. A conflict approaches. You are to bring settlement. Question."

"But what brought me here?"

The card slaps gently on the cloth. "The Tower. The old order is threatened. Do you perhaps threaten it? Question."

"How am I to know what to do when the time comes?"

The card slaps. "The Hermit. Look inside yourself. Question."

I look closely at Ripellino. Sweat is beading on his forehead, the muscles in his neck strained. "Are you well, Master Ripellino...?"

"Quite well," he snaps through clenched teeth. "Question!"

"Who is my enemy?"

The card goes down. "The Magician. The trickster. Betrayal."

The fortune-teller appears distressed, his eyes wide, but still he insists: "Question!"

"How shall I be betrayed?"

Ripellino bangs the card down. "The Lovers. F-failure to recognise... to recognise true nature...."

I am concerned for the seer. For some reason he appears in real pain. "Master Ripellino...."

"Question! Question!"

"But I still fail to understand! What will be the outcome of it all?"

Two cards fall from the deck; Ripellino looks aghast, but his mouth continues to work as though independent of his mind. "The

Wheel of Fortune. Beginnings. Endings. Dreams. The World. Completion. Birth. Endings. Beginnings. Too... too many possible outcomes...."

As though of their own volition, the remaining cards fly from Ripellino's hand, showering me. I throw up my arms to protect my face; the fortune-teller gasps as though exhausted and slumps into his chair.

"Sir," he breathes, wide-eyed. "I... I have never seen the like... my body was not my own... I...."

"Master Ripellino," I say softly. "You still hold two cards."

He looks down at them almost in surprise, clutched in his sweating hand.

"I have one final question."

He calms his breathing, looking at me with something approaching fear. I have seen the look before, in the eyes of the mercenary on the Charles Bridge. "Ask," he says.

"What must I do?"

Slowly he lays the first of the cards face up on the table with shaking hands. "The Sun," he says breathlessly. "Protection. Innocence."

He looks at me. He looks at me because he knows what the final card is. Ripellino lays it on the table with a loud exhalation of ragged breath.

"Death. Change. Moving on. New beginnings. Sir, I do not know who you are or why you have come to me, but the message is clear. You are trapped in a perhaps endless cycle of beginnings and endings, never quite achieving either. I do not profess to understand what has occurred here today, but I know what the cards tell me: There is only one way to break the cycle. You must save the innocents."

His head droops, he says no more. I stand to leave, and at the tent flaps I pause and look back at him. He is as a broken man. "Save the innocents, sir," he says weakly. "Save the innocents."

Before we enter the Ghetto, Hannah insists on buying me a mug of beer at a tavern near the Old Town Square. "You look terrible," she says, handing me the cool ale. I gulp it down thirstily. "What went on in there?"

I tell her, because I am sick of intrigue and distrust in this place. I tell her because I have to start trusting someone. I tell her everything.

When I finish my tale she is wide-eyed and animated; more so than I have seen her since I first met her.

"But what does it all mean? Who are the innocents? What do they need protecting from?"

I put my head in my hands. "I wish I knew. I am even more confused now than before I went in that damned tent. I wish I had never set eyes on Master Ripellino the fortune-teller."

Hannah finishes her glass of cordial. "We should get moving now. We need to find the Rabbi and get back to the castle before we are missed. The Chamberlain seemed suspicious of us."

We leave the tavern, and Hannah leads me around the corner to where great walls rise up, dividing the city. "The Ghetto," she says, leading me through huge rusted-open gates.

God knows Prague is filthy beyond the sanctity of castle, but I am taken aback by the squalor beyond the walls that bound the Ghetto. The first time I see a rat gambolling in the street I step back involuntarily; by the time we have walked for five or ten minutes I am so used to the vermin dashing in and out of the windowless hovels seemingly heaped upon each other that I ignore them.

"Welcome to the Jewish quarter," says Hannah wryly. "Nice, isn't it?"

"You live here?" I say, shocked.

Hannah nods. "I have to. We all have to. We have suffered generations of persecution and hatred, but we get by. If we keep our heads down and get on with our business, we do not get much trouble these days, apart from idiots like those guards. So long as we stay out of sight in our slums, of course."

I notice a change come over Jakob's daughter as we walk deeper into the degradation that is the Ghetto. Where she was subservient and anonymous in the castle and the outer city, here she is vibrant, confident. Beautiful. She greets people on the street, tosses a coin to filthy children rummaging in a stinking rubbish heap, waves to shopkeepers who wave back through doorless passages as raw filth runs past their windows. She points out a wall adorned with the fading mural of a dense wood.

"The only trees in the Ghetto," she says. "We are not without a sense of humour."

"Where shall we find Rabbi Loew?" I whisper to her.

She laughs, the first time I have heard her utter such a sound. It is far from unbecoming. "No need to whisper here, Poutnik," she says. I note she has dropped the Master, but do not comment upon it. "As to where we shall find the Rabbi...."

She stops and I look about us. Compared to the hovels in the tightly-packed streets, the building we stand before is a veritable palace.

It is tall with an intricate wood carving of fig-trees over the door, and has more space surrounding it than I have seen so far in the Ghetto. "The Old-New Synagogue, we call it," says Hannah. "The Rabbi should be inside. Wait here while I check."

Moments later Hannah emerges from the Synagogue. "He is inside. He shall see you now."

I am led into a small ante-chamber near the entrance to the gloomy Synagogue. There, in an austere room, Rabbi Loew awaits. He is small and frail, even with his tall, black cloth hat, his long beard is more grey than black, his face lined with years of woe. Yet his eyes burn bright and he regards me with a cool intelligence. "Master Poutnik," he says, inclining his head slightly. "Welcome to the Ghetto."

Remembering the introduction Jakob penned for me, I take the envelope out of my shirt and hand it to the Rabbi. He glances at the curious seal, tears it open, and reads it thoughtfully.

"So, Master Poutnik, you are on an errand from our dear Emperor Rudolf," he says. "Do you know why he would summon me to the castle in this manner?"

I am rather at a loss for words, not knowing how much to impart. "I am merely the messenger, sir," I say.

Rabbi Loew hobbles up to me and pats my shoulder. "Good boy. But Master Poutnik is much more than that, we hear, hmm? The Mirror of Prague, is it? A foundling, fell from heaven?" Loew cackles, not without good cheer. "It is good to see the Emperor still finds time for his little flights of fancy."

Loew wanders to the small window in the ante-room that looks out on the squalor. "Not so good, what goes on in the Ghetto, though, hmm? Not so good. Our dear Emperor and his courtiers have their fancies and flying rugs and clockwork mice, I dare say, but what of the Ghetto? What of Rabbi Loew's people?"

He turns his head with effort and winks at me. "No need for clockwork mice in the Ghetto, eh, Master Poutnik? Real ones as big as cats!" He cackles again.

Having seen the Ghetto with Hannah, who sits quietly by the fireplace in the ante-room, and compared it to the opulence of the castle, I am in no mood to push Rudolf's case for this man to run to Hradcany at the Emperor's beck and call.

"Still," muses Rabbi Loew. "It should do me good to get out, hmm? Maybe you can tell our dear Emperor that I shall be there... what was it, nightfall tomorrow?"

I express my gratitude to the Rabbi and he painfully limps to the door of the Synagogue to wave us off. “One more thing, Master Poutnik,” he calls as I walk down the muddy track with Hannah.

I turn to him. “Yes, sir?”

“Just remember, there are a lot of innocent souls could do with saving here at the Ghetto, hmm?” he shouts. And he winks at me.

“I didn’t say a word!” protests Hannah, before I can say anything. I glance back to where the Rabbi is closing the door of the Synagogue. Hmm indeed.

Interlude Two

Uriel listens, and speaks. He knows it is forbidden, knows that the game in the world beyond the shining silver city is not his to play, yet play he does. The risks are mighty, no-one has dared to do what he does, yet play he dares. The vengeance of The House would be swift and terrible, he is sure. Yet, he continues the game.

With his mouth of light he imparts secrets and wisdom that are not his to dole out. He speaks in the language of the birds, delighting the fragile sacks of bone and blood beyond. Yet, he reasons, why not? The knowledge of the silver city is infinite; much of it shall never be used again. It sits in the archives and the libraries, whispering dustily to itself, wonders filed in alphabetical order, mysteries heaped behind locked doors, marvels going to waste. Why not play the game?

He parts the water that is not water with his fingers that are not fingers, light slicing light, and allows an aspect of his beauty to manifest in the crude scrying stone of the bloodbones beyond. Were he to expose his essence to them, he would flay the mountains and freeze the seas. But he allows them a fraction, a side-on glance, a will-o'-the-wisp to keep them content.

Why? Because it amuses him. It amuses him to confound the rules of The House, it amuses him to play the game that is not his to play, it amuses him to cast wonders before the bloodbones and see them use his miracles for nothing more than obtaining rude coinage for themselves. He could pass on a whisper from The House, drop a pearl of light through the mirror, utter a single syllable of his own true name, and give the bloodbones a sword with which to smite the silver city with a single blow.

But he does not.

He leaves the singing pool, slip-sliding to the balcony and looking out over the silver city, encased in darkness beyond. He loves the city; it is his life. So as it ever been, so shall it ever be.

Nine
Adbusting

Cody can barely contain his excitement. He rushes into the living room brandishing a piece of paper. "I just got an e-mail from John! He's on his way back!"

Jenny looks up from her book. "What's he say?"

"Not much, really. He's in Bangkok now. He's been to Laos, Cambodia and even snuck into Burma! Man, he rocks."

"I guess he'll want to get right on with organising our contribution to N15," says Padraig.

"We've pretty much got everything in place now, haven't we?" says Petey.

"What exactly are we going to be doing?" I ask. Cody raises an eyebrow at my inclusion of myself in the group. The others glance at each other.

"It's a prank," says Karla with marked indifference. "We'd probably better wait until John gets back before filling you in properly. We all know what he's like for changing his mind at the last minute about stuff."

"He is not," scolds Cody. "Jesus, I wish you'd cut him some slack once in a while, Karla."

She shrugs and returns to her magazine. Cody goes on, "Anyway, I was thinking we might do something to welcome him back."

Jenny claps her hands. "A party!"

"Great," mutters Karla. "Place'll be wall to wall with fucking Wombles."

Cody shoots her a glare. "I was thinking something more appropriate, actually. There's a big fucking Esso hoarding gone up on the road from the airport. It's in English, too. Let's make the language of globalisation the language of revolution. Anyone up for a bit of adbusting?"

"Try to concentrate," says Jenny.

"I thought you told me to relax?"

She sighs and stands smoothly from the cross-legged position that I have uncomfortably and unsuccessfully tried to ape. Jenny had decided meditation might help me recall some of my invisible past. I have no shifts at the bar for a couple of days, and Jenny's lectures are sparse this week, so she has invited me to her room for some peace and quiet. We have been facing each other, eyes closed, matching our breathing for ten minutes or so now, but I can feel myself getting fidgety.

Jenny crosses the room and inserts a CD into the stereo. "Perhaps some soft music will help you chill out a bit."

She starts the CD playing and at the same time drags the curtains across the window, where bright light is slanting in. The flare of a match in the gloom startles me slightly; but it is only Jenny lighting candles which begin to waft scented smoke around the room.

She adeptly adopts the lotus position in front of me again. "There," she says softly. "That should help us to relax a little. Now breathe with me, Pooty. I'm going to slow it right down. Try not to think of anything at all. Nothing at all. No…"

No communication

"…interruptions. Follow my breathing, Pooty. Keep your eyes closed. Think of nothing for…"

Forbidden. Communication is forbidden

"…a few moments. Breathe... breathe...."

The quiet, calming music and the lazy smell of the incense and the tiniest hint of candlelight behind my eyes distil into a single sensation: the sound of Jenny's heartbeat, at first in slight discordance with her breathing, then absorbing the sound, merging with it, becoming all.

"...."

Jenny has spoken but I no longer feel totally here in the small dark room. My eyes are closed but I am beginning to see. The ghosts who walk beside me on my midnight rambles allow me to look through their eyes, to see what they see.

And it is death.

In a Paris bordello jackbooted soldiers in steel-grey uniforms unleash hot bullets on a huddle of frightened women as I can only watch and scream, a fourteen year old girl who I have brought to this place—to her doom—jerking as the gunfire slices through her, blood spewing from her mouth.

Under a blazing sun, slaves who have at my quiet instigation refused to lift one more block of back-breaking sandstone to complete the construction of a vast pyramid are mercilessly butchered by swarthy swordsmen; a good man who believed in my rousing claims that freedom is worth dying for looking at me with dull, accusing eyes as the light of life sputters and dies within him.

A frightened boy, far from the farm where he was born and raised with his four brothers and three sisters, weeps as he puts the barrel of his gun into his mouth, looking at me once with tear-blurred eyes before closing them tight and blowing the back of his head off, falling to the ground with his slaughtered comrades as enemy guerrillas abandon their stealthy progress through the steaming jungle and emerge, bemused at the unexpected self-sacrifice.

In the ruins of a once-great city, a man who had believed me to be the saviour of his dying race falls under the brutal blows of a barbaric horde as I hide in the rusted shell of a school bus, amid the bone-dry ashes of children long-since murdered in the ultimate war to end all wars.

All is death. All is my fault.

"Pooty?"

My mind ravels back into my body with the snap of twanged elastic. Jenny has crawled across the rug to me, peering with concern at my face, one hand resting on my shoulder. "Are you okay?"

I shake my visions away. "Jenny...."

"Did you see something? Did you remember...?"

Images crowd my mind, then the ghosts close their eyes, and they are gone. I pound the floor with frustration. "I could see...." I say helplessly.

Jenny has retrieved a notebook and pen. "Tell me what you saw, quickly, while you remember."

But it's no use. All that remains is a patina of death, the accusing eyes of those who died, the unshakeable knowledge that somehow it was all my fault.

Jenny sighs, putting the notebook to one side. "Well, at least we seem to be getting somewhere. We'll have to pursue this again."

There's a brief knock at the door and it opens. We look up as Karla stands in the doorway, nonplussed, returned from work on her lunch-break.

"Oh," she says, looking down at us on the rug, the room in darkness, the strong scent of the candles suddenly cloying. Composing herself, Karla runs a hand through her hair and says briskly, "Didn't expect to find you here, Pooty. Uh, Cody's called a house meeting. About tonight. See you downstairs in five minutes."

As Karla quickly closes the door Jenny lets out a low giggle. "Oops. That's set the cat among the pigeons."

"What do you mean?"

Jenny aims a playful punch at me. "Jesus, Pooty, there must be some things you remember! Karla's hot for you."

"Hot for me?"

"She fancies you, dickhead," grins Jenny. "And this cosy little tête-à-tête will have her fuming."

I'm not sure what to say. I think I'm blushing. "We should go downstairs," I suggest.

Jenny nods. "You're right. Better give Cody his last chance to play leader of the gang before John gets back. Come on."

We assemble in the living room, but I am too itchy with the detritus of my visions to take full notice of what is being said. We are to deface an advertising billboard, it seems. The reasoning behind this is lost on me, but I try to concentrate on what Cody is saying and push the death away.

"Fucking Esso, man, can you believe it? It's like Manna from Heaven."

"Johnny'll be impressed, right enough," says Padraig. He has assembled several tins of paint in the corner of the room.

"We'll split into three teams," says Cody. "Karla, you and…"

"Pooty," she says quickly. Everyone looks at her. Cody says quietly: "Well, I was going suggest you came with me."

Karla flushes slightly. "Pooty needs someone with him who's going to keep him out of trouble. I thought we could take the watch detail."

After a short, uncomfortable silence, Padraig speaks up. "She's probably right, Cody. Me and Petey are both going to want to be in the thick of it. Jenny's the best climber, so she can't partner Pooty."

Cody sighs. "Okay. Fine. Me and Jenny, then, on the ropework. We'll climb to the top and let the ropes down to Petey and Padraig. We'll pull you up and you can do the artwork. Karla and Pooty can keep watch."

"Sounds like a plan," says Jenny, glancing at Karla with the faintest of smiles playing on her lips. "What time are we heading out?"

"About three in the morning, I reckon," says Padraig. "Petey's checked the airport timetable; there's nothing coming in or going out between one-thirty and four-forty-five. Traffic should be low. Should give us plenty of time."

Everyone nods their agreement, and Cody hands out some Polaroids of the billboard in question. "I took these this morning. Any ideas?"

The ad is a huge poster depicting a photograph of a family in a car, all of them at turns flustered, angry, bored, while the driver unravels several huge roadmaps, with the legend ESSO: We're helping you plan it alongside. As far as I can gather, it refers to some kind of computerised route-finder device the oil company has manufactured.

We all study the Polaroids for a few minutes. Cody has a smug look on his face; evidently he has already had time to think of what we are going to do. He produces a sheaf of computer printouts from beside him.

"Had a tinker earlier on the PC," he says. "What do we think?"

We each get one of the pieces of paper. It shows the same billboard, but subtly altered. "We paint over a few letters, and hey presto," says Cody.

The slogan now reads: PISSOFF: We're raping the planet.

"Genius, man" says Petey. "Absolutely fucking righteous."

The rest of the afternoon strolls by lazily. Karla goes in to her newspaper, Padraig has a shift at the Leopold Bloom. Jenny ensconces herself with her medical text-books, Petey and Cody mull over the plan for tonight. I wander restlessly from house to garden, garden to house, eventually laying on my bed, trying to recapture the visions from my meditation session with Jenny without much success, other than conjuring an overriding feeling of horror.

Instead, I turn to thinking about my predicament. It occurs to me for the first time that no-one seems overly concerned about my presence here or my lack of memory; I have been assimilated into the house by a strange osmosis, become part of the population and its politics. Perhaps they are odd people, these who I find myself around, yet I have no yardstick to draw comparisons against. For all I know, they might as well be the only people I have ever met in my life. I have no frame of reference, no experience to measure my situation.

Are they good people? Bad people? Or maybe just people? I only know of them what they tell me, what they show me. They are as rough sketches to me. It is as though I am but a mirror, held up against them, reflecting the surface but not absorbing that which is hidden beneath. What part do I play in their dramas? What is my role here?

I sigh. It's pointless. There's a wall of fire preventing me from seeing beyond the moment I was found on Letna's green parkland by Karla just a few days ago. Whoever I was before, I have to re-invent myself now, based on what I learn of my world around me and those who inhabit it. It is to be hoped I am in good hands.

I am roused from the stasis that passes for sleep by Karla rapping at my door and opening it slightly. "Pooty? It's time."

I quickly dress in the black clothing loaned to me by the other members of the house and make my way to the living room. Karla and Cody are already there; Padraig emerges a moment or so after me, yawning, his hair sticking up in comical tufts.

"What time is it?" he says, pulling out his tongue, as Jenny joins us from the kitchen, sipping on a cup of coffee.

"Two-forty-five," says Cody curtly. "Where the hell's Petey?"

"Up in his room, sending a prayer to Ganesh," says Jenny.

"Jesus Christ," mutters Cody, and turns to checking a series of harnesses he has spread out on the sofa.

"Ganesh?" I say.

"Petey's god of the week," explains Karla. "Hindu guy with an elephant head."

Petey shuffles down the stairs. "The omens are good, dudes," he announces. "Doors are opened; obstacles removed. It's going to be a good jam."

"Well, if we're quite finished with cups of tea and Hindu elephant gods," snaps Cody, "we might want to get this show on the road."

We slip out of the gate into the dark chill. Padraig leads us to a squat, boxy car parked under a dull streetlight nearby. "It's going to be a bit of a squeeze," he says as he and Cody load the tins of paint and four rucksacks into the boot. "But I think we'll manage. Be quite cosy!"

"I presume the irony of us using a car to go and protest against the oil industry isn't lost on anyone," sighs Karla.

Cody rounds on her. "What the hell do you want to do? Get a cab, all dressed in black and carrying all this gear?"

"It's Noel's motor," Padraig says to me. "Bit of a compromise, I suppose, but Cody's right. Using the enemy and all that."

We bundle into the car, Padraig driving and Cody up front. The rest of us squeeze into the back, me wedged in between Jenny and Karla, Petey's lanky frame folded up on the end. Jenny squeezes my knee. "Exciting, isn't it?" she grins. Karla scowls but says nothing. Cody turns round in the passenger seat as Padraig crunches the car into gear and slips away from the kerb.

"Right, listen up. Here's the deal. This billboard's right on the main road, facing up the road towards the airport, maybe a mile away. It's a pretty busy road normally, but we should be okay at this time of night.

And if we stick to the plan, this should take no longer than fifteen minutes, tops."

"Fifteen minutes?" says Karla doubtfully.

"Fifteen minutes," says Cody firmly. "You drop me and Jenny off and do a U-turn further up the road, by the time you get back me and Jenny'll be at the top of the billboard."

"I do a lot of rock-climbing," says Jenny, squeezing my knee again.

"Padraig and Petey get out of the car with the paint, we drop the harnesses down and haul you up, and Karla and Pooty take the car to the other side of the road and keep their eyes peeled."

"And take care of the motor," pleads Padraig. "Noel'll string me up if there's so much as a scratch on it."

"After we've jammed the board we let Padraig and Petey down, they split, me and Jenny abseil down the back, dump the paint and meet the other two at the night tram stop, and Karla and Pooty bring the car back here. Fifteen minutes."

We continue the remainder of the journey in contemplative silence. Within minutes we're on the wide road that leads to Prague airport. Padraig suddenly pulls over to the kerb. "Okay," says Cody. "Jenny, out."

They head to the back of the car, haul out two of the rucksacks, and duck across the road, suddenly lost in the darkness. Padraig pulls away again, drives for two minutes, then executes a neat spin in the road and heads back down, parking in front of the huge billboard. There's a movement at the top and two ropes with the harnesses attached unfurl in front of the advertisement.

"We're on, Petey," says Padraig. He tosses the keys to Karla. "Take care of the motor, eh?"

Karla blows Padraig a kiss and he and Petey get the paint from the boot and disappear into the bushes at the foot of the hoarding. Karla slips out of the back of the car and into the driving seat. "Okay," she says. "We'll drive the car into a side street and get on the road and keep watch."

"What are we watching for?"

"Police. There are two kinds in Prague. The ones with the green uniforms are members of the national force. We don't want to run into them if we can help it. The black uniforms are the municipal cops for Prague; we should be able to get rid of them easy enough if they turn up."

We abandon Noel's car and walk to the road. Petey and Padraig are suspended in the harnesses at the face of the billboard; ESSO has already become PISSOFF.

Karla glances at her watch. "Not bad. Cody's on schedule."

I glance up and down the road, past the shuttered shops and the blank windows of apartments. All's quiet. Karla leans against the wall of a shuttered household goods store, watching the activity on the hoarding. "Do you even know what we're doing here, Pooty?" she asks, without hostility.

"Not really. I understand that you think the people who sell oil are wrong...."

She glances right and left. "The world runs on oil, Pooty. The global economy is fuelled by the internal combustion engine. Those who don't have oil want it at the lowest price and those who do have oil want to sell it for the most money. Countries like America thirst for oil more than most; so much that they go to war over it. Oh, they call it other things, such as war on terrorism or the fight to free people from tyranny, but at the bottom of it all is oil.

"It's the twenty-first century for Christ's sake. What happened to all the wind farms and solar power they promised us? There are renewable sources of energy out there, Pooty, but it's these guys—" she indicates the billboard and its rapidly disappearing original message "—who don't want to know. They'd rather spend billions digging deeper and deeper, searching for oil to put money in their own pockets rather than look at alternatives. And the Governments are in there with them."

Karla looks at her watch again. "The oil barons pay obscene amounts of money to finance campaigns to get Presidents elected, Pooty. Then the Presidents refuse to sign international protocols limiting the use of fossil fuels to halt the greenhouse effect. All nice and convenient, don't you think? Except for one small point: they're going to end up fucking killing us all."

I've rarely seen Karla so animated about the cause; up until now she has seemed less fervent than the rest of them. But her eyes blaze as she talks. This is something she believes in totally.

"Oh, shit," she says softly. I follow her gaze. Coming towards us is a police car. "Municipal cops," she says under her breath. "Just follow my lead, okay? And whatever you do, don't look at the billboard."

Within seconds the car is approaching us, slowing, and as it does so Karla lets fly with a stinging slap across my cheek.

"How could you?" she screams, as I stagger backwards in shock. "You bastard! You fucking bastard!"

The police car drifts to the kerb. I glance at it and see the two officers in the front, as Karla lets loose a volley of punches at my chest.

"Pig!" she hollers at the top of her voice.

The two cops in their black uniforms slowly climb out of the car. One of them, a young man with a pock-marked face, says in English, "Excuse me. What is going on here?"

"Ask this son of a bitch," shouts Karla, and I am shocked to see that she is actually crying now. The officers look at me expectantly.

"Uh, I...."

"The bastard's only gone and slept with my best fucking friend!" says Karla more quietly, dissolving into tears.

The two policemen look at each other, grinning openly. "Madam," says the younger one again. "You must be stopping the disturbance, please. Or we shall be forced to take action."

"Take action, then!" says Karla defiantly. "You'd better arrest this piece of shit for his own safety, or arrest me before I murder the little fucker."

"Madam," says the officer, although he is frowning now. Taking my cue I tentatively approach Karla, putting my arms around her shoulder.

"Oh, tell me it isn't true," she says dramatically, swooning in my arms.

"It isn't true," I say.

"Thank God!" says Karla, and begins kissing me. She pushes me against the wall, her lips on mine, forcing her tongue into my mouth. I close my eyes, and I can sense the embarrassed shuffling of the officers. Eventually, I hear one of them climb back into the car. "No more disturbances, please," says the other, then gets into the vehicle. It starts noisily and they pull away.

Karla is pressing up against me, her breathing heavy, and I feel my body respond to her. I open my eyes and glance over her shoulder. The billboard has been completed and the others are nowhere in sight. I pull myself away from Karla. "It's okay," I say. "They've gone."

"Good," she says, then begins to kiss me again. She pulls me into the shadow of the shop doorway. Her body feels alive and hot against mine, and I can feel her fumbling at the buttons of my jeans. My hands gravitate to her shirt, pulling it out of her trousers, her gasping as my cold hands slide up the warm curve of her back.

Abruptly she pulls back, her eyes searching mine. She seems to find what she's looking for, her gaze widening as she stares into me. "Poutnik," she breathes.

"Karla?"

"Fuck me."

I do.

We drive back in awkward silence, broken only by Karla muttering in an attempt to ease the atmosphere: "Well, that was all a bit Quadrophenia, wasn't it?"

I don't know what she's talking about. When she guides the car into the alley behind the house, all is in darkness. "The others aren't back," I observe unnecessarily.

"They've probably gone for a beer to celebrate," she says tightly. She swivels in the seat to face me. "Look, Pooty, I'm not sure what brought that on, but...."

"Don't worry. I won't tell Cody. I won't tell anyone."

"It's not just that, damn it, it's...." She trails off, her eyes widening. "Pooty. The gate. It's open."

I follow her gaze. In the blackness of the garden I sense a sudden movement. "There's someone there," I whisper.

Karla reaches behind the seat and feels around on the floor, her hand emerging clutching a tyre iron. "Open the doors very quietly," she mouths.

The click of the car door sounds like a gunshot and we both wince. As we ease ourselves out of the car, Karla slides noiselessly to the wall beside the gate, motioning for me to join her.

"We'll rush him" she whispers, then in a fluid movement kicks open the gently swinging gate and yells: "Stay right where you are!"

There's a scuffling movement in the garden and I glimpse a shape ducking to our left. Karla swings uselessly with the tyre iron, and I leap in the direction of the intruder, the wind flying out of me as flailing arms connect with my chest and I go down in a heap on top of the figure.

I regain my breath as the intruder wriggles beneath me, and Karla shouts, "Hold him, Pooty!" as she whips out a pencil-thin flashlight and clicks it on.

The strong beam reveals a face contorted in terror. A face I have seen before. As has Karla.

"It's that postcard seller," she says after a beat. "The one who gave you the evil eye on Charles Bridge that day I found you."

She's right. Terrified eyes shine out of a wind-burned face, a toothless mouth moving silently in fear. Then the eyes see mine, and the intruder at last finds his voice.

"Master Poutnik!"

Karla swears under her breath. My prisoner tries to push me off but I hold him tight.

"Master Poutnik," he says softly. "Do you not know me? It is I. Jakob."

"Jakob...." I repeat. "I... do I know you?"

As my grip slackens the old man brings up his knee into my crotch and I slide off him in agony. His wiry frame springs up and he swings out with his arms, knocking the flashlight out of Karla's hand. As the light spins crazily on the grass, I see through my pain the old man ducking out of the gate.

"Save the innocents, Master Poutnik!" he calls, his voice borne on frantic footfalls, disappearing down the alley. "Save the innocents!"

Ten
The Sea Monster

I am troubled by my journey to the Ghetto, not least by the fortune given to me by the mysterious seer Ripellino, which has raised more questions than it has provided answers. Rudolf, however, is delighted by my securing of the Rabbi's promise to visit him in secret at nightfall tomorrow, so much so that he pledges I shall be allowed to attend the summit meeting.

Upon our return to the castle Hannah abruptly pushes me into a shadowy alcove in one of the darkened corridors.

"Hannah....?" I say, but she places a finger on my lips, then replaces it with her own. I respond to her urgent kisses, my hands finding her breasts over the rough cotton of her shirt. She gasps softly, pushing herself into me, and then stiffens at a sound; bells.

Over Hannah's dark hair I see the odious dwarf Jeppe, one hand grasping his tinkling totem-stick, the other thrust brazenly down his breeches.

"Begone, fool!" I roar at him.

A hurt look comes over the dwarf's misshapen features. "A poor dwarf is Jeppe, of jokes he's the butt," he whines, then he bares his stunted, rotten teeth at us. "Do him a kindness, let him watch while you rut."

"Oh, God," says Hannah, and the dwarf giggles horribly, scuttling into the shadows. "I must go", she says and hurries back to the kitchens, but not before promising to meet me in the Royal Gardens when she ends her shift. Her coldness that characterised our first meeting has certainly thawed since our encounter with Ripellino on the Old Town Square, and, I am sure, my handling of the landsknechte on the Charles Bridge. There lies another mystery; what power cowed the soldier so? I resolve to quiz Masters Brahe and Kepler in Golden Lane, but their tiny room is locked when I visit. Bored, I seek out Sir Anthony and his men in their quarters, but I find only Percy, idly reading a book filched from one of Rudolf's libraries. He looks at me with disdain when I enter.

"I was looking for company," I confess.

"The men are whoring and Sir Anthony is making further entreaties to that Chamberlain, Lang, although why he bothers I just don't know," sniffs Percy. "For my money we should abandon the enterprise altogether, send a message to the Shah that we have failed and get back to England. Rudolf is too weak to take on the Turks."

He returns to his book, then looks up at me again. "I am not in the mood for company. You may go."

Nonplussed, I leave the quarters, as Percy calls behind me, "And I haven't forgotten you still have my cloak and boots!"

Burning to discuss my visit to the fortune-teller, I follow the shadowy corridors of the castle to the wardrobe rooms. Jakob is delighted to see me. "Master Poutnik! How was your errand? Hannah served you well, I trust? I know she can have a harsh tongue at times, and displays none of the respect for her elders and betters I brought her up with, but she's a good girl."

"Hannah was very helpful. Jakob, I would speak with you. Do you have a few moments?"

He puts down the brushes with which he is smoothing the ermine trim on a lustrous robe. "I was about to take a short break, Master Poutnik. Could I interest you in some tea?"

By the time I have told my tale, the tea has cooled, untouched, between us. I tell Jakob everything, from our meeting with Lang in the corridor, to the encounter with the guards on the Charles Bridge, to the episode with Ripellino, to my journey through the Ghetto.

"Master Poutnik," he says finally. "I thank you for being so open with me, although I doubt the wisdom of imparting so many secrets in this house of devils."

"I am tired of the intrigue, Jakob," I sigh. "I never asked to be brought to this place, never begged to be made Rudolf's pet. Ripellino only confirmed what I have begun to suspect; I am here for some purpose. I only wish it was clearer what it was."

"But the innocents," presses Jakob. "What could it mean? How must you save them? And from whom?"

"I have no greater idea than you."

"Perhaps it is the Jews who need saving," says Jakob slowly.

"The Rabbi suggested as much."

He looks at me curiously. "Master Poutnik, when you first told me your name, there was something I did not tell you. My people have a legend, a story, of one of our kind who criss-crosses the Earth. We know him as the Wanderer, the Pilgrim. Or, as they say in Prague, poutnik."

"I do not think I am your Wandering Jew, Jakob," I say sadly. "Surely I would remember that."

He shrugs. "Who knows? It's worth bearing in mind."

I stand, apologising for leaving Jakob's tea untouched. "I must be away, now. Thank you for listening, Jakob."

"Thank you for trusting me," he says, showing me to the door. As I step out into the empty corridor, he glances into the shadows and motions me closer to him. "Be careful of Chamberlain Lang," he whispers. "He is of a suspicious character. It concerns me that he addressed Hannah by name earlier today; it is not usual for one of his position to be so intimate with the personal details of a simple scullery maid. He may be watching us, Master Poutnik."

I promise him I will take care, and take my leave. Four bells sound at St Vitus's Cathedral, and I hurry to make my assignation with Jakob's daughter.

Hannah is waiting for me at the Powder Bridge as I hurry through the courtyards. "I had given up on you," she murmurs flatly, the confident, beautiful Hannah I had witnessed emerge from her dull shell in the Ghetto no longer apparent. A small smile does, however, play on her lips.

"I'm sorry, Hannah. I was talking with your father."

She looks slightly alarmed as we begin to walk to the Royal Gardens. "You did not tell him all of what we saw today...?"

"Should I not have? He seems to be trustworthy enough."

"Oh, he is," she says, stepping on to the paths through the fragrant bowers. "But he is old, my father, and has old ways. He harbours odd notions. He still thinks the Jews can yet be saved from our tormentors, still believes in saviours and such." She looks at me sidelong. "I bet he mentioned the Wandering Jew to you, didn't he?"

"As a matter of fact, he did...."

Hannah laughs lightly. "I knew he would. I must confess, the thought crossed my mind after seeing that display with the guards earlier."

To my surprise, Hannah stands on her tip-toes and kisses me on my cheek. "You're much too unworldly to be the Wandering Jew," she says, laughter in her voice.

I am in no mood to confront Rudolf's huge lion again, but Hannah leads me along quieter paths, alongside the battlements of the castle. Wooden scaffolding is ranged along them and stacks of great stone blocks are piled both at the foot of the walls and on the workmen's walkways above. They are evidently being raised, no doubt on the orders of Rudolf following some fever dream or astrological portent.

"I love these gardens," she says. "Staff aren't encouraged to walk here, but I am sure I will come to no harm with the Mirror of Prague as my escort."

The sun dips low in the clear sky, painting the straggling clouds blood red. Hannah pauses to pluck a flower from the ancient clematis climbing the walls. She holds it to her nose for a long while, glancing over the lilac petals at me. "You intrigue me, Master Poutnik," she says.

"I intrigue many, not least myself."

A sound startles me from beyond the trees. "What was that?"

"The parade ground. Rudolf's regiments must be mustering. Perhaps he is to send a legion to support Sir Anthony Sherley's Shah Abbas after all."

I glance sidelong at Hannah. For a scullery maid, she knows much of court affairs. Perhaps I was wrong to be so easy with my trust in her father.

Hannah joins me by my side, touching my cheek lightly. She withdraws her hand, suddenly embarrassed. "I apologise, Master Poutnik. I...."

"Hush," I say, taking her hand in my own. She looks at me, eyes expectant, then beyond me, over the wall at my back. Then her body is against mine again, her lips finding my own.

"I believe we have unfinished business," she murmurs, pushing me backwards until I stop short against the scaffolding.

"You look very handsome with the sun behind you," she says softly. "Let me take a proper look."

Hannah takes two or three steps back, watching me intently. The sun is sinking behind the walls quickly now, casting the dull shadow of the wall over the garden. Suddenly something catches my eye on the line of the shadow, an undulating, almost liquid movement, and the faintest tinkle of bells before Hannah shatters the air with a piercing scream.

The wind is knocked out of me and I am flung solidly to the right, landing in a tangle of limbs with another as a huge stone block hits the spot where I was standing with a sickening crunch. Dazed, it takes me a moment to realise what has happened; at first I think someone has leapt on me from the wall above, but then I understand as I disentangle myself from the huge body draped across me. Someone has deliberately pushed the stone block from the top of the wall, and I have been saved by some timely intervention. My rescuer is dressed in the uniform of

Rudolf's troops, and as he stands I catch the look of awe on Hannah's face.

My saviour is a giant.

He unfolds himself, brushing the dust from his leather tunic, and I squint up at him as his massive frame blocks out the last of the sun. He is perhaps nine feet tall, broad of shoulder, with a long face, lantern jaw and twinkling eyes. He reaches down, proffering a hand the size of a spade.

"You'll be this Master Poutnik we hear so much about then," he says in a lilting, smiling voice. "Pleased to be making your acquaintance. I'm the giant, Finn."

Finn takes me to the White Turnip, a tavern frequented by the castle guard and the fighting men, close to the castle gates. Hannah, to my disappointment, has business in the Ghetto to which she must attend. But I owe the towering soldier my life, and I am pleased to note that my status as the Mirror of Prague at least allows me two glasses of beer without charge in the tavern, albeit begrudgingly from the scowling barkeep.

"I cannot begin to thank you enough," I say as Finn clinks glasses with me.

"Ah, think nothing of it. I was just leaning on those trees there, having a pouch of baccy between running the troops through some exercises. I could see that block about to come down on you. I move pretty quick for a big feller. Surprises a lot of people."

He takes a look around the tavern and leans into me conspiratorially. "There was someone up on that wall, Master Poutnik. I fear it was no accident."

I nod glumly, recalling the unmistakeable bells in the instant before the stone almost killed me. The dwarf, Jeppe. But why? This is beyond mere bawdy peeping. Was he acting alone, and if not, on whose orders?

"Ah, but they reckoned without Finn," he booms, swallowing most of his beer in one gulp and waving to the barkeep for more. "Captain of Emperor Rudolf's feared regiment of giants!"

The other soldiers in the tavern glance at us but swiftly return to their beers and card games. "Regiment of giants?" I say, astonished.

The beers arrive and Finn's huge fingers nimbly flick a coin to the boy. "Aye, giants. A score of us at the last count. Not real giants, you understand, not as Rudolf believes us to be, supernatural creatures like elves or dragons or other nonsense. Big men. Freaks, if you will."

Finn, it transpires, was born on the west coast of Ireland, and grew up in a small fishing village. And kept growing. At the age of twelve he was six feet tall. By the time he was seventeen he had reached almost nine feet. He joined a travelling circus which eventually took him to England, and the court of Queen Elizabeth. There he heard of Rudolf and his predilection for freaks and sports, and began to make his way to Prague, working as a soldier for hire to earn coin along the way.

"The court of Emperor Rudolf is a good place to be a freak," he says agreeably. His voice drops again. "To tell the truth, the other soldiers don't have much truck with us. It's a fact the regiment of giants hasn't seen much in the way of real fighting; we're more of a show for Rudolf's court occasions. But nobody says anything to our faces." He grins broadly, his mouth as wide as my head. "Would you?"

I find I am having a good time in Finn's company, and I order two more glasses of beer. He gives me a sly glance. "So who was that colleen you were getting friendly with in the gardens before that stone interrupted your plans?"

"Hannah? She's a kitchen girl. The daughter of Jakob, the Emperor's valet."

"A fine looking woman," says Finn. "That's the problem with being a giant. The women like the idea of it, but won't let you near 'em when it comes to the crunch. 'Course, there's a couple of whores down in the New Town who'll do anything for the right price."

"How did you know who I was when we first met?"

Finn chuckles. "Everyone in the castle knows the Mirror of Prague, the foundling fallen from the heavens. Sir Anthony's men have been dining out on the tale since they arrived."

Conscious of having already spoken too readily about my situation with others, I offer no illumination to the giant, but he asks no probing questions, instead content to drink beer and chat aimlessly. "I don't get to talk to many apart from the other giants," says Finn. He laughs deafeningly. "I think people are scared of me!"

There's a commotion at the tavern door as a court messenger bursts in. The soldiers look up as a man, visibly disgruntled at the interruption to their drinking.

"All sober men to report to the Charles Bridge!" gasps the ruddy-faced page. "Bring arms!"

"What the devil's going on?" says a gruff officer, grabbing his arquebus from the weapons rack by the door.

The messenger can barely believe it himself. "There's a sea-serpent swimming up the Vltava!"

Finn winks at me. "Come on. Now this should be good."

I have to take three strides to match each one of Finn's, and by the time we run down from the inn and through Mala Strana with the other men, I am quite breathless. A crowd a dozen deep has gathered on the Charles Bridge, but they part readily enough as Finn, with me in his wake, pushes through to the balustrade. "By the Lord," breathes the giant, leaning between two of the statues which stand sentry on the stone bridge. "The lad was right. It *is* a sea-serpent."

I peer through the gloom of dusk. Moving slowly up the middle of the sluggish Vltava is a true sight to behold. It is brown and slimy, almost the shape of a whale, around twenty feet long and mostly submerged in the dark water. Beneath the surface I can make out what seem to be a row of fins, ranked along either side, lazily pushing the beast towards us. The realisation that it is moving straight for the Charles Bridge occurs to other people at the same time as me, and there's a collective gasp before the onlookers start to flee the bridge.

"I can see no head, or tail," mutters Finn. "It moves too steadily to be a thing truly alive."

The shape abruptly slows in the water, then clumsily changes direction until its nose is pointing to the bank on the Mala Strana side of the river. A scream goes up as the citizens ranked there try to climb back to the streets, fighting against the soldiers who are pushing towards the river.

"Come on," decides Finn. "Let's get closer."

I am about to question the wisdom of this action, but the giant grabs me by the arm and hauls me along with him through the crowd, until we are standing with the nervous soldiers on a small landing jetty in the shadow of the lamplight of the Charles Bridge. The sea-beast is but a dozen feet from us now, its skin gleaming in the dull light as it slows and stops, as though waiting for us to make a move. The soldiers thrust their pikes out, looking around for a senior officer to give them guidance.

What is the beast here for? Are we to be its supper?

But no; to a shocked gasp from the crowd, a hatch springs open in the top of the monster.

"It's no beast at all," mutters Finn. "It's a boat."

"Impossible," says a soldier beside him. "I have heard of no boat that can sail underwater."

But it appears Finn is correct for, like Jonah emerging from the belly of the beast, the thrummed sailor's cap of a young man, wild hair poking beneath it emerges from the dark hatch. The soldiers move forward as a man, brandishing their pikes, muskets and rapiers.

The man blinks twice, looking around him at the hushed crowd.

"Goodness me," he says, a smile breaking through his unkempt beard. "Quite a reception committee. I wasn't expecting this."

An officer of the guard steps forward, clearing his throat uncertainly. "Who are you, and what witchcraft is this?"

The man bows low as best as he is able perched in the hatchway, his doublet and loose trousers ill-fitting and sweat-stained. "Sir, I am Cornelius Drebbel, and this is no witchcraft. It is my amazing underwater boat, and I have journeyed here from the Low Countries to present myself to Emperor Rudolf II, ruler of the mighty Habsburg dynasty."

Drebbel's arrival in Prague has the castle in uproar. An audience is hastily organised, and very soon I find myself in the great hall, kneeling uncomfortably by Rudolf's throne, as the Dutchman is presented to the Emperor. The court is intrigued by Drebbel, and everyone has been allowed to squeeze into the hall to hear what he has to say. Lang grimaces by Rudolf's side, and though I glare at him, he gives me barely a cursory glance. Jeppe gambols by Rudolf's throne, leering at me from the shadows, shameless. Sir Anthony and Percy frown to each other at the front of the crowd. Brahe and Kepler are there, and Finn, and even Arcimboldo, who has allowed a sitting for his portrait to be interrupted for the audience with surprising grace.

Drebbel stands before Rudolf, the dozen or so men who were also hidden in the belly of his strange vessel at the rear of the room by a huge timber box. The atmosphere is quiet and expectant as Rudolf studies the visitor.

Eventually, the Emperor speaks. "Mr. Drebbel, you have caused quite a stir in fair Prague this evening. I am told that you sailed up the Vltava beneath the water; can this be so?"

Drebbel bows low again. "Indeed it is, Excellency. I have only recently perfected my underwater boat, and thought there was no more fitting a maiden voyage than to present it to Emperor Rudolf of Bohemia."

"I am aware many of my soldiers who were present for your most dramatic arrival had taken an ale or two in the taverns," says Rudolf, his eyes twinkling. "This is no extraordinary ramble of a drunken pikeman, you tell me?"

There's a sharp intake of breath from the soldiers present, but Rudolf is in good humour.

"Indeed not, Excellency," says Drebbel. "My device is so simple I cannot believe that others have not experimented before me; a wooden frame covered in waterproofed leather keeps the river out and a dozen oarsmen propel the machine forward, their oars moving within leather joints that allow no water in.

"But how do you all breathe under the water?"

Drebbel smiles. "I am something of an alchemist, Excellency, and I have devised a chemical liquor which purifies the air for my crew and myself, and a series of bellows and pumps to circulate it around the vessel."

Rudolf claps his hands together delightedly. "I must see this wonderful device. Have it brought to the castle immediately!"

Drebbel frowns slightly, glancing to Lang. The Chamberlain steps forward. "Your Excellency, the logistics of bringing the vast contraption to the castle are being worked upon as we speak. However, I believe Mr Drebbel has another device for the Emperor in the meantime."

Drebbel motions to his crew to bring the wooden box to the centre of the room, where they begin to dismantle it.

"I hope it is as amazing as the wonderful underwater boat I am seemingly not allowed to see," says Rudolf, sinking into petulance.

"It is perhaps more wondrous," says Drebbel as his men take away the wooden panels to reveal a huge contraption hidden by a white sheet. The Dutchman takes a corner of the cover and whips it off with a flourish, revealing a complicated array of coloured globes and elliptical tracks.

Kepler gasps in astonishment and recognition, and Drebbel announces, "Behold my perpetual motion machine! They said it could not be done, yet I, Cornelius Drebbel, have confounded the naysayers!"

"B-but...." interrupts Kepler, earning him a deathly stare from Lang. Drebbel bows low towards the scientist. "If I am not mistaken, this must be Master Johannes Kepler, the inspiration for my work."

"Inspiration?" drawls Rudolf.

"Certes, Excellency," says Drebbel. "It is Master Kepler's studies on the Laws of Planetary Motion which prompted me to make this machine. Voila!"

Drebbel swiftly releases two or three levers at the base of the contraption and lets several ball bearings free from their holsters. The machine begins to rotate uncertainly, then with more speed and smoothness, until each of the coloured globes is revolving around each other in a beautiful silent ballet. Rudolf watches enraptured, and I see tears forming in Kepler's eyes.

"Fascinating," breathes Rudolf.

"And it will go on forever," announces Drebbel. "As the heavens spin on into infinity, so shall this perpetual motion device. Excellency, I am your humble servant."

Drebbel bows low to show his presentation is at an end.

"Remarkable!" says Rudolf, breaking out into applause that is picked up a moment later by the rest of the court. "Rooms for Mr. Drebbel and his crew! They must be exhausted after their sub-marine journey. And a banquet tomorrow evening to properly welcome them to Prague."

The next morning Rudolf calls me to his chambers. "We must prepare cleverly for the Rabbi's secret visit tonight," he says. "The castle will busy itself with preparations for the banquet to welcome Mr. Drebbel and his crew. It is Lang we must confound."

I wonder aloud whether the Emperor could not merely command his Chamberlain to leave him be for an hour or two. Rudolf sighs. "Although Philipp is loyal to me, I am under no illusions. It is Rudolf the Emperor he serves, not Rudolf the man. He would not have harm come to the Empire, and I am afraid he would see me consorting with the Jews as not fulfilling my role as protector of the Habsburgs."

Rudolf muses for a moment while he takes his morning tea. "We will arrange a sitting for Master Arcimboldo," he decides. "Then you will tell the painter that I am unwell, and that the sitting is postponed. But he is not to speak of it to anyone."

"Can he be trusted?"

"As much as anyone in the court can," says the Emperor pointedly. "As much as a foundling dropped from Heaven."

Rudolf pauses for a moment, slipping into deep thought. Finally he stirs and commands me to leave. "Come to me at nightfall," he says. "I would have you present when I meet with Rabbi Loew."

I spend the rest of the day seeking out Hannah, and when I cannot find her I visit Jakob in his rooms. "I hope the Rabbi is true to his word," I say miserably. "I fear it would not be good for me if he fails to attend the castle this evening."

"The Rabbi will come," assures Jakob. "I do not think he would miss such an opportunity."

We are interrupted by a sharp knocking at Jakob's door. The valet opens it to a court messenger, leaning breathlessly on the door-jamb. "Master Poutnik! I have been searching for you. The Emperor requires your presence in the White Tower."

The White Tower is the tallest spire of the castle, overlooking Golden

Lane and the Stag Moat. I climb the many steep stairs to find Rudolf standing by the window, regarding the view from the bare chamber at the very top. Lang stands by as two guardsmen hold between them the dwarf, Jeppe, who looks terrified in his dirty red and green doublet and hose.

"Ah, the Mirror of Prague," says Lang.

Rudolf speaks without taking his eyes from the view of the Stag Moat, rich and green and teeming with wildlife and game. "Foundling, you did not tell me that there had been an attempt on your life."

I glance at Lang, who is wearing the same undulating black cloak he was when I first arrived at the castle. "I did not consider it necessary to bother your Excellency with the matter...."

Rudolf turns at last, his eyes red and rheumy. "Not necessary? Master Poutnik, I shall decide what is necessary when the lives of my courtiers are threatened. Lang, proceed."

The chamberlain clears his throat. The dwarf whimpers slightly.

"Jeppe has confessed to attempting to kill you, Mirror of Prague," says Lang.

The fool shakes his head. "N-no, Master Lang; it is not so; a fool is poor Jeppe, not villain or knave. To the Royal Gardens Jeppe did not go; speak Master Poutnik, my life you can save...."

"There was the sound of bells," I say, doubtfully. And something else as well. An unmistakable flash of black cloak.

"Murder is not the only thing on the dwarf's mind," says Lang, striding towards the fool. Jeppe flinches as Lang's fist flies to his chest, and surely I cannot be the only one who sees Lang's simple sleight of hand which allows him to appear to pluck something from the dwarf's doublet, which the chamberlain dangles from his gloved hand with a thin, satisfied smile.

"My scarab!" gasps Rudolf, and closer inspection reveals it to be a silvery beetle cast in amber, affixed to a thin leather thong. The item that the Emperor could not find in his Kunstkammer yesterday.

"A would-be murderer, and a thief into the bargain," says Lang. "What say you in your defence, Jeppe?"

"Emperor, chamberlain, Mirror of Prague," begins the dwarf. "I... I... please! Excellency! I am innocent!"

As the guards tighten their grips upon Jeppe's arms Lang smiles his bloodless smile again. "Your doggerel fails you, fool. A sure sign of guilt. What is your sentence, Excellency?"

"Your Excellency," I speak up. Everyone looks at me, hope burning in the dwarf's eyes. "I have no... evidence that Jeppe attacked me in the Royal Gardens." I look pointedly at Lang, but he just narrows his eyes at me.

"Do you deny the evidence of your own eyes? He has practically confessed."

Jeppe shakes his head, not taking his eyes from mine.

"Well, hardly…" I begin, but Rudolf waves a hand.

"Enough," he says. "There can only be one just sentence."

"The window, Excellency?" says Lang.

Jeppe shakes his head violently again. Rudolf merely nods, twisting the scarab this way and that, watching the light refract through the amber. "The window," he says softly, shuffling towards the spiral staircase.

Jeppe finally finds his voice again and I look on aghast as he screams, a terrible high-pitched sound as might issue from a child. At a nod from Lang, the two guards heft him up to chest level.

"It is such a long time since we have had a good defenestration," smiles Lang.

Jeppe is sobbing and kicking now, but the guards hold fast, and with little ceremony carry him to the window and haul him clumsily out. I can do nothing but stare numbly. Lang leans from the window and watches his descent, and long moments later there is a moist thud from below.

Rudolf has already begun to toil down the staircase, and the guards follow him, exchanging grins. Lang waits until they are out of sight then moves past me, stopping to glare at me. "You should feel much... safer, now, Mirror of Prague," he hisses, then follows them, leaving me alone in the bare chamber. Unable to help myself, I move towards the window and look out, to where a red and green stain blights the beauty of the Stag Moat far, far below.

By the time I have reached the Stag Moat, the mess that was Jeppe has been cleared away, with only a slight indentation in the clay to betray the brutal justice doled out by Rudolf and Lang. I decide to take a walk through the Stag Moat to clear my head of what I have just seen. It is wilder and more heavily wooded than the nearby Royal Gardens, and—as its name suggests—stags and other animals roam freely within its walled acres. I pick out a path through an overgrown meadow, pausing as I hear the sound of cursing a little way ahead of me. Hurrying on, I find the source of the oaths: Sir Anthony Sherley.

The mercenary holds in his left hand a matchlock firearm; his right he is shaking violently. "God's wounds!" he spits bitterly. "Ah, Master

Poutnik. How goes it?"

Without waiting for an answer, Sir Anthony begins to examine the matchlock and mutters, "Burned my bloody fingers on the coal yet again."

"How does this device work?" I ask, wanting to take my mind off the brutality I have just witnessed.

"Painfully slowly and with much fuss," says Sir Anthony. "I am much preferred of cold steel in close combat and the longbow for distance fighting, but Percy is enamoured of the arquebus. We have several men adept in its use but my lieutenant thinks it appropriate that we all master the weapon. Look here."

Sir Anthony shows me a small iron box in which he has hot coals, which he blows on to make them glow red. "This has to be touched to the match, here. This flash pan full of powder has to be kept level. And once you've fired it you have to stuff another shot into the barrel. I've been practising all morning."

Sir Anthony gestures towards a low branch of a tree where he has assembled three pots filched from the castle kitchens. There is no evidence of him having actually hit anything.

"Did you hear about what happened to the dwarf, Jeppe?" I ask.

Sir Anthony nods. "The poor wretch practically hit me on the way down. I think they've just taken his corpse away to the lion's cage."

"He tried to kill me, yesterday."

"So I hear," says Sir Anthony, peering down the barrel of the arquebus. "Do you believe that?"

"Do you not?"

Sir Anthony pauses, and rubs his beard. "I saw the stone that was pushed from the scaffolding; it would take much effort for a man that size to push it an inch."

"I feared as much myself," I say miserably. "I suspect Lang."

Sir Anthony nods. "I warned you to be wary of him, Master Poutnik. I'll watch your back as best I can, but it is perhaps best not to loiter near any windows when he is about."

Sir Anthony touches the coal-box to the match fuse and barks, "Stand back! I'm having another go. Watch that blue pot in the middle."

Resting the arquebus against his shoulder, Sir Anthony squints along the length of the weapon and slowly squeezes the trigger, bringing the match into contact with the flash pan. There's a loud crack and a flock of ravens rise noisily from the trees, as Sir Anthony is knocked backwards and loses his balance for a moment. I cough and peer through the smoke at the tree. All three pots are still standing.

"Arse," says Sir Anthony.

Then we both hear a heavy thud. Sir Anthony sets off at a run in the direction of his targets, and when I catch up he is staring down at the dead body of a muscular, impressively-antlered stag.

I cannot contain my mirth, and Sir Anthony cracks a wide grin. "I'll have it taken to the kitchens, give the men a treat. Better than that slop they've been serving us."

"And how goes your mission, Sir Anthony?"

"Poorly," sighs Sir Anthony, bending down to inspect the animal. "Rudolf is a stubborn old bastard. He refuses to commit a force to join Shah Abbas's campaign. It will be most unfortunate if we have to return to England having failed our mission."

I nod. "I suppose the Shah would not be best pleased."

Sir Anthony grins again. "No, especially as we've already taken his money. Still, I'll give it another few days. Then we'll head back to London. You are more than welcome to join us."

I thank Sir Anthony take my leave as he goes to collect his arquebus. Will I join them when they return to England? I feel no calling from London. Prague is the only home I have known. And there is the small matter of Master Ripellino's predictions. Save the innocents. I have already seen one innocent die this morning. Can I have already failed?

And yet... there is Hannah. I remember the gentle touch of her hand on my face in the Royal Gardens. Could she be the one I must save? Who else but Hannah can be innocent in this place? The realisation sends a shiver curling at the base of my skull. But what danger will befall her? And can I be sure I am able to fulfil the prophecy? I hurry to the kitchens in search of her.

By nightfall I have failed to find Hannah, but I must not be late for my appointment with Rudolf. I hurry to the throne room, where Arcimboldo is expecting the Emperor to sit for his portrait, and arrive at the closed double doors just ahead of the artist.

"A change of plan, Master Arcimboldo," I say breathlessly. "The Emperor is unwell."

The painter allows his easel to clatter to the stone floor, raising his eyes skyward. "How much more inconvenience must be heaped upon my head?" he cries. "I have already taken the trouble to set up two dozen candles in the hall because the Emperor requested a sitting at dusk. And now he has changed his mind?"

"He is unwell, Master Arcimboldo," I say sympathetically.

"This is too much," grumbles the painter. "I shall make my feelings known to Chamberlain Lang."

"Ah, no, I wouldn't do that," I say hurriedly. "The Emperor...." I search for some excuse that will appease the artist. "The Emperor has a woman with him," I whisper confidentially. "He would rather the Chamberlain not know."

Arcimboldo's eyes narrow. "Ah," he says, tapping the side of his nose. "I understand. Very well then, Master Poutnik. Tell the Emperor that we shall re-arrange for tomorrow, perhaps."

I watch as Arcimboldo gathers his equipment and staggers off down the corridor, allowing myself a small sigh of relief. When he has gone, I slip into the hall, where Rudolf sits on his throne, the glittering light cast by Arcimboldo's candles causing shadows to dance grotesquely in the dark room.

"Mirror of Prague? Has the artist gone?"

"Yes, Excellency."

"Good, then come sit by me while we wait for the Rabbi."

I perch nervously on a stool beside the throne. I am praying that Loew will be as good as his word. "How will the Rabbi get into the castle if the errand is so secret?" I ask, fearful of the answer.

"Oh, ways and means, hmm?" says a cracked voice, and Rabbi Loew emerges from the shadows, his eyes shining in the candlelight. "Ways and means."

The Rabbi bows low before the throne. Rudolf seems unfazed by his sudden appearance. "Good evening, Rabbi Loew," he says. "Thank you for keeping your appointment."

"The honour of your invitation was too gracious," says Loew, hobbling towards the throne. "How could I not attend?"

Rudolf bids me pull a chair up for the Rabbi, who sits heavily with a huge sigh. "Not as young as I was, hmm?" he smiles.

"Who is?" says Rudolf sadly. Wine has already been left by servants on a table near the draped walls. "Will you join me in a drink?"

I fetch goblets of wine for both Rudolf and the Rabbi. "You do not mind if Master Poutnik joins us for our meeting?" asks Rudolf.

"Not at all," says the Rabbi. "A most fascinating young man."

There's a lull as they both sip their wine, appearing to size each other up. Eventually, Rudolf says, "I suppose you must be wondering why I called you here."

Loew demurs with a wave of his hand. "Perhaps the Emperor wishes to talk about how to improve things for the Rabbi's people in the Ghetto, hmm?"

Rudolf shifts uncomfortably. "That is perhaps something we can speak about, at a later date. I am, of course, concerned for the well-being of all my peoples."

The Rabbi nods his head, but does not say anything. Rudolf sips more wine and says: "I would have knowledge from you, Rabbi. Knowledge of the Cabala."

Loew steeples his fingers and muses on this. "The Cabala. The sacred lore of the Hebrews. Perhaps the Emperor wishes to know the people in the Ghetto better, hmm? So that he can improve conditions for them?"

Rudolf can see he is being led into a corner, and smiles. "Very well, Rabbi. Tonight we shall talk about the Cabala; then we can talk about conditions in the Ghetto. That sounds like a fair bargain."

Loew acquiesces. "A little more wine, perhaps, then we can begin?"

As I refresh their glasses, the Rabbi begins speaking. Rudolf leans forward enraptured as the Rabbi talks, but his words mean little to me. Loew produces a piece of chalk from his robes and begins to sketch on the stone floor in front of the throne. With sudden interest, I note it is the pattern of circles and lines that was on the seal of the letter Jakob gave to me.

"The Tree of Life, the Sephirothic Tree," announces the Rabbi. "It grows downwards, rooted in Heaven and spreading through the Four Worlds. This is at the heart of the Cabala."

"Four worlds?" says Rudolf.

"Four Worlds," says the Rabbi. "The tree is rooted in Ain Soph, Nothingness."

The city is a paradox; itself infinite, though bordered at all points by inky black nothingness.

I jerk awake from the drowsiness that had threatened to overcome me. The words that had surfaced in my mind fade as quickly as they came.

"The tree grows down from Ain Soph through the Four Worlds of graduating spirituality, until it reaches Assiah, the Fourth World, our material plane."

Rudolf nods. "Go on."

"There are ten sephiroth on the Tree of Life; each ruled and guided by spiritual beings. Angels, you may call them.

"The sephirah which corresponds to our world is called Malkuth, which is ruled over by the Cherubim. Above that is Yesod, which is the vale of the moon, watched over by the Aishim.

"Beyond Yesod is the splendour of the cosmos, Hod, in which the Beni-Elohim are supreme.

"Each sephirah gets progressively closer to the ultimate of creation. Beyond Hod is the plane of victory, Netzach, ruled by the archangel Hamiel. Perhaps this is where the Emperor's soldiers go when they die, hmm?"

"What can be beyond victory?" muses Rudolf. "Some would say that is the ultimate."

The Rabbi cackles. "Beauty, Emperor. The realm Tiphereth, which is the terrible visage of the sun, in which the archangel Michael is supreme."

I know not if Rudolf is understanding the Rabbi's words, but each one hits me like a sledgehammer.

"Beyond Tiphereth is Geburah, ruled by the Seraphim, whose vengeance is swift and mighty. The next level is Chesed, which is mercy, for mercy is more divine than retribution, and this is the realm—"

Chesmalim

"—of Chesmalim. After Chesed is the Abyss. Some say that humans, no matter how mighty or divine, cannot cross the Abyss and reach the final stages of the Tree."

"I will cross it," asserts Rudolf. "Is there no known way?"

"The Bridge of Daath," says Loew quietly. "Daath is knowledge."

"Then I shall have knowledge," roars Rudolf. "More, Rabbi! More!"

"The first sephirah beyond the Abyss is—"

"Binah," I murmur, but neither of them hears me.

"—Binah," says the Rabbi. "This is the plane of understanding, it is ruled by the Aralim.

"And after understanding, comes wisdom. The realm of Chokmah, the final sephirah before the ultimate of creation. It is the domain of—"

"Ratziel," I say.

Rudolf and the Rabbi turn to me. "Did you speak, Mirror of Prague?" says Rudolf.

I am entranced by the Rabbi's words. "Chokmah is the realm of Ratziel," I say uncertainly.

"Impossible!" announces Rudolf.

"Intriguing," says Loew. "And does the foundling who was discovered in a ditch know what is beyond Chokmah?"

The words come unbidden, images of a shining silver city crowding the periphery of my vision, growing in intensity until I can barely see.

"Kether," I gasp. "The topmost sephriah, the root of the Tree of Life. The Primum Mobile, the First Motion that created all...."

"And who rules Kether?" asks the Rabbi urgently, as Rudolf looks on aghast. "Whose realm....?"

"Metatron!" I shriek. "Metatron! No, Metatron, not this, anything but…"

Then things go mercifully black.

I awake to find Rabbi Loew leaning over me and pressing a cold, damp towel to my forehead. Rudolf looks on sternly from his throne. "What happened?" I say idiotically.

"What do you remember?" says the Rabbi softly.

"I... I remember you sketching on the floor, then nothing."

Rudolf glances at the Rabbi. "You appeared to have a curiously full knowledge of the Cabala, Mirror of Prague," says the Emperor. "What make you of this, Rabbi?"

Loew muses thoughtfully for a long moment. "It has taken me a lifetime of study to merely scratch the surface of the Cabala, Emperor. Your Master Poutnik betrays an understanding I would have declared impossible in one so young and so evidently not of the Hebrew faith. You have chosen wisely in appointing your Mirror of Prague, Emperor. Wisely indeed, hmm?"

Rudolf struggles out of his throne and holds out a be-ringed hand to the Rabbi. "Our meeting is over, for now, Rabbi Loew. I have a state function to attend. We must meet again for further instruction, soon."

The Rabbi nods, rubbing the chalk drawings he has made on the stone floor with the hem of his robes, obliterating them from view. "And what the Emperor said, about my people in the Ghetto?"

"We shall talk on that also, Rabbi Loew."

"Very good, Emperor. Farewell, and also to you, Mirror of Prague."

The Rabbi melts into the shadows, and is gone. "Come, Master Poutnik," says Rudolf. "We are late for our banquet."

In the great hall at the centre of the castle Drebbel's underwater boat has been carefully placed on a huge plinth, the Dutchman and his crew standing before it, feted with wine and fine food and the fawning attention of Bohemia's nobles. Kepler hovers around the edges of the crowds, desperately trying to catch Drebbel's attention to speak with him further on his Laws of Planetary Motion. Sir Anthony is swapping military stories with Finn, but there is no sign of Percy. I wander around the hall, in no mood for festivities. I am perplexed by the encounter with the Rabbi, at the startling effect his words had on me. How is it I know more about the heavens and the cosmos than I do of the material world? I notice Lang watching me broodingly from across the hall, and would be away from his hawkish glare. Miserably, I realise I have not seen Hannah all day. I accost a serving girl and ask after her.

"She is in the kitchens," she says. Quietly, I slip out of the hall to find her.

Hannah is taking a rest outside the heat and steam of the kitchens when I arrive. "Master Poutnik," she says pleasantly.

"Hannah, I would speak with you," I say urgently. "Can we talk now?"

She glances into the kitchens. "I have half an hour of a break. I could do with a little fresh air."

"Perhaps the Royal Garden, then?"

It is cold in the gardens, and dark. We walk a little way into the arbours, and Hannah says, "Is this about what happened yesterday? The falling stone...?"

"No," I say absently. "No. Other concerns. Hannah, I fear for your life."

She looks startled. "My life? You think the stone was intended for me?"

"No. Perhaps." With frustration, I realise that I don't really know what I mean. The warnings from Ripellino are just too vague. "I just wanted to make sure you were all right," I say lamely.

Hannah smiles and moves closer to me. "Your concern for a mere scullery maid is very flattering, Master Poutnik," she murmurs, looking into my eyes. "And deserving of a token of gratitude, I feel."

Hannah leans forward on her tiptoes and plants a kiss on my lips, her hand moving to the back of my head and entwining in my curls. I return the kiss, and she presses her body to mine.

"How sweet," an unfamiliar voice interrupts. Hannah starts, and over her shoulder I see a figure emerge from the darkness of the fig trees. "Looks like there's plenty to share around, hey?"

The intruder is a fighting man of fearsome appearance. He is not dressed in the uniform of the castle guard, but rather anonymous leather armour and breeches. His hair is greying and straggly, his face battle-haggard. Perhaps most terrifyingly, his left eye is missing, a scab of scar tissue staring blindly from the socket. A cruel sneer plays on his thin lips.

Hannah moves behind me as he approaches, his hand resting on the hilt of his scabbarded-sword. "I have not been wenching for a while, and have heard the Bohemian whores are particularly lively," he says in a guttural voice. "Perhaps I get back in the saddle with you, eh, girl?"

"Come no closer," I warn the stranger, but am aware that I have no weapon to make good my threats.

"Oh, you are not willing to share then, boy?" says the intruder, a glint in his one eye. He moves so quickly that I do not see the hand that swipes upwards to my face, knocking me to the ground.

With strong hands he grips Hannah's arm as I lay dazed on the path, pushing her against the trunk of a tree and pawing at her skirts. "Don't worry, boy, I'll leave her alive." He grins. "Just about. You can make do with what's left."

Fortunately, Hannah proves more useful than myself. With her free hand she pulls a knife secreted in the folds of her skirt, and without hesitation plunges it into the exposed neck of her attacker.

The stranger winces, but no blood flows from the wound. Hannah looks on dumbly as the knife blade shatters as though thrust against a stone wall. Finally, I find my voice. "Help! Intruder!" I yell, knowing we are within hearing distance of the castle and that a guard patrol must be nearby. The man looks up, as though sniffing the air, and seconds later I hear the crunch of running boots on gravel. He throws Hannah to the ground and looks directly at me.

"This isn't over, boy. Not by a long shot," he whispers fiercely, and then disappears into the trees just as three members of the guard run up to us.

"He went that way," Hannah says, pointing into the trees, and the guards draw their rapiers and follow.

"Are you all right?" I ask Hannah, helping her to her feet.

She nods. "Did you see…? The knife, it just snapped...."

"I saw. Come on, let's get back to the castle."

Before we leave the Royal Gardens, though, a glint of reflected moonlight on the ground catches my eye. I stoop and pluck a small golden disc from the grass; a brooch or cloak-clasp that looks vaguely familiar. It depicts an ornate letter T. I pocket the brooch and escort Hannah back to the kitchens, promising to see if she is well tomorrow. Then I head back to the banquet, in search of Sir Anthony Sherley, for I think I have a mystery here that needs his attention immediately.

I find the adventurer still talking to the giant, Finn, at the banquet. They note my dishevelled appearance with alarm. "Master Poutnik, are you all right?" says Finn. "There hasn't been...?"

Sir Anthony glances to where Lang still stalks around the periphery of the hall. "Not from him," I say. "Not this time. I was with Hannah in the Royal Garden and we were confronted by an intruder."

When I reach the part in my tale about Hannah's knife snapping as she tried to plunge it into the stranger's neck, Sir Anthony looks troubled. "I have heard of this," he mutters darkly. "On my travels I have been told many tales of the so-called 'Hard Men', a band of mercenaries under the captainship of a merciless Croatian, whom they call Carlo Fantom. A cruel man, say those who have met him, although our paths have not crossed thus far."

"Hard Men?" says Finn. "Why do they call them that?"

"The tales say that they live in a forest community where they are given a mysterious herb as children, which makes them impervious to weaponry. I had not believed in them until now."

"You think perhaps this was one of these Hard Men?" says Finn worriedly. "I should perhaps organise a search of the castle grounds."

"It would be a good idea," says Sir Anthony. "If Fantom and his men are here in Prague, it cannot be for any good reason."

As Finn goes to organise a patrol, I delve into my pocket for the brooch I discovered where the Hard Man attacked us. "Why, that is one of Percy's," says Sir Anthony, turning the clasp over and inspecting the motif. "This is the seal of the Tremayne family. Where did you…?"

But we are interrupted by a commotion from the main doors of the hall. A small troop of castle guards enter, with a herald at their head. Rudolf, surrounded by his courtiers and inspecting Drebbel's underwater boat, looks up expectantly.

"Excellency," says the herald breathlessly as the conversation dies down in the great hall. "I apologise greatly for interrupting the court banquet, but the castle has a visitor."

"And who is so important that we should halt proceedings?" says Lang, materialising by Rudolf's side. The guards part to allow a tall dark figure through the doors. Sir Anthony swears softly beside me.

The herald clears his throat and announces loudly, "Rudolf II, Emperor of the Habsburgs and Ruler of Bohemia, I present to you Doctor John Dee."

Eleven
Direct Action

A wooden case. A snatch of conversation: "...fuses....". A package. An errand.

I turn these things over in my mind as I wander the streets of Prague in the chill pre-dawn light. Preparations are being made here, it seems. For what, I do not know. But Padraig, Karla and Jenny at least are involved, and I have no reason to doubt that Cody and Petey are part of the secret also, and, by extension, John, who I am yet to meet. A conflict is approaching. What is my role?

Save the innocents.

The weather-beaten old man who has been spying on the house since my arrival knew me. That much is evident. He called me by the name I had only been given since arriving here. How can this be? Karla was silent after our encounter with the mysterious Jakob. I was expecting her to call a house meeting immediately, but she kept the incident to herself. Perhaps she is afraid I will tell Cody about our urgent, passionate sex in the doorway on the night of the adbusting venture; a secret kept for a secret kept.

On my walks I have begun to notice posters pasted on the walls around Prague rallying support for the coming protest. N15: Say no to globalisation. Support Anti-Capitalist Action. November 15 - Wenceslas Square - Prague - DIRECT ACTION!

Karla's words from long ago strike a chord in me: *"It's an evil empire"*. Perhaps this is to be my purpose here. If only the details weren't so vague.

Back at the house, I tread softly to my room. What is to happen to me when John returns to reclaim his quarters? There is no other bedroom in the house. As I pass Jenny's room, I hear her voice in low conversation with another. I recognise the murmur that answers. It is Karla. Against what I know is the polite course of action, I stop to listen.

"You screwed him? Jesus, Karla."

"I know. I know. It was just... remember what you told me? After you kissed him on the Charles Bridge that first night?"

"Oh, Christ. Don't go there. I couldn't look Lisa in the face."

"You didn't tell her?"

"Fuck, no. But it was like she could see it in my eyes."

"I know what you mean. It's like... it's like, once you've touched him, you're changed, somehow."

There's a low giggle. "You telling me it was that good?"

Karla speaks slowly. "It was like touching light. It was warm and bright and... I can't put it into words."

A hush follows, then Jenny says, "Poor Cody."

"You just keep it zipped, okay, girl? Anyway, I'd better get to work."

I quietly hurry along the corridor to my room.

"The importance of oil is that everyone has some kind of opinion on it. It polarises society," says Cody. I have asked him for clarification on some of the issues involved in the protest; he seems to have little else to do so reluctantly agrees. "And not just people like us. Do you remember the fuel protests for cheap gas over in the UK a few years ago?"

I shake my head. "No."

"Oh, right," he says, glancing sidelong at me. I get the feeling he was trying to trip me up there. "Anyway, the haulage companies and the cab drivers and the farmers all got together because they thought fuel prices were too high. They blockaded fuel transfer plants, clogged up the freeways, that kind of thing. And they got things done. That's because people think cheap fuel is a fundamental right. Screw the fact that the tax they pay on oil goes to what little is done to combat climate change, pollution and the search for alternative fuel sources, 'cause let's face it, oil ain't going to last forever, they just wanted to fill their tanks up for less money.

"That's what we're up against. The oil companies got the whole world believing the hype, convinced they can't live without their cars."

"It doesn't sound like the protest is going to get much sympathy, in that case," I point out.

Cody shakes his head vehemently. "We don't go for sympathy. We go to get our voices heard. We can all stand with placards and shout slogans, but that ain't going to get on the nine o'clock news. That's why we smash up Starbucks and McDonald's and throw bricks at the police. Because out of every hundred people who watch the news and think what we do is a disgrace, there might be one person who thinks about what we're doing, and if we can get through to them, it's a start. See, the natural disasters—Hurricane Katrina, the floods in the UK, all that stuff—that actually helps us. It brings climate change home to people. It might take a while for them to equate what happens to them to their dependence on oil, but it's a start. It's a first step. Things are changing."

"What exactly will we be doing? On N15?"

Cody pauses. "Look, Pooty, no great disrespect or anything, but I'd rather not say too much until John comes back. It's his play, really. I'm sure he's going to include you and everything, but I'd rather just leave it until then."

I nod. "Fair enough." At least Cody seems to have thawed to me a little since the adbusting expedition. I feel a faint stab of guilt as I remember my hands on Karla's arching back in the shop doorway that night.

"I will say this, though," he grins. "It's gonna be fucking radical, man. We're gonna bring the house down."

Tonight we are to go and watch a performance by Petey's band at the club where they have a residency every Wednesday. I work a short shift at The Leopold Bloom, which is quiet. As I'm leaving, Noel calls me to one side. "Do you know when your man John is coming back to the house?" he asks.

"I'm told within a few days."

"Good. I might have some more gear for him, if he needs it for his protest. Top spec stuff. My brother's coming in from Derry next week. I'd have told Paddy but he's not on until tomorrow."

Noel taps the side of his nose and walks away. I too am, it appears, involved.

After my shift I return to the house as everyone is preparing for the gig. "We haven't had a night out together for ages," says Jenny, excitedly applying make-up in the living room.

Karla studiously avoids meeting my eyes, as she has done for the past two days since the adbusting night. I had hoped to speak to her, at least about the intruder, but she does her best to not be alone with me at any time.

We walk together in a group to the club. Petey is already there, setting up with his band. Tonight's performance is a benefit gig to raise funds for the N15 protest. "Everyone's going to be there," says Cody. "The Wombles, Reclaim the Streets, the Initiative Against Economic Globalisation. Everybody. I even heard that Deva's going to be at the protest."

Padraig sighs. "Deva's supposed to be at every protest. If he was everywhere he was rumoured to be, there'd have to be ten of him. A hundred of him."

"Who's Deva?" I ask.

"Deva's fucking hardcore," says Cody animatedly, as we cross the Charles Bridge, the biting wind taking our breath away. "He's like the ultimate anti-capitalism protester. No-one knows who he really is. He supposedly shot a cop in Seattle, and busted three Wombles out of a police van in Trafalgar Square."

"Petey calls him SuperAntiGlobalisationMan," laughs Padraig. "Reckons he's the superhero of the protest movement."

"Yeah, he always wears a mask, apparently," says Cody. "John met him, once."

"Yeah, right," mutters Karla.

"Anyway, you guys, what makes you think Deva's a man?" demands Jenny. "Are you saying a woman couldn't do what Deva's done?"

"I always kind of assumed it was an anagram of Dave," Padraig says doubtfully.

"Christ, no-one even knows if he—or she—actually exists," says Karla. "Deva's reached legendary status. He's a figurehead. Does it matter whether he's there or not?"

"Well, I think it would be cool," mumbles Cody.

"Forget it, anyway," says Jenny, bringing us to a halt outside a passageway set into a wall throbbing with the bass beat of music. "We're here."

We file into the club entrance and Karla pays the admission fee for us all before leading us down a flight of dark stairs. It's hot in the basement club, and loud. "Somebody get the drinks in," yells Karla.

"I'll go," shouts Jenny back. "Pooty, come and give me a hand. Budvar all round?"

We squeeze through the crowd at the bar, Jenny waving a wad of notes at the barman. There's a band on the small stage at the rear of the dark club. "Is this Petey's group?" I ask.

"No, the warm up," says Jenny, handing me three beers. "Tristessa are headlining tonight. Should be fun."

We find the others and distribute the beer. "I'm going to find Petey, wish him luck," says Padraig. "Anybody coming?"

"I'll come," says Jenny.

Cody shakes his head. "There are a couple of the guys from Reclaim the Streets over there. I need to speak to them for a minute."

They disperse, leaving me alone with Karla. She glances at me then looks away. I feel awkward, and sip the beer, racking my brains for something innocuous to say.

We both begin to speak at the same time, and give little nervous laughs. "You first," says Karla.

"No, you. I insist."

She takes a deep breath, leaning into me to shout into my ear as the band on stage reaches a deafening crescendo. "Pooty, about the other night...." She glances across the club to where Cody is in conversation with a group of people. "It wasn't right. Please don't tell Cody."

I shrug. "Don't worry, Karla. I don't want to mess things up for you."

She nods. "Thank you. And there's something else... that intruder...."

"I really don't know who he is. Or at least, I don't remember him if I do know."

She looks at me curiously. "What did he mean? All that 'save the innocents' business?"

I take a swig of beer. "I wish I knew, Karla. I've been thinking of trying to find him, see if he can shed any light on my situation."

"Good idea," she nods. "I'll help you, if you like."

She casts another look towards Cody, then quickly kisses me on the lips, her tongue probing for mine. Then she breaks off and looks away, just as Padraig and Jenny appear through the crowd.

"How's Petey?" says Karla brightly.

"Stoned," says Padraig, just as the other band finishes playing to whistles and applause. "Situation normal. Should be a good gig."

Suddenly Jenny lets loose a squeal and throws her arms around a young woman who emerges through the entrance from the stairs. "Lisa! I thought you had to work tonight!"

Jenny passionately embraces the blonde woman. "I managed to change my shift at the last minute. How are you, babe? Things going well for the protest?"

"Good," says Jenny. "We're expecting John back any day."

The others greet Lisa and Padraig goes to buy her a beer. Jenny's girlfriend sizes me up. "This must be the mysterious Mr. Poutnik, then," she says, extending a hand to me. I shake it, and she goes on, "So you're the guy who tried to turn Jenny het."

I struggle for a reply, but Jenny punches Lisa in the arm playfully. "Stop teasing," she admonishes, then says to me: "It's okay, Pooty. Lisa's just jealous."

"He is cute, mind," says Lisa, winking at me. "For a guy."

There's a murmur of expectancy from the crowd and a ripple of applause as one of the men Cody was speaking to earlier takes to the stage. "Before we get to the main event, I'd just like to say thanks for coming," he shouts through the mic. "We're having a great night here, but I want to remind us all that we're raising money for the N15 protest in a week or so's time."

A roar goes up from the crowd, and the man puts up his hands for silence. "The money we get tonight will pay for medical supplies and legal advice on the day. The eyes of the world are going to be on us, people, so let's make it count this time, okay?"

Everyone is cheering and clapping now, chanting slogans and stamping their feet. "Hold that thought," shouts the man on stage, "and keep making some noise for Tristessa!"

Four Petey clones shamble on to the stage. Petey blinks at the crowd and the lights, as though he was expecting to walk into his bedroom. He gives a nervous little wave at us and begins to strap on his guitar. The singer steps up to the mic and brushes his hair out of his eyes. "Like, wow," he says in a small voice.

Petey's band launch into a series of what seem to me to be identical bouts of squalling noise lasting around three minutes each. The singer announces each song with a mumble and every one is received with rapturous applause as the riffs fade away. I find myself beginning to enjoy the gig. What at first seemed to be chaotic mess of sound begins to coalesce into a tightly structured and highly melodic suite of music. I find myself idly marvelling at the fact that four human beings could make music of such intrinsic beauty, then wonder why I should have such a thought at all.

By the time the performance draws to a close I am applauding and cheering with everyone else. Petey and his band take awkward bows and shuffle off stage, and a hubbub of conversation strikes up.

Petey comes and joins us a moment later, accepting a bottle of beer from Cody and putting up his hands to fend off the congratulations. "We were okay," he concedes.

"You fucking rocked, man," insists Cody. Then his voice trails off. "I don't fucking believe it," he breathes.

Along with everyone else, I follow his eyes to the stairway that leads down into the club. Out of the curling smoke a dark figure is descending the stairs, and stepping into a pool of purple light cast by an overhead spotlight. It is a man, almost ageless looking, dressed in functional, plain clothes and with a neat beard and slicked-back, black hair. He casts around the club for an instant, then fixes a piercing gaze on us, his thin lips hinting at a smile of recognition.

"Well, look who's here," says Jenny quietly. Lisa sighs. "Don't tell me. House business coming up. I'll catch you later, babe." She gives her a kiss on the cheek and disappears into the crowd.

Cody waves his hand. "Over here!" he shouts. "John, we're over here."

John is being greeted by so many people at the gig that he decides to take us to a nearby bar. "Need to catch up with the latest news," he tells people apologetically, giving me a long glance and then steering us all up the stairs and out of the club.

"Damn good to have you back, man" says Cody. "There's so much to tell you. Hey, did you see our little welcome home present?"

"The Esso hoarding," says John, smiling. "I thought that had your touch on it. Good work, guys."

Cody beams with almost childlike pride. I have been studying John curiously since his arrival; there is a strange almost-familiarity about him that fills me with wariness and renders me silent. I cannot place his accent; not English, like Karla and Jenny, not American, like Petey and Cody, but somewhere in between. He says nothing to me until we are tucked around a table in a quiet, dark bar a street or so away from the club. He looks at me appraisingly, then says: "So this must be our mystery man. Mr. Poutnik, I am honoured to make your acquaintance. I have heard much about you."

I take his proffered hand and he grips mine tightly, his eyes boring into me. "I understand you have no memory. How very odd."

Jenny butts in. "I've done some cursory examinations. He's completely amnesiac. Not sure what brought it on; can't see any sign of a blow to the head or anything."

"And is our Mr. Poutnik fully appraised of our little group?" wonders John aloud.

"He came on the adbusting expedition the other night," says Cody. "I haven't told him too much about N15 yet."

"Guys, hello?" says Karla. "He's here, you know. You can talk directly to him, if you like."

John places his hand on his chest. "My apologies, Mr. Poutnik," he says, looking at me thoughtfully. "Hmm. Poutnik. The wanderer. So, where do you wander from? Or to?"

"I do not know, John. My mind is a complete blank up until I was discovered on Letna plain by Karla."

"A fascinating story," says John, draining his beer. "Well, if my team here trusts you, you're okay by me, Poutnik." A broad grin breaks out of his black beard flecked with grey. "Welcome aboard. It's going to be a long, strange trip these next few days."

"All right," says Cody, pumping his fist into John's solid shoulder.

"I'll get some more beers in," says Padraig, visibly relieved at John's reaction to me.

Jenny grins and Petey pats me on the shoulder. Karla says nothing, just meets my eyes for a tiny second then glances away.

"Oh yes," says John, accepting a beer from Padraig and clinking it against Cody's. "A long, strange trip indeed. Hope you're up to it, Poutnik."

As I sip my beer, I have the unshakeable feeling that whatever it seems I have been sent here to do is about to get underway.

Twelve
Doctor Dee

The party in honour of Mr. Drebbel is, it seems, over. Doctor John Dee has finally arrived in Prague. Rudolf hastily orders a formal reception in the great hall, and a disgruntled Drebbel and his crew are left to organise the removal of the underwater boat from the castle. Fickle Rudolf has a new plaything now.

If the court turned out in force for Drebbel's appearance, it has redoubled its efforts for Doctor Dee. All the familiar faces are packed into the hall and more I have never seen before. I am glad to have my front-row seat beside the Emperor's throne. Sir Anthony and Percy are present, and I wonder if the mercenary has quizzed his lieutenant about the brooch I discovered in the grounds when Hannah and I were assaulted by the so-called Hard Man, but I suspect all thoughts of that have been driven from Sir Anthony's mind by the arrival of Doctor Dee. He has made no secret of his distaste for the alchemist, and has indicated he would rather be away from Prague than resident in the castle at the same time as Dee. If their departure is indeed imminent, I wonder if I shall go with them?

Dee has with him a companion, a lanky man with narrow eyes and straggly, grey hair framing a gaunt, unshaven face. At first I think him to be some servant, but he never leaves Dee's side and whispers constantly in the conjuror's ear.

Dee himself has rather sad eyes, as though he carries the weight of his reputation with ill ease. His robes and ruff are tattered and dusty with days of travelling, a skull-cap hiding his white hair, a grey beard growing down to his chest. Yet his presence fills the room, and as he casts his gaze around, those who come under it fall silent, glancing at their feet and stealing sly looks at him from beneath their brows.

Rudolf regards Dee keenly, and once all are assembled in the room Lang clears his throat and steps forward. "You may approach His Excellency, Rudolf II, Emperor of the Habsburgs and King of Bohemia," he says loudly.

Dee and his companion stride forward, bowing low before the

throne. "Your Excellency," says Dee in a sonorous voice. "I am Doctor John Dee, philosopher to Queen Elizabeth, alchemist of some note, mathematician, hermeticist and Cabalist. This is my travelling companion and partner in study, Mr. Edward Kelley. Together we have travelled from Krakow to Prague, where we present ourselves most humbly to the Emperor and place ourselves at the disposal of Bohemia."

"Doctor Dee, Mr. Kelley," acknowledges Rudolf. "We have heard much about you, and your work, and are most delighted to welcome you into our court. There is much you can teach us, Doctor Dee, and under the patronage of the court here in Prague we are sure you shall flourish."

Lang steps forward again. "I am sure that Doctor Dee and Master Kelley are exhausted after their long journey, Excellency," he says. "I have taken the liberty of having quarters prepared for them, and shall arrange for their chattels to be transferred there at once."

"It is late," concedes Rudolf. "Doctor Dee, I would request the pleasure of your company at a private audience tomorrow afternoon, when you are rested and have settled into your quarters."

"That is most gracious, your Excellency," says Dee, bowing low again. "I would also request the presence of my partner Mr Kelley at the meeting, if that so pleases you."

"And I should have my Mirror of Prague present, if that so pleases you," says Rudolf, reaching down to ruffle my hair. "So we shall both have our pets with us."

The court erupts in laughter as I flush with embarrassment and Kelley scowls with his narrow eyes from beneath his unruly fringe of hair. Dee glances at him and bows again. "So be it, Excellency," he says, and the two of them turn and walk slowly out of the hall, every eye in the room on them.

As the courtiers disperse, I wander back to the hall where Drebbel is arranging for his underwater boat to be docked on the Vltava.

"I am a tad nervous," he confides to me over a nightcap of port as the hall is cleared and cleaned. "I was not aware that Dee was taking up residence at the castle. Trouble follows him like an albatross."

"Are you leaving soon, then, Mr. Drebbel?"

"I will remain in Prague for a few days," he says, sipping his port. "I would talk further with Master Kepler and discuss his Laws of Planetary Motion. But I would have my boat and crew ready for a speedy departure, should I need to." He glances around to see who, if anyone, is listening. "I have a bad feeling, Master Poutnik," he whispers. "Prague has an expectant air about it, like a place waiting for something to happen."

Drebbel goes to oversee the final preparations for the boat to be moved back down the hill to the river, and as I ponder retiring for the evening, Percy strides into the hall, casting about for someone. He sees me and raises his arm, hurrying over.

"Master Poutnik," he says. "I am glad to have found you. Sir Anthony returned to me the brooch that you found. I am grateful to you. I fear I lost it while walking in the gardens earlier this evening. While not of great value, it has sentimental appeal, being the seal of the Tremayne family. I trust you are well after your encounter with that brigand?"

Percy is almost babbling, and I am suspicious of his sudden good humour towards me. "It was nothing, Percy. I was pleased to have returned it to its rightful owner."

"I had been walking in the gardens," says Percy again. "Beautiful, are they not? I decided to take a walk there, before the banquet. It must have fallen from my cloak."

I nod, perturbed by Percy's insistence at this minor fact. "As you say, Percy."

"And the girl? She was not injured?"

"Through luck more than anything else," I say. "Is it true what Sir Anthony says? Of the Hard Men?"

Drebbel, who is walking back towards us to finish his port, looks alarmed. "Hard Men, did you say? Carlo Fantom's mercenaries? I have heard tell of them. Do say they are not here in Prague?"

"I should not expect so," says Percy. "Master Poutnik and the girl were confronted by a common criminal, I should think. There would be no reason for Fantom to be in Prague."

Drebbel still looks worried. "Perhaps my visit to Prague shall be even shorter than I had hoped."

Percy thanks me profusely again for finding his brooch before taking his leave. As Drebbel talks in low tones about this latest piece of news with his crew, I walk the castle corridors aimlessly, my feet taking me along dark passageways and across deserted torch-lit halls. On the west side of the castle Doctor Dee and Edward Kelley have been quartered, with rooms for their experiments and studies. Brahe and Kepler will be displeased at the attention paid to Dee, and Lang will undoubtedly have tried to talk Rudolf out of allowing them to carry out their alchemical practices within the castle walls. But it seems that Dee is the toast of Prague, inspiring awe, fear and respect in equal measures. Why he should stand out among the seers and mystics who are drawn to the city because of Rudolf's open patronage of the occult arts I am not sure, but I confess to being intrigued by him, not least by his claims to converse with angels through his magic mirror. Without realising it, I have wandered towards the west wing of the castle, and approach the suite of rooms set aside for Dee and Kelley. I pause, doubtful of why I am here, and am about to retrace my steps when a hand reaches from the shadows and grips my shoulder, causing me to start and cry out.

"Did I scare you, boy?" A face leers out of the shadows, criss-crossed with tiny scars and pock-marks, rheumy eyes sizing me up from deep within a pasty complexion framed by dry, grey hair. Edward Kelley, Doctor Dee's companion.

"Master Kelley," I say, regaining my composure. "I am sorry. You startled me."

Kelley emerges fully from the shadows, a half-eaten chicken leg in his hand. He tears at it noisily with his blackened teeth, watching me all the while. "What are you doing here, boy? Spying?"

I sigh inwardly. This seems to be a common accusation within the castle. "No, Master Kelley. I am merely walking."

"Hmm," says Kelley, biting into the chicken leg again. He watches me for a long minute while he chews, idly scratching his face with dirty nails. "So you're this Mirror of Prague I keep hearing about. What does this entail, exactly?"

"I...."

"Just as I thought," says Kelley with satisfaction. "Another charlatan."

He leans in close, exhaling his foetid breath into my face. "Look, boy, I'll be straight with you; I don't like the look of you, not one bit. Here, take a gander at this."

Grinning, Kelley pulls back the long hair that hangs beside his face, to reveal scarred, pustulous holes where his ears should be. "Had 'em chopped off by the Magistrates at Lancaster for being a bad lot. So you mark my words, boy: I'm not to be trifled with. There's only one show in town now, and that's Doctor Dee. So you be a good little foundling and keep out of our way, right?"

I am transfixed by the terrible sight of Kelley's ear-less head, and about to answer when a voice sounds from the nearest room to us. "Edward? Edward, who are you talking to?"

"No-one important, John," calls Edward, almost tenderly. He looks back at me pointedly. "Just some servant wanting to know if we want anything more to eat."

"I don't think so, Edward," sounds the voice again. "I think I would like to sleep, now."

"Good idea, John," says Kelley. "I shall turn in myself directly."

He turns back to me. "I hope the message is understood, boy," he says, pushing the greasy remains of his chicken bone into my hands before slipping back into the shadows of the corridor.

I spend a sleepless night turning over in my mind what little I know of Doctor Dee. Drebbel fears him; Kepler is in awe of him. Brahe thinks he is a charlatan, as does Percy. Sir Anthony, generally a down-to-earth sort, is wary of him and his reputation. Lang, I can tell, wants nothing of him in Prague. Lang sees Dee very much as he sees me, an unknown quantity over which he has no control, and which he fears may threaten the throne. Early in the morning I seek out Jakob's counsel.

"Ah, you think my opinion worthwhile Master Poutnik?" says Jakob, darning a pair of breeches. "I should be flattered, I think."

I take tea with Jakob, and he says casually: "Hannah told me of what happened in the Royal Garden last night."

"Ah," I say, feeling suddenly guilty. "I am sorry for putting her in danger, Jakob. I wasn't to know...."

He holds up his hands in a conciliatory gesture. "Of course you weren't, Master Poutnik. I was just wondering... do you enjoy Hannah's company?"

I feel myself flushing slightly. "She is a very interesting young woman, Jakob."

"A little headstrong," he sighs. "And modern. My generation, we accept our burden as Jews. We live in the Ghetto, and get by. Rabbi Loew tries his best for us with periodic entreaties to the Emperor, but we do not expect things to get any better. Hannah is different. She aspires to a better quality of life. I worry about her, sometimes. I worry about how far she might go to achieve her desires."

Jakob sips his tea thoughtfully, then sighs again. "But I am just being a protective father. And you wanted to know about Doctor Dee," he says, settling into his chair. "I confess to know no more about him than I pick up here in the castle. Dee is known to most as a magician, a conjuror who talks with angels through his magic mirror. Apparently—and I have this on good authority—it is not Dee at all who talks to the angels; it is that rapscallion compatriot of his, Kelley. Perhaps the great magician is not as powerful as he would have us believe, eh?"

"Kelley? I find that difficult to believe. I had a run-in with him yesterday evening."

"Not a pleasant man, I am led to believe. There are other rumours also," says Jakob, leaning in to me conspiratorially. "Dee and Kelley work for Queen Elizabeth's spymaster, the Earl of Walsingham, they say. All this magickery is merely a charade to enable them to get into courts across Europe and commit espionage for their paymasters in London."

"And others say that servants who talk too much are transformed by magic into frogs!" calls out a strident voice. Jakob groans silently; it is Lang. The Chamberlain is standing in the open door of the valet rooms, watching us. Heaven knows how long he has been there. Jakob immediately begins to apologise profusely.

"No time for this," says Lang, waving his hand dismissively. "Master Poutnik, your presence is required by the Emperor."

As I hurry after the Chamberlain down the corridors, he muses aloud, "Once again, the Mirror of Prague is requested to attend an important matter of state, while His Excellency's trusted Chamberlain is not."

Lang stops abruptly so I almost run into him, and whirls around, his eyes blazing. "I appear to be becoming more and more a simple messenger boy to fetch you at the Emperor's whim, foundling. It is not a change of affairs I greatly relish." Lang's eyes narrow and he hisses: "Rudolf is becoming dependent on you, boy. Was this your plan all along?"

I am growing weary of constant accusations and attacks in this castle. "I have no plan, Chamberlain," I snap. "If you have issues with the Emperor's wishes, perhaps you should take the matter up with him."

"Perhaps I will," says Lang mildly. "Now hurry along; you shall be late for the meeting with Doctor Dee. And take care around the castle, foundling. It can be a dangerous place."

I watch Lang stride away. There can be no doubt now that he was responsible for the stone that came crashing from the battlements and almost killed me; was he also behind the attack by the suspected Hard Man in the gardens? And if so, what is the connection between him and Percy Tremayne, who I am positive had been meeting the brigand before he attacked us and who has been going out of his way to put me off the scent ever since? But I have no time to ponder these questions now. The Chamberlain is right; I am late for the meeting with Doctor John Dee.

Kelley grins at me across the throne room, dragging back his hair to give me a surreptitious glance of his severed ears. I am in my customary position at Rudolf's side, while Dee and Kelley sit on stools before us.

The room is otherwise empty, apart from a small trestle table between the two newcomers covered by a dust-sheet that hints at some structure beneath. Intrigued, I try to concentrate on what Dee is saying and ignore his mischievous sidekick.

"There were certain... elements working against me at Elizabeth's court," says Dee sadly. "I served the Queen well, and was promised untold riches for my scrying and predictory work at the court. But certain agents endeavoured to have me cast out of favour."

"Is that when you decided to go to Poland?" asks Rudolf.

Dee nods. "Lord Albert Laski visited me at my home at Mortlake and invited me to Krakow, and there I carried out much good work with Edward, as ever, at my side."

Here Kelley bows his head at Rudolf, who says petulantly, "And what prompted you to come to Prague, if Krakow was so to your liking?"

Dee puts his head down and examines his hands curled in his lap. "The angels commanded it," he says in a quiet voice.

Rudolf leans forward, his eyes bright. "The angels," he breathes. "Then it is true. You converse with God's bright battalions. And the mirror...?"

"Not a mirror in the conventional sense," says Dee. "More a scrying stone. Polished obsidian. I call it my 'angelglass'."

Rudolf's eyes gravitate towards the covered table. "The angelglass...." he murmurs.

With a nod of assent from Dee, Kelley reverently removes the sheet. The angelglass is a remarkable piece of work. As Dee said, a lump of black obsidian, polished so deeply it darkly reflects all before it. A gold crucifix is mounted on the top of the stone; it rests on a cradle of brass legs. Rudolf looks at it greedily; another trinket for his collection.

"And the angels speak to you through this?" says Rudolf in awe.

"To be quite precise, they speak to Edward," replies Dee. "He has the gift, he can hear their unearthly voices. Through him they speak to me in the language that Adam was given by God in order to name the birds and beasts of Paradise; over many years we have been painstakingly assembling a lost alphabet which will eventually unlock the store-houses of Heaven."

This is all too much for Rudolf. His desire to breach the walls of God's castle is being made flesh before him. "Bid them speak," he commands in a whisper. "Bid the angels speak."

Dee looks doubtfully at Kelley. "Your Excellency, the angels do not suffer Earthly desires; they speak on their own whims. We can but try...."

"Then try!" roars Rudolf. "Am I not the absolute lord of the Holy Roman Empire? Bid them speak, Doctor Dee!"

Dee murmurs quietly to Kelley, who positions the scrying stone before him. We wait quietly for a moment as Kelley closes his eyes and begins to breathe loudly and slowly.

"He is going into the necessary trance to achieve the state of angelic communication," explains Dee in a whisper. "We must wait, and quietly."

After but three or four minutes, I can sense Rudolf becoming restless, and abruptly Kelley stiffens and gasps, his eyes opening and rolling back into his head.

"He has reached them!" says Dee excitedly, then to Kelley he commands, "Who comes?"

"It is Uriel," stammers Kelley through clenched teeth.

"Uriel," breathes Dee. "The greatest of the angels who deigns to speak to us. It is said that Uriel buried the body of the first man, Adam, when he died, and that he forewarned Noah of the great Deluge. He unveiled to Enoch, the father of Methuselah, the secrets of the heavenly zodiac. We are indeed honoured, Emperor, by the presence of an archangel."

Rudolf is wide-eyed, breathless, perched on the edge of his great throne. "What does he say?"

"What does he say?" repeats Dee to Kelley.

Kelley shudders as though in pain. "A message, a message for the Emperor...."

Rudolf claps his hands delightedly. "A message for me? From Heaven?"

Dee holds up his hand for quiet. "Please, Excellency," he whispers. "The angels are fickle beings; we must not upset them. Kelley, what is the message?"

"Betrayal," gasps Kelley. "False prophets. A warning. Beware!"

Then Kelley slumps, sweating and breathing heavily. "He's gone," he says in a small voice.

But it is more than enough for Rudolf. "A message from the archangel Uriel for me," he says wonderingly. "But what's this? A warning? Betrayal? Betrayal by whom? Who are the false prophets?"

Dee shrugs. "The words of the angels are often couched in mystery," he says. Kelley glances over at me meaningfully, but says no more.

"Will Uriel speak to us again?" asks Rudolf.

"Perhaps," says Doctor Dee. "Perhaps."

"Fascinating," says Rudolf. "Mirror of Prague, what say you to this?"

"Fascinating, Excellency," I agree. What I don't say is that I would stake my very life on the unassailable fact that we have just been treated to an elaborate but completely undoubted lie.

"But how do you know he was lying?" presses Jakob.

"I don't know. I just know that it was all trickery. Kelley was most emphatically not speaking to the archangel Uriel through that mirror."

"Another charlatan, then," sighs Jakob. "God knows, we could live without another one here in the castle."

We have taken care to close the door to Jakob's workrooms in case of another uninvited interruption by Lang. "However," I say slowly, "there was something... strange about that scrying stone."

"Oh? How so?"

I walk around the room impatiently. "I can't really say, Jakob. Just a feeling I had. I wish I could get a closer look at it."

"I should imagine it's kept pretty much under lock and key when Doctor Dee and that Kelley are not around," says Jakob.

"But there must be some way," I insist. "Jakob, I'm going to need your help."

"Oh, Master Poutnik," he groans. "I cannot get involved in anything…."

"I will not put you in danger, Jakob," I say softly. "I just need you to keep watch while I go into their quarters."

"But how will we know when it is safe to do so?"

"Tonight," I decide. "Dee and Kelley are to have supper with Rudolf. We'll go in tonight."

For the first time since arriving in Prague, I feel I have a purpose. I am empowered. Whatever conflict I am here to intervene in, and I fully believe that Ripellino's words are a prophecy that must be fulfilled, the stage is now becoming set. With the arrival of Dee and Kelley, all the players are now assembled. The pieces are all on the board. And I am sure that I will get answers from Dee's angelglass. If only I knew the questions.

I spend the afternoon with Hannah. She takes me on a walking tour of the city, taking me to the top of Petrin Hill and pointing out the five towns that make up Prague: Hradcany, the castle area; the Old Town, at its centre the bustling square of fortune tellers and hawkers;

the New Town, home of the nobles of Prague; Mala Strana, the lesser quarter, with its labyrinthine alleyways and snickets; and the Ghetto, its squalor walled and contained. The dying day is cold and fresh, and we walk the paths of the wooded parkland like young lovers, holding hands and laughing. Since making my decision to break into Dee's quarters, I feel as though a weight has been lifted from me. I do not tell Hannah of my plans, involving her father as they do.

"You seem a little less... serious," she says. "Has something happened?"

In reply, I kiss her. I kiss her lips and feel the warmth of her humanity. Surely, here in my arms I hold a true innocent, a child of persecution. Hannah must be protected at all costs. She must be saved. Of this, I am sure.

Later, when she has returned to the kitchens, I venture out into the Royal Garden again. I have a hankering to see Rudolf's lion again, to draw courage from the noble king of beasts who resides within the walled arbours. As I quietly tread the paths, I hear the low murmur of urgent voices ahead of me. For a reason I cannot place, I swiftly duck into the undergrowth and squat behind a huge flowering bush as two figures crunch up the gravel path.

From my hiding place I can see only Percy Tremayne, an angry look on his face. He stops right beside the bush, his companion obscured from view. "What do you mean by keeping me waiting for so long? If I am missed at the castle, if someone should see us...."

I shift as quietly as possible in a bid to identify the other person. Could Percy be again meeting the Hard Man who accosted Hannah and me on the night of Dee's arrival?

"Calm down, Percy," says the other. And I immediately know who it is, seconds before he moves into my sightline, his grey hair straggling down his back. Edward Kelley.

"We have to move quickly," says Percy. "Sherley would be away from here pretty soon, I fear. Rudolf is not budging on our pleas for help for Shah Abbas, thanks to that infernal chamberlain, and Sir Anthony is no great admirer of your boss. We only have days before he decides to take the company away from Prague."

Kelley moves a little way from Percy, and I can't make out the words he speaks. Percy laughs bitterly. "Yes, he gave that foundling and his little whore quite a fright right here the other night. He can't keep his tripe in his trousers, that one. That's another reason why we have to move quickly; the longer Fantom is holed up in the forest with nothing but venison to ravish, the more unpredictable he becomes."

Fantom. The leader of the Hard Men. Then Sir Anthony was right; they are here in Prague. But to what purpose? Why are Carlo Fantom, Percy Tremayne and Edward Kelley in league? And what should I do about it? Abruptly, the problem is taken out of my hands.

"About that boy, that foundling," says Kelley, walking back into earshot. My blood runs cold. "I don't trust him. There's something funny about him. We didn't legislate for him."

"Pshaw," says Percy. "He's nobody. Nothing. Just a piece of good luck we found on our way into Prague, thought he might jolly the old bastard up a bit. I must say, we didn't quite expect Rudolf to take him on board as much as he has. All this 'Mirror of Prague' business. But don't worry about him. He can't affect the plan one way or another now."

"Perhaps I'll have a quiet word anyway," sniffs Kelley. "It's possible he might stumble across something. I'll tell him that if he doesn't keep his nose out of things that don't concern him, that little Jewess he's running around with might be shown what a real man can do."

Hannah. No, I cannot endanger Hannah.

"Whatever," says Percy. "I'm going to brief Fantom the night after tomorrow, though God knows he makes me sick to even look at him. But I suppose he's integral to our plans. And we can't risk him coming to the castle after what happened last time."

"And the diversion? I have already laid the groundwork with Rudolf this morning. He really will believe anything, won't he? He's as gullible as Dee."

"That's up to you," says Percy. "I'd suggest waiting no later than tomorrow to make your move. Now, I must be back to the castle. I fear Sir Anthony is already a little suspicious since that damned foundling discovered my brooch. Farewell, Edward."

"Oh, I will, Percy. By the time this is over, we'll all be faring well, I hope."

As they crunch away in opposite directions along the path, my mind is in a whirl. What is the nature of this plot? And again, what am I to do?

The answer, for now, must be nothing. Who would believe me? Would Sir Anthony take the word of a stranger over his trusted lieutenant? I do not know Doctor Dee well enough to approach him. And Lang has already made an attempt on my life. Then there is the matter of the threats against Hannah; I cannot put her at risk. No, for the moment, I must act alone, at least until I know more of what is occurring. Perhaps I need to follow Percy to his meeting with this Carlo Fantom. But first, I have another mission. The angelglass of Doctor Dee.

"Master Poutnik, I fear we are making a terrible mistake," whispers Jakob. I have led him to the dark corridors at the west wing of the castle, much against his protestations. I feel guilt at involving him, but there is no time to waste.

"Just keep watch, Jakob, I shall be as quick as I can."

The old valet positions himself in the shadows at the top of the corridor, wreathed in darkness. As I expected, the door to Dee's quarters is locked. Dare I force it? Perhaps there is another way. I remember that guard on the Charles Bridge, the horror with which he beheld me and the look in my eyes. I try to summon up the way I felt as I forced him to submit to me, the feeling of unveiling, of exposing a little of something deep inside me. The door handle becomes warm beneath my touch, then hot. Then I feel the bolts click softly, and the door creaks open.

More mysteries, yet ones which I have no time to ponder. I am in Dee's quarters.

A small reception room gives way to a study lined with books. I brush their spines with my fingers as I make my way through the darkness. In an ante-room to the left is an alchemical laboratory, laid out much as Brahe's and Kepler's on Golden Lane. But where is the scrying stone? I feel my way through the room until I feel a coarse dustsheet covering a hard globe. I draw back involuntarily; it feels almost alive to my touch.

"Master Poutnik?"

I freeze. Jakob. Have we been discovered already?

"Master Poutnik, is everything well?"

"Yes," I hiss. "I thought you were keeping watch."

Jakob's shape emerges into the dark room. "You were taking so long, I was worried...." His voice trails off as his eyes become accustomed to the gloom. "Is that...?"

I look back at the hidden stone, my hand hovering above it. "Yes. I think so."

Carefully I remove the sheet as Jakob joins me. "It doesn't look too remarkable," he says doubtfully.

I squat before it, intently studying the polished obsidian. "It is... familiar to me, Jakob. Like I have seen or…"

No communication

"Master Poutnik?" whispers Jakob. "What is it?"

I am aware of having let loose a small cry. "I don't know, Jakob. I…"

Communication is forbidden

Pain strikes me in the head, splitting my skull. I cry out loudly.

"Master Poutnik, we should go...."

"Wait, Jakob," I command. The scrying stone seems to pulse with light, with life. "Can you not see this?"

I reach out, my fingers brushing the obsidian. Jakob mutters something under his breath as the room is suddenly bathed in rapidly intensifying light. It is the stone. It is on fire. I touch it harder and it seems to give way beneath my fingers, which are no longer fingers, but… Light slicing light……melting into the stone, impossibly, agonisingly. I can sense Jakob backing away behind me as the light that suffuses the room brightens and blinds. "Master Poutnik...."

Then a sound like light filters around me, a singing, a hundred musical instruments coming together in a concordance that whistles into my mind like a wind of knives, forming a single, perfect, heartbreaking sentence.

No, Uriel, this is not the time.

Then the light is hurting my eyes, and I can hear Jakob screaming, and I can no longer see anything other than the after-burn of the hot white light on my eyelids, and then I black out.

When I awake, which can only be scant moments later, the stone is just what it appears to be, a dead lump of polished obsidian, the room is in darkness again. And I am alone.

Jakob has gone.

Interlude Three

And yet... and yet... Uriel looks out at the shining silver city, at its perfectly-ordered lightways and neatly-cut lawns bordered by singing sunflowers, at the beings like himself who swim on the warm updrafts and chat aimlessly in the geometric meadows. So beautiful, so unblemished, so good and so great.

And yet...

So dull. Such infinite perfection and timeless beauty. Uriel secretly longs to see a weed bursting through the serried ranks of identical blooms, glances around for a welcoming shadow amid the endless light, perversely hopes for a harsh word or cry of frustration on the avenues below.

He looks towards The House at the centre of the city, rising high above all around it, emanating light, goodness and beauty. The House. Where all is made right, where order is maintained, where The Word is made flesh. Fireflies flit around The House, beings such as himself busying themselves with the affairs of the shining city. Affairs he has neglected of late, he knows. Though entitled to drift along the bright corridors of The House, he has been there little recently. The place has begun to disgust him.

His balcony murmurs agreeably as he leans on it, observing the unhurried yet orderly progression of his brethren in the temperate air around The House. One of them detaches itself from the parade and charts a course towards him, unerring and straight. Uriel straightens as the light grows larger, coalescing into a form he knows well as it approaches.

Metatron.

Thirteen
John

"It's time we talked," says John, stroking his beard and looking into the middle distance. "The day of action is approaching. We have less than two weeks until November fifteen now, and though we are only a small part of a massive protest, we have our duty to fulfil. I think it would be a good idea if we had a little progress update."

It is the next day after Petey's gig and we are gathered in the living room of the house. John has stayed up all night going over a dossier of newspaper clippings and reports that Cody has been compiling for him in his absence.

"Item one," he says. "Mr. Poutnik."

I flush slightly as everyone looks at me.

"Now, I don't need much sleep and jet-lag and Jenny's brilliant coffee meant I stayed up all last night, but I'm going to need my room back. That's my base of operations," he says to me, almost apologetically.

"He could stay with me," suggests Jenny immediately, ignoring the look that Karla shoots her. "It's a double bed and more often than not I'm either working nights at the hospital or over at Lisa's."

John frowns. "I'd like everyone to spend any spare time they've got back here at the house or preparing for N15, if that's okay. We've a lot to do in the next few days."

"What about the couch?" says Karla quickly. "We could make up a bed easy enough."

This sounds a better idea to me. Sleep is almost an unknown experience to me now, and I would not relish lying awake in Jenny's bed all night.

Jenny shrugs at Karla's suggestion. "Whatever."

John moves on. "Okay, that's sorted. Staying on the subject, and forgive me for speaking so candidly here, Poutnik, but... do we trust him?"

Everyone looks at each other for an awful moment. "Sure," says Petey nonchalantly, rolling a fat joint.

John looks around at the others. "Cody?"

"He's okay, I guess," he mumbles.

"He's in," says Karla decisively. "Definitely. He's one of us. For all we know, he could have been making his way to Prague to join in the protest anyway when he had his accident or whatever it was made him lose his memory."

"Fair point," says John, although Cody doesn't look convinced. "Then Poutnik is in. For his benefit, and for anyone else who's forgotten what we're supposed to be doing here while I've been away in the Far East, let's have a little look at the plan."

John settles back into the chair, taking a swig of coffee and accepting the joint from Petey. He seems to gather his thoughts for a moment, then speaks. "The thirty-first annual International Oil Industry Symposium. Almost two thousand representatives of every oil-producing nation and petroleum industry conglomerate in the world. The Excelsior Hotel on Wenceslas Square. November fifteen. These are the facts, people, as they appear on the delegates' programmes.

"What won't be down on there will be the small matter of the biggest protest in the history of the anti-globalisation movement. We did Seattle, we did London, we did Johannesburg. We've done Prague before, but nothing, I repeat, nothing, has ever been seen on this scale. Cody, the latest estimates, please."

Cody rapidly consults a clipboard on his knees. "Fifteen thou confirmed, John."

"Fifteen thousand," says John with satisfaction. "Fifteen thousand protesters from all corners of the world. And that's not counting the stragglers and the gawkers and the really deep underground groups who'll turn up. And guess what else I heard...?"

"You don't mean...?" says Padraig, ahead of him. John nods, a smile on his thin lips.

"Deva."

"All right," says Cody, slapping his thighs. "Didn't I tell you guys? Deva. This is going to be one fucking hardcore protest, dudes."

"How do you know Deva's coming, John?" says Karla levelly.

John shrugs. "SuperAntiGlobalisationMan wouldn't miss a chance like this. Am I right, Petey?"

Petey giggles. "Fucking A, John."

"Deva will be there," says John confidently. "But we've got our own plans to make. Everyone has their own agenda for the protest but we're all working towards one simple outcome: exposing the evil of the oil business to the world and driving home to people that climate change is here now and it's only going to get worse. There will be violence, there will be arrests. There will be damage, there will be vandalism, there will be marches and placards and petitions. We, however, are going for something a little more... visual."

I lean forward in anticipation as John passes the joint to Padraig. "It's an ambitious plan. Fuck that, it's audacious. It will get the protest on the front of every newspaper and on every evening news bulletin. People, the revolution will be televised."

John stands, pacing around the room with barely-suppressed energy. "At the height of the conference, as every scum-sucking delegate is round the table working out more and more ingenious ways to bleed the planet dry...

"BANG!"

His sudden shout makes us all jump. Bang? What are these people planning? I recall the boxes, the packages, the talk of fuses.

"Bang," says John more quietly. "Fireworks. Red and blue and green. Lighting up Prague. And as all eyes are heavenward, our banner unfurls."

"Banner?" I say, suddenly realising I have been holding my breath as John spoke.

"Don't sound so disappointed," laughs Jenny. "It's a pretty big banner."

"Fucking huge," corrects Cody. "We're going to unravel it all down the front of the Excelsior. It'll cover the front of the hotel. Beamed around the world."

John traces invisible words in the air. "DON'T SCREW THE PLANET."

"Pithy," mutters Karla. "Must have taken the best minds of the protest movement to come up with that one."

John is evidently amused by Karla. "By no means Chomksy, I'll admit, but I think it gets the point over. And I wouldn't have thought you'd have wanted anything more complicated, Karla, as you'll be helping to paint the banner."

"What?" protests Karla. "But I'm getting us into the Excelsior...."

"That you are," concedes John. "Without your press credentials we could never get you inside the hotel. And Padraig has secured the fireworks. And Jenny has obtained the floorplan of the hotel. And Petey has been selling dope to the concierge for the past three months. And Cody has been invaluable through his contacts with the other groups and his organisational skills."

"Okay, I get the point," sighs Karla. "We're all little cogs turning the great wheel of protest onwards. I just don't see why I…"

"Have to get your hands dirty?" says Cody sweetly.

John holds up his hands, frowning. "Let's not behave like children, please. Karla, what I was going to say, if you'd have let me finish, was that you'll be painting the banner with the rest of us. No-one's too big for this group. Now, if we could move on, I'd like to talk about the plan in more detail. Karla, I trust your press credentials are all in order, then?"

"Of course. I'm fully registered for the entire symposium. I can go in and out of the Excelsior as I please."

"Excellent. And Petey, this concierge of yours is fully on side?"

"Completely, man. He's buying an eighth a day. He'll be doing exactly what we want by the protest."

John sits down again, lost in thought. "We need to start getting the banner inside the hotel within a week."

"But doesn't that leave more chance for it to be discovered?" asks Padraig.

"Hotel plan, please, Cody," says John. Cody dutifully digs it out of his folders and John spreads it out on the coffee table. "This is where the hotel fronts Wenceslas Square," says John, indicating the plan with a pencil. "The banner needs to be supported at each corner at the top, basically from these two rooms at either end of the hotel. This room on the right is a store-room; the room on the far left is... what is this, Cody?"

Cody inspects the blueprint. "It looks like some kind of staff room or something."

"Hmm," muses John. "Could prove difficult. We'll need to secure that room early on. Karla, how many can you get in on your press pass?"

"Just me. But there'll be a photographer's pass as well."

"Will your paper be wanting someone inside the meeting legitimately?"

"Probably not, to be honest. It's the fourth day of the symposium, just another meeting as far as most people are concerned. I can probably get the snapper to go off for a few hours and get one of us inside."

John pauses for a thoughtful moment. "Poutnik, I think."

"What?" says Cody. "Wait a minute, John. I'm happy enough to have him involved, but…"

John holds up his hand for silence. "Poutnik. I've decided. You're going to be busy with me, Cody, and besides, you've been hanging around with the Wombles and the other groups. Your face might be known. Jenny's busy. Petey and Padraig will be creating the diversion."

"Diversion?" says Petey, looking doubtfully at Padraig.

"More of that in a moment," says John. "Petey, make us some more coffee, will you?"

Petey heads off into the kitchen. John says, "Karla and Poutnik will go in and secure the staff room. It doesn't matter how. Just make sure no-one else gets in. The banner will be in the store-room at the other end of the hotel, which Petey's concierge is going to take in for us and keep safe."

"And how do we get the banner strung out across a hundred feet of hotel?" inquires Karla.

"Our rope-man, Jenny," says John.

"And how's she going to get into the most heavily-guarded hotel in Prague on November the fifteenth?" asks Karla again.

John calls into the kitchen to where Petey is making the coffee. "Hey, Petey, how much does the concierge want to keep his job?"

"Like, totally, man," replies Petey.

"Jenny's in," grins John. "With her student doctor papers she'll have no trouble swanning around the hotel once the concierge gets her inside. She can say she's hotel medical staff or something. Then when we're ready, Jenny secures one end of the banner at this window, shimmies along this ledge with the rope, and into the staff-room where Karla and Poutnik are waiting. Then they pull the rope along and the banner unfurls. Simple."

"What about the fireworks?" remembers Jenny.

"Ah," says John as Petey carries a tray of coffee into the room. "Well, you remember I spoke about a diversion. That's it. And Petey and Padraig are on firework duty."

"Great," grins Padraig. "I do love a nice Roman Candle."

"'The only people for me are the mad ones, the ones who never say a common-place thing but burn, burn, burn," quotes John. "Jack Kerouac. Good choice of phrase, Padraig. Let's raise our cups, all we mad ones, and have a toast to Operation Roman Candle."

We sip our coffee as John orders. "Now," he says. "The diversion. Behind the Excelsior is a backpacker's hostel. Petey and Padraig are going to get into there a couple of days before the fifteenth. Now, the hostel will be subjected to numerous security sweeps, especially as it's going to be home to numerous protesters for the duration of the symposium. We'll keep the fireworks here and take them to the hostel in several trips on the day. When the time is right, Padraig and Petey will get on to the flat roof of the hostel and let them fly. That will be the cue to let the banner down while everyone else in Wenceslas Square is looking to the skies. The six o'clock news here we come."

"And what will you and Cody be doing while we're risking our necks?" asks Karla.

"We'll be in Wenceslas Square with the press," says John. "Someone's got to be ready to give our statement to the cameras."

"You mentioned security sweeps," says Padraig. "What can we expect?"

"Czech police, certainly," says Cody. "Muscle, probably armed, at the Excelsior. And agents."

"Agents?" I ask.

John takes a breath. "The oil companies have extensive private security. As well as the gorillas patrolling the place, they'll have a lot of armed agents dotted around the place. Most of them are ex-FBI, CIA, armed forces. Tough guys. They've probably already got several in deep cover trying to infiltrate the protest groups. That's why Cody can't be seen trying to get inside the hotel."

"Deep cover," murmurs Petey. I can sense people giving me sidelong looks. John laughs.

"I don't think for a minute our Mr. Poutnik is an agent for the oil companies," he says. He looks at me pointedly. "You wouldn't be sitting here if I thought that was the case."

Cody still looks doubtful. John goes on, "So that's where we're at right now. Get whatever rest and recuperation you need in the next couple of days, people, because things are going to step up a gear after the weekend."

After a short moment of reflection in the room, Padraig stands up. "Right, got to get to work. John, I promised I'd pay Noel for the gear when you came back...."

"No problem. I'll go and get some cash for you."

"Great," says Padraig. "Okay, I'm off for a quick shower. See you later."

We all stand and begin to move. John asks Cody to accompany him to his room to check on some information. Karla glances at her watch. "Better get into the office." Jenny nods. "There's an essay I've got to finish before the shit kicks off."

Eventually, as Petey shambles out of the room, I am left alone. So this is the big mystery, then. A banner and a firework display. I confess it feels something of an anti-climax after the tension that has been building in the house in recent weeks. I had the feeling of something big approaching, some climactic action, some conflict. Perhaps that is not how real life works. Perhaps we don't build to some defining event, but rather continue along life with minor landmarks to chart the way. Perhaps. But I cannot shake the feeling that I am not being told all of what is to come.

With no shift at the bar until this evening, I take a walk around Prague, stopping for a coffee in a cafe close to the Jewish Quarter. Despite veiled—and not so veiled—warnings from the others about John, I have found him agreeable and friendly. He is evidently committed to his cause, and I have noticed a subtle shift to a more business-like atmosphere in the house since his return. The protest obviously means much to them, and though I am being carried along by their enthusiasm, it is with a detached air. I wonder if I have ever had a cause to call my own, ever had an obsession I would die for or a standard to which I rallied. Or whether I have always been one of life's observers.

As dusk falls I make my way back to the house, pausing at the gate as I hear voices in the garden.

"I just don't trust him, that's all." That from Cody. "And I don't understand why you're letting him in so readily."

There's a pause, then John speaks. "You suspect him?"

"I just think it's unwise to let such an unknown quantity into the group so close to the N15 protest. Okay, yes; say I don't trust him. Say he is an agent for the oil conglomerates. What then? We could all end up in jail."

"For unfurling a banner outside the Excelsior Hotel? I doubt it."

"But that's not all we're doing, is it, John? I thought we were going to tell the others about... about the rest of it."

John sighs. "Perhaps I share some of your doubts about this Poutnik. I don't believe he's an oil agent, not for a second. He's too naive for that. But he got me to thinking. When everything goes up, he'll be right at the heart of it. Perhaps we can use him to our advantage."

"You mean set him up to take the blame?"

John laughs humourlessly. "What's left of him, maybe."

I freeze, my hand on the latch of the gate. So the banner business is all a smokescreen. I knew there had to be more to the protest than that.

Cody speaks again. "But I still don't see why we're not telling the others."

John sighs. "I'm not sure they can be trusted, Cody. Not even Karla."

"Karla? But she's…."

"I know, I know. But I don't want to fuck things up when we're so close. And it's not just Karla. It's Padraig and Petey and Jenny. I know they're all committed, but I've convinced myself that they might think what we're planning is going to be a step too far, even for them."

"But it's right," protests Cody. "It's just. It's the only thing to do."

"I know," says John tenderly. "You're a good friend, Cody. A good soldier. We'll go down in history for this, you know. Now come on, we've lots of planning to do."

I listen to their footsteps recede along the garden path and the slam of the door. John and Cody are planning something far more spectacular than we'd been led to believe. Something with massively far-reaching consequences. I'm at the heart of it... and I'm not expected to survive.

The question is, what do I do now?

On my makeshift bed on the living room couch I turn the question over and over in my sleepless mind. What am I to do now? The words of the intruder Karla and I caught in the grounds of the house come back to me relentlessly: Save the innocents. Save the innocents. What part does the wizened old man play in the drama that is unfolding? And who are the innocents that need saving? Karla, Padraig, Petey and Jenny? I toss and turn uncomfortably. Again, the question bores into my mind. What must I do?

I hear the click of the door handle being turned. Cody? John? I tense on the couch as a shape moves through the darkness.

"Pooty? You awake?"

Karla. "Yes," I whisper.

I make room for her on the couch and she sits down. As my eyes become accustomed to the darkness, I make out the curls falling over the shoulders of a small nightdress, her shape outlined against the thin light from the moon filtering through the curtains. "I couldn't sleep," she says unnecessarily.

We sit in silence for a while, and then Karla says softly, "So, what do you think about John's great plans, then?"

I hesitate. Do I trust her enough to tell her what I overheard in the garden earlier today? "They were... interesting," I say, erring on the side of caution.

"They were bullshit," she spits. "It sounded like a fucking fairy story to me. All this bollocks about clambering along the outside of a hotel and unfurling a banner. I think he's up to something else."

"He is," I say after a moment's pause.

"What?"

I tell Karla everything I heard today. I have to start trusting someone, and Karla hasn't told anyone of our confrontation with the intruder after the adbusting expedition. She is silent for some time when I have finished.

"Fucking hell," she breathes. "What on earth is he planning? It sounds like some kind of...."

"Bomb?" I say softly.

I can feel her looking at me in the darkness. "What makes you say that?"

"One time at the Leopold Bloom I heard Padraig and Noel talking in the cellar. They mentioned fuses."

"Of course," she whispers fiercely. "I thought something didn't sound right about Paddy getting the fireworks from Noel. Two blokes with Republican terrorist connections sneaking about for the sake of a few bangers? Puh-lease."

"What do we do, then?" I ask.

Karla says nothing. Instead, I feel her hand exploring under the duvet covering me. She strokes my nakedness and slides herself under the cover. I feel the warm wetness of her mouth on me and she expertly brings me to an urgent climax. She emerges a few seconds later, kissing me hotly on the mouth.

"Nothing," she whispers. "We do nothing, for now."

"What... what was that for?" I say breathlessly.

"There's trouble coming," she whispers, kissing me again. "I want you on my side."

Then she steals away, closing the door softly behind her.

The next few days pass quickly. I work at the Leopold Bloom and spend my free time walking around Prague or helping to stitch white bed-sheets together to form John's massive banner. Karla and I exchange loaded glances all the time, but we do nothing. Padraig is evidently with Cody and John; Petey and Jenny are as yet unknown quantities. I try to speak to Karla about our next move but we are never alone.

"People will die!" I hiss to her as we wash up together in the kitchen one evening. "I will die! We have to act soon."

"Soon," she agrees, then begins whistling as Jenny saunters into the kitchen in search of a snack.

On November the tenth I return to the house after my shift to find everyone sitting in the living room. Karla glances at me then looks away. It appears everyone is waiting for me.

"Poutnik, sit down," says John in a business-like tone. "We need to speak."

I perch on the edge of the couch uncertainly. What is going on now? Cody looks at me with something approaching hatred mingled with unalloyed joy.

"Me and John caught the intruder this afternoon," says Cody. I look at Karla but she is studying her feet. "The old guy who's been hanging around the house."

"And?" I say carefully.

"And he seems to know you," says John. "Seems to know you very well."

"This is good," says Jenny with a kind smile. "He might be able to help you remember."

"He told us quite a tale," says John, his eyes as hard as flint. "Do you remember living at the castle?"

The castle... I wondered why the collection of buildings perched on the hill at Prague had drawn me so. "No, I don't. The castle...." I say, excitement dulling my anxiety. "What did he say?"

"He said you'd appeared there one day, after being found in a ditch," John says. "That you'd been taken in and adopted by the court. That you'd been at the centre of intrigue and gossip."

"Intrigue...." I say wonderingly. Visions of court banquets and walks in arbours assail me. "When did this happen?"

"Fifteen eighty-four!" says John, bursting into deep laughter. Cody joins him, gasping: "He was mad as a fruitcake! Said he'd disappeared after you touched a magic mirror and woke up in the modern day!"

The atmosphere in the room suddenly eases. "Must have escaped from the bug-house," laughs Cody evilly. "Same one you came from, Poutnik?"

I flush. Jenny springs to my defence. "Aw, don't be awful, you guys."

Cody shrugs. "What other explanation is there? He knew Poutnik by name."

"He's been hanging about a lot," intervenes Padraig. "He could have heard any one of us refer to Pooty by his name. He's obviously just some nutter. Where is he now?"

"We let him go," says John. "Told him not to come back here or we'd turn him over to the police. I think it did the trick."

"Well, at least that's one mystery sorted out," says Jenny, satisfied. "Do you really think he'll stay away? Might mean I can have a shower in peace now."

"Oh, he won't be coming back," says John firmly. "We made sure of that."

But I'm barely listening to them. Magic mirror. In my mind's eye the room is filled with blazing cold light, my fingers sinking into hard stone, a cacophony of music distilling into a warning.

No, Uriel, this is not the time.

I don't know what it means, but I know one thing: The time is coming.

The next day the oil symposium begins in Prague. I wander down to Wenceslas Square after working at the Leopold Bloom to find every cafe and bar full to bursting, every hotel working to capacity. Police patrol the square and there are already knots of protesters gathering. A team from Reclaim the Streets cycles at low speed through the square, tooting horns and blowing whistles. A phalanx of Greenpeace activists is handing out leaflets. Suited men and women hurry between hotels and restaurants, heads down, trying their best to ignore the tumult around them. Across the baroque stone frontage of the Excelsior Hotel a banner has been strung advertising the Thirty-First Annual International Oil Industry Symposium. What will be strung across the hotel in three days' time? The banner John and Cody outlined to us? Dead bodies and carnage? Nothing? It is becoming difficult to know what to believe any more. Karla has so far failed to act upon our conversation, and I am conscious that time is running out. If John is indeed planning to plant a bomb in the Excelsior, there will be blood, and there will be death. Innocents, surely, will die. Something must be done. I could just walk away, I suddenly realise. Nothing is tying me to these people. Nothing except a burning desire to see how things turn out, that and the strange command from the intruder—what was his name? Jakob?—who implored me to "save the innocents".

Glumly I walk back to Mala Strana and the house. It is empty, the afternoon turning to dusk. I sit in the garden and brood. Padraig, I am sure, is in league with Cody and John. Out of Petey and Jenny, who should I approach? Petey remains an enigma to me, while Jenny has shown me much kindness. But what does that mean in this house of secrets and lies?

As I ponder, my eyes fall upon a patch of earth in the lengthening shadows by the back wall of the garden. Hidden by a shrivelled honeysuckle, the piece of garden looks at first glance like any other, except for a darkness of the soil. I push past the bush to investigate, poking at the soil with my booted toe. It seems freshly turned. I squat, frowning, running my hand over the moist earth. Freshly turned. Recently dug. I begin to brush the soil, absently at first and then with a growing urgency. I know what I will find here. I know what lies beneath the soil. "Oh, he won't be coming back," says John again inside my head. "We made sure of that."

By now I'm clawing frantically at the dirt with both hands, until I scrape something cold and clammy. I draw back in horror at what I have uncovered. A face, eyes staring imploringly through the cool soil, mouth set in a rictus of terror.

Fourteen
Blood Libel

I spend the night and the morning searching in vain for Jakob. His rooms remain as they were when we departed for our secret mission to Doctor Dee's quarters and no-one seems to have seen him since. He has seemingly been swallowed by the bright light that emanated from the scrying stone. I encounter Hannah but decide not to share the mysterious events of the previous evening. Hannah does not seem duly concerned. "I haven't seen my father for a couple of days," she shrugs. "It isn't unusual. Our work at the castle keeps us busy, Master Poutnik. Very often I do not see him for days on end."

It is my fear she will never see him again. I cannot make sense of what happened in Doctor Dee's rooms, but I have the greatest feeling of dread, and not a little confusion. Dee and Kelley claim to converse with a heavenly being named Uriel through their so-called angelglass. For reasons I cannot fully explain, I know in my heart that their summoning of Uriel for Rudolf was nothing but an elaborate trick. Yet I know I heard the voice within Dee's rooms: *Uriel, no, this is not the time.* Another trick from Dee or Kelley? Ventriloquism? If not, then who spoke? A voice from within the scrying stone, or from the heavenly plain that the enchanters claim to be in contact with? Not this Uriel, evidently; the voice was speaking to Uriel.

I have also the matter of the plot being hatched by Kelley, Percy and Carlo Fantom to address. Percy told Kelley to wait until no later than today to "make his move". And tomorrow evening Percy is to visit the Hard Man in his camp in the woods outside of Prague. I have elected to follow him to accrue more evidence to take to Sir Anthony. But first I must ensure that Hannah is safe. I seek her out again at the castle kitchens.

"Master Poutnik," she says, smiling. "Twice in one day. I am honoured indeed."

"Hannah," I say curtly. "You must away from the castle, at once if possible."

She frowns at me. "I cannot do that. I have my work here...."

"Please," I insist. "For me. I fear you are in great danger."

Hannah is silent for a moment. "What danger?"

"I... I cannot say. Not yet. You must trust me."

She shrugs. "I am not working tomorrow anyway, and I shall be returning to the Ghetto after my shift this afternoon. Does that please you?"

"Yes," I breathe. "Thank you."

"But you must come to me and tell me what this is all about. Do you promise?"

"I promise," I assure her.

Once again I am summoned to the great hall to see Rudolf. When I am announced, Dee and Kelley are already there, the scrying stone between them. It is a simple lump of obsidian now, not burning and glowing as it was the previous evening. Dee and Kelley betray no suspicions of me having tampered with the angelglass.

"Ah, the Mirror of Prague," says Rudolf. "You are just in time. Masters Dee and Kelley are about to summon the spirits to speak to us once more."

"Should the spirits be willing, of course, your Excellency," says Dee quietly.

"Am I not Rudolf?" says the Emperor pleasantly. "But first, we were talking of Empire, were we not, Doctor Dee?"

"That we were, Excellency," nods Dee. "Queen Elizabeth is a great believer in Empire. I myself have predicted that England shall one day rule most of the lands on this Earth. I coined the term 'Britannia' to describe this huge empire."

"An empire greater than that ruled by the Habsburgs?" says Rudolf doubtfully. "That would mean war between us and Elizabeth, Doctor Dee. Is that how you have advised her?"

Dee bows low. "Quite the contrary, Excellency. It is my belief that empires can be achieved through trade and economics as well as base warfare. A civilisation as grand as Britannia or indeed the Habsburgs can expand its borders by educating the rude savages to live as they do. Imagine, Emperor, a world where all are speaking the same tongue, all are wearing the same clothes, all are purchasing the same goods at the same prices. That is my vision, Emperor, be it Elizabeth or yourself who leads this great coming together of peoples and cultures, who forges it into a single nation spanning the globe."

Rudolf muses. "A great vision indeed, Doctor Dee. Do you believe it shall come to pass?"

"I do," says Dee. "Whether in my lifetime I know not, but one day I believe there shall be a beautiful homogeny across the Earth."

"And what of those who would be different, Doctor Dee?" I ask.

Rudolf looks at me in surprise. "You have an opinion, foundling?"

"What of those who do not wish to wear what is the fashion in London or Prague, who do not wish to watch the same plays or eat the same food? What of those whose own culture is more valuable to them than that of the Empire?"

Dee acquiesces with a nod. "As I said, Master Poutnik, Empire does not have to be achieved through warfare. But in some circumstances it may be the only way."

"Why do we not see what the angels would say on the matter?" suggests Rudolf.

Dee gives a small nod to Kelley, who closes his eyes and begins to enter the trance which he claims to help him converse with the angels. After a few moments he gasps and shudders.

"Contact," whispers Dee. Rudolf leans forward on his throne expectantly.

"Who comes, Edward?" says Dee softly.

Kelley's face contorts into a grimace, his eyes rolling, his teeth gnashing. His performance is, I admit, impressive. But I am as convinced as I was yesterday that this is nothing more than a fraud.

"Uriel," breathes Kelley through clenched teeth. "It is Uriel."

"The archangel," says Rudolf, eyes bright. "Ask him a question, Dee. Ask him who shall have the greater empire, Rudolf or Elizabeth."

There's a pause while Kelley undergoes much contortion and gasping, then he says, "Uriel remarks that an empire which lasts a thousand years on Earth is but a blink of an eye in the heavenly empire of God."

Rudolf is evidently dissatisfied with this, but Dee hurriedly says, "The angels cannot tell us too much of that which is to come, Excellency."

Kelley speaks again: "But Uriel has more to say. He has a message for the Emperor."

"For me?" says Rudolf, delighted. "What is the message?"

"He says... he says... to make Rudolf's empire strong, certain elements must be cast out."

"Elements? What elements?"

"Uriel says... the Jews, Emperor, the Christ-killers. He says they are against God. He says... they commit barbaric atrocities in their infernal ceremonies. He says they use the blood of Christian children in secret rites to the devils they worship."

Rudolf looks aghast; Dee glances doubtfully at Kelley. "Uriel said this?" murmurs the magician.

Kelley looks at him. "The word of Uriel cannot be doubted."

"The Jews," says Rudolf thoughtfully. "Ask him more, what should I do?"

But Kelley has relaxed his grimace. "Uriel has gone," he says simply.

Rudolf looks perturbed. "The blood of Christian children? What abomination is this? I must consult with my chamberlain."

The audience is at an end. As Kelley and Dee pack up the scrying stone, I can see hear Dee whispering in a disturbed manner to his assistant. Kelley shrugs, and replies, "I only repeat what the angels say."

Within an hour the word has spread around the castle like brush fire. Those from the Ghetto who work in the castle have fled by mid-afternoon. I seek Hannah, but her shift ended before the session with Dee and Kelley. She will know nothing of this. I have to speak with her.

As I make my way out of the castle, my way is blocked by a member of the guard. "I wouldn't go out into the city, Master Poutnik," he advises.

"Why not?"

"There's been a riot in the Old Town Square." I look to where he points and see a thin curl of smoke in the distance. "Some of the Jewish traders have been attacked. There's a mob trying to get to the Ghetto."

I push past him into the road that leads down the hill from the castle. Groups of worried citizens stand around, discussing in low voices the latest developments to leak out of the castle. Abruptly, I recall Kelley's overheard words from the Royal Garden yesterday: "And the diversion? I have already laid the groundwork with Rudolf." Is this pernicious lie part of the plot, then? If so, then it has certainly done its job; Prague is aflame with the words Kelley has passed off as the angel Uriel's. I see a woman hurry past, clinging two children closely to her. I pass a trio of hawkers talking in low voices.

"They say the Jews kidnap children every full-moon. My neighbour saw two Jews hanging around the school-room yesterday," says the first.

"But it's not even full-moon," scoffs his companion.

"Perhaps they're so desperate for child-blood they're taking them at any time," suggests the third.

How could such words have taken hold of the city so quickly and so efficiently? People seem ready to believe the lies without even checking on their validity. How many of them would believe the gossip if they knew it had come from the mouth of a man who claims to speak with angels? But as I look around the hate-filled faces in the street, and recall the rough treatment of Hannah at the hands of the guards on the Charles Bridge, I realise with a sinking heart that it is not the source of the words that is important, perhaps not even the words themselves. The citizenry have been given an excuse to hate the Jews. That is all that matters.

A diversion, then, and pulled off expertly. But the question remains: A diversion for what?

I hurry on towards the Ghetto. The crowds get thicker as I cross the Charles Bridge, and by the time I get towards the edge of the Old Town Square I'm fighting my way through the tightly-packed hordes. I can see a blazing hawker stall, the smoke curling up into the still air, and there's a lot of shouting. As I force my way through the crowd, I come across a group of angry citizens surrounding an elderly man curled up on the cobbles.

"Murderer!" screams a woman, kicking him fiercely in the back. A man hits him with his stick, and a young mother spits on his foetal, shaking form before hurrying away with her small son.

"What's going on here?" I call, pushing through. "Leave him alone!"

A dirty-faced man with no hair turns to me. "He's a stinking, child-killing Jew. He deserves no better."

A taller man looks at me. "Hey, is he a Jew as well?"

As one the crowd turns to regard me. The smaller bald man screws up his eyes. "He's a funny-looking one. Got the look of a Jew-boy about him."

"Child-killer!" screams the woman again, almost hysterical. The crowd advances on me, sticks and fists raised. I throw up my arms to defend myself as the first blow lands on my arm, and fear I am about to fall under the weight of the angry horde, when I suddenly feel something grip my shoulder strongly and haul me backwards away from my attackers.

The crowd fall silent and look up in awe. I twist around to see Finn, the giant, flanked by a small platoon of castle guard. "What occurs?" he rumbles.

"He's a child-killer," says the woman, slightly less hysterically.

"Go about your business!" roars Finn. The crowd disperses quickly and a soldier goes to the prone figure of the old Jew. He looks up. "Dead," he says quietly.

"I want the Old Town Square cleared," commands Finn to his

soldiers. "Master Poutnik, are you all right?"

"Fine, thank you, Finn. I fear I am once again indebted to you for saving my life."

Finn scans the Old Town Square, his normally jovial face set into a serious frown. "This is bad, Master Poutnik. Very bad. I have never seen the citizenry inflamed so. We were on our way to the Ghetto gates. I think you should accompany us until I can escort you back to the castle."

Leaving half of his company clearing the Old Town Square, Finn strides on through the alleyways towards the Ghetto. A clamour of voices greets us and we turn the corner to find half a dozen pressed soldiers trying to push a crowd of maybe three hundred or more back from the gates, which have been dragged shut but are hanging flimsily on their rusted hinges.

No. I have made a terrible error. I sent Hannah back to the Ghetto, thinking the danger to her came from within the castle. Now she is in greater jeopardy than I could have imagined.

Finn strides forward, brandishing his pike and calling for the crowd to fall back. They fall quiet and part nervously to let him through. "What's the situation?" the giant says to the harried commander of the soldiers at the Ghetto gates.

"Thank God you came!" says the guard. "We couldn't hold them back for much longer. They're intent on getting inside."

The guard lowers his voice. "For my money we should just let 'em in. The whole problem could be solved by this time tomorrow, if you know what I mean."

Finn gives him a withering look. "The people of the Ghetto are under my protection now. No-one shall pass by these gates. I have already seen one man dead as a result of this madness; I shall see no more."

The crowd are getting restless again. "Let us through!" calls a man, to loud agreement from the others. "The Ghetto should burn!"

"Return to your homes!" shouts Finn so loudly my head hurts. "There shall be no burning today. Return to your homes!"

As Finn's soldiers begin to disperse the crowd, he turns to me. "You are not safe here, Master Poutnik. I am to send two soldiers back to the castle to call for re-enforcements; you shall accompany them."

"But, Hannah...." I protest.

"If your girl is inside the Ghetto, I promise no harm shall come to her. Do you trust me?"

I nod reluctantly. "You have saved my life twice now, Finn. I trust you."

"Then go. And if you can use your influence in the court to do anything to halt this madness, I beseech you to try."

From the bare chamber atop the Whit Tower I look out over Prague as darkness falls. I can count at least half a dozen fires throughout the city, and scant minutes earlier I had watched the pressed castle guard fight running battles with scattered mobs in the streets below. At the instigation of his generals, Rudolf has imposed a curfew on the city, but it is proving difficult to enforce. Insanity has gripped Prague. I think of Hannah and my heart sinks to my boots.

I am interrupted in my gloomy introspection by a breathless messenger climbing the stairs. "Master Poutnik," he gasps. "I have been searching the castle for you. You are required in the great hall."

"Ah, Master Poutnik," says Lang with barely-contained anger as I rush into the hall. "We have only been waiting a half hour. At last we can begin our very important meeting."

"Philipp," chides Rudolf miserably. "I cannot have such a conference without the Mirror of Prague present. You know that."

Lang's eyes flash at me but he says nothing. Finn is in the hall, as are three or four other generals, as well as Sir Anthony and Percy Tremayne and Doctor Dee and Edward Kelley.

"If we can begin, then," says Lang. "Excellency, the city is in a state of panic. The message purporting to be from this angel which was passed on to you from Doctor Dee and Master Kelley has leaked out to the populace. We have reports of at least a dozen Jews murdered in the streets. Mobs are massing in the Old Town Square, ignoring the curfew we have imposed. Captain Finn, what is the situation at the Ghetto gates?"

"Grim," says Finn. "My soldiers have cleared the area but it is impossible to patrol the streets. We need more men."

"We cannot risk depleting the castle guard any further," interjects another soldier. "Should the hordes decide to turn on the castle, we shall need as much protection as we can muster."

"But we must protect the Ghetto!" says Finn angrily. "If that mob gets inside...."

Lang holds up his hands for calm. "Sir Anthony," he says. "Can you and your company help?"

Sir Anthony shifts uncomfortably, glancing at Percy. "With all due respect, Chamberlain, this is not our battle. But, ah, I suppose I could keep my men on alert at the castle, which could free up some of the castle guard to help in the city."

The captain of the guard frowns. He does not want his men in danger in the streets. Finn speaks up, "My men have been on duty for twelve hours now, Chamberlain. I need to relieve them soon."

"There is a school of thought that says we should let the rabble have their way," says Lang airily. "Help them, even."

"A pogrom?" says Rudolf slowly. "Burn down the Ghetto? Is that wise, Philipp? Are not the Jews my people, too?"

"Baby-killers," mutters the captain of the guard. "Let them burn."

"The Emperor is quite right," says Lang. "The Jews are as much a part of the citizenry as anyone else. I am just concerned that the longer the chaos lasts, the more damage it shall do to the Empire. Perhaps we must send word to Vienna for more troops?"

"No," says Rudolf flatly. "I shall not crawl to my family for help. I shall sort this out myself. Begone, all of you. I would think on this for a while."

As we file out of the hall in silence, I catch an unmistakable glance pass between Kelley and Percy.

"And meanwhile, Prague burns," says Lang quietly as the doors close behind us, leaving Rudolf alone in the shadows.

Feeling powerless, I wander the cold corridors of the castle, covering miles of carpeted, straw-strewn and bare stone hallways over the next two hours. Finn has refused to escort me back to the Ghetto, saying it is far too dangerous. But I must know if Hannah is well.

As I turn into a bright corridor I see a hooded figure rattling a door-knob halfway down. I realise it is the door to Lang's quarters. What transpires here? The figure looks up, the face lost in shadows, and starts at the sight of me. Then the hood is thrown back and it is my turn to be startled. It is Hannah.

I run up to her. "What on Earth are you doing here? How did you get away from the Ghetto?"

Hannah is breathless and has terror in her eyes. "I had to come to the castle. I was looking for you."

"But that is Chamberlain Lang's room," I say.

She looks at the door almost in surprise. "Is it? I didn't know where your quarters were. I was just trying anything. I was desperate."

"What is happening, Hannah? What is wrong?"

"You must come with me," she begs. "To the Ghetto. Someone must stop them."

"Stop who? The mob? Are they attacking?"

She shakes her head. "No, not the mob. Rabbi Loew and his cronies. They're raising the Golem."

Hannah refuses to answer my questions, instead urging me to be silent as we steal through the quiet back streets of Prague. There are distant sounds of shouting and fighting, and the smell of smoke hangs heavy in the still night air. Hannah leads me down narrow ginnels and alleys, taking us across a rickety wooden bridge a mile or two down-river from the Charles Bridge, then working through the city to the Ghetto. The journey takes almost two hours.

"But how will we get into the Ghetto?" I whisper fiercely. "The gate is guarded."

"There are other entrances, secret ones," she says softly. She leads us to the wall on the east side of the Ghetto, where a heavy locked door nestles in the brickwork. Hannah raps twice and it is opened swiftly to allow us in, then locked and bolted again. I note it is a good three inches thick and heavily armoured on the inside. "You didn't think we'd leave ourselves with just one gate into the Ghetto, did you?" she says to me.

"Are you going to explain what's going on now?"

"Come with me," she commands. I follow her through the rat-infested warren of streets, emerging at a familiar building; the Old-New Synagogue.

"Hannah," I say again. "Talk to me. What is this Golem?"

She pauses beneath the fig-tree carving that adorns the entrance to the Synagogue. "You'll see soon enough," she says, before rapping loudly on the door.

It opens a crack, a shadowed face peering out at us. "Hannah?" says the voice of a young man. "You should not be here. This is important business. Leave at once."

"Let me in, Ari," says Hannah. "Or I shall tell the soldiers at the gates exactly what is going on here."

The man sighs and opens the door. I follow Hannah into the gloomy entrance. "What do you hope to achieve by this?" he says.

"Rabbi Loew is making a mistake," says Hannah. "Raising the Golem is wrong."

"What's happening out there is wrong!" spits Ari. "They're killing us! They…"

He stops as the door into the ante-room where I met the Rabbi on my first visit creaks open. Loew appears, dressed in ceremonial robes. "Ah. Young Hannah. And Master Poutnik. I do hope this is not some vain attempt to put us off the only course of action that will save our people, hmm?"

"Rabbi, you're making a mistake," says Hannah again. "The carnage wrought up to now will be nothing to what the Golem will cause. I beg you to reconsider."

"She has threatened to tell the soldiers," says Ari sadly.

Loew muses for a moment, regarding us with his bright eyes, then clicks his fingers. From nowhere we are seized by strong arms, four men melting out of the shadows to hold us.

"Rabbi!" implores Hannah. "Please...."

"Bring them inside," says Loew. "And hold them tight." He gives me a twinkling smile. "I imagine you will find this interesting, Mirror of Prague."

We are pushed into the ante-room, which is lit by dozens of candles. As well as Loew and our captors, two men dressed in similar robes to the Rabbi await. The rough carpets on the floor have been rolled back and dominating the room is the crude figure of a man fashioned from what appears to be dried mud. It is prone, its face staring blindly at the ceiling, and it is some ten feet in length. The four men holding Hannah and myself drag us to a corner of the room and grip us tightly.

Loew turns to the two men. "Isaac ben Simson, my son-in-law, and David ben Chayim Sasson, my trusted friend, I am behove to point out to you the danger of this enterprise. If any one of us is found wanting, if our inner sanctification is in any way incomplete, then we shall have desecrated the Holy Name and the terrible vengeance of Heaven shall be absolute.

"Have we spent the day in earnest penitence? Have we purified our bodies and our souls? Have we taken the ritual bath of Mikveh?"

The two men nod. Loew says, "Then we are ready, hmm? You are brave men, and you shall have the eternal reward for what you do this night. We are to make a Golem to protect our people, and for this act we need the four elements of Aysch, which is fire, Mayim, which is water, Ruach, which is air, and Aphar, which is earth.

"You, Isaac, will be the element of fire. You, David, will be the element of water. I will be the element of air. Working together, we shall create out of the fourth element of earth, from the clay gathered on the banks of the Vltava, a Golem."

Isaac and David look terrified. I look at Hannah and she looks back at me, defeat in her eyes.

"Now we shall recite the Hazoth, the midnight lament for

Jerusalem," announces Loew, and the three men begin to chant in low voices. During the recitation, Loew takes a heavy leather-bound book and begins to read in Hebrew, his cracked voice mingling with the low chanting of Isaac and David in an almost hypnotic fashion.

"Isaac," says Loew softly. Still murmuring the prayer, Isaac begins to walk slowly in an anti-clockwise direction around the crude clay figure on the floor. Abruptly, the candles seem to dim in the small room. No, not the candles dimming, but a source of brighter light eclipsing them. The clay man has begun to glow from within, dull orange at first like embers, and brightening to a hot red like a blazing fire.

When Isaac has completed seven circuits he joins Loew at the feet of the statue.

"David," says Loew. The other man begins to walk in the opposite direction around the Golem, seven times. The fire within the clay giant is dulled, and the mud seems to smooth and flatten, the surface becoming shiny and undulating as though the lifeblood of water runs through it.

Loew walks once around the figure, pausing at the head and withdrawing a scrap of paper from within the folds of his robe. "The shem, hmm?" whispers Loew. "Inscribed with the true name of God."

He bends and places the shem into the mouth of the Golem. Base features are beginning to sharpen on the clay man's face. Loew stands at the head of the creature, Isaac and David at the feet, and together they recite, "'And he breathed into the nostrils the breath of life, and man became a living soul'."

I hear Hannah gasp and see what she has seen just seconds later. The pile of clay has become a thing alive, its chest rising and falling with heavy breath, its eyes open and staring heavenward.

"Stand up!" commands Loew. "Stand up!"

Uncertainly, the clay man rolls to one side, ungainly and unsure of itself, dragging its legs under it and rising to a towering height of ten feet or more, its smooth head brushing the ceiling of the room. I stare at it uncomprehending. Surely this cannot be. The crude clay has been smoothed and sculpted, almost like dark flesh, and the eyes blaze with dull light. Isaac and David look dumbfounded, as though they never believed what they were doing could possibly work.

Loew stands before the clay giant. "We have created a Golem," he says quietly. "From the crude earth we have summoned a champion to protect the people of the Ghetto. We are the victims of a terrible lie, and our people are suffering as they have never suffered before. I command you to seek out those that have perpetrated this evil libel, and deliver them to their punishment."

The Rabbi stands on tiptoe and withdraws a small knife from within the folds of his robes. He makes an inscription on the forehead of the impassive creature. "I have placed the word *emet*, which means truth, on your head to guide you in your task. Now go! Avenge the Ghetto!"

Rabbi Loew stands back, but the Golem remains unmoving. "Go!" he commands again.

The Golem does not flinch. Isaac and David look at each other doubtfully.

"Did I not create you?" says Loew angrily. "Did I not breathe life into you? Are you not beholden to me, the holiest man in the Ghetto?"

The Golem moves, and I sense Hannah tense. The creature tilts its head slightly, gazing down impassively at Loew.

"Am I not closer to God than any man here?" implores Loew.

The Golem gives the tiniest movement of its head. Left then right. No.

Loew looks aghast. "What treachery is this? Am I not the Chief Rabbi of the Ghetto? Please, I beg you, my people are dying. This cannot be. Who here is closer to God than Rabbi Loew?"

The Golem raises its head. And looks. At me.

Hannah catches her breath as she follows its gaze. "Poutnik, it's looking at you," she breathes.

Loew's eyes narrow. "What? Can this be? Master Poutnik, the Mirror of Prague?"

He hobbles over to me. "What trickery is this? What have you done?"

"Nothing, Rabbi," I whisper. "I don't understand."

"Command it," says Loew. "Tell it to do something."

I clear my throat. "Uh, walk," I say.

The Golem takes one step towards us. The men holding Hannah and me let loose their grip, backing into the wall.

"Unbelievable," breathes Loew. "You have mastery over the Golem, hmm? Again, command it again."

"Bring me that candle," I say, pointing to a candlestick in the corner of the room. The Golem turns clumsily, crossing the room with a single huge step. It grabs at the candlestick, its huge paws closing tightly around it, and with one stride it is before me, holding out the prize.

"I do not claim to understand this," says Loew. "But the path is clear. Command the Golem to protect the Ghetto, and to seek out those who have wronged my people."

"No!" says Hannah. "Poutnik, you must not. It shall cause chaos and death. There must be another way."

"There is no other way!" hisses Loew. "Why do you protect them so, Hannah? What are they to you?"

I look to Hannah for an answer. She gazes into my eyes for a long time, then lowers her face. "Do what you must," she says.

I look to Loew, and back to the Golem, still holding out the burning candle to me. Perhaps Hannah is right, perhaps it will cause more death and horror. But I cannot get out of my mind the face of the elderly man in the Old Town Square, kicked and beaten to death by the mob inflamed by the casual lies of Dee and Kelley. Whatever scheme Kelley, Percy and Carlo Fantom are hatching, there is no way they can have ever expected to deal with the Golem.

"Go," I say quietly. "Go. Seek the truth. Avenge the Ghetto. Save the innocents."

The Golem nods once, then ducks its head and crashes through the door into the Synagogue hall. We hear it tear open the doors and step out into the dark Ghetto streets.

"Oh, God," says Hannah softly. "What have we done?"

Fifteen
The Lovers

"How shall I be betrayed?"

"The Lovers. F-failure to recognise... to recognise true nature...."

I awake with a start. Sleep as others know it had not come to me, but merely the disconnected images that parade by whenever I try for rest. A card slaps down on a cloth-covered table... then it is gone. A painted image of two naked lovers, entwined, is the last to fade. The word betrayal hangs on the wind.

It is early. Dawn paints the sky pink through the un-curtained window. I am uncomfortable on the couch, and I have been mostly awake all night, pondering my next move. I have not yet signalled my discovery of Jakob, the intruder, to anyone—not even Karla. Her reticence to act on my information has made me suspicious of her motives. If John and Cody are indeed planning to bomb the oil symposium, many people could die. She seems to be not too concerned about that.

I wander to the window, immediately ducking back out of sight as I see two figures in the garden. I peer around the wall. Cody and John. Have they seen where I disturbed the shallow grave in the garden? Am I discovered? I can hear their low, urgent voices. Cody seems angry.

"I just wish we could tell the others, John. I don't see why we're holding out. It's only three days away now. I think we risk losing their support if we delay any longer."

John says something I don't hear. Cody rounds on him.

"For fuck's sake, why don't you trust Karla? She's as committed as any of us. I'm just worried that if we keep them in the dark, our people could be injured here. Can't you see that?"

John speaks again, and Cody throws up his hands. He begins to stalk back to the house, so I hurriedly get back on the couch, pretending to sleep as he quietly lets himself back in the house and pads up the stairs. A moment later John follows him, but he does not leave the living room. Instead, he perches on a chair beside me, and I can feel him watching me intently.

"Poutnik?" he says softly. "Poutnik? I don't think you're asleep, are you?"

I sigh and open my eyes. "John."

He smiles. "Poutnik, who's Ripellino?"

I sit up. "Ripellino? I have no idea. Why?"

He shrugs. "Just a name you were mumbling in your sleep earlier. Something about cards. No matter."

He pauses for a moment, studying me. "You heard me and Cody, didn't you? I saw you at the window."

So. The time has come for the confrontation. Am I to end up like Jakob, a corpse rotting beneath the honeysuckle?

"I think it's time we talked," decides John. "Come for a walk with me."

We wander through the dawn streets of Mala Strana, towards the river. "Prague smells wonderful in the morning," says John. "Human. It's a human city, Prague. Do you know what I mean?"

"I think so."

John throws up his arms. "Full of humanity. Seething with it. Every building, every brick, every cobble... it's seen so much. The history of the world's here, Poutnik."

We reach the Charles Bridge, leaning on the balustrade and watching the Vltava flow sluggishly beneath us. "What do you think you know?" says John.

I gather my thoughts, then speak quietly. "The banner is a front. You're planning to plant a bomb. I don't know how, but I'm to take the blame. I'm to die."

John nods thoughtfully. "That's one version of events," he agrees.

"Are there others?" I say, anger hardening my voice. "I'm not too keen on that one."

"Understandable," says John. "Just why do you think there's a bomb, out of interest?"

"Padraig got it. He's got terrorist links in Ireland, hasn't he? I heard him and Noel talking at the Leopold Bloom."

"Interesting," is all John says.

"Well? What are you going to do now that I know?"

John takes a pack of cigarettes out of his inside pocket and offers me one. I shake my head and he shrugs and lights one. "In one version of events there's a banner. In another there's a bomb. In another we save the world. In yet another we fail, nothing happens. Do you understand me?"

"No. I don't."

John sighs. "One's Cody's reality. Another one's Petey's. Jenny's. Padraig's. Can you spot which is which?"

"You're not making any sense!" I say, punching the cold stone balustrade. "Are you telling me that everyone has a different idea of what's to happen on November fifteenth?"

John breaks out into a smile. "Now you get it."

"No, John, I don't. I just want the truth."

John pulls a face. "You can't handle the truth!" he snarls, then begins to laugh. "Sorry. Little joke. Jack Nicholson, yeah?"

I shake my head in disgust. "I don't know who you're talking about."

John nods, his eyes narrow, appraising me coolly, then he turns back to the Vltava. We stand in silence for a while. John flicks his cigarette butt into space and we watch it tumble into the river below. "You didn't mention Karla," I say softly.

"What?"

"The different versions of events. Petey's and Cody's and Padraig's and Jenny's. But not Karla's. Why not?"

John looks at me for a long time. "You know something, Poutnik? I trust you. Fuck knows why. I don't know you from Adam. Three days from now I'm taking part in the most momentous event of my life. Telling you everything could screw it up big time. But for some bloody reason, I feel I can trust you."

"So tell me."

John lights another cigarette. "Okay. You want to know why I didn't mention Karla? You want to know why everyone has a different idea of what's going to happen at N15?"

"Yes."

"She's an agent. Karla's an agent for the oil companies."

"She's what?" I say, though I heard John perfectly well.

"An agent. For the oil companies. That's why I can't tell anyone exactly what's going to happen in three days' time. I'm not sure who to trust any more."

"But that seems...."

"Ridiculous? That's what I thought. At first. But then I started to get suspicious. Something about her didn't gel. I did some checking up on her. All these newspapers she claims to have worked for back in England... they've never heard of her. My theory is she's been inserted with a ready-made past, a back story, into the Prague Gazette by the oil companies. They probably paid the paper's owner a fortune to get her in. Hell, for all I know, the owner's a fucking shareholder in Exxon. It's classic deep cover stuff."

"But Cody...."

"Cody's screwing Karla," spits John. "I fucking told him not to get involved. Never take a lover in the field. It's basic. So until November fifteen, he doesn't get to know. Nobody does. Now, come on, let's get back before the house starts waking up."

As we start to walk back along the Charles Bridge, I say, "So what is going to happen?"

John laughs. "I trust you Poutnik, but I don't trust you that much."

The Leopold Bloom is busy with those who have come to Prague for the N15 protest. Noel isn't too happy. "I hope these fucking crusties aren't going to sit around all day nursing one bottle of beer between them," he growls.

Padraig seems quiet behind the bar. As I bring a tray-load of glasses back for washing, I try to engage him in small talk, but he just grunts in return. I remember what the others said about his quiet moments, evidently brooding on events in his past. Perhaps the imminent protest is bringing back bad memories.

As we both lean against the wall outside the pub, snatching a ten-minute break, I decide to break the silence. "Padraig, what happened to you back home?"

He shoots me a glance. "Who said something happened?"

I shrug. "Sometimes you're not your usual self. I just sort of put two and two together...."

"Well, your maths is shit," he snaps, looking away. We stand in silence for a minute or so, then he looks back at me. "Sorry, Pooty. You didn't deserve that. Look, something did happen in the North. Before the troops pulled out. Heavy shit went down in Derry. Two Brit soldiers died. It's why I came to Prague in the first place. I don't like to talk about it too much, okay?"

"Of course," I say quietly. But for a man haunted by demons of death, I am surprised that Padraig is so readily prepared to visit destruction on yet more innocents. But am I presuming too much? What exactly is the "version of events" that John has fed to Padraig?

"Are you looking forward to N15?" I say, trying to change the subject.

Padraig nods. "Bit nervous, to tell the truth. We've been working up to this for almost a year. I can't believe it's just days away. I hope to Christ everything goes okay."

"Why shouldn't it? It sounds simple enough."

Padraig casts me a sidelong look. "John's schemes always do in principle. That's if everything does go to plan, that is."

I'm about to ask him to elaborate when Noel pops his head around the door. "Can youse two get back in here? If these fucking wasters don't start buying beer soon, I want them kicked out, okay?"

Padraig pats me on the arm, smiling his broad smile. "Ah, don't worry, Pooty. I'm sure everything'll be fine."

After my shift, I'm sitting in the living room of the house alone, eyes closed, trying to recapture the feeling of calm I had during the meditation session with Jenny, hoping for more glimpses of my past which might make some kind of sense. But I'm too pre-occupied with the present. John is an enigma. He has almost convinced me that he has taken me into his confidence, that he trusts me and that I, in return, should trust him too. But I cannot push out of my mind the image of Jakob's face under the soil, eyes blind with terror.

"Pooty?"

I stir to see Jenny standing in the doorway from the stairs, her coat on.

"I was just dozing."

"It can't be too comfortable on that couch at night," sympathises Jenny, placing a pile of files and books on to the table. At that moment, Karla lets herself into the house. "Hi guys," she sighs. "Jesus, I'm beat."

"You're not the only one," says Jenny. "Just caught Pooty having a snooze. Hey, Pooty, why don't you go and crash in my bed for a bit? I've got to go to the hospital to sort some stuff out before N15, and I'm going to be gone at least three hours."

"Good idea," says Karla. "You're going to need your strength in the next couple of days."

I put up no argument. Jenny's room is cool and peaceful, and I can continue my meditations there. I settle on to her comfortable bed, arms folded over my chest, and try to empty my mind.

But the dead refuse to leave me in peace.

And neither do the living. I have been in Jenny's room for barely a few minutes when there's a soft tap at the door. It creaks open and Karla's face appears. "Pooty?"

"Come in," I say, sitting up on the bed. "I wasn't really sleeping. Just resting."

Karla closes the door and perches on the bed. "The house is empty," she says, a smile playing on her lips. "Fancy a shag?"

"Karla," I sigh. "Cody...."

"Cody's history after N15," she says firmly.

"I thought you said he loved you."

She shrugs. "He might. But I don't love him. After N15 I won't be here, anyway."

"You're leaving Prague?"

She nods. "What about you?"

I confess I don't know. I hadn't thought beyond the protest. Instead I say, "What did you mean the other night, when you said you wanted me on your side...?"

"What I said. I don't trust John. Especially after what you overheard."

I bite my lip, then decide to tell her. "There's more. You remember the intruder, Jakob? John and Cody didn't let him go. I found him buried in the garden. They killed him, or at least John did. I'm not sure if Cody was involved."

Karla pales. "He probably was. He's John's little lap-dog. Killed him? Jesus."

She shuffles up the bed, snuggling under my arms. "I'm a bit scared, Pooty," she says in a small voice. I wrap my arms around her, smelling her hair. She looks up at me, eyes wide, and plants a small kiss on my lips, followed by a longer one, until we're locked together, pulling at each other's clothes.

Later we lie together in Jenny's bed, breathing heavily, sweat cooling on our naked bodies. Karla sighs. "Jesus. You're a fucking good lay, Pooty."

I take her face in my hands and look into her eyes. "Karla, I need to know something."

She nods for me to go on.

"Are you an agent for the oil companies?"

Her face blanks for a moment, as if she's processing the question. Then she breaks out into a big grin. "An agent? For them? You're kidding, right?"

And somehow, somehow, I know she's telling the truth. As I look into her eyes and see something bright and shining reflected back at me, I know deep inside my soul that she's not lying. Which means only one thing. John is.

Karla pulls away from me. "An agent?" she says again. "Let me guess; John, right?"

I nod miserably. "Please don't say anything. I might not know exactly what he's up to, but I know I've got to stop him. It is like the intruder, Jakob, said; I have to save the innocents. John's planning something big. People are going to die. Perhaps you. Perhaps you're the innocent I must save."

Karla's hands explore my body underneath the duvet. "Oh, I'm not that innocent, Pooty."

I kiss her again and we move together. As I abandon myself to her, I know now my course is set.

John must be defeated.

Karla must be saved.

I have chosen sides.

Sixteen
The Hard Men

From the tower, I watch Prague burn. It seems a lifetime ago that Chamberlain Lang forced me against the precipice, warning that he would let me bring no harm to his precious city. And now, unwittingly, I have created the single biggest threat the city has ever faced.

No, not unwittingly. I could have commanded the Golem to throw itself in the Vltava, or walk to the ends of the Earth. Instead, I ordered it to protect the Ghetto, to seek out those who had wronged the Jews. Now it is rampaging through the city, chaotic and un-checked. Who knows how many have died at the Golem's hands so far? And are all of them guilty? Do all of them deserve the punishment? Or has the Golem taken the lives of the innocent and unblemished? Have children died at its mighty clay fists? Have I, in fact, made the false prophecy of the blood libel truth?

It is almost dusk, and the Golem has been abroad since midnight. At least it has deflected the citizenry's attention away from the Ghetto. The Jews are forgotten... for now. Those who have beheld the Golem's fearful visage have fled; I can see them streaming out of the city gates even now. The soldiers are powerless against it; pikes and swords merely bounce off its invincible hide. At Finn's instigation, the army has tried to create firewalls in the streets around the Ghetto, hoping to reduce the monster to the clay from which it was formed. But the Golem marches on relentlessly, impervious to the flames, while the hovels burn. Horror has been brought to the city.

And yet... is it any more terrible a thing than the hatred which was unleashed upon the Jews? Is life on this Earth not merely a succession of terrors and hatreds, each either slightly more horrible or slightly more bearable than the last?

I become aware that a figure is lurking behind me in the tower. Not another messenger summoning me to Rudolf's side, surely? I have been sitting in the great hall all day while the Emperor and his court have wrung their hands and sought solutions to the rampage of the Golem. I have told them a truncated version of events from the previous night, telling them I went to the Ghetto to seek an end to the war against the Jews, and accidentally spied on Loew creating the Golem. I have not told them of Hannah's or my part in the proceedings, but hoped that as much information as I could give would help the castle find some way to halt the Golem's progress. I turn wearily, but it is no messenger. It is Brahe, the alchemist.

"I thought it was you," he says his golden nose glinting in the setting sun. "Come here to escape, eh?"

I nod. "And to watch."

Brahe joins me at the balcony, squinting into the gloom. The firewalls are drawing closer to the banks of the Vltava. "It seems the Golem is heading this way," he observes. "Towards the castle. The latest news is that the troops have lost the thing. They had the Charles Bridge heavily guarded with cannons and pikemen, but it headed north. There are any number of fords or smaller bridges it could cross there."

"Perhaps you should flee?" I suggest.

Brahe shakes his head. "The Emperor has all his scientists and alchemists feverishly seeking ways to destroy the Golem. I fear the answer lies only with the man who fashioned it."

"Rabbi Loew," I say. "He created the creature to protect the Jews. In doing so he may destroy the city."

"I have been researching the Golem in the library all day," agrees Brahe. "It is an unstoppable force, a fury, a spirit of vengeance. If its mission is to murder every soul who has thought ill of the Jews, then I fear there will be little left of Prague by the time it has done. The Golem is an avenging machine of truth, say the books."

"Death, more like," I say quietly.

"Funny you should say that," says Brahe absently. "I looked up that word, emet, that you told Rudolf the Rabbi had carved on to the forehead of the beast. It does indeed mean truth. But I also noted in the books that there is a similar word in Hebrew, met, that means death. Perhaps truth and death are closer than we realised, eh, Master Poutnik?"

"Interesting, Master Brahe."

"I agree. But other than discovering interesting snippets of trivia, I am no closer to finding a solution."

"What do your Laws of Planetary Motion have to say on the matter?" I ask.

Brahe laughs mirthlessly. "Of little use in this situation, I am afraid. Other than to illustrate that bodies truly revolve around a centre."

I give him a quizzical look.

"Rudolf," says Brahe. "He is the centre of our universe, the figure around which we all rotate. He attracts wanderers from all over the world, as the Sun attracts the planets. On occasion a rogue might pass by the Earth, threatening life, attracted by gravitational power. The Golem is such a rogue."

"And myself, Master Brahe? Where do I fit into your equations?"

Brahe shrugs. "You have the look of a shooting star, Master Poutnik. You are drawn to the centre, yet you shall be on your way. Your journey does not end here, I think."

St Vitus's cathedral sounds four bells. At five I am due for another interminable conference with Rudolf. He has been taking advice all day but is no closer to stopping the Golem's carnage. Then I am to follow Percy Tremayne to his secret assignation with Carlo Fantom. I heard him speaking to Sir Anthony earlier, making up some lie about feeling unwell and planning to retire at seven or so. That is when he shall be stealing away for his meeting. And I shall be behind him.

I take my leave of Brahe and head to my quarters for a few moments' rest before the next meeting in the great hall. Waiting for me there is Hannah, wrapped in a long cloak.

"Hello," she smiles. "Surprised to see me?"

"Hannah, you should not be roaming the streets," I chide. "It isn't safe with that infernal creature on the loose."

She sits back on my small bed, pouring herself a cup of wine from a jug she has evidently brought with her. "I did try to tell you, Poutnik. You should not have commanded the Golem."

I punch the bed, startling Hannah. "Of course! I can command the Golem! All I need to do is find it and order it to call off its vendetta!"

Hannah shakes her head sadly. "If only it were so simple. Once a Golem is set a task, it will not be turned aside, not by its creator nor one who has mastery over it like yourself nor God in Heaven, until it has completed its task, or is killed. If only you had listened to me."

"Indeed," I sigh, deflated. "Well, now that you're here, you should stay. Promise me you won't go back to the Ghetto until the Golem has been stopped."

"The Ghetto is the safest place in the city, thanks to the Golem," she says, stretching back on the bed. "But I shall stay. If you can persuade me to."

I join her on the bed and she passes me the cup of wine, pouring another for herself. "Persuade you?"

Hannah leans in close to me, her sweet breath on my face. "I'm sure you know how," she whispers, kissing me lightly on my nose. "You have courted me these past few days, and I am not unwilling to lie with you, Master Poutnik. I might even forgive you for letting loose the Golem."

"Hannah, I must be away to the great hall soon...."

"Shush," she says, parting the folds of the heavy cloak to reveal her pale nakedness beneath. "Come to me." And I do.

I have dozed fitfully in Hannah's arms, and the sound of the cathedral bells awakens me. "Six!" I say aghast. "I have missed my appointment!"

"Hush," says Hannah softly, drawing me back into the bed. "They will make their decisions well enough without you. Come."

Half an hour later and Hannah is dressing.

"What will you do?" I say. "You are welcome to stay here for the night."

"Thank you," she says. "I thought I would seek out my father; I have not spoken with him for some time."

Guilt stabs at my heart. I fear Jakob is irretrievably gone. "If you do not find him, shall I see you here later?" I ask.

Hannah smiles. "Perhaps. Now, you have an errand to run, do you not?"

I have. Dressing in the darkest clothes I have accumulated in my wardrobe while at the castle, I bid farewell to Hannah and slip out to where Sir Anthony and his men are quartered. No sooner do I reach their corridor than I see Percy emerge from the rooms, glancing along the corridor before stealthily taking the stairwell to the ground floor. Hanging in the shadows, I follow him as best I can. The curfew is still in force for the general public, how will Percy manage to leave the castle?

I trot behind him as he heads to the main gate, ducking into the darkness as he approaches the heavily guarded courtyard. Two soldiers halt Percy and he announces himself to them. "Castle business," I hear him say. "I am on a mission from Sir Anthony regarding this dreadful Golem affair."

The guards shrug and let him through. I must hurry if I am not to lose Percy in the warren of streets outside.

"Castle business," I say as I rush up to the gate.

"Another mission for Sir Anthony?" says the guard, looking at me closely.

"No, I am on the Emperor's business. Secret business, I might add."

The guard lets me through. If half the castle is mad enough to want to be on the streets of Prague while the Golem is loose, then that isn't any of his business. He seems happy enough to be within the castle walls rather than on Golem duty in the Old Town.

I cast up and down the street in search of Percy, and see him labouring up the hill, away from the castle and the centre of the city. Fantom and his men must be to the north of Prague. Gathering my cloak about me, I set off at a light run to catch him up.

Beyond the castle the city thins out quickly, becoming little more than a series of small hamlets connected by a muddy road. I keep to the long grass beside the path, a hundred yards or so behind the dark figure of Percy hurrying on through the night. After an hour or so I see a black mass on the horizon against the starless cloudy sky, evidently some kind of wooded area. Percy pauses to take a tot from his flask, glancing back behind him, and I sit low in the damp grass. Satisfied he is alone, he sets off again in the direction of the forest.

At the edge of the forest the road turns off to the west, but Percy continues north, on the flat scrub-land. The long grass peters out, and I am forced to hide behind a bush until he reaches the trees. As his figure disappears into the blackness, I set off at a low run, ducking behind the thick trunk of an old oak as I see him ahead, standing alone twenty yards or so into the forest.

"Fantom! Fantom, are you here?" Percy curses and looks around him. "Fantom!"

"I am here," comes a rasping voice, the same one I heard when Hannah and I were confronted in the Royal Gardens. "I thought you were told to come alone."

"I am alone," says Percy, looking around. "Fantom, what are you talking about? And where the devil are you?"

"Here," says the voice, directly behind me. I have no time to even turn before something thick and heavy slams against my head.

I awake with a dull throbbing at the back of my head. My hands and feet are bound by rough ropes and I have been tossed into the centre of a large clearing some way, it seems, within the forest. A huge fire burns in the centre of the clearing, and around it I can make out several figures. Dozens of figures, I realise, as I come fully to. A small army, in fact.

Standing before me are Percy and Carlo Fantom, his grey hair scraped back into a pony-tail, his scarred face with its leather eye-patch peering down at me. "Seems we have caught a little spy," grins the mercenary humourlessly.

"I knew this one was going to be trouble," sighs Percy. "I suppose we shall have to kill him, now."

Fantom squats down beside me, peering into my eyes. "I told you it wasn't over, didn't I, boy? You'll wish you'd let me have your little bitch by the time I'm done with you."

"Fantom, we don't have time to torture him," says Percy. "Kill him and have done with it. We need to move tonight."

Fantom licks his lips and blows me a kiss, and stands to face Percy. "Tremayne," he says in a low voice. "This is my company and you are on my territory. Do not think to order me around here."

"I merely suggest it is perhaps time to strike. Tonight. The boy is here, who knows who else he has told? Perhaps others are aware of his mission. He has become quite thick with that freak at the castle, Finn the giant."

"Conditions would seem to be right," concurs Fantom, "with the army tied up battling this clay man. Kelley's diversion has worked better than anyone could have expected."

"Certainly better than he expected, I should think," sniffs Percy. "He caused well enough chaos with his ridiculously easy ploy to get the citizenry up in arms against the Jews; I don't think anyone could have anticipated this Golem business."

"My men are ready," says Fantom. I follow his gaze to where his company prepares. To my surprise they are smearing mud on their faces and changing into uniforms much stranger than any I have seen since I arrived in Prague; billowing pantaloons and tall helmets. Soldiers bring a rack of curved swords from a tent at the rear of the clearing and the soldiers begin to arm themselves.

"I must say, you've done a sterling job getting your men done up as Turks," says Percy.

"Turks?" I say, and they both look down at me.

"What's this?" leers Fantom. "Hoping to glean details of our plan so you can hop back to Rudolf and tell all? Too late, boy. For you anyway. You're not leaving here, except in the bellies of foxes and bears."

"But why Turks?" I say, playing for time as Fantom draws a cruel-looking blade from its sheath at his side.

"The plan was mine," boasts Percy. "I see no harm in telling you before Fantom slits your throat. While the city is in disarray, Fantom's men, disguised as Turks, are to attack the castle."

"But why? What do you gain by that?"

"What do I gain?" laughs Percy. "Sir Anthony will feel duty-bound to rally to the cause. He's such a hero, you see. And the men here have orders to run him through."

"But he's your captain," I protest.

"And when he's gone I'll lead the company," spits Percy. "And I won't be in thrall to that stupid pirate any longer."

"If there's any company left to lead by the time the Hard-Men have finished," I point out.

"We don't expect to take the castle, you stupid boy," says Percy as Fantom grins and runs a calloused thumb along the keen edge of his blade. "We just need to cause as much fuss as possible, getting rid of Sir Anthony in the process. The fact that a company of 'Turks' has managed to attack Prague's precious castle will be excuse enough for Kelley's Habsburg paymasters to oust that useless oaf Rudolf."

So Kelley is in the employ of the Habsburgs. But what of Dee? "All very neat," I agree. "But what do you get out of it, Captain Fantom? Whose cause are you fighting?"

Fantom throws back his head and laughs heartily. "I care not for your cause. I come to fight for your half-crown and your handsome women. My father was a Catholic and so was my grandfather. I have fought for the Christians against the Turks and for the Turks against the Christians. Now, enough talk. It's time you went to sleep, pretty little boy."

I try to shuffle backwards but Fantom catches me by the face, his iron grip squeezing my cheeks and exposing my throat. He licks the knife and touches its cold steel to my throat.

"Perhaps I'll fuck you when you're dead," he whispers gently, and presses the knife into my flesh.

I look deep inside myself for some shard of the power that frightened the guards on Charles Bridge and opened the locked door to Dee's rooms, but I am too panicked to focus. I feel the blade break the flesh, and fear that I am truly done for.

But it cannot be. I have been brought here to intervene in a terrible conflict. I cannot be killed before it has properly begun. I must save the innocents. I must save Hannah...

Something must be done.

And something is. I do not know whether I have reached inside myself and summoned the creature to me, or whether some unknown link between us has caused it to follow me out of the city, but at that moment a cry goes up from the men as a huge lumbering figure bursts into the clearing. The Golem.

"By my soul," whispers Percy. "I didn't quite believe it was true."

"It's true. It's here," says Fantom, abandoning me. By some quirk of fate or by dint of the power deep within me, the knots on the ropes binding me have loosened.

"Don't just stand there!" roars Fantom to his dumbfounded company as the Golem advances on us. "Attack it!"

Ignored for the moment, I shake myself free of the ropes. The pikes and curved swords of Fantom's men seem to be having no effect on the Golem as they quickly organise and launch themselves at its massive bulk, but their sheer numbers are forcing it back into the trees. With all eyes on the gigantic clay creature, I steal away into the darkness of the trees, then begin to run for my life through the black forest towards where I hope lie the dim lights of Prague.

Interlude Four

"We warned you in the strongest possible terms, Uriel," says Metatron gravely. "Yet still you persisted. Why?"

Uriel has no answers. He stands dumbly in the Shivering Gallery at the bright centre of The House, ringed by Metatron and the grim faces of the Committee.

"Such a transgression cannot be ignored, Uriel," continues Metatron. "You have betrayed one of our basic tenets. No communication."

He nods at the clerk, who opens a bottomless book of glass. "Here are your crimes, Uriel," says Metatron. "Collated, catalogued, filed. Not one, not a dozen. Hundreds!"

Uriel says nothing. He has become careless, he knows. He should have heeded Metatron's warning. But his communications with the bloodbags below have become something of an addiction, some blessed relief from the monotony of perfection.

"I have something to say," he decides.

There is a flutter of dreamflies around the heads of the Committee, a rustle of leaves as dry as cemetery earth. Metatron pauses, turning his visage to the centre of the circle.

"An explanation?" says Metatron. "An apology? A plea for clemency? The House shall hear you, Uriel."

"I shall not beg for mercy," says Uriel. "I shall say only this: why are we here?"

Amusement whispers around the circle. "That is a question for the baser forms, surely, Uriel. You, of all of us, should know that. Have they not asked that of you many times during your forbidden communications?"

"Again; why are we here?" says Uriel, his anger a prism. "We create, we tinker, we observe. Have we not a responsibility to the flesh? They did not ask to be created, Metatron, created and abandoned. Are there not innocents suffering? Is there not suffering we could alleviate?"

The whispers die down. "We have given them paradise and they have turned it into a cess-pit," flashes Metatron. "They are beneath us, Uriel. They are only human. Would you make them more? They would tear down the walls of the city if they could."

"So would I," whispers Uriel.

"Then we have no choice," says Metatron quietly. "Our punishment shall be swift and terrible. You believe there are innocents, Uriel? Then go to them. Save

them, if you can."

There is horror, then, on Uriel's shining face, as he realises what is about to occur.

"No, Metatron," he pleads. "Not this. Anything but this."

The Committee dims.

Metatron speaks a single word.

The Shivering Gallery shudders.

And Uriel falls.

Seventeen
N15

I do not sleep the night before November fifteenth, and for once I am not alone. Throughout the night I hear the sounds of movement from the rooms upstairs. Restless and anxious insomnia grips the house. We are to depart for the protest at two in the afternoon, and nerves are likely to be stretched taut throughout the day. I wonder when John will make his move? And when should I? Far away a bell strikes three times.

I hear heavy footfalls stumbling down the stairs. Cody emerges into the living room, breathing heavily, a three-quarters empty bottle of whisky swinging in his hand. "Pooty," he slurs. "You awake?"

I shuffle on the couch. "Yes."

He slumps beside me. "Karla's asleep. Been looking at her for an hour." He offers me the bottle. I shake my head and he takes a swig, grimacing. "Going to miss her," he mumbles.

I wait for a moment in the darkness, choosing my words carefully. "It's not too late," I say slowly. "The plan can be changed."

Cody shakes his head. "It is too late. John can't be stopped now. I'm scared, Pooty."

"What are you scared of, Cody?"

"People getting hurt," he says. "Didn't think people would get hurt."

"You're scared of Karla getting hurt, aren't you? She doesn't have to, you know."

Cody shakes his head and barks a little humourless laugh. "Karla'll be okay. She'll hate me, but she'll be okay."

"So who's going to get hurt, Cody?" I say carefully.

He empties the bottle and tosses it to one side. "I just wanted to show them, Pooty. That's all. Show everybody. You know how rich my folks are? They've got a ranch. I used to ride horses when I was a kid. Holidays in Europe. Private schooling. Trust fund. Everything I wanted all my life."

"So why this? Why the protest?"

"Everything I wanted all my life," says Cody again. "So long as they could send someone out with a credit card to buy it for me. Sometimes I just wanted someone to tell me a story and tuck me up. But they were too busy making money. As if we didn't have enough. Jesus, I was so lonely, Pooty. I am so lonely."

"But you've got Karla, and John, and the rest," I say.

Cody nods. "Family. Best family I ever had. That's why it's killing me what's going to happen. Killing me that John won't tell them."

"About the bomb?"

If Cody is surprised that I know, he doesn't show it. "The bomb," he agrees. He stares at the carpet for a long time, then looks at me.

"Get out of here," he hisses. "Go, now. Get out of Prague, out of the country. Go back to wherever the hell you came from."

"Why are you telling me this?" I say.

"It's out of control," he slurs. "Everything's gone crazy. Just go."

Cody stands uncertainly, steadying himself on the back of the couch. "Pooty, go," he says one last time, then stumbles back towards the stairs, leaving me alone in the darkness.

By eight everyone is sitting around the living room, sipping coffee and smoking cigarettes. Cody gives me a pitying look as he sees me still in the house, then glances away, his face a hard mask. He has given me my chance. He can do no more if I refuse to leave. Jenny busies herself in the kitchen, making pot after pot of coffee. Karla sets off for work to collect the press passes to get us into the Excelsior Hotel, Petey checks the ropes that will hold the banner. Padraig's mood is one of forced joviality, cracking jokes which no-one laughs at.

And John just watches, scrutinising each of us in turn, sitting quietly in the chair accepting coffee and cigarettes as the house bustles around him. There are just six hours to go.

After Karla leaves, Jenny goes to shower and Padraig says he is off to check the banner which is folded up in his room. Petey continues to add spots of oil to karibiners and to tug harnesses, eventually disappearing into his room to coil the ropes up.

Which leaves me and John, coolly regarding each other.

"Not long now," says John.

"No."

"I'm rather surprised that you're still here."

"You thought I would leave? Why?"

John pulls a face. "This isn't your battle, Poutnik. You can walk away. We can't."

I think about this. "I can't walk away, John. This is my battle. I'm here for a reason, I think."

John laughs. "Saving the innocents, is it? Perhaps that mad old guy we caught does know you, after all." He pauses. "Funny thing is, Poutnik, perhaps I do as well. There's something familiar about you. Have we met before?"

It is my turn to laugh. "I have no memory, John. You would know better than me."

He nods. "Maybe we have met. Just not in this life, eh?"

I shrug. John stands. "Well, things to do. Why don't you take a walk, think about things for a bit? If you're still here at two o'clock, you're in. For good. You know that, don't you?"

"Yes," I say. "I'll go for a walk. But I'll be here."

"Your choice," says John.

I put on my jacket and walk to the door. "No," I say, turning. "No, I don't think it is."

I wander through Mala Strana, across the Charles Bridge, and weave through the alleys of the Old Town towards Wenceslas Square. The streets are busy with protesters, different groups gathered under tribal banners calling for the world's rich to feed the poor, to plant forests, to not build dams, to produce food, to scrap weapons, to harness the wind, to not drill for oil. The police have tried to cordon off Wenceslas Square but the sheer force of numbers has rendered their efforts useless. As I get closer to the square it becomes almost impossible to move, and I become trapped in a bottle-neck of people shouting slogans and waving placards.

"Hey, look at that!" a voice goes up. I follow the pointing fingers to an advertising hoarding on the side of a hotel building. It has been painted over white and one word screams out in huge red letters from its centre: DEVA.

"I knew he'd be here!" someone says. "Deva!"

The shout is taken up by others, and becomes a chant. "Deva! Deva! Deva! Deva!"

Ahead of us, I can see the black hats of a small line of police officers, struggling to push the crowd back off the pavement. "Bastards!" a woman screams. "Why are you protecting them?"

Something whizzes over my head and lands with a crash ahead of me, where the police are. A shout goes up and the crowd becomes a single organism, pushing forward, heaving bottles and stones through the air. A whistle sounds and I hear the people at the front of the crowd scream.

"Fascist bastards!" a man close to me shouts. "Have you learned nothing in this city?"

The people in front of me part and a handful of protesters are ushered back through the crowd, blood streaming down their faces. Those around me pat them on the back as they are hurried away from the front line.

"Got me right on the nose with his truncheon," says a young man with long hair, smiling through the blood on his face. "Kicked the fucker right in the balls, though."

Sirens sound on the morning air, and I feel the crowd crush into me even more tightly. More black hats appear ahead, and a cry goes up as the police start hauling people out. I should not be here. I cannot afford to be detained. I turn and push through the mob, following the injured who are making their way to the back of the square. I push harder as screams sound and water spatters on to my head. The mass moves along with me, trying to get back from the powerful water cannons that have arrived in the square. A woman in front of me stumbles and falls, and is in danger of being crushed as the line of protesters becomes a fluid thing with no stability or structure. I haul her up by her arms and push her forward, panic rising within me as I am carried along. Then the crowd thins out and I can see the bars and shops, and suddenly I am standing with space around me. I strike out for the Old Town Square, away from the impending riot, hurrying through the streets and not pausing for breath until I am standing on the Charles Bridge, listening to the distant chanting and the wail of sirens. N15 has begun.

Back at the house, I see Petey in the garden, enjoying a solitary joint. "Poutnik," he nods, looking up with red-rimmed eyes. It seems he hasn't had much sleep either.

I sit beside him on the bench, forcing myself to not look at the stretch of turned earth underneath the honeysuckle. Whatever John's plans, whatever his motives, he has taken a human life. How can I not oppose him?

"I was just meditating, saying a little prayer," says Petey.

"For success?"

Petey shakes his head. "For forgiveness."

"Forgiveness?"

"I killed someone," says Petey in a very small voice. Involuntarily, my gaze snaps back to Jakob's shallow grave.

"A kid," goes on Petey. "Seventeen. Back home."

"You don't have to tell me, Petey," I say.

He looks at me with his bloodshot eyes. "I do, Pooty. I do. I have to tell someone."

He sucks tightly on the joint. "Back home. I was dealing in a bit of horse. Heroin. I had some bad shit, cut with all kinds of crap. But I sold it anyway. Needed the money."

Petey pauses, lost in his memories. "It was... awful. He was throwing up and bleeding from his nose and his ass and crying. I left him there in his bedroom. Didn't even call an ambulance. Took what money I had and got on the first flight anywhere. That's how I ended up here. And now I'm scared."

He looks at me, grabbing my coat with a weak hand. "What if I'm arrested at the protest, Pooty? They'll know what happened. They'll send me back. I don't think I can do time, man. It would kill me."

Petey starts to cry, burying his face in his hands. Not knowing what else to do, I pat him on the shoulder and walk quietly into the house, leaving him with his demons. Is anyone in this house not plagued by them?

By one we're all back in the house, save Jenny. Karla has the press passes which will get us both into the Excelsior. Petey is making last minute checks to the ropes. Padraig has gathered the banner in the living room. We are waiting for John to come downstairs, and when he does, Cody gives him a quizzical look.

"Nice suit," says Padraig.

John is wearing a sharply-cut three-piece pinstripe, his hair slicked back and his beard trimmed.

"Hello?" says Karla. "Earth to John. This is a protest, not a dinner party."

"Savile Row," says John, showing off the suit. "No need to let standards drop. I'm more likely to get on the TV and in the quality broadsheets dressed like this, don't you think?"

The house has an air of unreality about it, as though we are all players in a performance. Except I do not know my lines, I have not read the script. I look to John expectantly for stage directions.

"Where's Jenny?" asks Karla. "It's nearly time."

"In the Excelsior, with any luck," says John. "Petey's concierge friend should have her inside by now. She's going to ring my mobile to let me know she's in the store-room. Are you all set, Karla?"

She nods, producing a heavy tan bag. "I borrowed this from the office. Spare photographer's bag. We can get the banner and some ropes in here and cover them with lenses and stuff. Should get us in okay."

John nods. "Right, everyone go and get ready. We'll meet down here in half an hour."

I am the first down, dressed in my simplest clothing. John is waiting, smoking quietly. "So you decided you were in, then?" he says softly.

"I'm in," I say. "I have to see how this ends."

John glances at his watch. "Not long to wait now, eh? Not long to wait. Here come the others."

Karla comes down first, wearing a large bulky raincoat belted at the waist. "You look every inch a reporter," says John appreciatively. "This could be the story of your career, eh, Karla?"

She says nothing, busying herself with arranging the photography bag for me. Petey and Padraig comes down next, between them carrying the box of fireworks for the diversion. Cody is last, dressed casually.

"Right," says Padraig nervously. "Here we all are."

"Here we all are," agrees John.

There's silence for a moment as everyone glances at each other.

"Well?" says Cody, packing a small bag. "Should we not get moving?"

John looks at his watch again. "No, I don't think so," he says.

Petey looks up. Padraig meets Karla's eyes, a quizzical eyebrow raised. Cody stops what he is doing. "What did you say?"

John casually reaches inside his jacket and takes something out of the inner pocket. It takes me a second to find the right word for what he has in his hand.

It's a gun.

"I said, we're not going anywhere," says John, holding up the gun. "Are we, Deva?"

Eighteen
The Battle of Prague

The sounds of fighting recede behind me as I flee the forest, running blindly through the trees, falling into the damp shrubbery and scratching myself on thorns and branches. Through incredible good fortune, I emerge from the woods near the track that leads towards the city. Prague is not visible, but the thin glow of the fires burns the underside of the heavy clouds. Ignoring the cuts and scratches on my hands and face and the burning stitch in my side, I set off at a run for the castle.

The bells are tolling midnight by the time I stagger mud-splattered and breathless to the huge castle gates. There is a new watch on guard, and they regard me with as little sympathy as the statues above the gateposts. "Don't you know there's a curfew in place?" says the captain of the guard. "On your way before we arrest you and throw you in prison."

"Let me in," I manage to gasp. "It is I, Poutnik, the Mirror of Prague. The city is in grave danger."

The guard squints at me in the yellow light cast by the torches mounted on the gates. "I don't think so, boy. Off with you, now."

I lean forward with my hands on my knees in defeat, my breath coming in ragged gasps. I cannot be thwarted now. "Please," I beg.

"I've warned you," says the guard, beginning to unlock the gate. "We'd better take you to the gaol."

"Ah, I don't think that will be necessary," rumbles a deep voice. I look up gratefully at the source of the mighty shadow that falls across us.

"Captain Finn," says the guard, saluting. "I was just clearing this rabble from the castle gates."

The giant leans down to inspect me. "This sorry figure would indeed appear to be Master Poutnik of the castle," he says. "I think we'd better get him inside and cleaned up."

"No time, Finn," I say. "You must rally your men. An army marches on the castle."

"An army?" says Finn doubtfully, rubbing his huge chin. "But that makes no sense. Who...?"

A shout goes up behind us. The guards stand straight and look at each other. "The city warden," says Finn as a uniformed soldier runs up the road behind us.

"Captain Finn!" shouts the warden. "Sentries at the city limits are reporting a massive troop of Turks marching on the city."

"Turks," says Finn, straightening. "Not now. Not with the army tied up in the Old Town with this clay feller."

"No," I try to say. "No, listen to me, Finn, it isn't the Turks…"

But the warden cuts in. "And that's not all, Captain. At their head is the Golem."

No-one will listen to my protestations as Finn bundles me into the castle and alarms start to sound throughout the city. What madness is this? How have Percy and Fantom managed to recruit the Golem to their cause? I must find Sir Anthony at once.

The castle is in uproar, half of the court rushing to the castle walls to defend Rudolf, the others preparing to flee the city. With a start I realise that I ordered Hannah to stay in my room. Does everything I do put this woman in danger? How can I save the innocents when I am their biggest liability?

I fight my way to my quarters through a horde of panicking nobles who have suddenly decided Rudolf's court is not the easy life they had thought it to be for so many months. My room is empty. Hannah is not there. Perhaps she is at the kitchens, or maybe she has gone to look for Jakob again. I rush back into the corridor, my mind whirling, and run headlong into Cornelius Drebbel.

"Master Poutnik," he says. "Is it true the Turk is attacking Prague?"

"No," I say. "Well, there is an army, but it isn't the Turk."

"No matter. It is time for me and my crew to leave. You would be well advised to join us. We can be on the Elba by daybreak."

"I cannot leave, Master Drebbel, although your offer is most kind. I must find Hannah."

"Hannah? That servant girl? The Chamberlain's whore?"

I round on Drebbel angrily. "What did you call her?"

He backs off, his hands raised to calm me. "It is only what my men say, Master Poutnik. She shares Lang's bed, I hear. It is no business of mine."

Can this be? But Hannah professed love for me... was it all a charade? To what purpose, though?

Then I recall her insistence that I lie with her earlier this evening. Could it have all been a ploy to make me miss my appointment with Rudolf? So that Lang could meet with the Emperor without my interference? He has already made clear his distaste of Rudolf's insistence that I attend every meeting and conference. Could it all have been an elaborate deception to get me out of the way?

Abruptly I hear the clamour of the troops by the castle gate. I have allowed Drebbel to lead me to the courtyard, where his crew awaits anxiously. "Come," says the sub-mariner kindly. "You have nothing for you in Prague now. We can away to the Vltava before the Turks arrive. I will give you passage to where you like; England if that be your wish. It is time I tested my underwater boat on the open seas."

"No," I decide firmly. I cannot leave now, even if I am betrayed by Hannah. The conflict that was foretold by Ripellino has arrived. I must see it out. "Thank you, Master Drebbel, but I must stay. You had best be on your way."

"You are sure I cannot convince you?" says Drebbel, as his men urge him towards the gate. "Then good luck to you, Master Poutnik. Perhaps we shall meet again."

"Perhaps," I say. "God speed you, Master Drebbel."

Then they are gone, entreating the soldiers to let them through the castle gates.

I still cannot believe what Drebbel has told me. Surely it is just malicious court gossip. I head back into the castle, running through the halls and corridors bound for Chamberlain Lang's quarters.

They are, as I had half-suspected, empty. If Lang is going to be anywhere, it is with the Emperor. Exhausted and filthy, I set off again for the great hall.

Two guards bar my path at the closed double doors. "No-one is to enter," says one of them. "War council is in progress."

"Let me through!" I demand. "It is I, the Mirror of Prague."

The guards exchange glances. "The Emperor has been looking for you for hours," says the first again. "You had better go inside."

Before I can act the doors open from within, and Lang slips out. "Ah, the Mirror of Prague," he says, glancing at my ragged appearance. "I do not think your presence is required any more. The Emperor has discovered he can do well enough without you."

I glare at Lang. "All thanks to you, Chamberlain, and your infernal plots. Where is Hannah?"

Lang looks amused. "We have more pressing matters within the hall than the whereabouts of some serving girl. I suggest you run along now, Master Poutnik. Perhaps you can help at the castle gates. The Turk is attacking, don't you know."

"But it isn't the Turk!" I cry. "Why won't anyone listen to me? I have news of great importance…"

"Hush," says Lang, then to the guards he says, "See we are not disturbed again."

The two guards move towards me as Lang closes the doors. "Better do as he says," says one of them kindly. Exasperated beyond measure, I turn on my heel and stalk off towards the courtyard. Only Sir Anthony can help me now.

Barely half an hour has passed since I arrived back at the castle, but Fantom's army is already here. I must have spent more time lost in the forest than I thought. As many of the castle soldiers as can be mustered are manning the gates, and more pikemen have been called from their duty within the city. I push myself closer to the gates, and in the street I can see flames licking the sky where the mercenaries have evidently torched buildings around the castle. I stop dead as I peer through the ranks of soldiers to where Fantom's men stand maybe two hundred yards out of the castle gates. In front of them is indeed the figure of the Golem. Percy or Fantom cannot have achieved mastery over the automaton... it can only be Kelley. A silence has fallen for a moment as the two armies regard each other, then the Golem takes a step forward and the castle guard are galvanised into action. Archers let loose a flight of arrows and Fantom's men let out a roar and begin to advance. The Battle of Prague has begun.

In the flickering torchlight I suddenly catch sight of Sir Anthony, hanging back in the courtyard with his men. Percy is not with them. "Sir Anthony!" I call, pushing through the milling crowds towards them.

"Master Poutnik," he says, a grave look on his face. "This is bad. This is very bad. I would be away from here, but I cannot while the Turk is at the gate. You have not seen Percy, have you?"

"Yes," I say, relieved that someone is finally listening to me. "They are not Turks. They are disguised Hard Men. Percy is in league with Carlo Fantom and Edward Kelley. It is all a plot; everything, from the lies about the Jews to the attack on the castle."

"Percy, you say? What nonsense is this? Why would my trusted lieutenant plot against me?" says Sir Anthony angrily. "And in league with Kelley and Fantom? To what ends?"

"He wishes to take command of your company. He told me himself. Kelley is in the pay of the Habsburgs; that is why Fantom's troops are disguised as Turks, to discredit Rudolf so his family can oust him."

"Nonsense," says Sir Anthony again. "Your mind is addled, Master Poutnik. I…"

A huge cry goes up from the battlements. We turn as a man to see the castle guard fall back as the Golem, festooned with arrows, tears open the huge iron gates with a single movement. Fantom's men howl in triumph and follow the creature into the castle courtyard.

"God above," breathes Sir Anthony. He turns to his men. "We have no choice; we must fight."

Suddenly I am surrounded as the castle guard retreats before the Golem and the Hard Men whose mysterious herbs make them impervious to the arrows of the archers. I lose sight of Sir Anthony and his company as they join the fray. Looking for an escape to a safer vantage point, I suddenly come face to face with Percy Tremayne, decked out in the outlandish garb of a Turk, his face blackened with mud.

"Master Poutnik, we meet again," he says.

"Percy."

He holds out his scimitar, its cruel point touching my chest. "I believe we have unfinished business. Be thankful it is I who shall hasten your end and not Captain Fantom. It should be quicker this way."

"Just tell me one thing," I say weakly, the noise of battle all around me. "How have you commanded the Golem?"

Percy laughs. "We are in your debt for that one, Master Poutnik. The minute you escaped the beast ceased its attack on the camp and began lumbering back towards Prague. Unless I'm very much mistaken, the thing seems to be following you."

I slump, sinking to my knees before Percy. Of course. Did the Golem not turn to me for its commands in the Ghetto? All this time it has been working its way towards me, through the city, then to Fantom's camp, and now back here. I have brought it directly to the castle, aiding the plotters all the time. Perhaps it is better for everyone if Percy finishes me off now.

He seems more than happy to comply. "Enough chatter," says Percy raising his scimitar. "It is time I got you out of my hair, boy."

I feel myself plucked into the air. Is this death? I wonder idly to myself as I am hauled away from Percy's raised weapon. Then I see the grinning face of Finn. Once again, he has come to my rescue.

"Finn," I gasp, dangling from his huge fist. "You have saved my life three times, now."

"Ah, who's counting?" he smiles. Then his face registers brief surprise and his grip slackens, dropping me the four or so feet to the cobbles of the courtyard. Finn falls to his knees, the light fading in his twinkling eyes. Then he collapses, dead, as Percy stands behind him, his scimitar dripping with the giant's dark blood, an evil smile playing on his face.

"One freak down, one to go," says Percy, raising his sword again. "And nothing shall save you this time, boy."

My senses unravel at the impending slaughter at the hands of the traitor, and beneath the noise of fighting I focus on a half-familiar hiss, a whiff of burning coals. Percy seems to tune in to what I hear and his eyes widen for a moment, just as a dull crack sounds. His words die on his tongue and his chest convulses. He manages to turn his head and lay his eyes upon his attacker, the last thing he sees before crumpling to the ground. Sir Anthony, his face grim, the smoking arquebus in his hand, watches him fall.

"You were always a fool, Percy," he says quietly. "But I never thought you were a traitor. And look; I got the hang of the damned thing eventually."

Sir Anthony casts the weapon to the cobbles and looks at me. "It seems you spoke the truth, Master Poutnik. There is indeed a conspiracy at work. Come with me."

The battle has moved around us, the castle guard being re-enforced by troops from the city and managing to push the Hard Men back towards the gates. The Golem is nowhere to be seen. Sir Anthony commands his men to defend their horses in the stables and grabs me by the arm, making to haul me inside the castle. I pause only to boot Percy in his lifeless face, hearing the satisfying crack of his nose. "That's for Finn," I say, before heading off to catch Sir Anthony.

"Where are we going?"

"We must see the Emperor."

"I have already tried," I protest. "Lang barred my way. Besides, what can Rudolf do?"

"He's weak and feeble-minded, but he is still Emperor," says Sir Anthony, leading me towards the great hall. "And Chamberlain Lang would be wise not to get in my way."

The two guards standing outside the great hall let us pass as Sir Anthony rushes up. Within, Rudolf is alone in the darkness, slumped on his throne. "Philipp? Philipp, is that you?"

Sir Anthony clears his throat. "No, Emperor, it is Sir Anthony Sherley and Master Poutnik, the Mirror of Prague. We have distressing news."

"I know, I know," says Rudolf sadly. "The Turk is at the gate, as ever. Have you seen the Chamberlain? I fear he has deserted me."

Sir Anthony whispers to me, "Is Lang part of this conspiracy?"

"I do not know for sure."

"Emperor," calls Sir Anthony. "The situation is darker than it seems. It is not the Turks, but a plot against the throne. My own lieutenant Percy was involved, but he is no more. Doctor Dee's assistant Edward Kelley certainly is. You should take yourself to a safer place, your Excellency."

"A plot?" says Rudolf absently. "But the people love me, do they not? A plot? No, Sir Anthony. I have created a paradise on Earth here in Prague. Those sounds you hear are my people united in joy and worship. Should I call a banquet for my people, do you think? Should I declare a national holiday? I am loved and adored as a god, Sir Anthony. There is no plot, no attack, no Golem, no war. Come, Mirror of Prague, sit by me."

"Ah, this is hopeless," spits Sir Anthony. "The old fool is too far gone. Come on, Poutnik."

Leaving Rudolf proclaiming imagined glories to himself, I follow Sir Anthony out of the great hall. "But where are we going now?"

"I did not see Kelley among the fighting," he says. "Perhaps he is still in the castle, ignorant of the fact that the plot has been uncovered. Do you know where his quarters are?"

I lead the way through the dark corridors of the castle as servants and staff clamour around helplessly. On a whim I take a slight detour towards where Lang's rooms lie. As we approach I hold out my hand for Sir Anthony to stop and be silent, then kick open the door to the Chamberlain's apartments.

Lang and Hannah look up from a huge chest they are packing with treasures evidently looted from Rudolf's collections. Sir Anthony joins me at the door. "So, the rats prepare to flee the sinking ship, do they?"

"The Turks are attacking," says Lang, casting his eyes down to the floor. Hannah refuses to meet my gaze. "I must save the Emperor's collection."

I look at Hannah. "So it was all lies, then. You were merely a distraction, to keep me away from Rudolf. And all the while you were bedding Lang."

Hannah looks up at me, her eyes hard. "Think to judge me when you have spent a life-time in the Ghetto," she spits. "Am I to be cast as the villain for wanting a better life? Are you to tell me that a servant girl has no business loving a Chamberlain?"

"I thought you loved me," I say wretchedly. I think of Hannah in my bed, on our mission to the Ghetto, in the Royal Gardens... the Royal Gardens. Where she pushed me back against the wall as the stone was pushed from the battlements, the battlements where I saw a flash of expensive black cloth, of the type worn only by Chamberlain Lang. "You would go so far?" I ask quietly. "As to be complicit in my attempted murder?"

"Enough of this prattle," says Lang, eyeing Sir Anthony's sword in its sheath. "We should be away, Hannah. My carriage is being prepared. We can leave by the east gate and be off for Vienna within minutes."

"And I am surprised at you, Chamberlain Lang," I say levelly. "After all the lectures I received from you about your love for the Empire. And while Prague burns and your beloved Emperor sits in darkness and silence, you steal his treasures. So much for your loyalty."

Lang stands bringing his face angrily to mine. "It is the Empire I am loyal to, boy, not the Emperor. Emperors come and go, it is the Empire which shall last a thousand years. Rudolf is finished but the Holy Roman Empire shall endure throughout time."

"Oh, I doubt that," says a voice. We turn, Sir Anthony drawing his sword. In the corridor behind us stands the tall, thin, black-cloaked figure of Doctor John Dee.

"Your Holy Roman Empire is collapsing around your ears, wouldn't you say, Chamberlain Lang?" says Dee, leaning on his staff. "I rather think my plans have come together quite nicely."

Nineteen
Secrets and Lies

"Deva?" says Cody stupidly. "John, what the fuck are you talking about?"

We all follow John's gun as it rises in his hand and moves around the room, taking us all in its sights, then finally settles. On Karla. We all look to her, than back at John, still sitting casually in the chair.

"Deva," says John again. "Wanted by police in seven countries, on charges ranging from criminal damage to terrorism to murder. Isn't that right, 'Karla Stone', or whatever your real name is?"

Karla says nothing, just looks levelly at John, one eyebrow raised, her hair tumbling over her raincoat collar.

Cody holds up his hands. "Whoah. Whoah whoah whoah! Is somebody going to tell me what's going on here? John, are you really suggesting that Karla is Deva? Have you gone out of your mind?"

John laughs. "Not at all, Cody my boy. Not at all. The lovely Karla is indeed the mysterious Deva. The poster-boy of the revolution. Except Deva's a girl. Good plot twist, eh, people?"

Petey is looking wonderingly at Karla. "SuperAntiGlobalisationMan. Right here all the time. Like, wow."

"John," I say. Everyone looks at me. "Just one thing. Why the gun?"

"Simple," says John, raising the weapon again. "I'm taking Deva in."

And I am asking the fortune teller Master Ripellino, "Who is my enemy?"

"The Magician," he says, reading the card. "The trickster. Betrayal."

Dee seems to have grown, casting off the air of the frail, harmless old man he had been wearing throughout his time at the castle. He stands before us strong and tall, his eyes blazing with strength. Sir Anthony glances at me, confused.

"What are you talking about, man?" says Lang. "What plans?"

"I am here on official business," says Dee, taking a step towards us. "The Holy Roman Empire is becoming something of a nuisance to our dear Queen Elizabeth. We had thought that once that buffoon Rudolf took charge it would die a natural death, but it seems the Habsburg influence is clinging on to its territories despite the old fool's best efforts. I have been despatched here to hurry things along a little."

"Then you *are* in the employ of Walsingham," says Sir Anthony. "I confess I had disregarded the rumours, Doctor Dee. I had considered the Queen's spymaster too shrewd to employ a man condemned as a charlatan. I appear to have done you both a disservice."

Dee shrugs. "A common error. If I had a shilling for every man who called me a fraud, I should not have to work for the Earl of Walsingham, eh?"

"Then you are involved in the conspiracy, Doctor Dee," I say. "Percy Tremayne and Carlo Fantom are working for you."

Dee leans on his staff. "No, as a matter of fact. All that was dear old Edward's work. You see, he made the same mistake as many others have done. He thought to take me for a fool. He never realised I was pulling his strings all along, that I simply permitted him to stage his little conspiracies to further my own plans. Poor Edward."

"Where is he?" says Sir Anthony, his hand on his sword.

"Oh, Edward has gone," says Dee airily. "He has outlived his usefulness. As, I am afraid, have you."

And Master Ripellino slaps a card on to the soft velvet of the table covering. "Justice", he says. "A conflict approaches."

"You're taking me in?" says Karla, an amused look in her eye now. "I don't think so, John."

Cody holds his hands up again. "Okay, everybody, rewind. I still don't know what the fuck's going on here. Karla, are you telling me that for the past year I've been screwing Deva?"

Karla nods and sighs. "The things I do for the cause. Cody, you really should sort out that premature ejaculation thing."

Cody flushes and looks at John. "And what do you mean, you're taking her in?"

"I'll say this in words of one syllable, Cody, because I know you're not the sharpest tool in the box. Karla am big bad terr-or-ist. John am good guy with gun. John am arr-est-ing Karla. The end. Did you get that?"

"You're working for the oil companies, aren't you?" says Petey slowly. "Oh, man."

John presses an imaginary button the arm of the chair. "Bzzzzz! Keee-rect! Ten points to the dopehead in the corner! Next question, Petey: What the fuck are you going to do about it?"

Petey walks across the room, standing between John and Karla. "I can't let you do it, man. She's a hero."

John sighs and tightens his finger on the trigger. We all jump as the gun barks dully once, and Petey crumples to the floor, a mess of bones and tight skin and dark, spreading blood. Padraig swears softly and Cody leaps to Petey's side.

"If there's one thing I hate more than these crusty protesters, it's fucking junkies," John sighs.

Sir Anthony slowly holds out his rapier to Dee. "Doctor Dee, I do not mean to be rude, but I am a seasoned soldier and you are but an old man. Do not think to threaten me."

"Kill him," hisses Lang from the rear. "Run him through! He's a spy!"

"Shut up," says Sir Anthony from the corner of his mouth. He addresses Dee again: "Perhaps you should just leave, Doctor Dee. Chamberlain Lang and this girl mean to be away from Prague, as do I and my men. What you do concerns me not."

"Ah, but what you do concerns me, Sir Anthony. And it concerns the Queen. You have made no secret of your mercenary work; indeed, you are little more than a pirate, sir. England can well do without you."

"And how do you propose to do this, Doctor Dee?" grins Sir Anthony. "For you are but an unarmed man and I am a soldier with a sword."

Dee spreads his arms. "I am indeed unarmed, Sir Anthony. You are quite right about that. However, my compatriot is not."

"I thought you said Kelley had gone," I say.

Dee nods. "That I did. But I was not talking about Edward."

"No, he was talking about me."

We all turn to look. At Hannah.

"The Tower," says Master Ripellino. "The old order is threatened."

"He's dead," says Cody dumbly. "Jesus Christ. You shot Petey. In God's name, John, why?"

"It's what I get paid for," says John.

"And you really wonder why we do what we do," says Karla to John. "When there are people like you in the world."

"Oh, spare me," says John, turning his eyes to the ceiling. "Ninety-nine-point-nine-fucking-nine recurring per cent of the population of the world are like me. They just want to get on with their lives, buy a Big fucking Mac in any city in the world, fill their cars with petrol, wear their clothes without having to think about which little kid in which country had to sew the damn things, watch the TV, and get laid every now and again. It's people like you who are the fucking misfits. You want to save the world, but did you ever stop to ask the world whether it actually wanted saving?"

"I can't believe this," says Cody, tears streaming down his face. "You can't be saying this. You can't be shooting Petey. You're John, for God's sake. Everybody knows you. You're the fucking anti-globalisation supremo."

John grins. "Yeah, good cover, eh? Two years I've been 'John'. Two years living in shit-holes like this and spouting all this bullshit. And all to catch little old Deva here."

"But why?"

"Why? Why do you think? Because they pay me barrow-loads of money, you stupid little dipshit. And this time tomorrow I'll be back among civilised people, spending some of it. Shit, spending a lot of it. I think I might go to one of those all-inclusive resorts in India or somewhere. You know, the kind they chop down a hundred acres of rainforest to build and where they employ the natives to bring you drinks round the pool. I might enjoy that."

"But NI5...." says Cody, still unwilling to process the information. "The bomb, for Christ's sake...."

John sighs. "Jesus, Cody, how long is it going to take to get through to you? We're not a part of the protest. There's going to be no banner, no fireworks, no fucking bomb."

"You're wrong," says Karla, untying the belt around her raincoat. She lets it fall open. "There is a bomb."

"The Lovers. Failure to recognise true nature...."

"Hannah?" says Lang slowly. "What treachery is this?"

Hannah pecks Lang lightly on the cheek. "Not treachery, my love. I just had a better offer."

"From him?" says Lang, aghast, pointing at Dee. "I promised you riches beyond belief. You would have been a noblewoman in Vienna.

Yet you betray me for him?"

"I do like a big empire," says Hannah lightly. "But Dee's is bigger than yours. That's all there is to it."

"Elizabeth will never best the Habsburgs," declares Lang. "You have been taken for a fool."

"I think not," intervenes Dee. "Britannia shall rule the waves, and the mountains, and the plains. I have foreseen it."

"Foreseen it! Bah!" spits Lang. "Your magery holds no sway with me, charlatan. How, pray tell, did you foresee this web of lies?"

Dee shrugs. "The same way that I knew that the one person in the castle who could be bought with dreams of empire was not you, not Rudolf, not Sir Anthony, but a mere serving wench longing for a better life, Chamberlain Lang. The angels told me."

"But there are no angels in your magic scrying glass, are there, Doctor Dee?" I say. "Kelley fooled you as much as he fooled Rudolf. It was all a charade."

"True," says Dee. "Kelley purported to speak with the angels. He lied. This I know. But what Edward did not know was that I truly conversed with higher intelligences; it suited my purposes to think he was playing me for a fool. For some years now I have been communicating with the archangel Uriel, who feeds me nuggets and predictions."

Dee purses his lips. "Until recently, that is. For some reason, Uriel has been silent these past few weeks, despite my entreaties for him to speak. It is as though he has been cast out of Heaven itself."

Dee's eyes burn into mine. "What do you say, Master Poutnik?"

John smiles appreciatively at the device Karla wears around her midriff. A series of slender tubes strung along a webbing belt, a network of fuses connected to a switch running along the inside of her sleeve and hidden in the palm of her hand.

"Plastic explosives?" he says. "I suppose they were Padraig's doing."

I stare at Padraig. "You're with Karla?"

The Irishman takes a bow. "SuperAntiGlobalisationMan needs a sidekick," he grins. "Meet Paddy, the Boy Wonder."

Cody looks bereft. "Jesus. You two are in this together? Have you been screwing?"

John smiles tightly. "No, but she has been screwing somebody. Haven't you, Karla?"

She glances at me and Cody moans softly. Karla gives him a look of disdain. "Don't bother asking me how it was; you don't even shape up, baby. He's positively an angel between the sheets."

Cody slumps, his hands still on Petey's cooling corpse. "What about Jenny?" I say to Karla. "I suppose she's with you as well?"

"As a matter of fact, no," says John, his eyes still on the belt of explosives around Karla's waist. "Jenny's with me. How the hell do you think I know who's screwing who in this madhouse? She's been my partner for four years. A damned good operative. It's thanks to her the Seattle protest a couple of years ago never got off the ground. Right now she should be on her way back here. With Lisa and the others."

"Lisa?" says Karla, surprised. "Jenny's girlfriend?"

"Otherwise known as our CIA liaison in Eastern Europe. These dykes are pretty mean, you know. I wouldn't want to get on the wrong side of them," says John. "You might as well take that thing off, Deva, because you're coming in with me. Dead or alive, as they say."

"No," I say quietly. "No more killing. You've already killed Petey and Jakob. No more, John."

"Jakob?" frowns John. "The intruder guy? I didn't kill him. Just scared him shitless and let him go."

"Then who put his body under the honeysuckle in the garden?" I shout.

"Ah, that would be me," says Karla, an almost apologetic smile on her face.

I turn to look at her. "You?"

She shrugs. "He came back the day after John let him go. Thought I'd have a word with him myself. Got a bit carried away with the interrogation, I'm afraid."

"You killed him, Karla?"

"Not before he told me some interesting things, though," she says. "He was quite adamant about all that sixteenth century stuff. Says everyone thought you were a fallen angel."

"Enough of this nonsense," Sir Anthony says. "Master Poutnik, it is clear there is nothing to be done here. My suggestion is that we leave Dee to his machinations and Lang to his treachery, and that we flee Prague at once. My men are guarding our horses at the stables, it would perhaps be most judicious to go now while we still can."

The sounds of battle echo down the corridors. It seems that Fantom's men are driving the guard inside the castle. Without the relatively sensible voice of Percy to control Fantom, there is no guessing what the Hard Men will do. They will doubtless not stop until the castle is burning and they have plundered Prague.

"No-one is leaving," says Dee calmly. "I thought I had made that clear."

"And how do you propose to stop us, you old fraud?" says Lang.

"I don't need to," says Dee. "You shall not get out of the castle alive. Hannah, what time did you set the fuses?"

"About an hour ago," says Hannah.

Sir Anthony looks up. "Fuses?"

Dee nods in satisfaction. "Then there is but a quarter of an hour before the dozen barrels of gunpowder go up. I think our meeting is at an end, gentlemen."

"Gunpowder?" says Lang. "Fifteen minutes? But we can't get out of the castle in that time! We'll be blown to smithereens!"

"That is the idea, Chamberlain," smiles Dee.

"But neither can you make it out alive, Doctor Dee," says Sir Anthony. "Are we all to die, then, to protect and further the aims of Queen Elizabeth?"

"Not all of us. Hannah, to me, if you wish to take your payment for your efforts this day."

Hannah nimbly skips through the room and takes Dee's outstretched hand.

"We can still extinguish the fuses, if we can find the gunpowder," mutters Sir Anthony.

"And I am hardly likely to tell you where it is," says Dee, a strange, diffuse glow seeming to emanate from within his robes.

"Good God, it's impossible," breathes Lang as the light intensifies, blinding us. Hannah and Dee are enveloped by the sourceless brightness.

"Not impossible," laughs Dee from within the white light. "Did you not hear I was a sorcerer and a magician, Chamberlain Lang? Oh, but I forget, to you I am but a charlatan and a fraud."

"By my eyes," says Sir Anthony in wonder. "They're disappearing...."

And at that very moment, the Golem attacks.

"So, were you planning to bomb the Excelsior?" John asks.

"Of course."

"Dozens would have died. Hundreds."

"At least it would have been on the front pages tomorrow morning," says Karla. "A little more headline-grabbing than a banner, wouldn't you say?"

John straightens his arm, pointing the gun at Karla. "It's over, Deva. Take off the explosives. Your plan's thwarted. You're hardly going to blow us all up, yourself included, now are you?"

Karla holds up the trigger in her hand. "Oh, I wouldn't be too sure, John."

John looks with an air of bored detachment at the barrel of his gun. "You know, Karla," he says, "ten years ago, maybe, you might have gotten away with this."

Her thumb tightens perceptibly on the trigger. "I am getting away with it, John."

He sighs. "Whatever. You might well blow us all to kingdom come. Fine. No-one'll miss us greatly. But that's just the battle, Karla. I'm talking about the war. The war for hearts and minds. No-one has any great sympathy for terrorists any more. Oh, sure, people might privately agree with what you're trying to say. But not with the way you're saying it. That bunch of ragheads who took out the World Trade Centre have made sure that terrorism—no matter how young, white and beautiful those who commit it are—isn't something folks can get behind any more."

John pauses, scrutinising Karla's face. He nods at the belt around her waist. "However righteous you think you are, you press that button in your hand, and you're nothing more than a monster."

The Golem crashes into the corridor, staring at us.

"Good God," whispers Lang. "I didn't quite believe...."

"Stop them!" I shout at the Golem, pointing to Dee and Hannah. "They must not escape."

The Golem nods its rough clay head and lumbers forward to where Dee and Hannah stand in a haze of light. In panic, Hannah lets go of Dee's hand, and snaps back into focus.

"Doctor Dee!" she cries.

"Take my hand," says Dee, his voice distant. "I cannot come back for you."

But the Golem is between them, gripping Hannah tightly by her arms. "Dee!" she screams.

But the light has faded, and with it, Dee.

Cody looks up from Petey's body, his eyes red with tears. "Karla? You're not serious."

"Oh, I am, love," she says. "I'm expected at the Excelsior. If I'm not there my people will know something's gone wrong. They'll be making phone calls right now, and I should think the cameras and reporters should be rolling up outside any minute. If Deva can't go to the party, the party's going to come to her."

For once, John's mask of control slips. "Deva...." he says.

Hannah screams as the Golem squeezes the life from her. "Master Poutnik...." she gasps. "Please... call it off...."

Lang pushes past me, dragging a bag full of clinking treasures. "I shall take my chances," he says. "I have ten minutes to get clear of the castle. I think I can do it."

I look to Sir Anthony. "You too. I shall try to find the gunpowder."

"Poutnik...." cries Hannah.

Sir Anthony looks doubtfully at me. "Go," I urge.

"You are the bravest man I have ever met, Master Poutnik," he says. "May God welcome you into the kingdom of Heaven." Then, with a salute, he dashes off down the corridor.

"Deva, no," John says, standing.

"Back off," she shouts.

"Halt!" I command the Golem.

It ignores me.

"I'll do it, so help me God, I'll do it," says Karla, holding up the trigger.

John raises his gun. "I don't miss, Deva."

Brahe's words come unbidden to me. "Perhaps truth and death are closer than we realised, eh, Master Poutnik?"

Hannah is barely conscious now. My eyes fall upon the inscription on the Golem's head. Emet. Truth.

"Karla," I say as calmly as I can.

"Don't try to talk me out of this, Pooty," she says. She is panicked too, her voice high. Padraig is backing towards the door.

"Stay the fuck where you are!" bellows John.

The Golem is bending forward, wringing the breath out of Hannah. I reach up, softly touching its clay flesh, pulsing with life. Pulsing with innocent life. Life it never asked for, forced to serve causes it never believed in. Turned into a thing of evil through no fault of its own. And now it has to die. My fingers trace the letters. Emet.

I look at Hannah. I loved her, I think. And she betrayed me. Yet I have but minutes to extinguish the gunpowder fuses, or many will die in the castle.

I place my fingers over the first letter of the inscription.

And rub.

Padraig fumbles inside his jacket and pulls out a gun, but he's shaking, terrified. "Fuck, Karla," he says. "Fuck. You never said anything about this. You never said I was going to be blown to kingdom fucking come."

"I wasn't really planning on this happening!" she screams.

The Golem looks at me with its living eyes. The inscription on its forehead now reads met, death. It sags, and stumbles, releasing Hannah and falling to its knees. It looks at me, its eyes becoming more human even as its form melts and bubbles, its legs merging and spreading on the stone floor. Within seconds it is a puddle of clay, only the accusing, unbearable agony of its stare remaining in my mind's eye.

I crouch by Hannah, slapping her face. "The gunpowder, where is it?"

She stirs and moans. I slap her again.

"The gunpowder!"

"Your room...."

The door clicks and everyone turns. Jenny puts her head round and Padraig sobs and lets fly with the gun. Jenny jerks spastically and falls in the doorway. Outside, someone screams.

It takes me a minute to race down the corridor and on to the next floor to my rooms. By my reckoning I have only two minutes at the most to extinguish the fuses. Hannah has recovered and is following me, sobbing. I kick open my door and there they are: a dozen barrels of gunpowder, perilously short fuses fizzing at their heads.

"Oh, boy, you've done it now," says John. "Oh, shit, you two are going to swing for this."

"No we're not," says Karla, recovering her composure. "Say goodnight, everybody."

"How am I to know what to do when the time comes?"

Master Ripellino turns over the card. "The Hermit. Look inside yourself."

There isn't time to extinguish every fuse. Just one would ignite all the barrels, reducing the castle to rubble. *Look inside yourself.* The guards on the Charles Bridge... the dull clicks of the lock to Doctor Dee's room under the warm touch of my hand... I let the light shine out from my mind, focusing on each barrel in turn. I don't know for sure what has happened, but when I tear the lid off the nearest barrel, there is no gunpowder.

Only rose petals.

Hannah appears at the door, clutching her bruised arms where the Golem seized her.

"Poutnik," she says. "I am sorry. I...."

Her voice trails off, her head cocked as though listening. I hear the sound a second later; the faint yet distinct hiss of one last fuse.

"No," I say quietly. "No."

At the same time, Cody launches himself at John, and falls under the dull crack of the gun.

"Stupid shit," mutters John.

"Bastard," says Karla.

I squint. Too late, John's gun melts in his hand. He stares at it stupidly. Cody stops breathing.

"Bastard," says Karla again, tears blurring her eyes.

She squeezes the trigger in her hand.

I quickly count the barrels, the sweet odour of rose petals pervading the small room. There are only eleven.

"Under the bed," says Hannah.

I launch myself at Karla, screaming. "No! No! No!"

John casts the scalding metal away from him and pulls another weapon from inside his jacket. There's the sound of gunfire, whether from Padraig or John I have no idea.

Light fills the room.

One last card slaps dully on to velvet.

"Death. Change. Moving on. New beginnings."

The light becomes too bright to see. Far, far away, I hear the smothered sound of death.

I have failed.
    I have failed.

Interlude Five

The screams die away but the light shines on, and when he becomes accustomed to it a face emerges, one he knows. "Metatron," says Uriel weakly. "You have brought me back."

"Welcome home, Uriel," says Metatron kindly. "Your punishment is at an end."

Uriel sits and blinks and looks around. He is in his apartment, the bustle of the shining city outside his balcony. The air is clear and temperate, the hum of perfection all around.

"You have no need to thank me," continues Metatron. "The Committee has spoken. We trust you have learned much from your exile below."

Uriel stands and glides to the balcony. "I have," he murmurs. "I have learned much indeed."

"There are no innocents," says Metatron, amused. "That was our punishment. You were to save the innocents to halt the endless cycle of death and rebirth yet I am afraid we played something of a trick upon you, Uriel. But I am sure you agree it was for your own good."

"My own good?"

"All this talk," says Metatron, waving his hand airily. "All this talk of responsibility and protection. We cast you out into an infinite number of conflicts on the Earthly plane; pray tell us, how many innocents did you find?"

Uriel broods at the balcony, watching those like himself fly around The House, far distant. No, not like himself. Not any more.

"No innocents," he says finally. "None that we here in the city would call innocents."

"There you are," says Metatron with satisfaction. "Our punishment was worthwhile. Rest now, Uriel, for there is much work to do here."

Uriel turns his face of light to the other. "No, Metatron. Perhaps no innocents. But much, much more. We created them and abandoned them, Metatron, yet they have so much to teach us."

"They *have much to teach* us*? Uriel, you are still confused...."*

"No, Metatron. Not confused. Not any more. They know love and hate and fear and anger and they laugh and cry and shout and whisper. All the things we never knew, or perhaps have forgotten. I would rather spend a day among them than an eternity here."

Metatron frowns. "Careful, Uriel. Rash words may earn you yet more punishment."

"Then punish me!" roars Uriel. "Cast me out once more! Do your worst!"

"Uriel...."

"I have loved," whispers Uriel. "I have known betrayal and loss, but I have loved. Can you say the same?"

"This place is built on love, Uriel, you know that."

Uriel shakes his head. "Not love. Subservience. Slavery. Terror of the prospect of having to cope with anything different. Metatron, we have created a world of wonders, and we pretend it doesn't exist. Why is that?"

"They turned their backs on us," says Metatron doubtfully. "They were given life and all they were asked to do in return was love us and serve us. And they failed."

Uriel looks at Metatron sadly. "You really don't get it, do you? You never will. Send me back."

"What did you say?"

"Send me back. Send me back there. I don't care where or when."

"You won't remember your life here," says Metatron. "You won't recall your divine heritage...."

"I care not. It is as nothing to what I shall experience."

"And you can never come home."

"Send me back!"

Metatron purses his lips of light. "Very well, Uriel. If it is what you desire."

"Oh, it is, Metatron, it is."

"Then sleep."

And the light goes out for the last time.

Twenty
New Beginnings

I awake in a ditch, bereft of memories, naked, rested and fresh. I can taste the sunlight filtering through the trees, smell the sounds of a new dawn, see the beauty of birdsong all around.

I can touch life.

I have no recollection, save for the names of things. Of things other than myself. But I know more than I do not, I think.

I know more than I do not.

On balance.

Author's Note

Prague enthrals. Prague fascinates. Prague bewitches.

It's also, it seems, never the same place twice. Upon revisiting the city, a cobbled alley you are sure leads to the Charles Bridge unexpectedly spews you out somewhere quite different. An unfamiliar square you are certain you have never set foot on before will, surprisingly, be the location of the restaurant you ate at on your last visit, but which you were sure was on the other bank of the Vltava. And trying to relocate that bar where you whiled away the time until the small hours of that very morning can prove mystifying… retracing your steps just hours later can bring you to a faded wooden doorway; a dark shop selling pieces of vacuum cleaners; or, more disconcertingly, a blank stone wall.

For these reasons I make no claim that the Prague which provides the backdrop to *Angelglass* is anything other than a Prague of the imagination, a Prague of memory, a Prague of an unreliable narrator. The novel is not intended to be a guidebook to this most fascinating of cities, though it is not totally implausible that you might actually stumble upon the house of ex-pats or the Excelsior Hotel or the Leopold Bloom, given Prague's rather fluid nature. If you do, I'd be very interested to hear from you.

Similarly, *Angelglass* is not meant to be a definitive historical record of Prague in the last years of the 16th Century. The historical strand of the novel is based loosely on fact, and many of the characters who appear there did exist and were in Prague around or about the year 1584. The most notable liberty I have taken is the depiction of the Jewish Ghetto; for the purposes of this novel it is portrayed as a much less salubrious place than the rest of Prague, but in truth it was probably no worse than anywhere else in the city at that time. It did, much later, become a den of thieves and brigands of all creeds and cultures and a place where the unwary would be advised not to tread. The indignities visited upon the Jews, however, are based on fact and were probably much, much worse in reality than what I have documented here.

In the manner of the closing credits of a made-for-TV movie which appropriates real-life characters, it might be useful to document here some of the actual fates of those who appear in *Angelglass*.

Sir Anthony Sherley - Born 1565, and did indeed visit Prague on a mission from the Shah of Persia, but in 1605, from whence he was despatched on a mission to Morocco by Rudolf. Died in Madrid around 1635.

Doctor John Dee - Visited the court of Rudolf sometime around 1584, perhaps several times. Returned to England in 1589 and died around 1608. Did indeed have a scrying stone with which he claimed to converse with the angel, Uriel.

Edward Kelley - After parting company with Dee, Kelley stayed on in Bohemia and continued to spin promises of alchemy to Rudolf, who eventually tired of him and had him imprisoned. Legend has it he died in 1597 trying to escape from a high tower.

Tycho Brahe - The astronomer died in 1601 after falling ill a mere eleven days earlier. His final words to his assistant Kepler were apparently: "Let me not seem to have lived in vain!". His death has been ascribed to mercury poisoning; one school of thought suggests Kepler was responsible. He is interred in a tomb in the Tyn church on the Old Town Square in Prague.

Johannes Kepler - The German-born Kepler lived until 1630 and after Brahe's death in 1601 he became Rudolf's imperial mathematician, formulating his most important theories during this period. His Laws of Planetary Motion are world-renowned and formed the basis for many scientific formulae, including the laws of gravity. He died, curiously enough, on November 15.

Cornelius Drebbel - Drebbel visited Rudolf in Prague in 1610 and became Chief Alchemist for a while. He built his first navigable submarine in 1620, while working for the Royal Navy. He died in poverty, running a pub in London in 1633.

Philipp Lang - Described by one of Rudolf's biographers as "an evil genius", Lang was said to be a controlling, scheming politician who was eventually ousted from the court in 1609 or thereabouts

Rudolf II - The Emperor's life has been well documented and his legacy is three-fold: a bumbling ruler who directly caused the Thirty Years War which raged across central Europe, a great patron of the arts who ushered in something of a golden age in Bohemia, and a deep thinker in both scientific and occult fields who enabled great progress in both of those disciplines which lasts today. He died in January 1612 at the age of 59.

Rabbi Judah Loew ben Bezalel - He died in Prague in 1609, aged 84.

His tomb can be visited on the tourist trail in the city. The legend of his creation of the Golem often overshadows his other work, and he is a major figure in Jewish history.

Carlo Fantom - The most "out of time" character in *Angelglass*, being active in the English Civil War of 1642-1646, but I could not resist using him ever since reading his biography in *Aubrey's Brief Lives*: "Captain Carlo Fantom, a Croatian, spake 13 languages; was a Captain under the Earle of Essex. He was very quarrelsome and a great Ravisher. He left the Parliament Party, and went to the King Ch. the first at Oxford, where he was hanged for Ravishing." The bit about the Hard Men and their herb to make them invincible was, according to Aubrey, true.

Giuseppe Arcimboldo - The Milan-born painter was court portraitist to Rudolf's father Maximilian II in Vienna, and later to Rudolf in Prague. He died in Milan in 1593 and although he created a huge body of work, he is best remembered for his grotesque portraits of faces formed from fruit and vegetables.

I trust you will forgive the licence I have employed with these historical figures, and with Prague itself. Much as the famous black light theatre that can be found everywhere in the city offers a shadowy, magical experience of the Bohemian capital, so does *Angelglass* reflect Prague in a slightly distorted—but a hopefully entertaining—mirror.

David Barnett, West Yorkshire, October 2007

About the Author

David Barnett was born in Wigan in 1970. He's an award-winning journalist and has worked in newspapers in the North of England since 1989 as a reporter, a specialist correspondent, a news editor, a columnist, a features editor, and is now an assistant editor.

He has reported from Bosnia and Kosovo; once made a pilgrimage to Jack Kerouac's grave in Massachusetts; counts taking part in the "running of the bulls" at Pamplona's St Fermin fiesta as his most frightening experience ever; and spent most of the Nineties lying in a field at the Glastonbury Festival wondering if it was time to go home yet.

He is the lead singer with charismatic pop combo Choppersquad, who remain available for all festivals and functions.

David lives in West Yorkshire with his wife Claire, also an award-winning journalist, their children Charlie and Alice, and the inevitable two cats, Kali and Shiva.

He had his first novel Hinterland published by Immanion Press in April 2005, and is represented by the agent John Jarrold.

David can be found and contacted online via www.davidbarnett.org.uk

Other Recent Titles From Immanion Press

Oliphan Oracus
Neil Robinson
9781904853473
£12.99 paperback edition

IP0077 *Everyone is curious about the future. It would be a nice place to visit – but would you want to live there?*

In 2257 Keef is a television: a dishevelled, shamanic figure roaming a vast autumnal forest where big cats hunt, squirrels and monkeys teem in the canopy, and boar root in centuries of leaf litter. In 1995 Kate Wallis is a junior research assistant at a leading pharmaceutical company's laboratory complex, and she has no idea that she will soon find herself living the plot of a science fiction soap opera. She is accidentally exposed to an experimental longevity virus that causes a 262-year coma. Kate wakes in Keef's world and they begin a love affair that has profound repercussions for his community.

...Be warned: the resourceful heroes of science fiction stories are mythological figures, and technology might as well be magic.

Tourniquet: Tale from the Renegade City
Kim Lakin-Smith
9781904853350
£9.99 First edition

IP0072 Set in grand-gothika Renegade City, *Tourniquet* is a tale of dead messiahs, brutal loss, unrequited love, and blazing motorbikes. It incorporates all that is flesh and blood to Kim Lakin; the rock scene, alternative lifestyles, cyber-culture, bikes, hot rods, hard liquor, dark desires, and lurid living. Renegade City. Futurist Gothika. Mecca of the damned. Where über rock-band, Origin, is deified and the world's dark sub-cultures coexist under the umbrella faith of 'Belief'. Joining a black parade of freaks, geeks, and greebos, this living god and living-dead girl find their paths interlinked for a series of cataclysmic events that will tear at mutual bonds, unmask fresh hate, and forge new breeds of magick.

Digging Up Donald
Stephen Pirie
9781904853466IP0076
£12.99 Paperback/2nd edition

IP0076 It's the end of the world in Mudcaster, and the Mother is beset by family troubles – Maureen's unborn babies have been stolen by demons in the night, and Robert has taken to playing with dead Uncle Norman. The Father is talking to his pot plants again, which wouldn't be so bad if the Mother hadn't heard them answering back.

In dark times, the Mother knows that only by drawing the family together, the living and the dead, may they overcome the trials of Ending. Together they are strong; divided they are weak. Digging Up Donald is a gentle comedy – no demons were harmed in its writing.

The Fourth Cleansing
Book 3 of A Dream and Lie
Fiona McGavin
9781904853435
£13.99 Trade Paperback, first edition

IP0074 In the ancient city of Gel-Terridar, the enteri Nightshade, has been planning for centuries for the events that will lead up to the Fourth Cleansing. Now, with Alix's arrival in the city, it seems that nothing can stop his plans from reaching fruition. But Alix is determined not to do as Nightshade wishes, and together with a few loyal friends, he strives to fight the destiny Nightshade has planned for him.

But in Gel-Terridar everyone has their own agenda and Alix must find his way through a maze of plots and intrigues and false friends to find out if he is strong enough to resist Nightshade.

The third book in Fiona McGavin's acclaimed fantasy trilogy, ***A Dream and Lie***. The story of Alix Reste and the mysterious Enteri comes to a stunning conclusion.

Printed in the United Kingdom
by Lightning Source UK Ltd.
125290UK00001B/85/A